Praise for
The Shambling Guide to New York City:

"*The Shambling Guide* sets the wonderful world of the supernatural—and the slightly more esoteric world of travel guide publishing—on its ear, and the result is nothing short of delightful."

    —*New York Times* bestselling author Seanan McGuire

"Mur Lafferty's debut novel is a must-read book for those who like their urban fantasy fast, furious, and funny. Terrific stuff!"

    —National bestselling author Kat Richardson

"An engagingly funny, and fun, romp through NYC. You'll love Zoë...to bits."

    —*New York Times* bestselling author Tobias S. Buckell

"Shows exactly why so many writers have been buzzing about Mur Lafferty for so many years: an unbeatable mixture of humor, heart, imagination, and characterization. I want to live in Mur's New York."

    —*New York Times* bestselling author Cory Doctorow

"Without Mur Lafferty, the SF genre would be a much duller place. Mur is constantly inventive, always great fun, and deserves every success."

    —Paul Cornell

"A wild ride through the secret side of New York City, Mur Lafferty's mighty debut is urban fantasy the way it should be: fast, funny, with bags of action and characters you'll love. A total delight from cover to cover."

    —Adam Christopher

Don't let them intimidate you,

she firmly reminded herself. "Anyway, hi, I'm the human. Zoë. Good to meet you." She stepped into the room, but did not offer her hand to either woman to shake.

Morgen hooted with laughter. "Awesome! How long does he expect you to last with the zombies and vampires here? And did he tell you about the incubus?"

"Oh, they're not allowed to touch her," the other woman said. "That much is clear. I am Gwen, Zoë. I'm your head writer. Morgen is in sales and marketing." She stood, her long black skirts rustling somberly, and extended her hand.

Zoë shook it and immediately her mind filled with whispers of numbers: *2,015; 20 percent; 2,023; 30 percent; by 2,067; 100 percent.*

Zoë dropped Gwen's hand as quickly as she could without appearing rude. "Uh, I don't know how long he expects me to last, honestly," Zoë said to Morgen. She shook her head to clear it. "Maybe he's testing me somehow."

"Why would he do that?" Gwen asked.

Morgen shrugged. "He's a vampire. Wouldn't put it past him."

Gwen sniffed. "Bigot."

BY MUR LAFFERTY

The Shambling Guide to New York City

The
Shambling Guide to
New York City

Mur Lafferty

www.orbitbooks.net

Orbit
Hachette Book Group
237 Park Avenue, New York, NY 10017
HachetteBookGroup.com

First Edition: May 2013

Orbit is an imprint of Hachette Book Group, Inc. The Orbit name and logo are
trademarks of Little, Brown Book Group Limited.

The Hachette Speakers Bureau provides a wide range of authors for speaking
events. To find out more, go to www.hachettespeakersbureau.com or call (866)
376-6591.

The publisher is not responsible for websites (or their content) that are not owned
by the publisher.

Library of Congress Cataloging-in-Publication Data

Lafferty, Mur.
    The shambling guide to New York City / Mur Lafferty.
        p. cm.
    Summary: "An exciting, witty urban fantasy series from podcaster Mur Lafferty,
about a travel writer who takes a job with a shady publishing company in New
York, only to find that she must write a guide to the city—for the undead!"
—Provided by the publisher.
    ISBN 978-0-316-22117-7 (pbk.)—ISBN 978-0-316-22116-0 (ebook)
    1. Women editors—Fiction.   2. New York (N.Y.)—Fiction.   I. Title.
    PS3612.A3743S53 2013
    813'.6—dc23
                                                              2012032172

10 9 8 7 6 5 4 3 2 1

RRD-C

Printed in the United States of America

A good spouse encourages you to chase your dream.
A great one will flat out refuse to let you settle for a dream that's "almost as good."
This book would literally not be in your hands if not for my husband, Jim Van Verth.

Send him cookies.

CHAPTER ONE

The bookstore was sandwiched between a dry cleaner's and a shifty-looking accounting office. Mannegishi's Tricks wasn't in the guidebook, but Zoë Norris knew enough about guidebooks to know they often missed the best places.

This clearly was not one of those places.

The store was, to put it bluntly, filthy. It reminded Zoë of an abandoned mechanic's garage, with grime and grease coating the walls and bookshelves. She pulled her arms in to avoid brushing against anything. Long strips of paint dotted with mold peeled away from the walls as if they could no longer stand to adhere to such filth. Zoë couldn't blame them. She felt a bizarre desire to wave to them as they bobbed lazily to herald her passing. Her shoes stuck slightly to the floor, making her trek through the store louder than she would have liked.

She always enjoyed looking at cities—even her hometown—through the eyes of a tourist. She owned guidebooks of every city she had visited and used them extensively. It made her usual urban exploration feel more thorough.

It also allowed her to look at the competition, or it had when she'd worked in travel book publishing.

The store didn't win her over with its stock, either. She'd never heard of most of the books; they had titles like *How to Make Love, Marry, Devour, and Inherit in Eight Weeks* in the Romance section and *When Your Hound from Hell Outgrows His House—and Yours* in the Pets section.

She picked the one about hounds and opened it to Chapter Four: "The Augean Stables: How to Pooper-Scoop Dung That Could Drown a Terrier." She frowned. *So, they're really assuming your dog gets bigger than a house? It's not tongue-in-cheek? If this is humor, it's failing.* Despite the humorous title, the front cover had a frightening drawing of a hulking white beast with red eyes. The cover was growing uncomfortably warm, and the leather had a sticky, alien feeling, not like cow or even snake leather. She switched the book to her left hand and wiped her right on her beige sweater. She immediately regretted it.

"One sweater ruined," she muttered, looking at the grainy black smear. "What *is* this stuff?"

The cashier's desk faced the door from the back of the store, and was staffed by an unsmiling teen girl in a dirty gray sundress. She had olive skin and big round eyes, and her head had the fuzz of the somewhat-recently shaved. Piercings dotted her face at her nose, eyebrow, lip, and cheek, and all the way up her ears. Despite her slouchy body language, she watched Zoë with a bright, sharp gaze that looked almost hungry.

Beside the desk was a bulletin board, blocked by a pudgy man hanging a flyer. He wore a T-shirt and jeans and looked to be in his mid-thirties. He looked completely out of place in this store; that is, he was clean.

"Can I help you?" the girl asked as Zoë approached the counter.

"Uh, you have a very interesting shop here," Zoë said, smiling. She put the hound book on the counter and tried not to grimace as it stuck to her hand briefly. "How much is this one?"

The clerk didn't return her smile. "We cater to a specific clientele."

"OK…but how much is the book?" Zoë asked again.

2

"It's not for sale. It's a collectible."

Zoë became aware of the man at the bulletin board turning and watching her. She began to sweat a little bit.

Jesus, calm down. Not everyone is out to get you.

"So it's not for sale, or it's a collectible. Which one?"

The girl reached over and took the book. "It's not for sale to you, only to collectors."

"How do you know I don't collect dog books?" Zoë asked, bristling. "And what does it matter? All I wanted to know was how much it costs. Do you care where it goes as long as it's paid for?"

"Are you a collector of rare books catering to the owners of... exotic pets?" the man interrupted, smiling. His voice was pleasant and mild, and she relaxed a little, despite his patronizing words. "Excuse me for butting in, but I know the owner of this shop and she considers these books her treasure. She is very particular about where they go when they leave her care."

"Why should she..." Zoë trailed off when she got a closer look at the bulletin board to the man's left. Several flyers stood out, many with phone numbers ripped from the bottom. One, advertising an exorcism service specializing in elemental demons, looked burned in a couple of places. The flyer that had caught her eye was pink, and the one the man had just secured with a thumbtack.

Underground Publishing
LOOKING FOR WRITERS

Underground Publishing is a new company writing travel guides for people like you. Since we're writing for people like you, we need people like you to write for us.

(continued)

Pluses: Experience in writing, publishing, or editing (in this life or any other), and knowledge of New York City.

Minuses: A life span shorter than an editorial cycle (in this case, nine months).

Call 212.555.1666 for more information or e-mail rand@undergroundpub.com for more information.

"Oh, hell yes," said Zoë, and with the weird, dirty hound book forgotten, she pulled a battered notebook from her satchel. She needed a job. She was refusing to adhere to the stereotype of running home to New York, admitting failure at her attempts to leave her hometown. Her goal was a simple office job. She wasn't waiting for her big break on Broadway and looking to wait tables or take on a leaflet-passing, taco-suit-wearing street-nuisance job in the meantime.

Office job. Simple. Uncomplicated.

As she scribbled down the information, the man looked her up and down and said, "Ah, I'm not sure if that's a good idea for you to pursue."

Zoë looked up sharply. "What are you talking about? First I can't buy the book, now I can't apply for a job? I know you guys have some sort of weird vibe going on, 'We're so goth and special, let's freak out the normals.' But for a business that caters to, you know, *customers*, you're certainly not welcoming."

"I just think that particular business may be looking for someone with experience you may not have," he said, his voice level and diplomatic. He held his hands out, placating her.

"But you don't even know me. You don't know my qualifications. I just left Misconceptions Publishing in Raleigh. You heard of them?" She hated name-dropping her old employer—

she would have preferred to forget it entirely—but the second-biggest travel book publisher in the USA was her strongest credential in the job hunt.

The man shifted his weight and touched his chin. "Really. What did you do for them?"

Zoë stood a little taller. "Head researcher and writer. I wrote most of *Raleigh Misconceptions*, and was picked to head the project *Tallahassee Misconceptions*."

He smiled a bit. "Impressive. But you do know Tallahassee is south of North Carolina, right? You went in the wrong direction entirely."

Zoë clenched her jaw. "I was laid off. It wasn't due to job performance. I took my severance and came back home to the city."

The man rubbed his smooth, pudgy cheek. "What happened to cause the layoff? I thought Misconceptions was doing well."

Zoë felt her cheeks get hot. Her boss, Godfrey, had happened. Then Godfrey's wife—whom he had failed to mention until Zoë was well and truly in "other woman" territory—had happened. She swallowed. "Economy. You know how it goes."

He stepped back and leaned against the wall, clearly not minding the cracked and peeling paint that broke off and stuck to his shirt. "Those are good credentials. However, you're still probably not what they're looking for."

Zoë looked at her notebook and continued writing. "Luckily it's not your decision, is it?"

"Actually, it is."

She groaned and looked back up at him. "All right. Who are you?"

He extended his hand. "Phillip Rand. Owner, president, and CEO of Underground Publishing."

She looked at his hand for a moment and shook it, her small fingers briefly engulfed in his grip. It was a cool handshake, but strong.

"Zoë Norris. And why, Mr. Phillip Rand, will you not let me even apply?"

"Well, Miss Zoë Norris, I don't think you'd fit in with the staff. And fitting in with the staff is key to this company's success."

A vision of future months dressed as a dancing cell phone on the wintry streets pummeled Zoë's psyche. She leaned forward in desperation. She was short, and used to looking up at people, but he was over six feet, and she was forced to crane her neck to look up at him. "Mr. Rand. How many other people experienced in researching and writing travel guides do you have with you?"

He considered for a moment. "With that specific qualification? I actually have none."

"So if you have a full staff of people who fit into some kind of mystery mold, but don't actually have experience writing travel books, how good do you think your books are going to be? You sound like you're a kid trying to fill a club, not a working publishing company. You need a managing editor with experience to supervise your writers and researchers. I'm smart, hardworking, creative, and a hell of a lot of fun in the times I'm not blatantly begging for a job—obviously you'll have to just take my word on that. I haven't found a work environment I don't fit in with. I don't care if Underground Publishing is catering to eastern Europeans, or transsexuals, or Eskimos, or even Republicans. Just because I don't fit in doesn't mean I can't be accepting as long as they accept me. Just give me a chance."

Phillip Rand was unmoved. "Trust me. You would not fit in. You're not our type."

She finally deflated and sighed. "Isn't this illegal?"

He actually had the audacity to laugh at that. "I'm not discriminating based on your gender or race or religion."

"Then what are you basing it on?"

He licked his lips and looked at her again, studying her. "Call it a gut reaction."

She deflated. "Oh well. It was worth a try. Have a good day."

On her way out, she ran through her options: there were the few publishing companies she hadn't yet applied to, the jobs that she had recently thought beneath her that she'd gladly take at this point. She paused a moment in the Self-Help section to see if anything there could help her better herself. She glanced at the covers for *Reborn and Loving It, Second Life: Not Just on the Internet,* and *Get the Salary You Deserve! Negotiating Hell Notes in a Time of Economic Downturn.* Nothing she could relate to, so she trudged out the door, contemplating a long bath when she got back to her apartment. Better than unpacking more boxes.

After the grimy door shut behind her, Zoë decided she had earned a tall caloric caffeine bomb to soothe her ego. She wasn't sure what she'd done to deserve this, but it didn't take much to make her leap for the comfort treats these days—which reminded her, she needed to recycle some wine bottles.

The Shambling Guide to New York City

THEATER DISTRICT:
Shops

Mannegishi's Tricks is the oldest bookstore in the Theater District. Established 1834 by Akilina, nicknamed "The Drakon Lady," after she immigrated from Russia, the store has a stock that is lovingly picked from collections all over the world. Currently managed by Akilina's great-grandaughter, Anastasiya, the store continues to offer some of the best finds for any book collector. Anastasiya upholds the old dragon lady's practice of knowing just which book should go to which customer, and refuses to sell a book to the "wrong" person. Don't try to argue with her; the drakon's teeth remain sharp.

Mannegishi's Tricks is one of the few shops that deliberately maintain a squalid appearance—dingy, smelly, with a strong "leave now" aura—in order to repel unwanted customers. In nearly 180 years, Akilina and her descendants have sold only three books to humans. She refuses to say to whom. ∎

CHAPTER TWO

October seemed completely unaware that she was having a shit day. The crisp weather and the blue sky couldn't help but cheer Zoë a little bit. She had simply loved coming home. Full of people and secrets, cities were three-dimensional, rising high in the sky and creating labyrinthine tunnels underground. She'd come from the suburbs of the Research Triangle in North Carolina, a sterile, impotent metropolitan area of three million people stretched over several counties. That was not a city.

She'd moved with her parents when she was in grade school, but nowhere had ever felt like home the way the city did. She reflected she should have returned when she got out of school, but she got a job traveling for a magazine, and then got the job in Raleigh with Misconceptions and decided that was worth it.

After that ended, it seemed obvious that there was nowhere else to go except home. Ever since she was a child, she had felt cities, especially New York, were alive. Cities had a heartbeat. When she wasn't in a city, she felt soulless, with an ever-present itch telling her something was missing.

New York was a *city*.

Zoë prided herself in her ability to seek out the perfect hidden gems in a city. She fancied herself an urban explorer of a sort, and desperately avoided chain restaurants and stores. She enjoyed getting to know cities as if they were friends; you visited the Targets of your acquaintances, but the mom-and-pop stores of your friends.

Her fifteen or so years out of New York had seen the city change a lot, both from time and from 9/11. She loved wandering the streets, getting to know it again.

So what if she'd left Raleigh in shame and now counted on one hand the unemployed weeks she had left in her savings account before she had to give up and move out? She was where she'd always wanted to be.

When she spied the little café a few doors down from the bookstore, she knew where she wanted to be right then: Bakery Under Starlight. It was perfectly placed, facing south on Fifty-First Street so that the fading afternoon sun of early autumn cut through the trees and into the café. The café had orange-red walls with antique, mismatched chairs and tables. Behind the counter a cappuccino machine hissed. Racks of bread and pastries assaulted Zoë's nose, and she took an appreciative whiff of freshly baked goodies.

"Suck it, Starbucks," she muttered as she got in line.

The only people Zoë saw working the shop were a mountain of a man whose baker's jacket said "Carl" and a petite woman who shouted obscenities at the customers when their coffees were ready.

Zoë stood in line behind a fat man with sallow skin and limp brown hair. He wore a very nicely tailored pinstripe suit, but it was ill-fitting, straining at the buttons and baggy in the shoulders. She felt a little sorry for the suit, thinking that if it had had any say in the matter, it would not have chosen this man to fill it.

Carl greeted the customer by name. "'Morning, John, you're looking well."

John smiled and winked at Carl. "I found a new club the other night. Things are looking up."

"Oh really? I'd check it out, but, you know." Carl gestured

widely, encompassing the café, and John nodded as if he understood.

The John person got his coffee and scone—"Latte for the son of a demon and a whore!" the small woman cried out in accented English—and nodded again to Carl before taking a table against the wall.

Zoë nodded to the barista as she approached the counter. "Doesn't that drive away customers?" she asked Carl.

Carl shrugged. "Tenagne's Ethiopian," he said, as if that explained it.

"That's a little stereotypical," Zoë said.

Carl glanced at Tenagne, who steamed milk with her back to him. "Not for her family, which is pretty large. Don't worry, she only yells obscenities at people she likes. You should be safe. Now what can we get you?" Zoë blushed and gave her order—plain coffee and a croissant—and then snagged the only free table by a window, which happened to be along the wall next to John's.

On the wall above her hung another corkboard with missing-cat notices and job postings. She saw the Underground Publishing flyer, and snatched the whole thing off.

As she contemplated the job description again, she caught John staring at her. She tried to ignore him, reading the flyer a couple of times, looking for any clue that would lead her to what Underground Publishing wanted, but finding nothing.

When she looked up, the man was still staring at her. She sighed. "Do you have a problem?"

He did not flinch at the obvious irritation in her voice, but instead put down his coffee and wiped his mouth, a silver bracelet peeking from inside his cuff. Despite his lugubrious appearance, he sat up straight and met her eyes with no sense of shyness. He gestured toward the flyer. "I'm not sure if that's a good idea for you to pursue."

Zoë pursed her lips. "So I've heard. Is there a campaign against me? You don't even know me. Neither does that Phillip guy."

John raised an eyebrow at her. "You know Phil?"

She nodded. "I just met Phillip Rand at that nasty bookstore down the street, and he told me the same thing. So what is the problem? Why are you people following me to make sure I don't apply? Why do you fucking care?"

The fat man considered her for a moment, smiling. "Paranoid, and quick to anger. That's very attractive." He didn't sound sarcastic, and his tone made her squirm slightly inside. "To answer your question, Phil is my boss. Our office is nearby. We're hanging flyers in area businesses. Your encountering both of us is nothing but a happy coincidence." He ignored her snort of derision. "And about your qualifications, Phil is looking for someone with experience you may not have," he said, seeming to choose his words carefully.

Zoë sighed. "Why not? I've got experience, I'm a native, I'm an excellent researcher, surely I'm worth an interview at least."

He sipped at his coffee again, sizing her up over the mug's rim. His muddy brown eyes weren't undressing her, but she still had the uncomfortable feeling that she was a slab of beef and John was a butcher, deciding where to make the first cut. "You're still probably not what they're looking for."

"So what do you do? What makes *you* so perfect for the job?"

He extended his hand. "John Dickens. Public relations, Underground Publishing."

She shook it, his warm hand strangely dainty in her own.

"Zoë Norris."

"Well, I'm not in editorial; it's not my decision. Go ahead and apply. Who knows? Phil might change his mind and take a liking to you. You're...appealing."

Zoë didn't like the way he said that. Did she want to work

with this asshole? "Thanks for the advice, I guess." She sat at her table and pushed her chair pointedly to put her back to John. She got out her BlackBerry and pulled up the template for her standard job query. She made some pertinent changes, attached her résumé, double-checked for mistakes, and then sent it to Phil's e-mail address as given on the sheet.

She sat back and relaxed. Despite the comments to the contrary, she felt good about this one. Of course, she'd felt good about all the jobs she'd applied for; she'd been convinced that every publishing house in the city had at least one open job whose description read so perfectly the ad might as well have said, "WANTED: Thirtysomething woman from Raleigh, NC, petite, heartbroken, fleeing a scandal at a publishing company. Names starting with 'Z' preferred." But she had been overqualified for one, under-qualified for another, and too laid-back for a third—although she was pretty sure her lack of any structured religion was the real reason, even though by law they couldn't say that. That was her worry about Underground Publishing: that it was focused toward Jews or Christians or bisexuals or people who had lived through the heartbreak of psoriasis or some other group that she didn't belong to. But why were John and Phil so secretive?

Zoë fiddled with her phone, ignoring the other patrons, especially the man behind her. She went through news feeds, reading her favorite websites, checking in at the weirder science news sites just for fun, and then checked publishing blogs. She was *tsk*ing at another book deal for another celebrity who'd made a name for herself by doing drugs and sleeping with producers and now felt qualified to write, when she realized that an old Kool & the Gang song was playing very loudly.

No, Carl hadn't cranked the volume. Instead, everyone in the café had stopped talking. Zoë looked up and saw a dirty, wide-eyed woman standing in the middle of the café. She looked to be older, like seventy, and had white hair and Asian features. She wore a pink shawl, a grimy T-shirt that said "I 8 NY" over a silhouette of Godzilla, and dirty jeans. Out of place on her ragged form was a pair of very high-quality black combat boots. She pirouetted slowly and stared at the patrons in the café. The patrons stared back.

"Well, this should be interesting," John whispered behind her.

Zoë frowned. The tension in the café was palpable; there was none of the usual discomfort or pointed ignoring reactions New Yorkers did when faced with something or someone they didn't want to deal with. The people in the café seemed completely terrified of the old woman, even though her thick braided hair swinging at her hip was the strongest-looking thing about her. Zoë felt a sudden kinship with this woman, feeling outcast and friendless as she had been. She stood up and glanced around the coffee shop. Even Carl looked petrified.

No one moved to talk to the woman, to take her order, or to usher her out. Zoë couldn't take the tension any more, so she turned on what she had learned of Southern charm. She heard a small gasp behind her as she approached the woman.

"Hi, honey, can I help you? Are you meeting a friend, or do you need a cup of coffee?"

The woman fixed her wide brown eyes on Zoë and seemed to think for a moment. "You want to buy Granny Good Mae a cup of coffee?" Her accent was flat and difficult to place, almost the generic American accent Hollywood actors had.

Zoë shrugged. "Sure, why not?"

"I always knew you were a good one," she said, glaring at Carl, who blanched, his dark skin turning ashy. "I don't do coffee. I drink tea."

"Sure." Zoë walked to the counter. She waved her hand in

front of Carl's face. "It's OK, she won't bite. Just get her some hot tea. I'll pay for it and get her out of here."

"That's Granny Good Mae," Carl whispered, but he moved to fill a to-go cup with hot water. "She's not welcome here."

Zoë shook her head in amazement. "She's not hurting anyone. What's your problem?"

"You both batshit crazy," Tenagne said to Zoë, tossing Carl a tea bag. "Her 'cause she talk to the air, and you 'cause you listen to her."

"Yeah, whatever," Zoë said. She paid Carl for the tea. The customers still watched Granny Good Mae, who looked them over as if she were a general surveying the enemy. Neither seemed willing to make the first strike.

Zoë walked up to the old woman and put her hand on her elbow. "I'm sorry, ma'am, I'm not really sure why they don't want you here, but I think it might be best if you go. Here's your tea."

"I got what I came here for," Granny Good Mae said, turning to leave.

"Does this café have especially good tea?" Zoë asked, opening the door for the woman.

Granny Good Mae looked at her, startled. "What? No, the tea here is garbage tea. Comes in bags. Like garbage. And goldfish crackers. I came here to see how you've grown up." She tossed the full cup of tea into a garbage can on the street. "And you grew up real nice."

Bemused, Zoë said, "Uh, OK. I'm Zoë. Nice to meet you."

"Life! Life! This city needs life!" Granny Good Mae cackled as if she'd made a good joke, then her face fell. "Remember, Zoë-Life, watch your back. Some people in this city will eat you right up."

Before Zoë could ask anything more, the old woman turned and wandered down the street, laughing again about "Zoë-Life."

15

Zoë shrugged and went back into the café. A couple of the patrons shot her sidelong glances, but the room had returned to its former light and friendly atmosphere.

"You're really not looking to make friends, are you?" John asked as she sat down.

"I don't know what the problem is. She's just a harmless old woman. She didn't even shout obscenities or urinate on the wall," Zoë said, not looking at him and taking her phone out of her pocket. The light on top was blinking, and she switched it on to read her messages.

"You don't know what you're talking about, but that's not your fault," John said. He retrieved his own mobile phone and started typing something on the screen.

"Holy crap," Zoë said, as she read her messages. She had already gotten a reply from Underground Publishing. She read the e-mail quickly.

She finally looked at John, a triumphant smile on her face. "Phil wants to talk to me. I've got an interview."

John nodded absently, checking his own phone. "Yeah, but don't worry. We have time for another cup of coffee. You want a refill on me?"

Zoë blinked at him, her triumph melting into a feeling of stupidity. "Uh, what?"

"Didn't you read your e-mail? Phil wants to see you at four o'clock. It's three fifteen now."

Zoë gasped and called up the e-mail again. There it was, four o'clock. She looked down at herself. She wore her favorite (read: old) beige sweater, which now had a grimy streak across the front from that foul bookstore. Underneath that she wore an old Pearl Jam T-shirt with an ink stain on the shoulder and a hole by the neck seam. Jeans, purple Chuck Taylor sneakers, and her vintage denim jacket completed her wardrobe. She hadn't even washed her hair that morning. "I'm not dressed for an interview."

John shrugged. "Phil is likely trying to catch you off guard. I told you, you won't fit in with us. He's going to try to find any reason not to hire you. Here's a hint: Phil likes confidence."

Zoë narrowed her eyes. "Why are you helping me? You clearly didn't want me to get the job ten minutes ago."

John's eyes widened and he shook his head. "Oh no, I'd like nothing more than to work with you. You seem intelligent and willing to take risks. You're also not shy. I hate shy women." Zoë frowned, but remained silent. "I'm just saying, I agree with Phil: you won't fit in. Once you learn more about the job, you probably won't even want it."

Zoë sat back. "We'll see. And yes, I will take that coffee." Her heart pounded in anticipation of her interview. "But make it decaf."

Zoë had demanded John keep silent as she frantically searched the Web on her phone, looking for any information on Underground Publishing. She pulled up a page with a slate-gray background saying "Under Construction," complete with a circa-1997 animated gif of a little stick man in a yellow hard hat digging the same shovelful of pixelated dirt over and over. She groaned.

Well, there's a place to start with suggestions for the company. It gave her nothing to go on, though.

She began to make notes about what the website needed, surfing to other publishing sites to see what common elements they contained. She bit her lip and typed in the URL for Misconceptions Publishing. Godfrey's trim, bearded face smiled at her from the home page, and she hit the back button and closed her eyes.

She knew what was on its site. She'd designed the damn thing back when Misconceptions was a little company with a skeleton crew. It had been her idea to put his face on the front page, giving the company a figurehead, someone to trust.

Just as I trusted him.

She took a deep breath and then a big gulp of her coffee. Now was definitely not the time to think about Godfrey. She frowned, and then rooted around in her leather satchel. She dug out a little silver MINI Cooper (a gift from Godfrey, its once-comforting weight now feeling like a heavy reminder) and put it aside, firmly telling herself to stop pining like a brokenhearted teen. After a little more rooting through papers and two novels, she found what she was looking for: one copy of *Raleigh Misconceptions*, the book she'd edited (not to mention that the entire *Misconceptions* line was her baby). She put the little car back in her satchel and then looked at her watch.

"How long does it take to get to Underground Publishing?" she asked John, who was reading the *Times*. "Should we catch a cab?"

"Nah. It's around the corner," John said, putting his newspaper into his briefcase.

Zoë raised her eyebrows. "A publishing company in the Theater District?"

He grinned. "Phil rented and refurbished an old off-Broadway theater and put a publishing company there. But working in an old theater won't be the weirdest thing you encounter today, I promise."

Zoë shrugged. "All right, then. Lead on." She bused her table, dropping the dishes at the counter.

Carl stopped her before she could go, his hand touching her wrist lightly. "Listen, Zoë, isn't it?" She nodded. "If you're a friend of John's, then I'll warn you, we've had...trouble with

18

Granny Good Mae in the past. I'll serve anyone who can pay, and sometimes if they can't. But Mae is a different story."

Zoë frowned. "I still don't see what's so harmful about the old woman."

"I hope you never have to know," he said. He stuck his hand out. "Water under the bridge?"

She shook it, surprised. "Sure, I guess."

She followed John into the afternoon sunlight, and he led her around the corner and down an alley. John proudly waved his hand down a rickety staircase that led to a below-street-level theater. "And here we are."

The doorway had no signage, and had a board nailed across it, even though it opened inward.

Zoë nodded calmly, looking around for possible exits. "So you're bringing me here to kill me."

John's eyes widened. "Oh, goodness no. I'm pretty sure in a one-on-one match, you'd end up on top, easy."

Zoë gripped her satchel and planted her feet, but John made no aggressive moves toward her. She hadn't studied martial arts in a couple of years, but she still remembered the basics. "So you just expect me to go into a condemned theater with a guy who I just met, who's been checking me out for the last hour?" she asked.

John grinned ruefully. "I can't help my nature, Zoë. And you're the one who wanted the job, remember?"

He had her there. She pointed down the stairwell. "You go first."

John shrugged. "Sure."

She watched him walk all the way down the stairs and reach under the board to push the door open. "Now just duck under the board, and we're in."

Zoë swallowed hard, curious despite her fear. She pulled out her phone to check if she still had cell service, and dialed 91 and kept her finger over the 1. She followed John down the stairs and, saying a prayer to whatever god might be listening in a disused alley near Fifty-First Street, she slipped under the board and followed John into the dark hallway.

The Shambling Guide to New York City

THEATER DISTRICT:
Nightlife

One of the best things about New York City is how coterie have insinuated themselves into the culture. Broadway wouldn't have started without the fae queen, Titania, establishing the New Amsterdam at West Forty-Second Street, but infighting among the fae made the palace fall into squalor. Peaseblossom, who has held power for the past four decades, has restored the palace to its former glory. He's welcomed vampires, succubi, and incubi, and even some of the fresher zombies, into Broadway auditions.

The coterie-friendly cast and crew may imply that all coterie are welcome to audition or attend, but you need to remember the dress code is key: make sure to blend in.

As with all auditions, don't expect your coterie status to get you in; they still want the best, and they'll choose a human over you if you don't measure up to their standards. ∎

CHAPTER THREE

There was a distinct lack of smell in the hallway. Zoë realized it didn't smell musty or even overly clean and bleachy; it didn't smell like anything.

Dim lights along the wall lit the sad, worn red carpet. Her logical mind told her that following a stranger into a condemned building was about as smart as climbing trees during a lightning storm, but for some reason Zoë felt no sense of panic. Something told her that this was legit, and a certain, curious part of her was eager to see what a publisher would do with an old theater.

The lobby was small and empty, with an ancient popcorn machine at the leaning candy counter. John led her around to a side door and into another hallway. Zoë realized they were going backstage. She peeked through one of the portholes in the wall and saw a woman sitting in the theater, by herself in the dim light, reading a book. Zoë frowned and picked up her pace to catch up to John.

Once she got backstage, Zoë realized that, yes, they had actually renovated the old theater to house a publishing company. The wings held a fridge and a freestanding cupboard, and the stage looked to be the set of a break room complete with a table and chairs, and easy chairs. Shelves filled with colorful books sat next to the easy chairs, with reading lamps on top of them. If not for the hundreds of dusty, empty seats facing the area, it might even have been cozy.

"That's the break room," said John. "Everyone works in the dressing rooms backstage. Editorial in one room, marketing in another, the boss gets his own dressing room. The star, you know." He winked at her.

Zoë managed a smile. Her fear had mostly left her, but she still didn't trust this guy. She glanced at him as he led her down another poorly lit hallway. He definitely didn't look as if he could take her; he looked like an unsure nouveau riche who had bought an expensive suit without having a tailor measure him.

"Phil wants to see you before you meet anyone else," he said over his shoulder.

"Mysterious," she said, trying to sound amused. They had reached the dressing rooms at this point, all of them closed, and headed for the one with a big star on the door. John knocked on the door twice.

"Come!"

John raised his eyebrows. "Ready?"

She made a face at him. "You take me this far and ask me if I'm ready now?" She moved past him and put her hand on the doorknob. "Stop trying to psych me out."

Zoë nearly laughed as she opened the door. She'd expected the publishing company to have taken over the theater and made it look sterile and corporate, but Phil Rand had apparently not done anything to modify the star's dressing room. It was still lit largely by a vanity, which he had apparently repurposed as his desk. Instead of makeup and hair products, he had books and notebooks and pens, but the abandoned theater still apparently boasted a good deal of its costuming and set pieces; a corner held trunks, armoires, and hat racks. Phil stood as they entered and left his seat at the vanity to walk forward and shake her hand. He still looked unassuming and bland when lit brightly by the clear bulbs. He was maybe thirty pounds overweight, with a red ponytail and thin glasses. He was more casual than John, still wearing his T-shirt. He seemed even taller than he had in the bookstore. His clean-shaven face was freckled and mature, yet unlined, so she guessed his age at around thirty-five.

"Zoë, how nice to see you again," he said, his voice seeming friendlier than it had in the store.

She smiled at him. "It's my pleasure, Mr. Rand. Thank you for agreeing to meet with me so soon."

"I appreciate tenacity. If you're so interested in this job, far be it from me to dissuade you with words. I'm so glad that John was able to lead you here. You may not have been able to find the place on your own; we don't advertise very much."

Zoë felt she was being tested already, and decided not to be thrown off. "I wouldn't worry about it, sir, your business isn't direct retail. As long as employees can get to work, there's no issue. While I might worry about OSHA getting upset at a few of your more…eccentric design decisions, I love your offices. They're unique."

"OSHA. Right. I'll make a note of that," Phil said, scribbling something on a pad. It was literally a scribble. Zoë caught sight of it when he put the pad down, and the scrawl was completely illegible.

This is decidedly weird.

"Have a seat," he said, inviting her to a plush pink couch. Zoë joined him. Phil looked pointedly at John, who looked slightly startled, then nodded and left the room. "I want to know what John told you about the company," he said.

Zoë remembered what John had told her and sat up straighter. "Not much more than what you said. He said I wouldn't fit in, that I am not like the rest of you."

Phil sat back. "He was telling the truth. And he told you nothing else?"

She frowned. "No. He refused to, even though I thought it was jumping to some pretty extreme conclusions. And now you're doing it again. Why interview me if you agree with him?"

He smiled at her. "Because when you find out what this company is all about, you're going to leave. And I want to make sure you remember that you could have left this whole time."

"Sheesh, either you guys are baby-eaters or I'm really making a bad impression!" she said.

He laughed, his voice echoing in the large dressing room. "I just want you prepared. I honestly am interested in your credentials, I just know you won't take the job."

Zoë glared at him. "Reverse psychology?"

He shrugged. "Simply the truth. Now. Your résumé is impressive. We don't have any of the *Misconceptions* line here yet, do you happen to have one of your books on you?"

She handed over *Raleigh Misconceptions*. "I led the team on *Raleigh*, and launched the *Misconceptions* line, actually."

He flipped through the book. "Impressive, I have to say. I still—"

Zoë interrupted him, her voice desperate. "Please, Mr. Rand, I have no idea what you have against me or what you think I may be, but please just give me a chance. I'm really open-minded, it's hard to shock me."

He cocked an eyebrow at her and stared, his brown eyes studying her. She felt blood rise to her face, but she knew she couldn't back down. He handed the book back to her. "I'm hungry and it's quitting time. Let's go get a bite to eat."

Echoes of the situation she had recently exited ran through her mind. She pursed her lips. "I'm sorry, Mr. Rand, but I'm not going on a date with you—or doing anything more—for a job."

He gave a close-lipped smile, amused. "Oh, Zoë. You're delightful. I am merely hungry, I don't require anything else from you except companionship. Do you want to work at Underground Publishing?"

The unconventional work space was intriguing, and she needed a job in a bad way. If she honestly did end up standing out among her coworkers like a redheaded stepchild, she could always turn him down, or quit later. She nodded firmly. "Yes, sir."

He checked his watch. "We can leave in about half an hour. I'll wrap up what I'm doing here, and John can show you the rest of the office. I think everyone has gone home; everyone except Kevin and Opal, anyway."

He got up and moved to his office door. Zoë admired the graceful way he handled his somewhat heavy body before she caught herself. *Not again.*

John was at the door as soon as Phil called for him. They spoke quietly, and then John peeked into the room. "Zoë, can I show you around?"

She got the tour for the next twenty minutes, seeing the large dressing rooms with dressing tables serving as desks. Zoë found out that about ten people worked at Underground Publishing, that it had been around for about a week, and that it still didn't have computers. It had PR, marketing, and writers, but no managing editors yet. She and John settled in the "break room," which had a decidedly non-relaxing atmosphere, with the whole of the theater spread out before them. The woman in the audience had gone.

"There was a woman here before," Zoë asked. "Who was that?"

"If she was Japanese, that was Koi. She likes to read the papers in the audience."

"I didn't see her face, but her hair was really long and dark," Zoë said.

"Yeah, that's Koi. She's in charge of our operations. Office manager, distribution, she handles about seven different tasks at once."

"Gotcha. Koi. Operations."

John looked at her curiously. "Do you like what you've seen so far?"

Zoë weighed how honest she should be. "It's definitely interesting," she finally said. "I'm dying to know what the dreadful secret is that separates me from all the rest of you, though."

John looked over to where Phil had joined them onstage. The big man had barely made a sound while walking. "I expect you will find that out tonight. Right?"

Phil carried a briefcase, and a dark coat hung over his arm. "She certainly will. We're going to the little Italian place around the corner."

John blinked. "Ah. Well. Yes, that will do it. Can I come?"

"No." Phil was matter-of-fact, but his voice held a no-nonsense tone. Zoë was surprised at the sudden change in demeanor. "You're not even hungry."

How does he know how hungry John is? Zoë looked from one man to the other. "Is everything all right?"

Phil smiled. "It's best if it's just the two of us. You'll be fine, Zoë. I won't let any harm come to you."

"Is that a possibility?"

Neither man answered.

They said good night to John, who smiled mischievously at Zoë and said he hoped to see more of her in the future.

"He's a little forward," Zoë said.

"Well yes, what did you expect?" Phil said, leading them down Fifty-First Street toward Broadway.

"Uh, a little respect? If he talks like that all the time, someone could sue you for sexual harassment," Zoë said.

Phil frowned. "It's his way. Everyone we work with understands that."

It made no sense, but Zoë shrugged it away, refusing to rise to the constant "You're not like us" bait. She just made a mental note to throat-punch the guy if he ever tried to touch her. "So where are we going?"

"A little Italian place on Ninth Avenue. My favorite place to eat. It's a little hole in the wall, something you wouldn't find in mainstream tourist guides."

Zoë nodded and prepared herself to survey the place. Food, atmosphere, and service, not to mention clientele. Maybe a write-up of the restaurant after the meal would impress Phil.

"Is it the kind of place you'd want written about in your travel guide? For 'your kind' of people?"

"Most assuredly," Phil said. He looked at her then, his face inscrutable in the city lights. "Do you honestly think you could fit in with *any* office environment?"

She blanched. "Well, sure. I mean…" She thought briefly of hard-core bondage fans, or people who ended each conversation with "God bless," but shook her head. "No, I can't think of anyone I couldn't work with. Maybe the Ku Klux Klan or Westboro Baptist Church PR departments, I guess."

"Oh, we're not bigots. We like all kinds of people. But you may change your mind. I will not judge you if you do."

"So if I turn out to be an unintentional bigot, it's OK?" she asked, laughing.

He didn't share her mirth. "Actually, yes. You can decide not to take the job, and you move about your life in the city, and we work on our books."

Zoë stopped laughing. "Look. I'm no racist or whateverist. You have a job that needs doing. I can do it. Let me prove it to you."

"Let me show you whom you'll be working with first," he said.

Zoë was all ready to look at the restaurant with an appraising eye in hopes of impressing Phil with her keen observation skills. Gothic decorations covered the walls, wrought-iron twisted into curlicues on top of red wallpaper decorated with dusty weeping flowers. She squinted into the low light as she realized the only illumination came from candles.

Was he planning something romantic after all?

A tall, willowy woman, looking to be in her late forties, swept up to them and embraced Phil. She wore a long blood-red dress that clung to her shapely torso and then draped gracefully in a fuller skirt that hung to her feet. Black lace peeked out from her sleeves and collar. She reminded Zoë of something gothic, only much more authentic than the goth girls she'd gone to college with.

"Phillip, it's so good to see you again. I had begun to fear that you had forsaken us!" she cooed.

Phil returned the hug with more warmth than Zoë had seen him show, but cleared his throat quickly as he let her go. "Sylvia, I'll need a table for two tonight."

Sylvia stepped back and glanced at Zoë and then turned back to Phil. "A table in the back, perhaps? And would you like to see a wine list, or did you bring your own?"

"Wine list, please. And my companion will take the standard menu." He said "companion" with a little bit of emphasis, as if telling Sylvia that they weren't on a date.

"Of course! Only the best for you," she said, and swept through the shadows to the back of the restaurant, motioning them to follow.

Zoë surveyed the other patrons as she followed Sylvia. A handsome couple dressed in a fashion that spoke of older days, almost Victorian ones, returned her gaze coolly, and she flushed. Sylvia led them to the table and asked Phil if he wanted his usual server. He paused and then nodded.

Zoë sat and put her napkin, a fine piece of linen that she feared dirtying, in her lap. She grinned at Phil. "I feel a little underdressed."

Phil inclined his head. "That is nothing to fear." The question of whether there was anything else to fear hung between them, but Zoë refused to ask it. She was tired of his enigmatic attitude and wanted him to just come clean with her.

Admittedly, something about the restaurant had thrown her off her game, and she was desperately trying to regain her footing. She opened her mouth to speak, but a dry voice over her shoulder interrupted her.

"Mr. Rand, lovely to see you."

"Eric, the pleasure is mine. I'll have my usual vintage, but my companion will need a wine list."

"Ms. Stoll already indicated this to me," the voice said, and Zoë craned her neck back and took the proffered menu. She did a double take when she saw the waiter, and then looked back at Phil, who watched her closely.

She took a look around the restaurant and then again at the waiter, who loomed calmly over her. She laughed. "Is this what you were worried about?"

Phil stared at her, his mouth slightly open. It was the first time she had actually surprised him, and it felt good. "Well. Frankly, yes."

"I told you, I don't judge. Is that what the book will be? A view of New York for cosplayers?"

"Cosplayers," he repeated faintly.

"Yeah, people who are really into costume play. Storm Troopers or Slave Leias or Master Chiefs from that video game. Or"—she surveyed the waiter who shuffled away from them—"makeup. That was some seriously good zombie makeup."

Each of the patrons now made sense. It was a room full of sore thumbs; but together they all seemed to fit in. A man ate alone in the corner, dipping his spoon into a bowl full of a black liquid. Small demon horns were glued to his forehead. The handsome couple she had noticed earlier had fangs that glinted as they talked and laughed. And three hulking men devoured plates of meat in a way that made Zoë think they were being a bit too true to the role-playing aspect of their costuming. And their waiter— wow. He waited for her order, hunched over, gray skin peeling from his face. She worried that it wasn't terribly sanitary, but she figured the management would have taken that into account.

She took a look at the pathetically short wine list and decided to go with the house red. She looked up. Phil was still staring at her. She laughed. "Come on, did you think I would be so judgmental about it? I played Dungeons & Dragons in college, and a lot of my friends were into live-action role-playing and cosplay. Some were even furries. I've been to cons with guys just like these people. I didn't get the memo that we'd need to come in makeup. I can do a good vampire if I can find my fangs."

Phil smiled at last, then laughed loud and long, startling the patrons near them. "I would make a safe bet that you can do just that."

The shuffling waiter looked at Zoë. "And the lady would like . . . ?" he asked her in his dry voice.

"A glass of your house red, please," she said, smiling at him.

31

"You would not enjoy our house red, ma'am," the waiter replied. "It's... clear your tastes run to a much finer vintage."

"Well, what would you recommend?"

"We have a lovely shiraz that many of our human customers enjoy. I will bring you a glass." He shuffled off.

Zoë grinned at Phil. " 'Human customers'? This is so cool. I really wish we'd dressed the part. This is exactly the kind of restaurant I'd love to write about in the guidebook."

Phil nodded, picking up on her segue. "Let's look at your book again."

He perused the book on Raleigh, nodding in some areas and frowning in others. Zoë pointed out her specific work, whether it had been editing or writing, and he read in silence for several minutes. Their wine arrived without further comment from the zombie, and she sipped her red and tried not to fret.

Phil closed the book and handed it back to her. "I'll be frank. You are nearly perfect for the job. And it bodes well that you are not put off by the various customers we hope to reach. But I admit I haven't been one hundred percent honest with you."

At that point, time seemed to slow for Zoë. Four waiters had gathered around the table where the three burly men sat after devouring their meat. Two were dressed as zombies, one was much cleaner and his fangs indicated he was probably a vampire, and the fourth had some superb scaly makeup covering his face and hands. They all began to sing "Happy Birthday" to one of the men, who beamed and didn't bother to wipe the juice from his steak off his face. A fifth waiter approached from the kitchen, this one wearing stuck-on demon horns and carrying...

He carried...

Zoë swooned for a moment, a memory hitting her like a fist to the jaw. When her family had moved to the suburbs of North Carolina, she would often ride her bike around the development.

During one mid-morning Sunday ride, she came across a scene that took her brain a full ten seconds to process. Nothing she saw was otherworldly, but it was so out of place in a peaceful suburb that she refused to see it. A family stood in the backyard watching a man butcher a deer they'd hung on their kids' swing set. The skin lay in a discarded pile to the side, and the man approached the pink muscles and sinew and started to carve off hunks of venison with a long knife. Zoë stopped and stared and her brain attempted again to process, but it failed.

They're slaughtering a deer. A deer. In the suburbs. A skinless deer is hanging RIGHT THERE.

Nope. Still the brain didn't acknowledge. She moved on, worried the family would notice her blatant staring, and only about a minute later did her brain work out what had happened. She slammed on the brakes and toppled from her bike into a hydrangea bush, where she vomited, clutching her stomach and voiding her mother's signature hash browns. She had not expected to see a skinless deer hanging from a child's swing set, and when she did, her brain rejected it until forced to understand.

And her brain was rejecting what she saw now, utterly refusing to acknowledge that the demon waiter carried a terrarium that was half-full of hedgehogs. The little creatures moved against one another, each trying to get to the top. The mound positively writhed, and the men at the table watched eagerly. At the end of "Happy Birthday," while everyone in the restaurant applauded, the waiter placed it in front of the man, who reached inside and grabbed a hedgehog. He opened his mouth impossibly wide—his head hadn't been that big before, had it?—and popped the hedgehog in as if it were a marshmallow. He chewed and grinned and nodded to his companions, who both went grabbing for their own desserts.

This scene played out in front of Zoë's eyes, and her brain

tried to process it, but eventually it refused and it decided instead to focus back on Phil. Phil watched her with the same intent gaze he had fixed on her all night. He took a sip of his very thick red, the legs of the wine sliding into the glass as he righted it. His freckled face had gained a little color.

"Now do you understand?" he asked.

He smiled at her, showing teeth that slowly elongated into fangs. Zoë nodded once and then toppled slowly out of her chair as her brain decided that the best way to deal with the situation was to check out completely.

Wake up.

When Zoë opened her eyes, it was as if she were looking through a television. She had no emotional reaction, and felt slow and stupid. She was sitting awkwardly in the chair, unable to move, slumped oddly to the side.

Phil swirled the blood in his glass, contemplating it. "You're interesting, Zoë. You went a completely different way than most humans do. Most deny it first, not even attempting to find a plausible explanation. I wonder if you've encountered others like me."

She felt her head move from side to side. "I don't think so."

Eric shambled over and looked down at Zoë. "Are you going to eat her here, Mr. Rand, or should I prepare her to go?"

Zoë expected a jolt of adrenaline, but it didn't come. Phil frowned. "Bring her some water. She will need it when I let her go."

"So you won't be dining on her?"

"No. I'll have another glass, though, same vintage please."

Eric helpfully propped her more upright in her chair, push-ing her slightly so that she slumped against the wall instead of out of the chair. Phil handed the zombie his wineglass and he trudged off.

Phil tapped his finger on the table. "For this moment, you are mine," he said, staring into her eyes.

"You're the boss," she answered, blinking.

"I want to ask you some questions, and I need you to be truthful to me. You will be under my control for only a few minutes."

She frowned, realizing her face was answering some of her commands. "You don't have to be so dramatic. I'll tell you anything you want." Her words were slow, though, as if she were drunk.

He tapped his finger again. "The truth is, hiring a human might be what we need, if you can take the stress. Do you have any phobias?"

"No." Zoë rubbed her face, still disoriented.

"How do you work under extreme stress? Have you ever been in a position to find out?"

Zoë's face stilled. "Yes," she said softly. "I was terrified. I threw up. But I handled it the best I could. I guess."

"Tell me what happened."

"My boss seduced me. I didn't know he was married. No one did. When his wife found out—" She stopped.

Don't tell him. Something—instinct?—told her not to give him the details, and although it was an effort to resist, she managed it.

"What happened?"

"No."

Phil pursed his lips over his fangs. "Are you in league with Public Works, do you have any history with zoëtism, fortune-telling, or anyone in coterie society?"

"Does a fing look swart to the zooloofills?"

Phil stared at her blankly. "I have no idea—"

"Exactly," she interrupted. "I don't know what you're talking about either."

Phil's tongue ran over his fangs, and Zoë got the sense that it was a tell he used when he was thinking, not something that indicated his hunger. He tapped his finger on the table again. "How are you resisting me? All other humans have been malleable."

"I don't know," she said. "I'm being truthful. I just don't want to tell you everything about me."

"What do you have to hide?" he demanded.

"It's not a matter of hiding something. I don't need to hide the age I started my period, but you don't need to know it. I just don't want to tell you. You don't need to know the model of my first car or the fact that I thought Lionel Ritchie rocked pretty hard when I was a kid. Although I did just tell you that. If you want to know everything about me, we're going to have to be here a long time. I'll tell you what you need to know." Her eyelids drooped suddenly, exhaustion taking over. Keeping them open had taken almost as much effort as resisting him had.

"You don't know how you're resisting me," he said slowly.

"Honestly, I don't," she said. "I wish I did."

Eric brought Phil his refilled wineglass. "The bill, please, Eric, and have Ms. Stoll call me a cab." He took a deep drink.

"As you wish," the zombie said.

"Why are you asking all these questions? Don't you want to know my history with publishing?" Zoë asked, looking at her napkin and fingering the seam. "What does my incident of dreadful decision-making with a married man have to do with anything?"

Phil put his hand on *Raleigh Misconceptions*. "No, I'm satisfied there. It truly is a remarkable book you've written. I needed to know if you'd fit in. I needed to know what scared you. Now, do you remember anything that's happened tonight?"

"Sure. There are monsters here."

"And how do you feel about that?"

"Scared. But no one has threatened me. If you wanted to eat me, you probably would have done it by now."

Phil dabbed a bit of blood off his lips with his napkin and put it on the table, neatly folded. "Zoë, you're too cool, too quick. We need you on our side before Public Works finds out about you. I fully expect that after this initial shock, you will accept our world with as much grace as a human can."

Eric brought the bill and Phil paid it with two bright red-and-yellow bills. He led the groggy Zoë out of the restaurant, waving to Sylvia as he left.

He helped her into the cab. She went along pleasantly, feeling rather drunk. As they pulled away from the curb, she said, "You're a vampire."

He smiled wanly. "And how do you feel about that?"

"It's a lot to take in. Are we going somewhere for dessert?"

"No. I'm taking you home. You will have a job offer tomorrow. I can give you a day to sleep on it."

She frowned. "Now wait a second, I never said I'd take the job. I mean, you eat people, don't you?"

He smiled at her, his face looking rather handsome now that the blood had given him a ruddy complexion. "Now, Zoë, you've already learned far more than the average human. I can't give you any more information unless you agree to work for me."

She felt she should be freaking out more. Or at least fainting again. But the calm Phil had forced on her was still washing over her, leaving her pleasantly buzzed and peaceful. Monsters in the city? Sure. No problem.

The cab screeched to a halt in front of her building. How had they gotten to Brooklyn so fast? She shook her head. "This is too weird."

"It's been a pleasure, Zoë. I look forward to your answer tomorrow." Phil took her limp hand and shook it. She stared at him blankly. He got out of the cab, walked around, and opened the door for her. "This is your address, is it not? It was on your résumé."

"Oh. Yeah. Right." Zoë let him help her out of the car, wondering when she'd be able to move on her own. Phil got back into the cab, and it roared down the street.

Reality snapped back into place as she stood alone on the street. Reality and a sense of acidic hunger. Zoë put her hand to her stomach, where a glass of red wine sat alone and forlorn. "Hey. You were supposed to buy me dinner. Asshole."

"Bad date?" asked a voice behind her.

She jumped and turned, a small scream escaping from her lips. Zombies? Frankensteins? Harpies? "Jesus, don't do that!"

The man held out his hands in apology. He was much taller than she was, dark and muscular. He wore a black sweatshirt and worn jeans. "Sorry. Zoë, isn't it? You live in twenty-seven A?"

She frowned in suspicion. "Who wants to know?"

"I'm Arthur, just moved into twenty-seven B." He held a dirty hand up in an awkward wave. "Uh, I'd shake your hand, but…"

Zoë fought the urge to interrogate him to find out if he was human. *Stop being paranoid. If the world is the same as it was, there's no reason to think that anyone else knows about this.*

If it's even true.

She grasped his hand. "I'm pretty sure it's cleaner than some of the things I've seen and touched tonight. In fact, I'm probably getting you dirty."

Arthur looked at her hand in surprise. It was clean. "Dirty with what?"

Zoë managed to shrug. "It's a long story. It's been a weird-ass night. Nice to meet you." His grip was firm and warm, which she appreciated after feeling the vampire's cool touch.

Together they headed for the door of their building.

"So, bad date?" he asked, unlocking the hallway door for her.

"Eh. It wasn't a date. It was a professional dinner, I guess. An interview. It didn't turn out to be a dinner. I had a glass of wine. We talked about the job. We came back here and he dropped me off."

He screwed up his face, his glasses shifting on his nose. "You went to dinner but you only got a glass of wine?"

"Yeah. It's complicated." She didn't meet his eyes.

"It's not Facebook, it's dinner. Even interviews should provide at least a pretzel from a food cart. What do you do, anyway?"

"Nothing, now," Zoë said, misery welling up to fill the empty cavity in her stomach. "I'm unemployed and seem to have a habit of finding myself in really weird situations." She scrubbed her hands over her face. "I'm sorry—Arthur, right?—I think I just need a sandwich and to go to bed. Thanks for checking on me."

Arthur smiled at her. "No problem. I've been in the unemployment line before. Finally got a new job that brought me to Brooklyn. Unemployment sucks. I hope tomorrow's better. See you around?"

"Yeah, sure," Zoë said, fumbling with her keys and opening her apartment.

She stumbled to the couch, and despite its being eight thirty, fell asleep immediately.

The Shambling Guide to New York City

THEATER DISTRICT:
Restaurants

Italy's Entrails *****
    While fine dining is one of the best reasons to come to the city, many "old-school" coterie prefer not to ape the humans by forcing civilized actions on themselves, like eating in restaurants. There are many prime hunting grounds in the city, but this is not one of them. If you have, or miss having, human sensibilities, then you can do much worse than Italy's Entrails. For coterie, Italy's Entrails is the place in New York where everybody knows your name. Literally. Owner Sylvia Stoll is a vampire from the seventeenth century who has an eidetic memory: if you tell her once who you are and what you like to eat, then she'll remember forever. Tell her how you died and you'll get a free dessert. And this place has the best hedgehog delight in the city. ■

CHAPTER FOUR

The sun crept across Zoë's face and assaulted her eyes. She shielded them and squinted. Morning. She blearily looked around. She was in her apartment, fully dressed, still in her coat, even, lying on the couch. She tried to remember the events of the previous evening, but as she passed her hand over her face, the memories were slow in coming.

Had she had too much wine? She didn't feel hungover. She did a quick body check in a brief panic, but her clothes were only sleep-rumpled and didn't have the look or feel of having been shoved aside or removed. So that Phil guy hadn't taken advantage of her. So... what had happened? And how had he returned her home without her knowing?

She got off the couch and stood, swaying slightly. Had there been something in the wine? Why had he wanted her so drunk? She had a horrifying thought and looked around wildly for her satchel, which happened to be sitting by the door with everything she'd had in it, including her wallet and credit cards. So no sexual assault, no robbery, and no apparent apartment distress. What was going on?

She trudged down the hall to her bathroom and started the shower going, hot. As the bathroom filled with steam, she peered into the mirror and examined the dark circles under her eyes.

As the steam obscured her image in the mirror, her memories reluctantly organized themselves into some sort of chronological blurry sense. There had been the woman in the red dress. The wine. The gross waiter. The strange cosplay. And the hedgehogs. Zoë gasped. *The hedgehogs.* And the man with whom she'd dined, his teeth elongated into fangs. She brought her hands to her head and pressed, as if that could stifle the strange, insistent memories.

Had he bitten her? She couldn't remember, but her neck seemed fine.

Was it true? Could it be true? Vampires and zombies and those weird, horrific men who chowed down on little nocturnal darlings? She'd thought it was cosplay, but by the end of the evening it had been pretty clear something else was going on. Shaking her head, she stuck her hands in the pockets of her pants to remove her valuables before stripping. She found a small folded piece of paper in the front left pocket. Her fingers shook as she peeled it open. In very neat handwriting were the words: *If you are still interested, I'd like to make an offer. Call me. Phil Rand, Underground Publishing.* A phone number followed.

She left the note on her bathroom counter to gather condensation—maybe it would blur the ink and she could pretend she couldn't read the number—as she finished removing her clothes and stepped into the hot shower. She gasped as the water hit her back, and grudgingly stayed under the too-hot spray, allowing it to melt the rest of the cobwebs in her mind. The zombies had been dropping bits of flesh on the carpet. The vampires—even Phil—had been drinking blood instead of red wine. How had she not noticed that Phil's wine was so viscous? And those demons and the hedgehogs...

She shampooed furiously, hoping to scrub the images from her mind, but succeeded only in tangling her curly black hair. She tried to focus completely on scrubbing, rinsing, conditioning, shaving, turning the water off, exiting the tub, and toweling dry.

Vampires. Monsters. In the city.

Then it hit her.

She sat down with a thud on the toilet seat, the breath leaving her. Phil was publishing a travel book for monsters. And his coworkers had to be monsters as well.

I guess they were right about my not fitting in.

How would monster tourists view the city? The implications were fascinating. And terrifying. Were the monsters coming here to take over? Devour everyone? The patrons of the restaurant last night hadn't seemed to have any interest in devouring her, even though they clearly could have. Something nagged at her—Sylvia had asked Phil if he had brought his own vintage that evening. Zoë realized with a sick jolt that the hostess had been talking about her.

She could easily become a personal vintage if she took this job. But if monsters were already here, how was that different from any other day? Why was she in more danger now than she had been last week?

Well, she conceded to herself as she slipped on some jeans and a T-shirt, every day she wasn't walking knowingly into a vampire lair. She didn't think she was, anyway. She'd been happy in her ignorant belief that gangs and rapists and serial killers were the greatest threats in the city. She hadn't considered the living dead, or any other monster, until yesterday.

And was she now considering *working* with them? Really considering? The concept was insane. And yet it still intrigued her. What would they do? How do you write for monsters? She wondered what it paid. If Phil would—or even could—guarantee her safety. And what kind of benefits she'd get.

Zoë exited her building with a frightened lump in her throat. She'd had a small fear of being mugged or raped when she'd returned to the city, and always carried the pepper spray her mother had given her. But now she had a new fear.

Would pepper spray stop a zombie? A vampire? Those hedgehog-eating demon guys? And if those existed, what else was out there? Werewolves? She had forgotten to check the moon phase on the calendar. Ghosts? She'd have to keep an eye on any cemeteries she passed. Banshees? Now everything about Britney Spears made sense.

Zoë looked at the people on the street, trying to identify each one as human or not. Many didn't notice, but some returned her gaze with interest, nervousness, or hostility. Plain green eyes, blue eyes, brown eyes looked back at her.

If there were monsters in New York, where did they hide?

She had done some urban exploration in Raleigh, but she had been too young to do any in New York when she had first lived there. She did know there were miles of unused tunnels under the city.

Bet they're not unused.

She walked on. The city was full of people. Gangs, celebrities, upper-crust society, poor, homeless, artists, clubbers, and the ordinary folks: those just wanting to get by. New Yorkers didn't look at one another, they didn't stop to help strangers, and they certainly didn't ask what time it was. Who knew what could be lurking underneath the overcoats and hats? Who were the ones who walked with their heads down, at a slightly swifter gait? And who came out at night?

Zoë entered the massive front doors of the main branch of the Brooklyn Public Library and sniffed around for an occult section. A pale young man with black hair and a thin face sat behind an information desk. He was helping a college student find a book on elves when Zoë entered the room. It was disappointingly not the dark corner with a musty collection of books she'd been expecting; it was clean and boring. Why couldn't there be a happy medium between the horror that was the terrible, unwelcoming bookstore she'd found yesterday and a sterile library?

She smacked herself in the forehead as she realized that the bookstore had been for monsters. They didn't want to sell to humans.

H. P. Lovecraft had written about dark, forbidding libraries and book rooms; those had books worthy of chronicling monsters.

Had Lovecraft been a fiction writer, or had he been writing the true histories of New England towns? Zoë shook her head: *One mind-blowing item at a time.*

When she smacked herself in the head, the librarian turned at the sound.

"You don't look like you read much occult," he said, looking her up and down. Zoë was suddenly aware of her lack of wild hair color or facial piercings. "Are you looking for anything in particular?"

"Um. Books on vampires, I guess. And Lovecraft."

"You know that Lovecraft didn't write about vampires, right?"

Zoë glared at him. "Yes. I know. Thanks."

"We have *Twilight* in our young adult section," he said dismissively, pointing down the hall.

Zoë placed her hands on the desk. The startled librarian sat back. "While I'm sure your patronizing attitude has gotten you quite far in your career in library science, I'd like you to give me the benefit of the doubt and think that perhaps I know that *Twilight* is easily found at a bookstore, and perhaps I am here for a book that is a bit more difficult to find."

He swallowed and looked at his computer screen, which, Zoë saw, was blank. "Ah. If you want some rare Lovecraft, our collection is pretty good, but you should check out the library in Red Hook—he lived there for years, you know. Of course, he hated it, but any community will claim someone if they end up being famous. The library's tiny, but it's got some amazing texts. What we have here isn't too shabby, though, so it's not a bad place to start. To get the authentic stories, you're going to have to find books that weren't edited by August—"

Zoë nodded politely for as long as she could stand it, then put up a hand to stop him.

"Really, I just want to start with whatever Lovecraft you have. Just point me to where they are."

He frowned at the interruption of his display of Lovecraftian history and motioned for her to follow him. He left her unceremoniously in an aisle near the back wall and pointed to a shelf. "Vampires: here. Lovecraft: on that wall. Other undead or otherwise otherworldly monsters are one aisle over. I'll be at my desk working on a new shelving protocol."

She nodded to him, and when she didn't seem impressed with his very important task, he sighed and walked off, his boots sounding poutingly loud.

Zoë perused the books: they focused on vampires in general, Dracula in particular, and vampire hunters. There was a great deal of vampire fiction, vampire comics, and vampire role-playing games. She grabbed several at random and then went to the wall where several Lovecraft collections sat on the shelves, along with many copies of the *Necronomicon*, each by a different author. Zoë added a collection of Lovecraft's stories and two different copies of the *Necronomicon* to the pile. She carried her stack to the counter and set it in front of the librarian.

He took the top book, *The Dunwich Horror and Others*, from the stack. "Good choice. Why so much interest in Lovecraft and vampires?"

Zoë peered at him closely. He seemed human, but so had Phil and the girl at the bookstore. And that flirty fat guy, John. The librarian stood in a dusty shaft of sunlight, though, so he was probably not a vampire.

"I have heard a lot about Lovecraft," she said. "I wanted to learn a bit about him. And I'm curious about how different authors treat the vampire myths."

"Weird focus for a thesis," he said, scanning the bar codes in the backs of the books.

"It's not a thesis. I'm not in school. Just interested."

He shrugged and finished scanning her books and then her card. "Due back in three weeks. Let me know how you liked 'The Dunwich Horror.'"

She nodded at him and stuffed the books in her satchel. Time to do some reading.

Damn, but Lovecraft was dull! Zoë shut *The Dunwich Horror and Others* with a sigh and put it beside her on the couch. She had been able to get through only a few pages. She'd heard her friends in college talk about elder gods Cthulhu and Ithaqua, and the stories had sounded awesome, but she'd never actually sat down to read Lovecraft's words. The anecdotes had been better than the stories.

She had already looked through several of the vampire books, making notes when they seemed to correspond with—or contradict—what she had observed about Phil. As the books said, he'd seemed to avoid sunlight. But how had he gotten from the bookstore to the publishing offices? He seemed fine with being awake during the day. He drank a glass of chilled blood (Zoë had assumed it was chilled, but she realized with a jolt that it might not have been) instead of needing to drink from a living victim. And the worst part, he'd enthralled her. Although she'd managed to fight him, at least a little bit.

She looked through the books to find information on people fighting thralls, and could only find information about humans bending entirely to vampires' wills.

She had little memory. At least she didn't have a burning need to go to him or be by his side or open a vein for him. She didn't really want to serve him—beyond the publishing job, of course.

Which still intrigued her. Dammit.

She had to face it. As much as this whole thing scared her, the sheer fact that she had an opportunity to write for these creatures, to see New York City in a way that few humans ever would, was exciting to the point of making her punch-drunk. She picked up *The Dunwich Horror and Others* again and tried to read it not as fiction, but as history. Telling herself she wasn't supposed to get pleasure out of it made it a little easier to read.

Finally, after getting through the first two parts of the titular story, she slammed the book shut and looked at the clock. Two thirty. Phil would be expecting her call soon. She needed to come up with an answer.

She stood and grabbed her jacket. For once, she needed things to be on her terms. Time to visit Underground Publishing.

The Shambling Guide to New York City

MANHATTAN:
Business Travel

Any coterie with business in the city will want to go to the Hell's Kitchen area first, but avoid the Javits Center, which banned coterie after an unfortunate vampire gathering had a miscommunication with the catering company and many humans died. Your goal is a mere two blocks away. That's where the Flight of Pigeons meets.

An empty lot on Thirty-Eighth Street is the gathering point for the finest business minds in the city, and they welcome coterie—bearing breadcrumbs in exchange for advice on business-related questions. While not exactly scrying the future for accurate answers (or obscure prophesy), these brilliant birds work together as a hive mind to come up with the best decision.

The incredible usefulness of these birds has caused their section of New York to be deemed neutral territory, and woe to anyone who injures or threatens them.

The decree came after tragedy hit Boston on January 15, 1919. An angry zombie killed fourteen pigeons that were trying to broker a deal between the zombie and her chief business rival. The ensuing destruction done to the city caused all cities to declare the territory of the Flight of Pigeons neutral. ■

CHAPTER FIVE

Phil looked up, startled, when Zoë opened the door to his office. She walked in, sat down on the pink couch, and waited.

"Hello, Zoë," he said. He glanced at a barefoot woman wearing a light-blue sundress who was standing at his desk. Her skin had a bluish tinge and her hair was pink. "Morgen, we can talk later."

Morgen, thin and almost childlike with her frizzy hair captured in two ponytails, looked at Zoë with her head cocked. "Is this the human?"

Zoë studied her with equal curiosity. The woman clearly wasn't a zombie, but didn't have the gravitas of the vampire.

"You have me at a disadvantage," Zoë said, standing and holding her hand out. "I am in fact the human. Zoë."

The woman grinned broadly and shook her hand. "Hello, Zoë the human. I'm Morgen the water sprite." She looked at Phil. "I like her!"

"I'm sure you do," he said dryly. "Hiring her would add to the chaos you seem to enjoy. Would you leave me with her?"

"Sure thing, boss. See you later, Zoë!" She stepped lightly from the room, barely touching the ground.

"I was expecting a call," he said as Zoë sat down again.

Zoë snorted. "And I was expecting you guys to be human. Life is full of disappointments." Phil didn't react. "Anyway, I have a lot of questions for you. Are you prepared to answer? Or should I just leave now?"

Phil's eyes narrowed at the challenging tone to her voice. "I will answer what I can."

She crossed her arms. "What happened last night? After I figured things out?"

"You fainted. I had to explain to Sylvia that I hadn't brought you there to eat you. We talked a bit when you woke up. I paid for the wine and blood, looked at your résumé to find out your address, and took you home."

"And did you enthrall me?"

Phil dropped his eyes. "I tried. You're somewhat resistant."

She pulled *Dracula* from her satchel. "I read about it."

Phil took a look at the book and laughed out loud. "You're getting your vampire information from *Dracula*?"

Zoë frowned. "What, did you want me to just walk blindly into working with you without doing any research beyond what you told me last night—while I was hypnotized by you? That's real smart, there. So I got some books. But then I thought you could probably tell me more about monsters than I need to know, right?"

"Coterie."

Zoë blinked. "What?"

"'Monsters' is pejorative. Nonhumans go by the term 'coterie.'"

"OK, sure, whatever. You can tell me about coterie, then?"

He extended his hands. "Indeed."

"So I can research who I'd be writing for here."

He nodded.

She swallowed but tried not to let her nervousness show. "These coterie, they eat humans, right?"

"Many do, yes."

"How am I going to survive? Isn't that like a chicken working with foxes?"

Phil paused for a moment. "Field research may be difficult. I

51

can't guarantee your safety that way. But you will have a chaperone on most assignments, likely one who doesn't eat humans. And you can always delegate the field research." He paused. "I can guarantee your safety in the office, though. No one under my employ will touch you."

"How can you guarantee it?"

Phil looked at her for a moment, then smiled, his incisors elongating and his eyes becoming bloodshot. Zoë gritted her teeth against the intense desire to turn and run. When he spoke again, his voice was deeper. "Coterie businesses have a different and more...primal management structure than human ones. If I guarantee your safety, you know you will be safe. The staff know what will happen to them if they disobey."

And in an instant, he became the pleasant Phil again, although his eyes still looked as if he'd been up all night in a smoky club. "Besides, they're a good crew, I think you'll like them. As long as you can, as you mentioned, be accepting of their 'alternative lifestyles.'"

"So you're really offering me this job."

Phil nodded. "You were right: we need someone who knows travel book writing. I know book publishing and distribution and advertising in coterie circles, but when it comes to the writing, I need someone who knows what she's doing. I have some very passionate writers on staff, but you're the only one with the experience I need. I figure I'll have you research some history and details on your audience, and then come in and outline the book, get to know the staff. Then you can set the book assignments. Even though you'll be managing editor, I'll want you in the field with some of the writers to get to understand the world we live in."

Zoë held up her hand. "This is too weird."

Phil continued as if she hadn't spoken. "About your compensation; coterie have a different monetary system than humans. We deal in hell notes, blood tokens, or occult favors. Sometimes all three. But no one could exist in a world with humans without some currency, so there is an exchange rate to dollars—money changers are in Chinatown, and the World Bank is in New Orleans. I will offer you a straight human salary to start off with, but in three months we can renegotiate. I think once you learn more about our world, you will want the monetary ability to participate in it."

"How can I pay my rent with occult favors or that other stuff?"

"Occult favors can get you things like a windfall of cash from unexpected places, or cause your landlord to assume you've already paid. And while no, you likely wouldn't want blood tokens as they're usually best spent at restaurants and blood banks, don't discount hell notes till you see how they're spent."

Zoë mentally filed this information away under Freak Out About This Later. "OK, and what about benefits?"

"Sad to say we do not offer benefits, as the normal life insurance, health insurance, et cetera don't apply in our world. But I am prepared to make sure your salary is high enough that you could cover that on your own."

Zoë forced herself to say, "So I guess a 401(k) is too much to hope for?"

Phil grinned. "I think you'll want to invest in an IRA."

"And why did you just assume I'd take the job?" she asked.

Phil leaned back and put his arms behind his head, the casual power pose. "I can read people. I know a sure thing when I see it. You're scared, but you're also unemployed, you know it's a good job, and you're burning with curiosity about it. You will take the job."

"I don't think—"

"And besides," he interrupted. "I don't take no for an answer very well."

The actual negotiations were brief. The salary nearly made her choke, but she remembered she'd be paying for her own health insurance. Phil ran through some other details, such as that if she got attacked in the field and turned into a coterie—zombie, vampire, et cetera—she could retain her job. Then he pulled out his phone and called Koi in operations to tell her the company was getting a new employee.

And it was done. She was employed. In the strangest job she'd ever had.

Zoë stared out the window of the train as she rode back to Brooklyn and thought about her situation.

Phil had not introduced her to anyone, but did say she'd be working with vampires, zombies, Morgen the water sprite, a Japanese fox spirit (a *kitsune*, he'd called her), a death goddess, a succubus, and an incubus. He had told her about some websites and books that he promised would give her more reliable information than Bram Stoker.

Stoker was a wannabe, according to Phil, and no self-respecting vampire would turn him. H. P. Lovecraft had been a frightened chronicler of current events, and Mary Shelley had been the first zoëtist to write down her methods.

"Read *Frankenstein*," Phil had said. "Carefully."

"Zoëtist? Like my name?" Zoë had asked.

He grinned. "Yes, 'Zoë' means life. 'Zoëtist' is what we call those who create life—in ways other than procreation, that is. Anyone from voodoo practitioners who raise zombies to rabbis who work with the ancient golem creation techniques are zoëtists. And they're almost always humans—one of the rare human coterie you'll encounter."

As he wrote down the book titles for her, he added, "Most of the existing books in our society are poorly written and outdated. You're going to have to trudge through some dense stuff to find out what makes some zombies mindless, ravenous husks and others intelligent and functioning undead."

Zoë frowned. "I don't suppose you can tell me?"

He shook his head. "You will learn more if you read it yourself."

"Thanks, Dad. And I guess there's no handy *Human's Guide to the Coterie in New York City?*"

Phil paused, then smiled slightly. "No, there's not. That might be a good idea for a limited-run book. And now I know that it was a good idea to hire you."

"Yeah, hope you keep that opinion after I get through all of this."

This was not her world. She was not the target demographic.

Later that afternoon, Zoë poured two glasses of wine and lined them up on her coffee table. She needed liquid fortitude. She sat in her large comfy blue chair and pulled her knees to her chin. Her hands were sweaty as she dialed her cell phone. Sometimes the admin assistant answered the phone, but often—

"Godfrey Sullivan." The voice on the other end was buttery and rich. The voice that had once made her stomach turn over and disregard her better common sense.

But now it seemed far away, without power.

"It's Zoë Norris. I got a job in New York but I need to talk to you to extend COBRA benefits for three months."

There was a pause, then he said, "And you didn't even need a recommendation! That's just great, Jenny."

She wanted to correct him; his use of her middle name no longer felt secret and intimate; now it felt like an intrusion, something he wasn't allowed to do anymore. "It's Zoë, please. Yeah, I got a job, so can you connect me to HR? I need to talk about some benefits stuff."

"Hang on a second, Jenny," Godfrey said. "It's good to talk to you."

"Yeah?" She was surprised to realize she didn't agree. The knot in her chest loosened a little.

Godfrey's voice dropped. "Do you...ever think about me?"

"Yeah, I thought about you today when I was relieved that I was going to have a boss who wouldn't seduce me."

Silence on the other end.

"So how *is* Lucy?" she asked, driving the knife home.

His voice lost the sultry tones. "I'll connect you to Tony in HR."

"You do that."

She found herself smiling as Tony, the HR guy, answered the phone. As they discussed how long she could continue to pay for her health insurance under COBRA, she was amazed that she no longer ached for Godfrey. Maybe she was finally growing up.

Her mind went to the night Lucy, Godfrey's wife, who, by the way, was a fucking *police officer*, had arrived at her apartment. The enraged cop had stood outside her first-floor window, screaming and throwing rocks. When the glass shattered, Zoë had called 911, but once she identified herself, the connection was cut and the police never showed. Of course not; the police were already there, screaming at her. She broke down the door and Zoë hid in the empty chest at the foot of her bed. Heavy footsteps trudged through her house; she couldn't even tell how many people were with Lucy, but none of them found her, and they finally left.

Zoë stayed in the chest for the rest of the night, tasting sour bile in her mouth and wondering how she had gotten into this mess. Godfrey wore no ring and brought no one to company events.

The next day she called into work and talked to Tony in HR, who had already spoken with Godfrey and prepared a severance package. Tony told her that resigning would be her safest avenue, and before she could let the word "lawsuit" leave her lips, he named the amount that Misconceptions would pay her for her agreeable and quiet exit. It was a large number.

Very large.

At that moment, Zoë realized that she had a price. And perhaps Raleigh wasn't the place for her.

She asked Tony if he would pack up her desk, and he paused, then said that Lucy had been there and, ah, had made packing her desk largely unnecessary. He mentioned that part of the dollar amount was the estimated cost of her broken decorations, torn books, and destroyed plants. Tony would pack what had survived, along with copies of the books she had worked on to ensure her future employment.

She rented a hotel room for the next two days, staying in pajamas and remaining stunned. She couldn't hold food down, and despite frequent showers, her body odor took on a tangy, metallic odor, the scent of her own anxiety. She called a packing company, a repairman, and a real estate agent, and gave them as much information as they'd need to finalize her affairs. She didn't want to return to her house. Ever.

On the third day, when her Misconceptions severance was deposited directly into her account, Zoë packed her emergency backpack full of books and underwear and got online to buy a one-way ticket home to New York City.

Unlike Raleigh, which had always felt a bit hostile, even before the Lucy incident, New York seemed to welcome her with open arms. And it was in New York that she got the job with the monster publishing company.

No, sorry, the *coterie* publishing company.

She couldn't deny feeling trepidation—or outright fear—when she thought of her first day at Underground Publishing. And yet facing real supernatural beings who literally ate humans seemed less stressful than facing Godfrey—or Lucy—ever again. Phil at least guaranteed her safety. Godfrey had not been able to do that.

Zoë sighed and stretched, feeling a hundred pounds lighter. She sipped her second glass of wine and pulled out one of the books Phil had told her about. She had two weeks before her first day, on November 2.

The Shambling Guide to New York City

FINANCIAL DISTRICT AND HARBOR ISLANDS:
Places of Note

While many coterie find visiting human crypts and graveyards relaxing, the Statue of Liberty is not such a crypt. Coterie visit her island with solemn reverence. "Lady Liberty" is the sarcophagus of the great French demon Chandal L'énorme, and she stands forever at Liberty Island as a reminder to coterie everywhere that once only humans were welcome in America. While that is no longer true, the humans celebrate the poor demon's crypt as a symbol of freedom, a truly ironic interpretation. ■

CHAPTER SIX

Zoë would not have described herself as an anxious person, but when things did manage to faze her, she had to admit to a nervous stomach. After the Godfrey/Lucy incident she had lost five pounds hiding in her hotel room, her digestion rebelling against her. She tried to look at it as a positive, as she needed to slim down a little anyway, but she wouldn't be writing books recommending the "anxious bulimia" diet.

In the few days leading up to the start of her coterie managing editor job, she managed to vomit only twice, both times after waking up from anxiety dreams involving working in a dungeon, and Phil chaining her screaming, drooling coworkers to the wall to keep them from devouring her—only to attack her himself, biting her neck and draining her dry.

Other than that, she was fine.

Phil had said her first day would be Tuesday, November 2, to get her started on a new pay period. November 1, he informed her, was the Day of the Dead, and a coterie holiday.

She took advantage of her time in October to do research, bemoaning the fact that there was very little current coterie information. Part of her panicked at that—how was she going to deal with modern coterie?—but another part, the writer, the editor, began to think and wonder what holes were there and how she could fill them. There were hints that many coterie in the eighteen hundreds had developed a new, peaceful relation-

ship with humans by striking deals with undertakers and sometimes even doctors to get food from corpses so they could avoid
murder.

Did that still happen? Someone had to supply the coterie in
Italy's Entrails with their fare. If they worked with humans in
morgues and, she guessed, blood banks, then there had to be
more humans who knew about the coterie.

Was that why Phil had brightened up (as much as he did
brighten) at the thought of a book on coterie intended for
humans? Perhaps, but it wouldn't serve a large audience.

She also learned that many undead needed to feed only once
or twice a week, as the life they fed on was quite sustaining to
their limited needs. They were metaphysical needs, the human
remains representing a life force that drove the undead. Their
food wasn't like her food, which needed to constantly create
energy to make her organs run.

Never a spiritual or religious woman, Zoë had to shake her
head at this. A pint of blood kept a vampire going for four days?
She got woozy if she didn't have a mid-morning snack. And
it wasn't the blood at all, but what the blood represented: life
force. If vampires were so passionate and depicted as sexy beasts
because they fed on life force, why were zombies not depicted as
the scholars of the coterie world?

Her reading showed that zombies were different beasts alto-
gether. The lurching, mindless state only happened when they
reached a certain level of hunger; as long as they always had a
good supply of brains on hand they functioned just fine. Zoë
learned with a smile that they *were* considered the brainiacs of
the undead world, due to their frequent consumption of "brain
food."

She found depressingly little information on the economics of
the coterie world, and still had only a passing understanding of

what hell notes and blood tokens were. She wondered if a book on coterie economics might be useful at some point.

On the Sunday before her first day, she actually went to a Catholic church, but didn't spend much time in Mass since she knew next to nothing of the rituals. She thought about filling an eyedropper with holy water, but didn't know if it would work— or, if it did, if her employer would look at her as if she were carrying a loaded gun into the office.

She didn't steal the holy water, but she did note the address of the church for future reference. Best to be safe.

That night she took it easy, going over basic rituals. Dealing with the coterie would be like being a page at the United Nations trying to keep up with all the different protocols. Take greetings, for example. Zoë read that vampires were, on the whole, formal and preferred to shake hands. Zombies didn't want to be touched, they didn't like their flesh sloughing off. *Can't blame them.* Many demons were eager to touch you, but would usually see it as an opportunity to suck your life force out, so it was best to meet them with your hands full to avoid any skin-to-skin touch.

There were so many other races to worry about. Zoë had been shocked to note that there was more than one kind of vampire: those that sucked blood, those that sucked the will to live, those that sucked life force...she began making notes in her notebook to keep with her to remind her of what to do—or, in many cases, what not to do.

Never look a brownie in the eye. Never accept an invitation from one of the fae folk. Never sleep with an incubus.

(Had Godfrey been an incubus? It would explain a lot. It would also take all responsibility away from Zoë...she felt like a coward thinking that.)

She finally made herself some tea, took a hot bath, and went to bed early. Plenty of time to worry about faux pas on her first day.

Zoë got up early on November 1 and headed to the train station for a dry run to see how long it took to get to Fifty-First Street. (And when she got there, might as well get breakfast at Bakery Under Starlight. She didn't know what Carl put in his croissants, but she was convinced it had to be pure crack.)

In forty-five minutes she exited the train and figured giving herself an hour's commute time would work. She headed north to Bakery Under Starlight, people-watching as she went.

People in cities were so anonymous. She realized they could be anything and she wouldn't have noticed if she hadn't really been looking. It made a weird sort of sense: hide a zombie in a crowd of people who don't look at one another, even if a lot of people are around, and it's bound to blend in. Put it in a rural environment with people who know everyone and everyone's business, and a zombie stands out like a necrotic thumb. Cities were perfect for coterie.

A man wearing dark sunglasses despite the cloudy November day passed her on the sidewalk. He had a quick gait that she would have assumed was a precise, metrosexual style of walking, but something reminded her of that water sprite from the office, Morgen. They were walking in the same direction, so Zoë didn't have to deviate from her path to watch him. He was dressed well, but a little underdressed for the weather, wearing only a linen suit and no coat, while everyone else was bundled against the unseasonable cold.

The man, to Zoë's delight, walked into Bakery Under Starlight. She followed him and took her place in line behind him.

Zoë had a hunch that one did not come out and ask if someone was coterie. It probably had the same etiquette-ignorant grace as asking someone what race they were. Still, she was dying to know.

When it was the man's turn in line, he smiled at Carl. Behind the glasses, he was quite handsome. "Morning, Carl," he said. "Can I have a Tibetan Blue tea?"

Carl nodded and got a mug ready. "Can I tempt you with a pastry?"

The man grinned wider. "You know you always can tempt me, Carl."

Zoë shuffled her feet, suddenly trying not to eavesdrop on this blatant flirtation. The man bought two scones along with his tea, and then it was Zoë's turn. She greeted Carl by name.

"I didn't think to see you again," he said, his voice losing its flirtation.

"Your pastries are unmatched, how could I not come back?" she said, smiling, hoping to mend the tension between them regarding the incident of the old homeless woman. "So, do you know everyone?" she asked.

He shrugged. "Pretty much. I've got a lot of regulars. What can I get you?"

Catching the cue that he had no desire to talk to her, Zoë made her breakfast order and then sat down with her coffee and pastry.

The café was crowded, but Zoë looked around and realized that a lot of the patrons had a similar...*oddness* about them, like the man she'd stood behind. Some moved with an unearthly grace. Some had hats that sat oddly on their heads, ill-fitting hats that looked as if they had a more important job than just being fashionable. Others had coats with collars pulled up high, and one man looked gray and ill, like a zombie that hadn't started peeling.

Zoë was the odd woman here. She realized with a start that it was a coterie establishment, like Italy's Entrails. *That's why Carl knows everyone. That's why John was in here.*

She looked at the man behind the counter again. There was absolutely nothing otherworldly about him; he seemed like a normal, tall, muscular man, flour dusting his shirt, making his dark hands much lighter than the rest of him.

Zoë shrugged. She had a lot to learn. Maybe she'd be able to tell coterie from humans after working with them for a bit. *It would make life easier, that's for sure.*

A couple of hours drifted by as she read more books on coterie. She sat at the same table she'd been at when she had applied to the job at Underground Publishing. After getting a refill, she checked the bulletin board again. Beside the Underground Publishing flyer now hung a notice about a lost hellhound, a request for a carnivorous-plant sitter while the owner was on vacation, and a flyer advertising the grand opening of a Chinese restaurant, the Jade Crane.

Zoë frowned. That seemed rather out of place among the other, more specifically coterie-focused flyers. Was the Chinese food more tailored to coterie? Chinese coterie? Or was it for coterie who preferred eating Asian people? Zoë shuddered. That one was a little too morbid for thought. She took note of the restaurant's address and realized it was just a few blocks north. Lunch sounded like a great idea.

For a restaurant celebrating a grand opening, the Jade Crane looked pretty dead, not to mention that the storefront looked thirty years old instead of new. Zoë squinted through the dirty window. A Chinese hostess sat behind a register, wearing a traditional red brocade shirt and black slacks, flipping through a *Vogue* magazine and glancing at the clock. She looked to be about twenty-five, short and thin.

Zoë poked her head in. "Are you open?"

The woman looked up and narrowed her eyes briefly. After she gave Zoë the once-over, her face broke into a petite, toothy smile and she stretched her hands out. "Of course! Grand opening! Please, come in, sit where you like!"

Zoë smiled back at her and took a seat at the back of the restaurant, where she could people-watch. Or monster-watch. (*Coterie*, she had to remind herself.)

The woman brought her a menu and a glass of water. The restaurant was different from other Chinese restaurants in that it didn't have the classic bamboo, lucky cats, or scrolls on the wall. Instead the walls were blood-red, making the room dark even in the sunny midday, and decorations were nonexistent. Zoë was the only person in the restaurant.

The woman came to take her order. Zoë ordered some soup and some fried rice. The woman nodded and jotted down the order on a pad. Zoë noticed there was a large scar on her wrist, a burn that looked like a symbol, but she didn't get a good look. Two Asian women came in, laughing. The hostess bowed briefly to Zoë and ran to attend to them.

While she had been friendly and welcoming to Zoë, she practically groveled before these women. She bowed low several times and spoke in Chinese to them. They were older, one with a bun on top of her head, the other with a graying bob cut. Both were slightly overweight and dressed like upper-middle-class ladies who looked, honestly, out of place in this dirty restaurant. Zoë watched them carefully.

There. A red piece of paper switched from one of the women to the hostess, and she brightened and became, if possible, even more obsequious. *A hell note*, Zoë thought.

The hostess sat them in the middle of the dining room and called a young man from the back room to wait on them, whispering swiftly in low, tense Chinese. His eyes widened and he nodded.

Through all of this, Zoë was dying to find out who, or what, these very important women were. But the dining room began filling up for lunch, and Zoë became busy watching other people, trying to identify the men and women as human or not. The coterie began standing out once she knew what clues to look for. Ways of moving, ways of dressing, and the biggest clue: how the hostess treated them. She welcomed humans, but worshiped the coterie.

After that, the only question was whether they were vampire, zombie, fae, demon, or something else Zoë hadn't learned about yet.

She pulled out her book and read it discreetly as the food came. She jumped when the empty chair at her table scraped across the floor. In an instant, she was looking into the wide eyes of the homeless woman from the café, who had sat down across from her without an invitation. What had Carl called her? Granny something?

"How did you hear about this restaurant?" the woman asked.

Zoë swallowed her mouthful of rice. "I saw an ad for it at Bakery Under Starlight," she said. "I was craving Chinese, wanted to check it out."

The woman nodded and looked pointedly at Zoë's book, a manual for the Wraith role-playing game. "And the books?"

Zoë bit her lip. She glanced at the woman, then the other patrons, who had to be 75 percent coterie, and then back at the woman. "I'm doing research for my new job. I'm editing a travel book."

The woman's eyes widened. "And this travel book is focused on New York City?"

Zoë nodded.

"And the travel book is for...?"

Zoë looked at the patrons and swallowed. She couldn't be obvious yet, she would sound ridiculous. She finally said, "I'm betting you know the answer to that."

"Are you a zoëtist?" the woman asked, voice even lower.

"No, just an editor," Zoë said.

The woman reached over and snagged the edge of Zoë's hot-and-sour-soup bowl and dragged it across the table. She took a bite and chewed on a mushroom. "She said you weren't a zoëtist. If that's true, you should have a talisman. Where is it?"

Zoë was too shocked at the theft of her soup to respond right away. She signaled the waiter and asked for another bowl of soup, then asked the woman if she wanted anything else to eat.

"I have soup," the woman said, as if Zoë were stupid. "I don't need anything else."

Zoë shrugged, and after the waiter left, she told the woman, "I have no idea what a talisman is."

The soup was going into the woman's mouth faster than Zoë could track, and she didn't spill a drop. "You are human. Working with coterie. You have no talisman. You carry no weapons. You're going to last one, maybe two hours."

"Hey, how do you know I'm unarmed?" she asked, forcing her voice to stay a whisper.

The woman stopped eating long enough to meet her eye. "I can always tell."

"I can take care of myself," Zoë said, hating how petulant she sounded.

"You ever fight a hungry vampire? A mad zombie? An incubus?"

Zoë's eyes flicked to the other patrons again, and she sighed. "No."

The woman nodded. "You're stupid. But I will teach you. Come with me, I'll keep you alive."

She stood then, and left the room, her braid swinging. A few of the patrons looked at her with fear on their faces.

Emotions warred within Zoë: irritation at this woman's audacity in insisting Zoë would die, annoyance that she fueled the fear Zoë had been fighting, and a small, intrigued glee that she had, perhaps, found a kindred spirit.

She dropped a twenty-dollar bill on the table and ran after the woman.

Zoë caught up with her halfway down the block. The woman walked with purpose, not meeting anyone's eyes, more like a Wall Street broker than a homeless woman.

"So what's your name, anyway?" Zoë asked, putting her hand on the woman's shoulder to slow her down.

Immediately the hand was trapped in the woman's strong grip and twisted in a way that caused shooting pains up Zoë's arm. The woman kept walking. "You don't grab someone in the city. You just died."

"I just died?" Zoë asked, trying to get her hand free.

The woman let her go. "If I had been something else, you would have died. You have no reaction time, no common sense. She has faith in you, Zoë-Life, but I do not."

"Who are you? Who is *she*? Where are we going?" Zoë shook her hand, trying to get feeling back into her numb fingers.

"I am Granny Good Mae. You will meet her in time. Right now we're going to the park."

They made it to Central Park, which was sparsely populated on the cold day. Granny Good Mae found a good-size rock with a view of the Lake and sat down. "You have many questions. So do I. We must get to know each other."

"Uh, OK," Zoë said, and sat down beside her.

Granny Good Mae watched a jogger run past in a sweatshirt, shorts, and gloves. "You came with me—not without question, but you came with me. Why were you so trusting?"

"Because you are the only other human I've met who knows what's going on. I wanted some answers from the outside."

"How do you know I'm not one of them?"

"Because they practically wet themselves when they see you," Zoë said bluntly. "When I first saw you, I thought they were just mad because they didn't want a homeless person in their swank café. But at lunch today it was more obvious—you terrify them.

"And now it's my turn," she said before Granny Good Mae could reply. "Why have you taken an interest in me if I'm so hopeless?"

"She told me to," the woman said simply. "And maybe I needed someone too. But I don't think so."

She again. Zoë wondered if Granny Good Mae was a schizophrenic.

"OK. How do you know about the coterie?"

Granny Good Mae lay back on the rock as if it were a feather bed. "Ahhh, how indeed. I was the child of an American soldier and a Japanese woman. A zombie bit my mother when I was a girl. My mother was a doctor. She had me serving the coterie of my village, stealing brains from the mortuaries, mostly. I returned her to death when I was twelve after she tried to attack me when the food supply ran low. At that moment I dropped the name she had given me, I was No One, and began studying how to hunt them."

Zoë listened in rapt silence. Was this for real?

"I had tried to understand the balance of the human-and-coterie relationship, but if one of them attacked a human, there was no more balance. At first, my skills were self-taught. It was a matter of necessity. After I killed my mother, the food supply was fully cut off for the coterie in my village. They started attacking humans. Since I knew the coterie, I was the only one who could protect my people."

She paused and stared at her hands, with their short chipped nails and many scars. "I failed. The coterie doomed themselves when they finally overtook the village, once they had eaten everyone, there was no one left to eat. This is why they need a balance with humans, you see. They can't overfish their ocean. I escaped into the mountains. I was faster than the zombies and the vampires couldn't follow me during the day. I ended up at a monastery that was under siege from zombies. I had my grandfather's sword, and I easily identified the alpha zombie and destroyed it. This distracted the remaining zombies, allowing the monks to leave the fortress and attack. Together we defeated the horde, and the monks took me in as repayment. They taught me their martial art, sǐshén lièrén, death hunting, which is focused on coterie hunting. They also taught me the branch of herbalism that uses hell note magic combined with herbs to support people attacked by coterie. When I was seventeen, they called me an adult and sent me to my father, who worked at the Pentagon."

"Did you tell him what you knew about the coterie?"

"No, no one would have believed me. When I was older, I got a job in the CIA thanks to my father's connections. I became an assassin. I left China in shame and ended up, later, here. Which is where I call home." Her eyes had gone misty.

"Wow," was all Zoë could think to say.

"How were you planning on staying alive while working with creatures who think you're a walking, talking cheeseburger?"

"Phil told me he would keep me safe in the office." Zoë felt very naive.

71

"And outside?"

"I hadn't thought that through," she admitted.

"You're dead again, then."

Zoë shivered. "What was this talisman you asked me about?"

Granny Good Mae extended her arm, and her ragged sweater pulled back. On her wrist was a brand, a circle with a curved icon like a fang in the center. "My mother gave me this after she turned. If you work among coterie, this labels you as a human who is an ally, one who should not be touched. Of course, they are not supposed to touch any human against their will, but we wouldn't need police if humans did what they were supposed to, so why do we assume the coterie will do what they are supposed to?"

Zoë winced at the puckered skin surrounding the brand. "That can't have been pleasant," she said lightly.

"Your story now," Granny Good Mae said.

Zoë was almost afraid to tell; she felt like Roy Schieder looking at his appendectomy scar while shark hunters told their war stories. "Mine isn't nearly as interesting, but"—and she told her story, complete with Godfrey and Lucy—glossing over some of the more shameful, hiding-in-a-chest details—and ending with the decision to check out the Jade Crane restaurant.

"My boss, Phil, the vampire, has promised I'm protected inside the office," she said again, trying to convince herself more than the old woman.

"Here is your problem," Granny Good Mae said, staring into the cloudy sky. "No matter how much they trust you, they will never teach you how to protect yourself against them. They don't want you to learn how to turn on them. They are not like us. They'll even tell you that if you ask them. Any coterie who tells you otherwise is trying to get something from you, probably food. Even if you're working with them, or for them, you can never forget that. To most of them, you are a talking bowl of noodles. Sentient noodles that can be useful, but still more tasty than anything else. And if you forget that, you will be doomed."

Doomed. She didn't like the sound of that.

"But I will teach you," Granny Good Mae said. "Come see me. Mornings. After work. Weekends."

"All of that?" Zoë asked, hoping she had misheard.

"You should have been training since you were ten. We have some catching up to do."

Zoë groaned.

The Shambling Guide to New York City

INTRODUCTION:
Weather

Winter is a prime time to visit New York, as people are bundled up to the eyes against the cold. Coterie with more nonhuman features have a better chance to wrap coats and hats around themselves and blend in with the humans in the daylight.

In the summer, the city's oppressive heat makes movement easy only under the dark of night, as most people are wearing as little as possible. Bundling up for camouflage attracts more attention than horns and a tail.

The downside to this is that if your body normally runs hot, making a coat and hat oppressive, then in the winter you're forced to settle for the nightlife. But you're probably here for the nightlife anyway, right? ■

CHAPTER SEVEN

Zoë rubbed the bruises on her forearms and ribs; training with Granny Good Mae had been more intense than she had expected, and she wasn't really in shape for a two-hour workout. But the woman had put her through the paces last night in Central Park, learning what she knew, then showing her the attacks of the different coterie. Zoë had been amazed that the woman had told her more about coterie in two hours than she'd learned in two weeks of research.

This morning, all she'd had to do was run three miles. At least Granny Good Mae had met her in Brooklyn so she could get a shower afterward.

Zoë still wasn't sure where the woman slept.

Unless you got her on the topic of "she," Granny Good Mae seemed more like a zealous trainer than an insane homeless woman. Zoë considered telling her she could make a lot of money as a personal trainer, but after an hour with the woman, it became clear that she was exactly where she wanted to be, dirty clothes and reputation and all.

After her vigorous workouts, Zoë was aching and exhausted as she walked into the destitute theater that was her new office. She left the sunlight behind and entered the tomb-like basement full of monsters, with few exits.

Good lord. I'm crazy.

"Hello?" she said tentatively into the theater, and immediately felt stupid. She had every right to be here, and she knew where to go. She quickened her pace and went through the door leading backstage.

An irritated voice drifted out of one of the dressing rooms. "Morgen, will you ever learn to respect my space?" The voice was feminine and booming and frightening, as if being sent over a loudspeaker. This was a woman Zoë would never want to cross.

She poked her head into the dressing room. This one was much larger than Phil's, as if for the chorus, with a line of lit mirrors and dressers down a long wall. Only two people sat in the office at that moment: Morgen, the pink-haired sprite, who perched on the edge of a desk, grinned down at a black-clad, black-skinned gothy woman with long black hair, who gripped a heavy book in her hands and glared up at Morgen. Her dark eyes glinted. She was black, not like of African descent, but black like a shadow. Inky, almost. Zoë's eyes swam briefly as if they wanted to get lost in the void that was this woman's skin.

"This is my sacred area," she said. "You have to ask first."

The water sprite shrugged. "If I had asked, you wouldn't have let me in."

The woman put her book down. "Fine. What do you want?"

Morgen leaned over, and the woman tried not to flinch at her disrespect of the space. "The new managing editor. She's human."

"Aye, that's what Phil says," the woman said, moving a philodendron away from Morgen's encroaching backside. "He said she's strangely astute and has lots of experience with publishing. She's not affiliated with Public Works. He said it'll be nice to get new blood in here."

"That's good to know," Zoë said. "Although I don't like the phrase 'new blood.'"

76

The women's heads whirled around to look at her. Morgen grinned; the gothy woman's eyes narrowed. Zoë nearly took a step back: the woman didn't have any whites; her eyes were all black. Zoë could barely determine features on the shadow in front of her.

Don't let them intimidate you, she firmly reminded herself. "Anyway, hi, I'm the human. Zoë. Good to meet you." She stepped into the room, but did not offer her hand to either woman to shake.

Morgen hooted with laughter. "Awesome! How long does he expect you to last with the zombies and vampires here? And did he tell you about the incubus?"

"Oh, they're not allowed to touch her," the other woman said. "That much is clear. I am Gwen, Zoë. I'm your head writer. Morgen is in sales and marketing." She stood, her long black skirts rustling somberly, and extended her hand.

Zoë shook it and immediately her mind filled with whispers of numbers: *2,015; 20 percent; 2,023; 30 percent; by 2,067; 100 percent.*

Zoë dropped Gwen's hand as quickly as she could without appearing rude. "Uh, I don't know how long he expects me to last, honestly," Zoë said to Morgen. She shook her head to clear it. "Maybe he's testing me somehow."

"Why would he do that?" Gwen asked.

Morgen shrugged. "He's a vampire. Wouldn't put it past him."

Gwen sniffed. "Bigot."

Morgen laughed again. "Come on, Zoëlife, I'll show you your office." She said "Zoëlife" as one word.

"Now maybe we can start to get some work done around here instead of wasting time at other people's desks," Gwen said, turning her back on them.

Despite the chill in the fall air, Morgen wore a light clingy summer dress that hugged her slight curves. Her bare feet brushed the carpet lightly, and her skin was a paler blue than Zoë remembered.

Zoë wondered where Morgen was leading her, but relaxed a bit when they reached a modified closet pleasantly lit and even decorated with a little plant.

"Wow, I rank a solo office?" she asked, hanging her coat behind the door.

"Closet office, yeah. Managing editor and all that. Writers, sales and marketing, research, et cetera are all grouped in the big dressing rooms." She jabbed her thumb over her shoulder down the hall. "Now, there are some things you need to know." Morgen closed the door behind her. She indicated the desk chair for Zoë and took the guest chair facing the desk.

"Now listen. Everyone knows a human is going to be working with us, but some don't believe it. They don't want to believe it. Phil told me that you will have done research, but there are some things you need to know that the books will not have told you. Some people see their personal space as sacred—literally sacred ground. They mark it off with tape, or plants, or sometimes just dirt spilled on the floor. Do not enter these spaces unless you're looking to piss off a coworker. Which"—she grinned again—"I'll admit sometimes is fun. But I know how to deal with them. You don't."

Zoë pulled out her notebook and began taking notes. Morgen continued.

"Let's see, what else?" She counted things off on her fingers. "Eventually you'll probably share a meal with people—don't freak out on what others eat. They don't like it."

Zoë smiled. "That's true in any culture."

Morgen nodded. "Sure, but rarely in other human cultures will you encounter someone eating human remains."

"Point taken."

"Some of us don't eat at all. Gwen the gothic princess gets her sustenance through...well, different means. But we do employ zombies, and you've already shared a meal with Phil, so you know human bits will be eaten in front of you."

Zoë nodded.

"OK, your first week is essentially orientation. We currently don't have anyone in CR, so till we get someone, Phil's assigned me to help you out. Sprites don't eat people, you know, so I'm not meant to be a threat to you. Feel free to ask me anything. Are you threatened?" Her head quirked to the side like a dog's.

Zoë held up a hand to stop the fast-talking woman. "Um, I do have some questions. 'CR'?"

"Coterie resources instead of human resources. We're not human."

Zoë felt stupid. "Of course. Here's my big question. I've studied a lot of different coterie, but I'm missing one bit of information—how to identify people by sight. For example, and please understand I mean no disrespect, but when I came in I was surprised to realize that you and Gwen both could have passed as human. I know you're a sprite, but I still don't know what she is. How am I to avoid offending someone if I don't know what they are?"

"Gwen? She's a psychopomp." Zoë stared at her blankly. "Oh, right. You wouldn't have heard that word. She's a death goddess. Welsh, I think. She used to ride the countryside, gathering up errant lost souls and taking them to the underworld."

Zoë sat back heavily in her chair, feeling the color go out of her face.

Morgen laughed. "I wasn't trying to scare you, just wanted you to know. She doesn't do that anymore, you know; publishing pays better these days. Not as many Welsh souls needing escorting into the underworld anymore, even in Wales."

"Do not a lot of Welsh die these days?"

Morgen shook her head. "No, it's not that. As far as I can tell, after Christianity came to the British Isles, most of the population chose Heaven as their goal instead of the underworld of their ancestors. And get this, Gwen tells me their ancestors are seriously pissed about that. Spend all that time creating a family to endure through the ages and BAM!—your descendants change religions and you don't even get to talk to them in the afterlife. But there's not much they can do to them, so they pretty much sulk. She says it's a pretty depressing place to go, in honesty."

"I suppose that's another bonus to taking this job? No moping souls?"

"Exactly. But to answer your question, you're right, asking someone what they are is pretty rude. But it's a little more important in this situation to find out if a coworker is going to freak out if you turn your back in his presence, so if you have any questions, ask me. There are going to be some coworkers who will be looking at you to find the flaw so they can convince Phil to boot you, and you'll want to not give them that. But let me tell you who you'll be working with." She began ticking off her long fingers as she counted.

"There's me, Gwen, and you know Phil's a vampire. We have two other vampires, Kevin and Opal, they're also writers. Oh, another bit of protocol, never ask a vampire who her sire is. That's a private thing to them. Koi is our operations, she's a kitsune, a fox spirit. I think she's likely the oldest person in the office. Nine thousand years or something." Morgen paused to grin mischievously. "Get her drunk and ask her to take her spirit shape. It's pretty awe-inspiring."

"Anyway," she continued. "Paul, Rodrigo, and Montel are our zombies. Paul is a writer and Rodrigo is our office assistant. Montel is an executive VP under Phil. Montel is his go-to guy.

"Oh, Ursula and John, the siblings—look out for them. They're 'buses. Succubus and incubus. They feed on sexual energy. They're both in PR. John will give you the best night of your life, but then you'll feel like you have the worst hangover ever for about a week. Unless you're a lesbian, then you're safe. Ursula's tastes run to men. Regardless, watch out for them. They're sexy and dangerous and very good at what they do."

"John, an incubus," Zoë said. "Really?"

Her disbelief must have registered. Morgen raised an eyebrow. "You've met him?"

"Yeah, and, well." Zoë felt uncomfortable, not sure how to mention someone wasn't as sexy as myths described him to be. "I didn't feel the draw," she finally said.

"Really. Huh." Morgen looked amused and interested. "That will be a first."

"And anyway, I don't want an office romance. I don't need another—" Zoë bit her lip. "It's bad news," she finally said.

"Really? You know this for a fact?" Morgen asked.

"Yes," Zoë said, stony-faced.

The water sprite got the hint. "So anyway, that's everyone. We are hiring more writers and editors right now, and some section editors that will work directly under you, but we needed you before we hired them."

Zoë blanched. That she might be involved in the hiring process hadn't occurred to her. "What does one look for in a coterie employee?"

Morgen thought for a moment. "Having never been human, I'm not sure how they'd compare. Hang on." She got up and left Zoë's office.

Zoë let out a breath she hadn't realized she was holding. Had she really been chatting with a water sprite? About a death goddess and a succubus? She shook her head to clear it. Morgen

81

swept back into her office, followed by a slow-moving man who had been, at one time, a tall, thin, handsome African-American, but now was clearly an ashen-green walking corpse.

"Zoë, this is our executive VP of Operations, Montel. Montel, Zoë is our new managing editor."

Zoë remembered not to extend her hand and instead smiled warmly, trying not to let the man's peeling facial skin pull her gaze from its firm place on the man's lifeless eyes.

He smiled slowly in return. "Phil had told me we were hiring someone with experience. I have a history in business, but not publishing, so we're quite glad to have you here."

Montel formed each word deliberately, reminding her of her grandfather who, after his stroke, had spoken painfully slowly. Zoë tried not to fidget while the zombie spoke.

"I'm excited, but I know I have a lot to learn," she said. "Morgen mentioned I would be interviewing section editors once we get the New York book set up, and I was curious what you look for in hiring."

"The same thing as when you're hiring a human. Strong work ethic. Preferably experience, or knowledge. And don't judge based on coterie clan. A bleeding flesh golem might dirty up the carpet, but we can work around that. An ifrit could set things on fire if he gets angry, but if he's a strong writer, I don't care."

Zoë nodded through this laborious speech and wondered if e-mail would be a better communication tool with a zombie. "Understood."

"That's leaping ahead a bit, though," Montel said. "For now, get familiar with the office, your coworkers. You and I have a meeting with Phil at ten to discuss the first book." His face screwed itself into an attempt at a thoughtful expression, and then fell back to the drooping neutral. He shuffled out of the office.

Zoë wrote "learn different body language cues" and "ifrit?" in her notebook.

Morgen motioned for her to follow. "Come on, I'll show you where everyone sits."

Even though Zoë had gotten to work fifteen minutes before Phil had suggested—at 8:45—she had still arrived after a lot of coworkers. Gwen quietly pointed out the two vampires lurking onstage in the break room. A peek as she walked by showed that Kevin preferred more traditional vampire garb than Phil did; he wore all black. Opal, however, wore a long-sleeved T-shirt and jeans complete with high heels. Neither looked up at her as she walked by.

In the writing room, Gwen sat at her desk, writing furiously in a notebook. Another zombie, Paul, had arrived and was shuffling toward his desk at the end of the row. Paul wore a fedora and an overcoat, and when he reached his desk, began the laborious work of undressing. Zoë saw the festering, peeling wound on his neck, and averted her eyes.

Beside Zoë's office sat Montel in his gloomy room, which apparently he shared with Rodrigo, the executive assistant zombie who hadn't arrived yet. Koi also ranked her own office, and a small administrative office had been converted into one for PR and marketing. John and Ursula usually got in at ten, Morgen explained. On the other side of the backstage was another closet with a closed door. Then Phil's large office.

"Those who need to, use the bathrooms in the lobby," Morgen said, gesturing past the rows of seats. "And that's the tour."

Zoë checked her watch. "I've got half an hour before my meeting with Phil. What do I do till then?"

Morgen shrugged. "Get familiar with your office? Bother the writers? Change your mind about this whole thing?"

Zoë made a face. She found herself liking the water sprite. "I think I'll choose option A. I need research books, I guess I will head out at lunch and get some. Will Phil reimburse me?"

"In hell notes, yeah," Morgen said. "He's pretty easy with the checkbook, he's looking for an accountant. He wants a dragon"—she rolled her eyes at this—"but there aren't a lot of dragons in New York City who don't already have hoards, and it's really hard to find a dragon who will look after someone else's money. But they are the absolute best with money, and Phil always wants the best."

A dragon. Zoë nodded, feeling a buzzing in her ears. She realized that was the sound of the reality portion of her brain checking out, and that she would likely hear it a lot.

She went to her office and shut the door. It was cozy, not claustrophobia-inducing, she told herself firmly. She had room for a desk, a guest chair, and a bookcase. She made a mental note to get a grow lamp for her plant. If she didn't have a window, at least she could bring a little nature in.

The door locked. That was very, very good. Although if something tried to get her through the door, there wasn't anywhere she could go. Still, it gave her some relief.

She got out her notebook and a pen, and sat at her desk, occupying herself with making lists until ten o'clock.

When she and Montel entered Phil's office, he was sitting at his desk. Zoë realized with a start that he was in front of the vanity mirror and cast no reflection. She mentally shook her head: she should have seen that coming.

"Zoë, great. I trust you've gotten the tour and met everyone?" Phil asked, getting up from his desk.

"Yeah, well, I've learned about everyone and gotten the tour, but not met everyone."

Phil nodded. "Perhaps that's best, we don't want to overwhelm you."

He gestured to the couch, and she and Montel sat down. She tried not to act as if she was trying not to touch him, even though that was exactly what she was doing.

Phil pulled his desk chair to face the couch. "So we're about to do what no one ever has—chronicle the city through the eyes of the coterie. Which is why, Zoë, I need your expertise, but you need to let the writers do their jobs."

"Naturally," Zoë said. "But can you give me an example of how you see the city?"

Phil thought for a moment.

Surprisingly, Montel spoke first. "Liberty."

Phil clapped his hands once. "Yes! Humans look at the Statue of Liberty as a gift from France and a symbol of freedom. But it's really the horrific sarcophagus of a great French demon who was killed and sent to America as a gift and warning."

Zoë felt the spit in her mouth dry up. "Warning? Of what?" She thought of the time she had gone to Liberty Island—had she really been wandering around the insides of a demon?

"It's there to keep immigrating demons out of New York. It's a symbol of the might of the coterie hunters. A 'Look what we did to the last demon who came here' warning."

She started writing things down. "All right. That is different. So I outline the book, assign writers, and then set them free?"

"You will need to go with some of them," Montel drawled. "You will get a better sense of what the book must contain if you see our field research."

"But—" Zoë stopped herself. Phil had said she wasn't as safe outside, but she knew she had to accept the risks if she was to accept the job. "Right. Field research."

"This week we're doing interviews, and I'll need you to help interview the writers," Phil said. "You won't have to do it alone, but you must remember—"

Zoë held up her hand, pen wedged between her fingers. "I know, Montel already told me. Don't judge people by their, uh, race, do you call it? Or something else?"

Phil raised his eyebrows. "That's very good, but I wasn't going to say that. I meant to say that if we interview someone who feeds from humans, you can't judge them on that basis. And they may not respect you as a boss right away, and you will need to assert yourself. The stronger you appear, the fewer problems you will have, especially outside the office."

"OK, no judging, be strong and stuff. Got it," Zoë said. On her notepad, where Phil and Montel couldn't see, she wrote, in very small letters, "help."

MANHATTAN:
Lodging

New York is one of the older cities in the United States, and New Amsterdam was built on an island after a battle that still-existing coterie call the Day the Sun Caught Fire. The treaty that sprung from that battle, with the water sprite Angah and the vampire Dark Sun signing, allowed for the humans to settle their city on the island with small concessions to the coterie to continue existing.

One thing the coterie made sure of was to leave enough existing underground tunnels to accommodate its survivors, as well as creating elaborate tombs to make the already dead feel at home. We recommend Grant's Tomb, as some of the inner sanctums are quite lovely. But perhaps the best secret lodging is the New York Marble Cemetery in the Bowery, with hidden catacombs offering luxurious safety to visiting coterie. ■

CHAPTER EIGHT

The next week was a blur.

Zoë fit in better than she'd thought she would. Once her coworkers became used to her, she began to relax a bit.

She was impressed with her writing team, especially Gwen, who had a clear geographic knowledge of the city. Opal was a native New Yorker whose specialty was her home, the Bronx, while Kevin had been turned while visiting the city and had spent most of his undead existence in Manhattan.

Zoë got a sense that Opal was annoyed with his preference for Manhattan, but couldn't figure out why. She got along well with Opal, who was open and friendly, but while Kevin never threatened her, he was short with her.

"Don't take it personally," Opal said one day in the break room. "He was only turned a year ago and has a tendency to resent humans still."

"Is that normal?" Zoë asked.

"Sure, we all did. It doesn't take long to acclimate to undeath, though. He should be used to it in five years or so."

Paul, the zombie on her writing team, was the hardest to get to know. He was a fresher zombie than Montel, apparently, but didn't have the other man's flair for conversation. Instead of having been turned by a simple bite, Paul had actually had parts of his brain devoured, which left him a little slow. And that was compared to most zombies.

Zoë asked Phil, in private, why they had hired him in the first place.

"Oh, the speech center in his brain was damaged, but the man can write beautifully. He also observes very well, and catches things people usually do not. I've put him on writing about 'Things to Do' since he can go and watch people and see who's best at entertaining coterie."

Ursula, John, and Koi were on some sort of business trip to Boston, and Zoë was glad not to have more complications. She could get used to only so many new creatures at once.

However, one thing she had to do that week was interview new writers. She found it illuminating, as she met coterie she had never even heard of. Since the company had little need of marketing yet, Zoë begged Morgen to act like her assistant so she could warn Zoë of what kind of coterie was coming through the door.

She interviewed a scab demon, a minor Norse deity (Eir, goddess of healing, she had said), and Bertie, a wyrm, who called himself a baby dragon at "only" two hundred years old. He was a knowledge devourer, and wanted to eat as much of the city as possible, and he assured her that he could maintain his human shape for some time. He almost never lost his human shape when it was "really important."

Almost never, thought Zoë.

All of the applicants looked human, in fact, except that the scab demon was covered in hideous scabs, and Zoë tried very hard to calmly meet her eyes without staring.

"Why are you not working at a hospital? Why a publishing company?" Zoë asked Eir.

The goddess, a tall, broad woman with spiky yellow hair, pulled herself up even taller in her chair. "I failed out. To work in a hospital, I must go through years and years of medical school that I don't need, learning practices that are pointless. Why should I learn the strains of syphilis if I can cure it with a wave of my hand?"

"You can cure syphilis but can't conjure up a medical degree?" Zoë asked without thinking. The goddess's eyes grew wide and she gasped. She stood up and looked very tall while Morgen and Zoë stayed seated, stunned.

Is she going to throw lightning at us? Zoë thought wildly.

Eir stomped out.

"Don't worry about it. The Norse are prickly. At least you didn't piss off a thunder god," Morgen said as Zoë banged her head on her desk. "What's this one going to do after being offended, anyway? Heal you *really hard*?"

Zoë was more careful with the baby dragon and the scab demon, and decided that the dragon deserved a second interview. The scab demon was new to the city and wasn't sure which island was Manhattan and which was Long Island.

During the afternoons Zoë researched New York guidebooks for humans, making notes of the best things to see and do. She left lodging and restaurants to the writers' discretion, as she doubted a scab demon could get into the New York Athletic Club or a table at Sugiyama.

She took her lunches outside and alone, needing sunlight and human contact.

All in all, it wasn't a bad job.

Training with Granny Good Mae was another thing. Every morning she had to get up and run through Prospect Park to increase her endurance, and every evening Granny Good Mae would meet her after work and drag her to some private area for training. Every time Zoë messed up, Granny Good Mae would hit her on the head and yell, "Dead! You're dead now."

She was learning a mix of kung fu, self-defense, and dirty street fighting. Each day they focused on a different coterie type, its fighting style, and how to defeat it.

"Fire demon," Granny Good Mae said on Thursday after she took Zoë to the train station.

"Yeah?" Zoë said, fearing the woman would attack her with a branding iron. She still had healing puncture wounds where the woman had hit her with a stick covered in thumbtacks to imitate a vampire.

"No defense. Unscrew a fire hydrant. Lesson over!" She turned to go.

Zoë reached out to catch her arm, then thought better of it. She ran after her instead. "Wait, that's it? No beating me up, no calling me dead?"

"No. With fire demons you either burn or you open a hydrant. You can't punch a bonfire."

"I don't even know how to open a fire hydrant! Don't you need a giant wrench?"

Granny Good Mae stopped and looked in Zoë's eyes, the matter-of-fact look that always made Zoë feel very stupid. "Then carry a big wrench. You should be armed anyway."

On Friday, Zoë saw no sign of the woman. She looked around on the block where Granny Good Mae usually intercepted her, saw no one, then shrugged and went home.

She slept a lot that weekend.

Between working with monsters and training with the crazy homeless kung fu master, Zoë didn't have many chances to work on her social life. She managed to get Carl to be a bit warmer to her, and his barista, Tenagne, called her "pale as butter on a cockwaffle" one day, which left her feeling accepted and pleased. Morgen accompanied her to coffee breaks and to lunch once, and seemed to be the closest thing she had to a friend.

What really bugged her, however, was that her neighbor Arthur never seemed to be home. She had hoped to run into him in the hall, naturally, as neighbors do, as she had on the night she'd gone out with Phil, but she and Arthur never seemed to be home at the same time. She even went to his door after work once, with the lame "cup of sugar" excuse, but he wasn't home.

She wasn't looking for love, or a fling, but dang, if you had a cute neighbor, it was a shame if you couldn't look at him from time to time.

"All right, what's with Public Works?" Zoë asked the following Tuesday, waving one of her writers' first reports of the Upper East Side. "I've heard you mention them once, now my writers are mentioning them, and I have no idea who they are. I thought they did, like, the sewers and water and power lines?"

Phil winced and looked up from his desk, where he had been reading a newspaper. "Did I fail to explain them?"

"Yes," Zoë said, her voice stony. "And it sounds like they're a big deal."

"The humans and coterie live in a balance, that much should be obvious. If we ate everyone, we would be out of food. If the humans drove us out—well, they would probably be fine, but we don't support our own extinction. Centuries ago, the humans invented Public Works to control coterie movement."

"The dirty guys in the sewers? They're Buffy?"

Phil snorted. "Forget sexy vampire hunters; today's slayers are the same guys about whom the term 'plumber butt' was invented."

Zoë winced. "OK...that's news to me. How does it work?"

"Ideally, they keep an eye out for when coterie break the rules, murder humans, et cetera. In reality, they have spies everywhere, and whenever one of us attacks one of you, they assemble. We're supposed to go to the legitimate places for food, blood banks, morgues, et cetera. But everyone wants to hunt. It's our nature. When we do, then they have to act." His voice sounded slightly bitter.

"I thought they just handled water and sewer and stuff? Hard hats with lights on them?"

"First, where do you think the majority of coterie live? Above ground?" Zoë blushed; the number of coterie living in the sewers should have been an obvious thing, she realized. "Secondly, it's been this way for years. Colonization. Humans try to establish a new city; those whose job it is to develop the foundation of the new city encounter the coterie first. They clear the land and find the sprites, they dig up the subterranean demons. There are battles. If the humans hang on long enough, they can manage to do ethnic cleansing on a city. Seattle is sterilized, for one. So is Belfast. More likely, the humans and coterie eventually draw up treaties, create rules for living in balance. They provide us with food, we don't eat them. Often the coterie understand that if humans move in, their food supply will increase, so a balance is in their best interest."

He frowned. "Although having a police force watching one is less desirous. Anyway, during these battles, if the coterie win and drive the humans out entirely, then places like the Mayan ruins can happen."

"How much does Public Works know about the coterie?" Zoë asked.

"We aren't sure," Phil said. "Sometimes they can track a hunting zombie and kill him in a single evening. Other times they are woefully ignorant of hunters at large gatherings, like New Year's Eve. I hear we have a mole inside, keeping the balance but throwing the organization off the scent just often enough to keep too many coterie from being falsely accused, but I don't know enough to know who that is."

Zoë paused, and then had to ask. "Would that be a literal mole?"

Phil smiled. "I don't think so, but I try never to assume."

Zoë didn't tell any of her coworkers about her meetings with Granny Good Mae; they were, as far as she knew, unknown to Phil and the others. She felt it was safest if no one knew she studied with the strange woman.

When they met on Monday night, Zoë asked where she had been at the end of the previous week. Granny Good Mae laughed. "You're not the only thing there is."

"What can you tell me about Public Works?" Zoë asked as the woman lunged at her, slowly, like a zombie. Zoë countered by nimbly stepping aside and touching the back of Granny's head lightly with her hand, trying to imagine she was holding a heavy weapon or knife.

"Dead!" Granny Good Mae said brightly. "That was your first kill! Congratulations!"

They paused for some water. They worked out in a clearing of Central Park. Every once in a while someone would look at them and Granny Good Mae would transition seamlessly into a slow tai chi movement, and Zoë would attempt to ape her.

It was cold work, but the workouts soon warmed Zoë up. They kept walking through the park to keep warm as Granny Good Mae talked.

"Public Works are good people. Keep the peace, keep the balance. Balance is very important to her."

Zoë had stopped asking who "her" was.

"They pay well, too," Granny Good Mae continued. "I do contract work for them now and then."

"Contract work?"

"Assassinations. Hunting. The odd coterie member who gets out of hand."

"Assassinate? Jesus, don't they even get a trial?" Zoë asked.

"Who would be judge? Who would be jury? If a city is lucky enough to have a neutral truth deity, they can get confirmation, but not every place has one. Or they're not neutral. Anyway, yes, we go for the assassination path. It's easier for all. Besides, most of them we're simply returning to the grave. So it's not murder."

"I guess that's why they're so terrified of you?" Zoë asked. She wasn't sure she liked the casual way her mentor talked about killing the people Zoë worked with, but she swallowed her protestations and indicated that Granny Good Mae should continue.

"Public Works has to care for the sewers, too, so that's their day job. You knew that, right?"

"Right, I know. Do the coterie consider them enemies?"

The old woman shrugged. "Only as much as you people consider your police to be enemies."

"Good point," Zoë said. They finished their walk and continued training.

Only later that night did Zoë realize that Granny Good Mae had said "you people" and "your police."

The Shambling Guide to New York City

MANHATTAN:
RESTAURANTS:
Introduction

Of course, not all coterie feed on humans and need special establishments in which to feed. Deities and other human-looking coterie can fit in quite well in most restaurants, but will want to choose carefully regardless. If you feed on belief and worship, any of the trendy places are recommended, such as Nobu and Abboccato. Humans go to these places to see and be seen, making it easy to find worshipers, even if only for the night.

Fair folk will find any of the city's vegetarian or vegan restaurants welcoming. Red Bamboo Vegetarian Soul Café, Red Bamboo Brooklyn, and Chennai Garden will also serve raw food or flowers if you ask special. Kajitsu has, as of this writing, a wood sprite working as an assistant manager; she does everything she can to accommodate fair folk and other coterie customers. She accepts either human currency or hell notes, making her stand out among working coterie.

Succubi and incubi can feed at any of the many sex clubs in the city. Chemistry and La Trapeze are two favorites, but the best by far is Tastiest Dish as it specially caters to the 'bus lifestyle. It has a strict "no-kill" policy as it depends on repeat human customers, but it is the easiest and most popular place to eat. The cover charge is minimal, but renting a private room—or watching a semiprivate room—is where you'll spend your hell notes. An adjacent club holds a strip bar where most of the dancers are succubi, feeding on many more humans, but not as deeply as in the sex club. ∎

CHAPTER NINE

The following Monday, November 16, Zoë met her new coworkers. First there was Zoë's own hire, Bertie the wyrm, who she was convinced could handle both Queens and Harlem. She was pleased both that she had managed to hire a very capable person, and that she hadn't dreadfully offended anyone other than Eir during the interviews.

When Zoë had told Phil of her hire, he had nodded and said that maybe in a hundred years Bertie could transition to accounting. She had just nodded, trying not to let her amazement show. *I wonder what kind of watch you get for a hundred years' service.*

She got Bertie settled into the writing room, and then went to her office, where she met some other new hires. Each desk/vanity had a gleaming new computer, but in Zoë's office, tiny little men and women crawled over it like caterpillars.

"Hello?" she asked carefully when she came in.

One of the people, a four-inch-tall woman, snapped to attention. She had green skin and pointed ears, and wore blue overalls. "Greetings!" she shouted through a tiny bullhorn up to Zoë. "We are your IT staff. I am your sysadmin, you can call me Cassandra. We're almost done setting up your system."

"Great, thanks so much," Zoë said, and hung her satchel behind the door. "I'm just going to get some coffee while you finish."

Morgen met her in the break room and opened her mouth, but Zoë held up a finger. "Let me guess. Gremlins?"

Morgen grinned. "Got it in one! You're getting good at this!"

Zoë allowed herself a small feeling of pride. "I think you might be right. This weekend I'm pretty sure I spotted a succubus, a fire demon, and a vampire while I was at the deli. And I wasn't even trying."

Morgen patted her shoulder. "Don't let your guard down."

Montel came into the break room, shuffling across the stage slowly. "We hired a new coterie relations person. You each need to meet with him." He handed each woman a schedule and shuffled away.

"So what do we talk about with coterie relations if we don't get benefits?" Zoë asked, seeing her name second on the list, after Gwen, to meet with Wesley, their new CR manager.

Morgen filled a glass with water and then leaned against the counter. "He'll plan our parties, he's in charge of stocking the break room, and if we have a problem with a coworker, we go to him. Most of them are pretty good, with extensive coterie knowledge. He may be good to interview for your own benefit."

The gremlins were still in Zoë's office setting up her computer, so she trudged down to meet the new CR person. She met Gwen backstage exiting the one door she'd never seen open.

"Hey, how's the new guy?" she asked in a low voice. Aside from Morgen, Gwen was the person she felt closest to in the office. She found herself drawn to people who didn't eat humans. Self-preservation.

"He could be better," Gwen said, frowning. "He's a construct."

Zoë blinked. "Construct? That's not one I've come across."

"Construct, Prometheus, they have several names. You'd call him a Frankenstein's monster, but of course that is pejorative. Also, people were making constructs and golems much longer than that book has been out. They're made by zoëtists."

"Oh, right, I think Phil told me about them," Zoë said.

"For being in CR, he's somewhat cranky and not good with people, but from the looks of his stitches, he's fairly fresh. His head probably had something to do with HR in his former life, and Phil wanted someone with experience. He should have hired the health goddess."

Zoë was glad the low light hid her blush. "Right. Thanks for the warning."

Gwen left for the writing room as Zoë knocked on the closed door. A strange, fabricated voice sounded from inside. "What is it?"

Zoë opened the door into a brightly lit closet office—which was a little too brightly lit—and said, "Hi, Wesley, I'm Zoë, the new—" She stopped cold.

She squinted in the bright light to see if he was an illusion. The man behind the desk stood up and stared at her. For a moment Zoë panicked as she realized she had no idea what the protocol for greeting constructs was, but Wesley extended a hand.

Zoë took it, forcing herself not to blanch at the fact that the hand Wesley had extended was clearly a woman's, with long, thin fingers and smooth skin. He'd even had the nails manicured and painted a subtle pink. The slim wrist and arm were lost in the man's dress shirt that clearly had to be at least a large to fit his barrel chest and his beefy left arm and hairy hand. Chest hair peeked out over his necktie, but ended abruptly with a scar joining the shoulders and the thin neck that stretched up to hold the familiar head of a blond, bespectacled man.

Oh God.

Wesley did not smile at her, but shook her hand professionally. "Close the door and sit."

Zoë did so, commanding her heart to stop its pounding. She sat, gripping the chair arms. What she was really doing was trying not to vomit. She couldn't bring herself to look at him.

Wesley spoke again, and the voice sounded strange, coming from huge lungs and a small head, deep and high at the same time. "Zoë Jennifer Norris, managing editor." From his mouth it sounded like an insult, especially when he ended it up with "Human."

She forced a smile and tried to meet his eyes again, her stomach tightening. "That's me."

"How are you liking your job among coterie?"

"It's fine. Nice, I mean. It's nice. I like my coworkers." She laughed. It sounded very high-pitched, so she stopped.

For the love of God, stop babbling.

Wesley opened a folder on his desk and looked at the one piece of paper inside. He peered at it and said, without looking at her, "You seem nervous, Zoë."

"I, well, it's just." She took a deep breath. "You look like someone I knew once. That startled me."

"Really? That's not a statement I hear often," Wesley said without smiling. "Zoë, I will be honest with you. I was surprised to hear a human was on staff who wasn't being farmed for food. I don't know what you think you're doing here, but I don't expect you to last very long. The coterie benefits plan does not fit for humans, so I won't need to work with you for anything except salary issues. Phil has ordered that your safety within the office is to be guaranteed, so if someone threatens or attacks you, bring the issue to me. But if you have a problem with the odor of the zombies, or the way vampires might look at you during lunch, or if someone makes a disgusting smell, or"—his voice took on a mocking falsetto—"even if someone reminds you of someone else, I *don't* want to hear about it. I expect, honestly, not to speak to you again until you tender your resignation."

Zoë bit her lip and stared at a spot on his forehead, still unable to meet his too-familiar eyes. "That's unbelievable."

A thin eyebrow arched. "Oh?"

Zoë smiled. "Unbelievable that you would expect me not to say hi to you in the halls. It's an underestimation of my ability to be friendly. Thanks for the information, Wesley."

His face might as well have been carved from stone. "That will be all, Zoë."

She forced a laugh. "I'll see you around."

She closed the door behind her and ran onto the stage and up the aisle. She made it to the lobby bathroom and finally allowed her composure to break. When Morgen came in looking for her, she was still dry-heaving into the toilet.

The water sprite blinked, checked her watch, and said, "Let's go out for coffee. Gwen knows a lovely human place around the corner."

Zoë was feeling much better with a latte in front of her, sitting by the window of a nice, generic Starbucks. She took a deep breath and forced the trembling to subside.

Gwen sat with a cup of tea, patiently watching Zoë.

Morgen fidgeted, playing with the straw in her ice water, then finally said, "So. The new guy's a prick, isn't he?"

Zoë winced, and Morgen frowned as her joke tanked. "What did he say that made you lose your shit? I thought you were tougher than this."

Despite the backhanded compliment, she appreciated Morgen; annoyance with the sprite let her focus on something besides the shock and fear. "I can accept all of this shit you've thrown at me. Vampires. Zombies. Goddesses, sprites, whatever. Fucking *dragons*. I got it covered. No worries. But what you really didn't prepare me for was working alongside my college boyfriend's head."

Gwen didn't react. Morgen stopped fidgeting. The noontime sun glinted off her eyebrow ring.

"Your ex-boyfriend? Wesley's head? Seriously?" Morgen said. "But when did he die?"

"That's just it," Zoë said, grasping her mug tightly. "I didn't know he was dead. Scott and I haven't talked in years."

Morgen tapped her chin as she thought aloud. "So not only is this a 'Hi, welcome to work, here's a construct with someone from your past working with you' shock, you're also dealing with the fact you didn't even know he was dead, cut up, and reanimated."

Zoë nodded. Her stomach rolled over again, trying to make a decision on the latte, but she firmly told it to stay put.

Outside the coffee shop a flock of sparrows roosted in a tree, waiting patiently for Gwen. Apparently they followed her everywhere; she had explained they were her heralds.

These coterie, Gwen and Morgen, were not looking to eat her or taunt her, and didn't bear body parts from people she'd slept with. So they couldn't be all bad.

Gwen sipped at her tea. "This is unexpected. I mean, I don't really keep track of humans much anymore, except to feed, but the few humans who have connection with us in the world haven't come across this."

Zoë looked up from her coffee. "Wait, what? You feed on humans?"

"I mean, of all the people who die, only a tiny percentage are made into constructs. And of humans, only a tiny percentage are introduced to the coterie. What are the odds those two would intersect?"

Morgen grinned at Zoë's discomfort. "Gwen, I think you distracted her."

"What?"

"Zoë wants to know what you eat, as a death goddess." She settled back and grinned, enjoying this a bit too much for Zoë's taste.

Gwen's eyes grew wide. "Oh! Oh, my dear, don't worry. I feed off the life force of the dying. Dying humans give off an air of desperation that sustains my kind. It doesn't hurt them at all. All I need to do is sit in a crowded area and that's my lunch."

"But how do you know who's dying? Are you talking about cancer or something?"

"Cancer, heart disease, AIDS, but I can also get a sense of who's about to be killed in an accident. But really, the moment you're born, you begin dying. I could eat comfortably on a room full of healthy children and they wouldn't even feel fatigued. And as for how I know, I'm a death goddess. It's my nature to know."

Zoë shifted in her chair and tried to focus on the horror of the morning, not the horror here at lunch. Morgen leaned forward and looked at Zoë with eyes the color of a Pacific-island bay. "Go on. You know you want to ask it. Come on!"

Zoë made a face at her. "And you must feed on social discomfort?"

Morgen laughed, a beautiful bubbling sound. "No, I'm just obnoxious. I eat plants, preferably water-grown. And fish. I'm insatiable at sushi restaurants. I could blow a week's wages on one good night. And don't change the subject. You want to ask her when you'll die."

Gwen focused briefly on a pale young woman sitting at a table nearby, and then gave a satisfied sigh. "Oh, she wants to ask, Morgen, she's just afraid of the answer. Don't worry, Zoë. I won't tell you."

"Well, if you can diagnose stuff, if I get hit with cancer or AIDS, I'd appreciate you telling me."

She smiled. "I think that's better left to your physicians. Now back to the matter at hand. You're sure our new guy is made of your boyfriend's head?"

"Ex-boyfriend, and yes, I'm positive. He even has a picture of my ex in life behind him on a shelf."

Morgen rounded on Gwen. "Yeah, I noticed that. Creepy. What the hells is up with that? Do constructs always keep pictures of the people who they're made of? An homage or something?"

Gwen frowned. "I admit I don't have a lot of experience with constructs. But it seems a little odd."

Morgen thought for a moment. "Was your ex a fun-hating prick as well, Zoë?"

"Not at all. He always told bad jokes and gave me tacky gifts, kitsch that you get in airports—spoons that say 'Denver' and snow globes from LA. He was a good guy; we didn't even have a big breakup. College ended, and we just sort of drifted apart. And seeing him this morning was almost a bigger shock than finding out that people like you two exist."

"I guess you need to do some research on constructs," Morgen said, sucking on her straw. "Then you might better understand Wesley. Maybe *you* can tell us why he's such a prick."

Zoë shrugged. "What about the little issue of him being my dead boyfriend?"

"I wouldn't recommend rekindling that flame," Morgen said, thinking. "Constructs are creepy bastards. Even by our standards. How does his personality get created, anyway, Gwen?"

Gwen raised her hands in an "I surrender" gesture. "Why am I suddenly the construct expert?"

"You're a death goddess," Zoë said. "And they're made from dead people. Of everyone here, you're likely to know the most. Do souls get plucked from the underworld when a construct is made? Or is it a new one? Or a shadow of an older soul?

Gwen shook her head. "I know very little about them. I just

know that he doesn't have any kind of soul that I could feed off of or usher into the underworld."

Zoë sighed as they fell into silence. Gwen began people-watching—or feeding, Zoë assumed—and Morgen finished attacking her glass of water. Zoë looked at her companions, a part of her brain still disbelieving this whole thing, and said, "I guess I have to go talk to Phil. Maybe he'll know who created Wesley and I can start there. I'm not wrong in thinking it's a weird coincidence, am I?"

Gwen frowned, and for a moment her face took on the shadow of a leering dog skull. Zoë blinked. "My kind doesn't really believe in coincidences. I'm not sure why someone wanted to freak you out with a construct made of someone you loved, but someone did this on purpose."

Zoë shivered despite the warmth of the coffee shop. "Then I suppose I really need to talk to Phil."

Phil looked up in surprise when Zoë stormed into his office and slammed the door behind her. "Zoë. Is there a problem?"

She crossed her arms and glared at him. "Did you plan this? Was it a mean initiation, or are you just trying to scare me into quitting?"

Phil frowned. "All right. What did Morgen do?"

Zoë shook her head. "No, not Morgen. She didn't do anything. I'm talking about Wesley."

Phil relaxed. "He's not the most pleasant fellow, but he's good at what he does. He comes with great recommendations. I'm sorry if he put you off, but I would find it hard to believe that he actually scared you. That's not really his way of operation."

Zoë gaped at him. "Are you kidding me? Do you seriously not know what I'm talking about?"

"Unless you're upset about the fact you're working with coterie, then no, I don't."

"Phil, Wesley's made in part from my ex-boyfriend who I didn't even know was dead. Specifically his head. So my meeting with him this morning was a little shocking."

Phil's jaw dropped. "You can't be serious. The odds against that are astronomical."

"You think? I've been thinking you did it to freak me out or make me leave."

Phil leaned back in his chair, baffled. "Zoë, I've known you for a month. I'm taking a chance on you; why would I want to sabotage that?"

Zoë shook her head. "Someone wants to sabotage something, that's pretty clear. Who created him?"

"I don't know. It's not something you ask. This is ridiculous, I can't imagine forces at work to create Wesley to scare or hurt you."

"Gwen said she didn't believe in coincidences. I find it very hard to believe myself. It's weird you don't know who created him; that sounds important, like where you went to college. You could ask CR about the protocol behind hiring constructs and knowing their history but, oops, the construct *is* CR."

By the end of this, Zoë was nearly shouting. Phil stood with surprising speed and latched his hand onto her shoulder. "Calm down, Zoë. This was totally unexpected, I am honestly sorry. We can talk to Wesley about this—"

"No," she interrupted. "I don't want to talk to him. He's been pretty rude to me already. If it *is* somehow a weird coincidence, then this fact will just make him hate me more. And if it's not, then I don't want him knowing that I've figured something out. Besides, he doesn't want me to talk to him until it's to tender my resignation."

He sighed and pulled his hand away. "So what are you going to do?"

Zoë set her jaw. "You wanted me to learn more about the coterie, right? I'm off to learn."

He frowned and thought for a moment. "I may be able to help here." He sat down and dialed a number on his office phone, putting it on speakerphone. The other person took a while to pick up, but he waited patiently. Finally the slow voice of Montel filled the room.

"What up, Phil?"

"We have a little bit of a situation, Montel," he said. "Turns out Wesley is the construct of a zoëtist who may have it in for our new managing editor."

"How do you figure that?" Montel asked.

"He's made out of her dead ex-boyfriend."

"Oh. Shit, that doesn't make us look very good, does it? Are you sure she has no coterie connections?"

"No, I don't know anyone except you guys," Zoë said.

Phil tapped his fingers on his desk. "I'm beginning to think that there's something bigger going on here. Have any visiting zoëtists been through here recently?"

Montel paused. "I don't know of any," he finally said. "Benjamin Rosenberg usually keeps up with that, doesn't he?"

Phil winced. "Right. Listen, I'll get in touch with Benjamin, you put someone on Wesley, see if we can find out some things about him."

"Paul can do it," Montel said.

"That's fine," Phil said.

"You really believe in this woman? A human?" Montel asked.

"Dude, I'm right here," Zoë said.

"She's got experience. And there's something hard about her, something that makes her fit in with us. I can't explain it," Phil said, looking at Zoë. She fidgeted under his gaze.

"Going with your gut?"

Phil chuckled. "Guess so. OK, get Paul on that, I'll get in touch with Benjamin next. Thanks, Montel."

"Got your back." Montel hung up.

"Sorry about that. For some reason he speaks better on the phone than in person. It's faster to just call him," Phil said.

"Who's the Rosenberg guy?"

"He's a zoëtist. But he doesn't like other coterie, even other zoëtists. I don't know how much he practices anymore. He also doesn't like people dropping in on him unannounced, so we should call." He fiddled with his cell phone, looking for a number. He then picked up the handset of his office phone, looking at Zoë as he hit the speakerphone button. "I'm not happy with where this is going."

The Shambling Guide to New York City

DEDICATION

The publisher said dedications were not standard in travel books, but I told him to go suck on a hobo. We went through a great deal to get this book published, including dealing with the events on December 8, and I wanted two people memorialized for being instrumental in the creation of this book.

So, with love, this book is dedicated to Scott Andretti and Granny Good Mae. May they rest in peace wherever they are now. ∎

CHAPTER TEN

A deep-voiced man answered the phone. "Rosenberg-Caldwell residence."

Phil grimaced. "Is Benjamin available?"

"Who may I say is calling?" said the voice.

He sounds like a graduate of Phone Etiquette 101, thought Zoë.

"This is Phil Rand. I need his...expertise."

The voice grew exponentially colder. "I will let him know."

Phil put the phone on mute. "Benjamin's husband is not as open to coterie as he is."

"I thought you said Benjamin didn't like coterie in the first place."

"Exactly. Now imagine someone who hates us more." Phil switched off mute. They could hear the two men talking in tense, low tones.

"Phil. Hello." This voice was higher, more agitated.

Phil smiled. "Ben. Thanks for taking my call. I have a bit of a problem and it might be of interest to you."

The man paused. "That is debatable. I don't do much in coterie circles these days. It upsets Orson."

"I don't need to visit you, and I don't need to bother Orson. I just need to talk to you."

Ben sighed. There was a muffled sound as he put his hand over the phone. "Orson, honey, I'll be in the kitchen."

The deep voice floated back. "Is it . . ." He stopped, and there was a meaningful pause.

"Yes, but it won't take long."

A pause. "All right."

"This had better not take long," Ben said, and they could hear footsteps down a hall.

"He knows of your past, does he not?" Phil asked.

"He does, but he doesn't like it cutting into family time. I try to keep them separate. What do you want?"

Phil shrugged and rolled his eyes at Zoë. Then he focused on the phone again. "I hired a construct last week to work for a new company I'm starting. I also hired a human. She's coping with the coterie quite well, but when she met the construct, she said he had been constructed in part of her dead ex-boyfriend."

Ben spluttered. "The odds of that—"

Phil interrupted. "Astronomical, I know. She's understandably upset about it, and convinced someone is doing this purposefully. She only found out about us about last month. I didn't ask any questions about the construct's past in the interview, as I didn't think I needed to know how old he was, or where he was from. He could do the job, it was enough for me."

Ben's voice was all business. "Did you hire the human first, or the construct?"

"Human."

"And was this her first exposure to our world?"

Phil looked at Zoë, eyebrows raised. "You know it was!" she whispered, annoyed.

"Yes, it was," Phil said.

"All right, let's get this out of the way, why are you so concerned about a human? I don't get really concerned about the chickens that hit my table. You're not sleeping with her, are you?"

111

Zoë made a face. "What a prick! I thought he was human!" she whispered.

Phil waved her silent. "She has experience that I can't find among coterie. We're doing something new, and she fell into my lap, and managed to accept the reality of the world with surprising aplomb. But it's a larger issue: if someone makes me lose this editor, they're messing with my business, and therefore me." His fangs elongated, making Zoë step back. "And that is a threat."

"I see. Well, he's not one of mine. I don't mess with constructs, haven't really done so beyond when my master taught me the basics. But each zoëtist puts a mark on her work, I might be able to tell you more about the creator if I could meet him."

"Would you?"

Ben paused for what seemed like a long time. "You have been a decent enough vampire, Phil," he said at last. "Others haven't treated me so well in the past, but there have only been two, and Orson killed one, and the other one moved away. Property taxes, you know. It's how we met, Orson rescuing me, but understandably why he doesn't like my associations with vampires, or any of the coterie." *

"You are coterie."

Ben chuckled bitterly. "He doesn't see it that way. Anyway. I'll help you. All I need to do is get a good look at your construct, so you can e-mail me a picture or something."

"Thank you, Ben. Do not hesitate to call on me if you need a favor."

"I will make a note of that." Ben sighed again. "Listen. This is serious; zoëtism is a skill one should not take lightly, or use to sow mischief. I guess I'm involved with this as much as you are, because if a zoëtist is threatening you, she's messing with the art itself, and that offends me. Let me know what you need."

"I will," Phil said, and ended the call.

Zoë felt suddenly impotent. Everyone else was working on her problem, but she had nothing to do. "Why did he keep saying 'she'? I'm all for progressive language, but you don't see 'she' as a general pronoun, well, ever."

"Women make life. Ninety-five percent of zoëtists are female. You just met one of two male zoëtists that I know. It's easier magic for women, for obvious reasons. We just assume zoëtists are going to be women.

"Anyway, get back to work. Make a book for me. Let's meet tomorrow morning with the writers and we can start brainstorming different series. I want something even better than your *Misconceptions* line."

Zoë groaned inwardly. The *Misconceptions* travel book line had taken weeks to plan out. But she did have a job to do.

"You got it, boss."

As she headed back to her office Zoë nodded to Morgen, who got up to go get Gwen. Something else dragged at Zoë's attention to the left, someone she hadn't seen in the office before, but she ignored it and went to her office to wait for her friends.

Gwen and Morgen came in, closing the door behind them. Morgen perched on the back of the guest chair, Gwen stood silently by the door.

"Phil swears he knows nothing," Zoë said.

Morgen made a face. "Vampires don't swear."

Zoë sighed. "Fine. He says he knows nothing. I don't know if vampires can lie any better than people, but he seemed pretty floored. I don't think he's behind it."

"Vampires aren't zoëtists, anyway," Morgen interrupted.

"Which I can understand," Zoë finished. "Why would anyone want to mess with me?"

Gwen shrugged, the black cape across her shoulders moving gracefully. "You're a human working with coterie. If you're not a zoëtist or a thrall, most think you don't fit in."

"But I didn't know I would be doing this until last month!"

"Yes, but many coterie can scry the future and get hints of what is about to happen."

Zoë collapsed into her chair, suddenly too tired to deal. "Shit. Maybe I should quit. This is too much."

Morgen glared at her, and the room became thick with humidity. "Look, girl. You work with coterie. With monsters, to your eyes. You have taken everything in stride until you saw your ex-boyfriend's dead head being a prick to you. That's pretty damn impressive. It's clear you can work with us if we can just get past the Wesley thing. Don't let him drag you down. You can work with people who would eat you, but you can't work with a guy whose only scary aspect is his head?"

Zoë smiled in spite of herself. Morgen continued, "Anyway, Wesley knows the rule. He steps out of line, he'll have to deal with us. And"—she shuddered—"Phil."

A knock at the door interrupted Zoë's response. Gwen opened the door and in strode the most beautiful man Zoë had ever seen. He was of average height—around five foot eleven—and had dark brown hair and brown eyes, a narrow face, and a body that looked as if it had been made to fit his suit, not the other way around. Her breath caught in her throat and a flush crept up around her neck and onto her cheeks. Her nipples tingled as they hardened inside her blouse.

Whoa. What's going on?

"Sorry for interrupting, ladies, but we just got back and I wanted to officially welcome the new managing editor." His voice was smooth and low, as if he had just finished making love to all three of them and wanted to make sure they were satisfied.

His eyes fell on Zoë and he stuck his hand out. "Hi, Zoë. Good to see you again."

John. This did not look like John. There was a slight resemblance; this man could have been John's hotter, fitter, younger brother. But it clearly wasn't the heavy man in the ill-fitting suit she had met the day she found out about coterie.

He smirked as she stared at him, heat rising in her face. Then she remembered his own advice to her not to let anyone throw her off. She smiled back and stood, extending her hand. A wild part of her mind craved nothing more than the touch of his bare hand on hers.

Morgen knocked his away. "Very funny, John. You lay a hand on her and the boss will drain you dry."

His brown eyes traveled lazily over Zoë's face, breasts, hips, and legs. She blushed harder, feeling her body respond, and sat back down. "It's good to see you again, John. I wanted to thank you again for helping me get this job."

He ignored her words, his eyes lingering on her as if cataloging all her attributes. She waved a hand to get his attention away from her breasts. "Are you done?"

"Not even close to being done, Zoë. Not at all. It is absolutely lovely to see you again. I hope we can have lunch sometime soon. I'm looking forward to working with you." Morgen punched him in the shoulder. He made a pained expression and rubbed the bruise. As he raised his arm, Zoë caught sight of the same bracelet he'd worn the other day, a slim silver chain held closed by a tiny padlock. "I meant just spending time together. Not that I would be feeding on her! Cut me a little slack, please."

Zoë laughed, startling them all. John grinned at her, this time in a friendlier and less erotic way, and he nodded to her and left the office.

Zoë collapsed into her desk chair and motioned for Gwen to

close the door. When she did, a small smile creased the goddess's usually stoic face.

"What the hell was *that*?" Zoë asked. "And why did he look so different when I met him last month?"

Morgen looked at her as if she had asked if Prince Charles rode a Kawasaki motorcycle. "We *told* you. He's an incubus." She said it as if that answered all Zoë's questions. Zoë stared at her. Morgen sighed and continued, "And that means that when he's hungry, he appears to you as the sexiest thing in the world. When he's not hungry, he settles back into a dumpier model. He must not have eaten on the road."

"I do not recommend allowing him to seduce you," Gwen said. "As they feed on sexual energy, humans find encounters with them quite...tiring."

A shiver went through her. That sounded *wonderful*.

"Seriously, Zoë. Incubi and succubi are bad news," Morgen said. "Think of him as forbidden fruit. You don't want to sleep with a coworker anyway, do you?"

That snapped Zoë out of her lust. *No. Not another Godfrey.*

"No," she said. "I definitely don't want that."

The Shambling Guide to New York City

BROOKLYN:
Shops

If your thrall has been forgetful and didn't bring his talisman with him on your trip to the city, there are several shops that can help you out. The most popular store is actually a Target on Gateway Drive in Brooklyn, because the jewelry counter is run by an earth sprite by the name of Horace who will get you what you need if you ask him nicely. It is considered polite to tip him with a vial of dirt from your hometown. So come prepared!

The local talismans are created from silver or gold and the black fang is etched in carbon that has been ground by human slaves who should have known better than to take off their talismans. The sweat of desperation gives the talismans their power. ■

CHAPTER ELEVEN

One thing that Zoë was proud of was her ability, regardless of life stress, to dive into work. So far she'd found two coworkers she rather liked and one she disliked a great deal, her boss wasn't bad, and there was one coworker it seemed safest to stay away from at all costs. Damn, but John was hot.

Her ability to keep her head and stay outwardly cool when her insides were screaming, *Run now, run far, run fast* was also a trait she was proud of. If only her stomach wouldn't rebel...

However, considering she'd used most of her coping strength by two p.m., she realized she wanted nothing more but to go home and see if wine and a bath would make it all go away. She had a hunch that they would not, but there was no way to know without trying.

She figured she'd be better off closing her door for the afternoon than cutting out early in her third week. When the door clicked, her soul felt somewhat lighter. She could almost fool herself into thinking that she'd gotten a cushy job at a mainstream publishing company, complete with corner office.

A small, windowless corner office that smelled vaguely of bleach, but Zoë had a strong imagination.

She stared at the blank wall, knowing that the underbelly of the city, not the glorious skyline, lay beyond it, and sighed. Time to make a list. She rummaged in her desk and pulled out a paper and pen. She drew a line down the center and labeled the left side "WORK" and the right side "PERSONAL."

In the "WORK" column she wrote, "Outline book series," "Get Bertie settled and researching," "Research constructs," and "Shop for office enhancements."

In the "PERSONAL" column she wrote, "Buy more wine, paper towels, houseplant." She had brought her only plant into the office to brighten her space; now her home felt devoid of life. She paused, knocking the pen against her teeth as she thought. Then she added, "Investigate occult shops," "Go cross shopping."

Then she wrote, "crucifix?" beside it. What was the difference? Someone religious would know.

Then below that she wrote, "Go to church."

She wondered what denomination would be best. Did it have to be Christian, or did the Star of David repel vampires as well as the cross? Somehow she thought Phil wouldn't tell her. When the vampires themselves wrote the books, strangely they didn't write about their weaknesses.

And this was probably something she shouldn't ask her boss about anyway. It might affect her first review. And she needed this job. Who knew—even wearing a religious medallion to work might be against policy. Although if they actually employed a death goddess...

Zoë put her head in her hands. It was all so confusing.

She made it through the rest of the day without incident, actually working on a rough outline of the series she decided to tentatively title "The Shambling Guide Series." Not all coterie shambled like zombies, but no humans that she was aware of did so. She ran the idea by Montel, and he loved it.

At least, she thought he did. His gray face spread in a slow smile and he said, "That would definitely work. You have a knack for this already."

That night, Granny Good Mae didn't meet her again, and Zoë gratefully went to her apartment after a quick stop at the corner store where she got a bottle of wine, a box of spaghetti, a roll of paper towels, an orchid she bet herself she could keep alive at least a week, and two veladora candles (one of the Virgin Mary and one of Jesus crucified). She wasn't ready to buy a necklace yet, but she figured the candles were so ugly and so popular that they had to have some kind of power.

She got home, lit both candles, poured the wine, and got into the tub while the stove heated water for the spaghetti. She tried to meditate on the characters on the candles, but then started to feel creepy that these holy figures were looking at her in the tub, and turned them around so they faced the bathroom door.

She was only two weeks and one day in and suddenly buying religious trinkets. She fully expected to let wine carry her to sleep tonight. Tomorrow she needed to find out about Wesley's creator, and zoëtists in general.

But for now she decided to forget about Wesley. She needed to focus on the coworkers she dealt with regularly. One thing she'd avoided doing was dining with them in the break room, choosing to go out to lunch instead. Tomorrow she decided to go for the scariest prospect and invite the vampires to lunch. According to Phil and the office rules he assured her he put in place, eating with Kevin and Opal should be safe enough, but she'd have to ready herself to not get disgusted at their choice of food. With Phil's guarantee, she figured extending the invitation would not hint to them that she was offering herself for lunch.

After her third glass of wine, she fell asleep on the couch to an episode of *CSI* in which the characters were trying to solve a murder whose victim looked suspiciously like a werewolf. She thought in a drunken panic that she should ask about lycanthropes, but forgot as she fell into a wine-induced sleep.

She woke at one o'clock in the morning to an infomercial, completely convinced she should get involved in real estate. With a start she realized one of the salespeople on the TV was a fae of some sort. She wondered if all infomercials employed coterie. No wonder the products labeled "As Seen on TV" were so popular.

A door closed in the hall, and she wondered blearily why Arthur was coming home so late on a weekday, and if he had anyone with him. She couldn't just knock on his door at one in the morning. She wasn't in college anymore.

Her sleep-addled mind refused to believe anything that had happened the previous day.

She stumbled to bed.

Zoë didn't know whether she should be proud of herself for having the foresight to set her alarm or if she should hate herself for drinking before bed during a weekday, but she woke at five o'clock with a completely addled hangover. Oh yes. She was going to run this morning. *Great.*

She stumbled around Prospect Park in the dark for about a mile before she trudged back home, thinking she needed a chapter in the *Shambling Guide* on how to catch idiot humans who ran in the dark with a hangover.

She stood in the shower for far too long, trying to sweat the last of the alcohol out of her body.

That day she was going to meet with the writers, some of whom were vampires. Vampires, Granny Good Mae had told her, could smell her very well. She avoided strong lotions and any fragrances, trying to keep from offending them. On the other hand, would she appeal to them more the more she smelled like good old-fashioned plain human? She looked at her deodorant (*fresh spring scent!*) and contemplated. She finally decided that she'd rather be offensive for a reason she was unused to than offensive for being too sweaty. She also didn't want to smell like lunch.

She packed up her leftover spaghetti as well as the Virgin Mary veladora and headed out the door.

Around nine thirty, Zoë was fueled by Tylenol and coffee, and working hard to function. She was surprised to see Paul shamble into her office and shut the door. They hadn't talked much, communicating solely through e-mail and chat since they had gotten the computers. Phil had been right, he was a very good writer. Not so good with in-person communication.

"Hey, Paul. Is there a reason you needed to meet in person? I thought typing was better for you?" she asked, motioning for him to have a seat.

He carried a pad and scrawled some words down, then held the pad up so Zoë could read it.

"PRIVACY."

He took it back and wrote a bit more.

"MONTEL SAID YOU NEED HELP. HAPPY TO BE OF SERVICE."

Right. He was supposed to tail Wesley. Zoë had gotten used to seeing Paul, but it still made her want to wince in sympathy. He wasn't just dead and peeling like Montel; this guy had died horribly with holes gouged in his head and large bites taken from his neck and shoulders. He stared at her with wide, dead eyes and she tried to put a pleasant look on her face.

"Yeah, thanks a lot. I believe Phil and Montel were going to have you look into something for me."

The zombie scrawled on the pad again.

"FOLLOW WESLEY. DON'T LET HIM SEE ME. FIGURE OUT WHO MADE HIM." Paul picked at a stray flap of skin on his wrist while she read, but then wrote again. "WHAT DID HE DO?"

Zoë thought for a moment. Should she tell him? "We're just unsure of his loyalty and origin."

"WE COULD KILL HIM AND THEN FIND SOME-ONE WHO WORKS IN HR IN ANOTHER COMPANY AND BITE THEM."

Zoë studied him for a moment, wondering if he was serious. A smile played at his lips, and she laughed out loud, realizing for the first time that a zombie could have a sense of humor. "You just go for the straight solution, don't you? While that would be one answer, I don't think it falls under the covert work we need."

He wrote again.

"OK, BOSS. WILL FIND OUT WHAT I CAN."

He flipped the page on the pad and began writing again. He wrote for so long, Zoë shifted impatiently. "You writing a book there?"

He glanced up, then showed her the page.

TO DO

EAT BRAINS

MEET WITH ZOË REGARDING WRITING ASSIGNMENTS

LEARN WHERE WESLEY LIVES

FOLLOW WESLEY

REPORT BACK TO PHIL, MONTEL, OR ZOË

BE DISCREET

MORE BRAINS

Satisfied, Paul sat back.

Zoë smiled and said, "Impressive. You always so meticulous?"

"I FORGET OTHERWISE," Paul wrote, touching the back of his head, where a gangrenous hole was where his skull used to be.

Zoë winced. "I'm sorry."

Paul shrugged. He wrote, "I WAS ALWAYS A LIST MAKER."

Zoë thought for a moment. "Do you know if Wesley's in yet?"

Paul glanced at his watch. He shook his head.

"HE USUALLY COMES IN AT TEN," he wrote.

Zoë checked her watch. "Good. As for your writing assignments, I'd like to see a sample of your work, so just write up a review of your favorite lunch place, and your favorite place to get clothes, and that will give me a good idea of where to place you."

Paul nodded, then heaved himself to his feet. He opened her door and shambled away, nearly getting run over by a buoyant Morgen, who danced into Zoë's office. Her energy made Zoë's hangover tired.

Morgen reminded Zoë not so much of a water sprite, but more of a tree sprite. A monkey, to be precise. Zoë didn't like monkeys. She knew they appealed to the child in people, the anarchic sense that it was delightful that someone could just throw some poop if displeased. But Zoë always felt like the person who would get the poop thrown at her, and that she would probably have to be the one to clean up.

Morgen perched on the back of Zoë's visitor chair, feet in the seat and butt on the back of the chair. "So you're having meetings today with people who would eat you," she said.

Zoë leaned back and rubbed her forehead. "Word gets around."

"Well, sure! You're the odd one out here, the prey in the middle of the predators, just walking around giving writing assignments. You fascinate us. We want to know all the dirt."

Zoë felt the analogy a little too keenly, as if she were identifying with a child who had wandered into the lion's den. "I am just trying to get to know people. I have to talk to Paul about assignments. And lunch with Opal and Kevin seemed like a good idea."

"But why start with the coterie most likely to eat you? Why not me and Gwen?"

Zoë smiled. "Would you believe it if I said I wanted to make a statement?"

Morgen cackled. "I knew you had brass ovaries when you took this job, but that one is a move I didn't anticipate. You do know that not every vampire eats at Italy's Entrails or even has a contact with the Red Cross or local hospitals, don't you? Some still hunt or drink from willing victims."

Zoë's mouth grew dry, but she nodded. "I figured as much. I'm not lucky enough to find out that monsters are real and find out that they're all fluffy bunnies and soft kittens too."

She had chosen her words carefully to gauge Morgen, to see if she would take offense, but the pink-haired sprite just laughed again. "No shit, girlfriend. Hey, I'm going out after work to a little bar that's out of the way. You wanna come? I can take you to a coterie restaurant that's friendlier than Italy's Entrails, too."

Zoë's stomach clenched at the thought of going out again. She felt bad, but she shook her head. "I'm sorry, Morgen, I'm not up to it tonight. Rain check?"

The sprite shrugged and grinned. "Sure. You shouldn't drink alone, by the way."

Zoë groaned. "Is it that obvious?"

"To coterie, yeah. Also, you look like shit."

"Thanks." Zoë checked her watch; according to Paul, Wesley

wouldn't be in for another fifteen minutes. "I've got to go check on something. I'll catch up with you later, OK?"

Biting her lip, Zoë pushed the closet/office door gently open and slipped inside, hitting the overhead light. Careful not to touch anything, she approached the pictures on the shelf behind the tiny desk. There, next to the picture of the woman with small, delicate hands, was the picture of Scott, her ex, grinning from a fishing boat. Emotions warred within her: she missed him, she wondered how he'd died, but already the sight of him brought up negative connotations of Wesley. She gritted her teeth at the desire to punch her sweet ex, and straightened.

"Wesley's really not going to want you going through his things," came a voice from behind her, and she jumped.

"Dammit, you just scared ten years off my life! I didn't hear you at all!"

Kevin the vampire leaned against the doorjamb with his arms crossed over his black turtleneck and blazer, grinning at her. He didn't bother to hide his long incisors.

Zoë turned back to the photos. "It interested me that Wesley kept pictures of those people he was created from. I wondered if all constructs do that."

He shrugged. "Some do, some don't."

She brushed past him and turned off Wesley's light, careful to pull the door closed. "Anyway, did you get the note I left on your desk? I wanted to meet with you and Opal at lunch today. We need to talk about books and eventual assignments."

He shrugged again. "I figured you wanted to learn about vampires."

Zoë smiled. "That too. Are you and Opal free?"

He nodded slowly.

"Great. Noon it is." She walked away from him, trying not to think that he was looking at her and wondering how she tasted.

Zoë had to be honest with herself: it was never a good idea to overindulge in alcohol. But there were times when it was worse to do so than others. Like, for example, when you had plans to meet vampires for lunch. When you needed to be sharp. Her stomach still sour from the wine, she decided on coffee for lunch. Opal and Kevin both came into the break room with thermoses at the ready.

Kevin sat next to Zoë at the table and slowly unscrewed the top of his thermos, taking care to inhale the scent of the blood inside. He tipped it over so the blood flowed slowly into the thermos lid.

Zoë tried to inhale the coffee scent, but with her sour stomach it seemed like a dreadful proposition, and when the coppery scent of Kevin's lunch hit her, she carefully walked to the fridge to get a stomach-settling soda instead.

Her stomach turned again when she saw Tupperware containers full of gray, ropey things that she guessed were brains.

When Zoë returned, Kevin was still pouring. She wondered if he had stopped pouring until she got back to witness it.

"God, Kevin, pour that away from her. Are you trying to make her ill?" Opal said. She pulled Kevin back so there was a good three feet between him and Zoë's chair. When Zoë sat down, Opal said, "Pardon my son, Zoë. He has no manners yet."

Kevin glared at Opal with red eyes. "Does my lunch offend her? I find it difficult to believe she didn't know what she was getting into." He made a show of taking a long gulp from the thermos lid.

Zoë refused to take the bait and made a face at him. "No, I

drank too much wine last night and my stomach isn't treating me well. I'm new to coterie food choices, but I'm pretty sure that vomit is not one of the bodily fluids you enjoy."

Opal laughed, tweaking Kevin on the cheek. He brushed her off, and she sat on the other side of Zoë at a respectful distance. Sweeping her long blonde hair away from her face, she poured her lunch, a lot more efficiently and less obviously than Kevin, into a coffee mug.

"I'm sorry, did you say Kevin was your son?" Zoë asked. She knew they were immortal but it still boggled her that Opal looked to be in her twenties and Kevin solidly in his thirties.

She nodded and sipped delicately at her thermos. "I got very sick with a fever when I was a girl and it made me sterile. I grew up in a large family, always wanted a ton of kids. What life couldn't give me, immortality has given in spades." She looked fondly at Kevin, who ignored her and gulped more blood.

Zoë watched him with interest. "So does the Rh factor make a difference? Do you prefer A over B, and is O like the chicken of the blood family, in that it doesn't taste like much of anything, but everything tastes like it?"

Kevin looked, for the first time, as if he was listening to her and considering her as more than a meal. "I prefer A, but it's nearly impossible to choose. You can order at a restaurant, if you want to pay for it. If you're getting a handout at the hospital or Red Cross, you get what they give, and if you're hunting, it's rare you can smell their type unless they're injured. And if you're hunting, you're not going to be choosy."

Zoë found herself morbidly fascinated. "So you can't tell my type?"

Kevin inhaled deeply, then shook his head. "No, you're dehydrated and we both are already eating, so that's all I can smell."

"Huh," she said, secretly relieved. Her blood type was A. "Tell me about hunting versus handouts. How do you decide which to do and are there some vampires who prefer one over the other?"

Kevin's lips were very red as he lowered his thermos lid. The blood left in the lid dribbled down the inside slowly, like the legs of a good wine. She wondered if he'd added an anticoagulant.

"All vampires prefer to hunt. It's in our nature. Hunted blood is sharper, fresher. But it's illegal. Public Works has eyes everywhere. We have to have a truce with the city to feed, we become gatherers to survive. Most of the Red Crosses in the area have someone coterie-friendly on the inside, and a handful of the hospitals do. We pay in hell notes and they give us blood."

Zoë made a note about the establishments that gave out blood. "How often are these insiders replaced? Are they people you can count on to hang around?"

His eyes narrowed. "Why?"

"Well, if we publish their names in the book, and they leave, then the book will be out of date. If there's high turnover, then a link pointing to an up-to-date list of names online is the best way to go. Anyway, we can worry about that later. Let's talk about the book. So if you get blood from the humans, does that mean there are no hunting grounds?"

"Oh, we didn't say that," Opal said, and smiled at Kevin as he drained his thermos lid and licked his lips. "We all still hunt. How do you think I got my beautiful Kevin here?" She touched his hair fondly, and Zoë became uncomfortable, unsure whether the touch was one of a mother or a lover.

"We just are extremely careful," she continued. "There are always ways to get fresh blood. Hunt, yes. There are some safe places; places that are already violent rarely notice coterie movement, but we have to be careful not to hunt too much in any one place. Then there are those who love coterie and wish to become our thralls. While it's not something we do more than once a month or so, the prudent ones anyway, every vampire will drink from the living if given a chance."

Kevin moved from under her hand and got up from the table. He rinsed his thermos out at the sink. Zoë made the final notes on her pad and realized Kevin had come to stand behind her, quite close. She could hear him breathing deeply, and realized he was smelling her. She didn't look up from her notes. "I think I'm going to assign you the write-ups of the Red Crosses and hospitals in your areas. Kevin, you have Manhattan, Opal, you have the Bronx. When you're done, we'll think about the rest of the city. Maybe I'll see if Bertie can do that. I'll get a more detailed outline to you soon. Unless we hire more writers, I may need you to cover the feeding details for other coterie races in your areas."

She paused and looked up at Kevin, who still stood over her, silently, blood wet on his lips. She met his red eyes. "Any questions?"

He licked his lips. "What about hunting grounds?"

She sat back and considered. "I'm not sure. If hunting is illegal, will we want to list them? Would we get in trouble, or cause Public Works to focus on those areas?"

"Ask a human police chief who the drug lords are in his city. He can name names. Knowing where the grounds are doesn't make it easier to control," Kevin said, still looking at her as if she were a price piece of meat. "Also, thank you for wearing little personal scent today. You smell wonderful."

Color rose to her cheeks and she forced a smile. "I'll trust your judgment on the hunting grounds reporting then. It was nice talking to you both. Thanks for your help." She dropped her eyes and went back to her notes. Kevin stood there a moment longer, then left the break room.

"Is he always like that?" she asked Opal, who still sipped at her blood thoughtfully.

"He's a baby yet, and chafing to be his own man," she said, her voice slightly mournful. "He wants to turn his own companion. I think he's moving away from me."

Zoë made another note. "That's got to be hard for you."

"It is, but unlike when I was human, I can always have more babies," Opal said, her voice soft. Zoë looked up and found the vampire staring at her.

She smiled. "I'm not ready for immortality yet. I have yet to master this life."

Opal nodded. "I'll abide by Phil's demands, but you never know. You might like it. Just say the word."

She left the table and finally Zoë was alone.

She put her head in her hands. This was just getting better and better.

On her way out of the break room, she caught Wesley's voice drifting from behind the cracked door to his office. "I'll be ready to accept your resignation this afternoon, Zoë, if you'd like to talk."

The Shambling Guide to New York City

BRONX:
Events

A growing group of humans have decided to live in symbiotic relationships with vampires, giving the coterie a chance to drink from live hosts, and it is beneficial to the hosts as well. Humans suffering from the genetic condition hereditary hemochromatosis have an abundance of iron in their bodies, and the treatment is bloodletting.

With the advent of adventure races among the humans, some enterprising coterie have started the Tough Blooder. You are welcome to enter with a small registration fee, and the humans enter the race for free. They run through the woods and obstacles, and you buy a place on the course to attack and feed from them. This gives the humans the treatment they need and gives the vampires adrenaline-fueled blood.

You are barred from the race if you kill your host, or drink more than one and a half pints. This event is sanctioned by Public Works. ■

CHAPTER TWELVE

John came to see Zoë that afternoon as she was working on her outline and swearing at her body's inability to process Tylenol quickly.

"I hear you're not feeling well," he said, gliding into the office with unnatural grace.

No, not unnatural. Just *inhuman*. Zoë couldn't help but wonder how it would feel if he touched her with those graceful hands, and shook her head to clear it. "Rough night. No matter."

"Ahhh," he said, exhaling in just the way she'd expect him to do after climaxing. "I understand. Job stress?"

She grinned despite herself. "A little." His direct stare made her weak in the knees. She inhaled and said in what she hoped was a businesslike way, "What can I do for you, John?"

She immediately regretted the question as he smiled slowly and widely, sitting down in her visitor chair and leaning back. She fancied she could see every contour of his body underneath his white shirt and khakis. She had met dangerous men before. She'd let her last boss seduce her. She had been threatened by a construct. And yet John was the first man—or rather, sentient being—in a while who had made her fear for her well-being. Probably the first person since she'd encountered Godfrey's wife.

With John in the room, Zoë felt as if she were looking over the edge of a cliff thinking that the wind through her hair would feel so good on the way down. That image was immediately replaced with the image of John's fingers in her hair, and she gritted her teeth and focused again. She realized he was speaking, and watched his lips form the words.

"I know you're researching the coterie world. I'd love to teach you a little about the 'bus lifestyle. Are you free for dinner?"

With every fiber of her being screaming *yes*, Zoë managed to laugh. "John, I'm new here, but I have done *some* research. I know what you eat for dinner, and although you are very good at creating the reaction in me that you're looking for, I prefer not to suffer the consequences. I'd love to learn whatever you can teach me—about your world," she added. "But I would prefer not to learn about your feeding habits firsthand."

He leaned forward and looked at her intently. "Oh, you would. You would be very interested to learn about my feeding habits. It's only the aftereffects you would rather not experience. But the feeding habits? Yes, you would enjoy those very much. You would be keenly aware of each bite I took, each morsel I devoured, each droplet I would lick up. And once you had recovered, you would come to me again for the research opportunity."

Zoë sighed, feeling very much like a trembling rabbit under a circling hawk; instincts screamed at her to run, but if she ran, he would strike. If she had to guess, there were no sexual harassment laws in the coterie world, especially for those working with sex demons. "No means no, John. And regardless of my interest or lack thereof or even just my common sense, I have plans tonight."

He bowed his head, acquiescing. "Another time, then." He stood, then paused with his long-fingered hand on her office door. "Oh, and don't worry. I will never attack you or try to take you by force. That is not a taste I enjoy. You will come to me of your own accord."

"Will I?" she said flatly.

He grinned at her again, making her heart quicken. Was he

even hotter today than yesterday? Zoë stared after him as he left, then sighed, willing her body to stop reacting to him like a teenager's. She pulled out her to-do list and wrote, "Talk to GGM about battling incubi" in the "PERSONAL" column. Then she added, "Buy vibrator." Anything to lessen John's impact on her.

Morgen came in soon after John. "I saw John in here. Is he bugging you? Want me to kick his ass?"

Zoë ran her fingers through her hair. "How do you hurt an incubus? He looks like he works out."

"Oh, water droplet," Morgen said sympathetically, "he looks like whatever you want to see in a guy."

Zoë hadn't thought of that. "What do you see?"

"Oh, I just see an average guy, brown skin, black eyes, somewhat heavyset. His power doesn't have any effect on me. He just wants human sexual energy. Pity, though. Water sprites are pretty wild."

Zoë laughed. "Let me guess. Asphyxiation games?"

Morgen nodded vigorously. "You don't know the half of it."

"And yet less than half is all I want to know, which works out just fine. But I need to come up with plans for tonight, since that's how I got out of seeing him. What are you doing?"

Morgen clapped her hands. "Oh, I get to show you the city from a sprite's point of view? Yay! Let's see. First we'll go to Blossoms on Fifth Avenue so you can see where the fae eat, and then we'll go to a club. Has Phil given you a talisman yet?"

Zoë frowned. "No." She was about to say that she'd meant to remind him, but then remembered that no coterie had told her of the talismans; she was not supposed to know about them yet.

Morgen sighed. "He wanted to hire a human and didn't prepare her for anything. A talisman is a mark that humans who work with coterie wear, to let others know they didn't wander in by accident, and that they're not available for feeding."

"I thought coterie weren't supposed to hunt?" Zoë asked.

Morgen dropped her easygoing attitude. "Zoë. If a tiger gets out of her cage at the zoo and eats someone, they shoot it. But if a human is stupid enough to get into the cage with the tiger, do they begrudge it the meal?"

Zoë swallowed. "So how do I use, or get, one of these talismans, then?"

On his way out, Phil informed them that he had indeed left a talisman for Zoë, but he'd left it in her employee folder for Wesley to give to her upon orientation.

Morgen frowned like a rainy afternoon. "Well, it's beginning to make sense now. Let's go bully Wesley."

Zoë groaned.

The abandoned theater was mostly empty, it being after dark and safe for everyone to leave. Only the zombies remained, congregating in the onstage break room.

Morgen poked her head into Wesley's office, then grinned back at Zoë. "He's gone."

Morgen stepped into the room. "I know where he keeps employee files, let me deal with this."

She went to the file cabinet beside Wesley's desk and pulled briefly on the top drawer, showing no surprise when it proved locked. She nodded and then put her finger against the keyhole.

Zoë gasped as Morgen's hand turned watery and translucent, flowing into the keyhole. The water sprite bit her lip in concentration and twisted her wrist slightly, and the drawer popped open. The water flowed back out and formed again into Morgen's hand.

Zoë leaned against the door, knees weak with shock. "That was amazing."

Morgen looked up and grinned at her. "Buy me a drink and ask me what happened to the stuff inside Al Capone's vault. The water sprites know."

She flipped through the different files and pulled out Zoë's. "Ah! Zoë Norris. What do we have here? A talisman!" She pulled a black ribbon from the folder and tossed it to Zoë. It was a velvet choker necklace with a silver medallion hanging from it, the medallion engraved with the same symbol she'd seen on Granny Good Mae's wrist.

"And your typed-up resignation letter, waiting for your signature," Morgen continued. "I guess he really does have it in for you."

Zoë had been wrong; aside from the zombies, John was also still in the office. He stood onstage with them, discussing something. Their voices were low and tense.

"What does Wesley have against me?" she asked, mostly rhetorically.

"Oh, what does anyone have against anyone in this world? Some resent a human hanging out here. Some want to see you squirm. Some want to eat you. It's no big deal. You can handle yourself. Also, don't stress about it. It may not even be Wesley who's got it in for you, it's probably his creator. So work should be a little easier, huh? Knowing it's not Wesley that hates you?"

Zoë made a face at her. "Yeah. Much better. Thanks."

The zombies kept mumbling at each other, and Morgen finally raised her voice. "What the hells is the matter with you guys?"

John came over, his strong jaw set. Even concerned, he looked hotter than ever. His brown eyes swept over Zoë briefly before he focused on Morgen.

"Do you guys know anything about missing brains? The zombies' stash is gone."

Morgen blanched, looking nearly translucent. "Are they sure? I mean, couldn't someone have just forgotten to bring some today?"

"They claim not. And they're getting close to losing their shit."

"Losing it?" Zoë asked.

John nodded. "Zombies get more mindless and animalistic when they don't eat. You don't know that yet?"

Zoë knew. She just found higher thinking hard with John next to her. She grimaced. "Right. Of course."

John looked at Morgen and pointed at Zoë. "We'd better get her out of here. They're hungry and I don't know if they're going to revert or something."

"Well, yeah, but we can't just leave them. If they go hunting like this, they'll get caught. Can't they go home and eat?"

"They live in Queens."

Morgen swore—Zoë assumed—in a language Zoë didn't recognize. "And they're that bad off? So fast?"

"Yeah. I can't understand it," John said, putting his hand on Zoë's shoulder. He pressed slightly, sending a message of more than simple concern for her. "They don't usually get this hungry."

Rodrigo, the short office assistant whom Zoë hadn't talked to much, turned and focused on them. "The brains are missing. Paul brought in new brains this morning. We should have had enough for the week. Are you sure you didn't take any?"

Zoë's heart hammered when she realized all three zombies were looking at her pointedly, but she rolled her eyes. "Yeah. I'm going to accidentally eat brains. And keep eating them once I realize my mistake."

Rodrigo looked at the trash can. "You could have thrown them away."

"Why in the world would I want to throw away your food, when I know that I'm the only other food source you have in the office?" Zoë asked. "I know you're hungry, dude, but use some common sense and give me a tiny bit of credit."

John started pulling on her. "Come on, Zoë, don't taunt the people who are thinking about that gorgeous pink brain of yours," he whispered, his low voice tickling her ear. She shivered.

"All right. Listen, the brains were there at lunch, I saw some when I got a soda. I didn't touch them. I didn't see who took them." John pulled on her again. "Good luck finding brains, guys!"

The zombies didn't register her leaving. That was probably a good thing.

Once the three were outside, John pulled his coat around him. "We'd better follow them, just to make sure they get what they need and don't start hunting."

"Shouldn't Phil do that or something?" Zoë asked.

John rolled his eyes. "Phil's on the phone doing a business deal. You don't interrupt Phil when he's doing business."

Morgen looked at Zoë. "Are you up for this?"

Zoë was quite hungry, but realized she would get a chance to see how coterie food worked within the city twice, if they followed the zombies. "Sure. I'm game."

As they waited for the zombies to exit the theater, Zoë studied her talisman so she wouldn't have to look at John's silhouette against the streetlight.

"A choker? Seriously?" Zoë asked Morgen.

"What's wrong with a choker?" Morgen asked, taking it from her and fastening it around Zoë's neck.

"Look at me, Morgen. Am I goth? Even slightly?" She wore a red sweater, khakis, and brown boots under a tan overcoat.

"Not even slightly," the water sprite said. "But people in this city don't notice the fact that zombies walk the street with them, not to mention other coterie. Do you think they'll notice the one goth necklace standing out of your mundane wardrobe?"

Zoë made a face. "Yes, actually! The fact that zombies are wandering the streets is so far outside the concept of the human world, it just flows out of their mind. At the very least, people will think they're going to a costume party. But bad accessorizing..." She shuddered.

Morgen rolled her eyes. "You'll deal. Better than getting eaten." She pointed to the door where the zombies were exiting, and she, John, and Zoë slunk back into the shadows. "Come on, let's follow them."

Each zombie wore an overcoat and a low-pulled hat. To Zoë's eyes, they looked painfully obvious, but it was the city's way to ignore passersby, so no one took notice. The zombies were clearly hurrying, but still walked slower than Zoë, John, and Morgen, so they followed at a leisurely pace far behind.

"I think the necklace is lovely on you," John said. "It may look better with a more revealing top. May I suggest a button-down blouse?"

In the dark, Zoë wondered if by his very nature he could tell when her face reddened due to his attentions. "You can suggest all you want. But I think wearing revealing clothing around you is a bad idea."

He laughed, a low chuckle. Then his hand was on her shoulder again and his breath was hot on her ear. "Then perhaps you should wear none at all."

I walked into that one, she thought. Her legs turned to jelly. "Sheesh, John. It's really good that you're a supernatural being.

I figure if I can hold you off, I can handle any temptation." She laughed, determined not to show the cracks in her armor.

He just smiled at her, his gorgeous, full lips promising much in the way of pleasure.

Morgen slipped between then, forcing them apart. "Come on, you two. John, if you mess her up so she can't come to work, Phil will have your head. Zoë, I told you, he's sex on two legs. He's programmed to turn you on. You've got to be strong."

Zoë blushed harder and stared firmly ahead. She'd forgotten Morgen was there. *John really is powerful. I shouldn't underestimate him simply because he doesn't want to eat my brains or blood.*

They stepped up their pace, as the zombies had gotten farther ahead of them. Zoë remembered she'd meant to contact an old college friend to find out if she knew how Scott had died, which might lead to some clues about Wesley's goals.

Putting dead people out of her mind was difficult as the zombies led them through an alley and to a garage door on the side of a hospital annex. It took Zoë a moment to realize they were at the hearse entrance for the morgue. "Ohh..." she said. Morgen grinned at her.

"Where did you think we were going?" she asked.

Zoë shrugged. "A coworker is made of an ex-boyfriend and an incubus is trying to seduce me on the streets. I was kinda distracted."

"OK, we need to keep quiet. But," Morgen added, pulling at Zoë's jacket collar to show off the choker, "if we're seen, make sure anyone can see this."

"But aren't they humans?"

"Doesn't matter. They'll have one too. Watch."

The zombies pounded four times on the door, and a hum came from inside and the door lifted. An older, heavyset Hispanic man came out, glaring at them. He rolled up his sleeves in the chilly night, showing a talisman set into a frayed leather strap around his wrist.

"Jorge, we need replenishment," Montel said without preamble.

"You're not supposed to be here for another week or so. What makes you think I have any stash left?"

Zoë had the bizarre feeling of being present during a drug deal, and felt the need to look right and left for any lurking cops. No one noticed them; no one was present except for a homeless woman pushing a shopping cart and muttering to herself.

"This is worse than I thought," John whispered.

"How so?" Zoë asked.

Morgen watched the zombies with shining eyes. "Montel's nearly lost all humanity. He's seriously feral at this point. If we tell you to run, do it."

Zoë nodded, biting her lip.

"We require food," Rodrigo said. He switched to Spanish, and spoke a moment longer. Jorge's face went slack with shock and he took a step back.

Montel groaned, then said, "You should always be ready to provide."

"I don't have anything ready, you'll have to hit another supplier," Jorge said, his voice going high with panic. He tried to close the door, but Montel blocked it with his arm. The zombies shuffled closer.

Just go inside! Zoë thought, her heart hammering. She opened her mouth to call to him, but Morgen stopped her. "If you speak up, all they will hear is another meal. Keep quiet. I'm going to call Phil."

"But—" Zoë said, and Morgen ran out of the alley to the sidewalk.

Jorge held up his hand, showing his talisman. "I'm neutral!

You can't harm me! You kill me, you lose this hospital and call Public Works down on your nasty heads!"

Montel shook his head as if to clear it and stepped back. His dead eyes caught Zoë and John in the shadows, and then the homeless woman. He put his hand on Paul's shoulder and pulled him back too. "He's right. We need to calm down."

Montel's arm was out to grab Rodrigo, but the shorter zombie reached out with one decayed finger and hooked Jorge's leather strap. It had frayed too much, and one quick tug pulled the talisman off. Zoë caught sight once more of Jorge's frightened brown eyes, and then Rodrigo was on him, chewing on his head and ripping at his clothing.

Zoë staggered back, her hand clasped to her mouth, John's hand over hers. This was supposed to be a stop as benign as a grocery trip. Even after the bloody meeting with the vampires, she had nearly convinced herself that coterie were just people too. She'd never seen them hunt. But the scene in front of her rivaled Friday nights when she'd worked as a waitress at Applebee's and belligerent customers had nearly bitten her head off for bringing the wrong drinks.

Well (her frantic mind tried to calm itself with logic), that biting of her head had been metaphorical, even if a customer had sprayed her with infuriated spittle one time. Jorge was getting his head literally bitten off, and Zoë pressed her fingers into her mouth to stop herself from screaming.

Then John's mouth was at her ear, his hands on her shoulders, he was pulling her away, whispering, God, whispering things, filthy, seductive things, shocking things, but his coterie power had the desired effect. Lust surged in Zoë and she nearly swooned, falling into his arms. His lips were on hers then, crushing her, and she could feel something boiling inside her, and then being removed from her. The screams and hungry moans behind her faded, and all she could hear was her own pulse in her ears, and her own roaring need.

Then she was on the street, with no idea of how she'd gotten there. Morgen was shutting her phone and frowning. "Voice mail. This is not good." She looked at Zoë and then at John. "Fuck, John, what did you do to her?"

He looked affronted. "I got her out of there. She was freaking and I had to . . . distract her."

"Why was she freaking out?"

"Rodrigo is feeding on his supplier."

"Shit. Did the others go native, too?"

"I think they're all right. They pulled him off the man, but the damage is done. Rodrigo is mad with hunger, and Montel and Paul have enough to deal with controlling their own hunger." John pointed down into the hospital's parking deck. "Rodrigo ran that way."

Morgen looked grimmer than Zoë had ever seen her. "Phil's not answering. Montel can't help. And I'm not leaving Zoë alone in order to run them down."

"Should we call—" John asked.

Morgen made a cutting motion with her hand, interrupting. "No. They will know about it. They always do. That's why we shouldn't be caught here. Let's just go."

The Shambling Guide to New York City

APPENDIX:
The Post-9/11 City

The city became a somber place, a safer place, for the humans after the 9/11 attacks. But for coterie it got a lot more dangerous.

First there was the ifrit and djinn hunting. Any coterie with Arab or Muslim origins were hunted down, as Public Works became convinced that the terrorist attacks were too well orchestrated to be pulled off by humans alone. The ifrit and djinn were rounded up and interrogated, and some disappeared. Coterie investigators tracked some to a closed-off area of Guantanamo Bay, but others simply disappeared and, as of this writing, are assumed dead.

This was a dark day for the city's coterie, as war with Public Works threatened. It was averted when a group of ifrit from New Jersey traveled back to the Middle East and dug up information about the attacks, sending proof back to Public Works that they were a human job. Public Works never fully believed coterie hadn't been involved—at the very least, it assumed gremlins had been hired to take over the planes—and tensions have been high since.

The buildings that have been closed off to the public since 9/11 (such as the New York Stock Exchange) have also had most of the coterie entrances blockaded. ∎

CHAPTER THIRTEEN

"This feels wrong," Zoë said, staring dumbly at the menu.

"Why?" Morgen asked, her menu down.

"We just saw a guy get killed. Eaten. We shouldn't be... going to a fancy restaurant. It feels disrespectful. Also I'm pretty sure I'd be freaking out right now if someone didn't practically molest me in the alley." She glared at John, but her words lacked venom.

He sipped a glass of water and leaned back, utterly delicious. "Tell me you didn't enjoy it. Tell me it didn't save your life by keeping you focused on something other than the zombies feeding." He leaned forward and his fingertips brushed her knee under the table. "Tell me you don't want more."

Morgen reached over and pushed him back. "Hands on the table, perv. Are you honestly trying to make a case that you used your powers for good?"

John crossed his arms. "As a matter of fact, I am."

Morgen rolled her eyes and focused on Zoë, who blinked stupidly at her. "Anyway, Zoë, there's nothing we can do. We told Phil, I know that Public Works knows about it already, we got you out of there, and now we're feeding you. Have you eaten all day?"

Zoë scanned the menu again, realizing that part of her light-headedness was from low blood sugar. Despite her utter need for the man (*not man*) beside her (*not man, incubus*), Zoë felt a small disquieting tremor in her chest. (*Not man. This is wrong.*)

She blinked a couple of times and then took a deep breath, as if she had been holding hers for a long time. She rubbed her face and said, "OK. I'm back. Thanks for the rescue, John. I think." She smiled at John, who looked, for the first time since she'd met him, unsure.

"So is there anything for humans to eat at this restaurant?" she asked.

Morgen picked up her menu. "Yeah, there should be some salads you can stomach. But let me order for you. Some might think you're my playtoy. Or John's. Let them. No one will mess with you if they think you're a lover of ours, and they won't question you either."

Inside, Blossoms looked exactly like a dance club without the music. Soft neon tubes snaked up the walls, casting blue and pink light everywhere. The bar was made of mirrored glass, which made sense, as everyone in the establishment was painfully beautiful. Among them, Zoë felt awkward, lumbering, and human, the ugly duckling that could never hope to grow up. No one cast her a second glance once seeing her horrible choker, though, and the hostess had led them to a table decorated with glass flowers and a burning oil lantern.

Morgen noticed Zoë's discomfort. "Nice, huh?"

"Are you talking about the clientele or the restaurant?"

"This is a favorite watering hole for most sprites and other fae folk. Those who accept city life, anyway. Others will just hang in Central Park or the river." Morgen paused to shudder. "While that is unappetizing at best and horrific at worst, it is, at least, cheap."

"Aw hell, how am I going to pay for this? I haven't been paid yet and I doubt these guys take credit cards," Zoë said.

John waved her hand. "Dinner is on me, ladies. You both have had quite a shock."

Morgen made a rude noise. "Dude, the chivalry thing won't work here. I'm perfectly fine. But we'll take the free food, right, Zoë?"

"Huh? Oh. Right. Free food. Thanks," she said, her cheeks reddening. She had just been thinking how terribly nice John was being, quite gallant, actually.

A waiter drifted over to them—literally drifting, as his lower half seemed to dissipate. He looked liked a ghost, but held on to a very real notepad. He focused entirely on Morgen.

"I'll have whatever kelp is on special, the scallops, and my friend here will have whatever aboveground salad you have going on, and another order of the scallops. I'd like some sparkling water, and"—she raised her greenish eyebrows to Zoë, who nodded—"she'll have the same."

John ordered a bottle of wine, "The most expensive red you have," and nothing else.

Was this going to be a perpetual state with him?

The waiter nodded and drifted off. Zoë watched him go. "So is he a ghost?"

"Nope. Air sprite."

"Oh. Duh. What do they eat?"

"Clouds, mostly. Although some do get addicted to perfume. Those are some sad bastards. They hang out in malls, follow rich women around, try to get people to buy them the stuff themselves. Some get high off of cheap shit like deodorants, but we don't really like to talk about them."

At other tables, diaphanous beings opened vials and sniffed appreciatively at the air inside, while darker, brown wisps ate a black liquid from bowls. Brightly colored women with sharp features and eyes of strong primary colors—with no pupils—munched on flower petals.

"I still feel like we could have done something. I mean, we just stood there and let that man get...eaten," Zoë said, sipping the mineral water the waiter put down in front of her.

John leaned back in his seat, relaxing like a panther, and sniffed appreciatively at his wine. "And what should we have done about it? Are you some sort of secret zombie hunter?"

Zoë said nothing. She remembered what Granny Good Mae had said about zombies: just avoid fighting them; you could survive a vampire bite, but once a zombie bit you, you were pretty much toast. But she didn't want her coworkers to know that she was training in self-defense, so she just shrugged.

"No, not at all, but I feel like there's something more we should have done." Zoë was rummaging around in her bag. She pulled out a notebook. "I still feel pretty low. I mean, are the zombies coming into work tomorrow? What's going to happen to Rodrigo if Public Works catches him? Will the other zombies be accomplices?"

John's eyes lingered on her choker, and Zoë could almost feel his lips on her skin. "If our people get to him first, then he will be fed, brought back to common sense, and probably sequestered till it dies down. If Public Works gets him first, then, well, we find a new administrative assistant."

"And if what you guys say is true, Montel was smart to hang back. That probably saved him and Paul," Morgen said. "We will find out tomorrow, in any case."

"And how will Public Works know what happened? We were the only ones there," Zoë said.

"Nope," John said, grinning. "You missed one."

Zoë frowned. Then she remembered. "That homeless woman?"

"Public Works agent," John said. "Most homeless, and some gangs, work as spies."

"Yeah," Morgen said. "They're ubiquitous and ignored, and if they talk about zombies eating a guy, people think they're insane so if there's ever a security breach, no one believes them anyway. But that agent in the alleyway pretty much cements the fact that Public Works will find Rodrigo first."

Zoë cleared her throat, really wanting to change the subject. "So what brings the fae to New York?"

Morgen thought. "The same thing that brings everyone else. They come for the lifestyle, the people, the change of pace from wherever they came from. Nature spirits love it here, believe it or not. You'd think we wouldn't, but honestly it's a change of pace from the boring life among the trees. Sure, not many of us actually move here, and those who do don't last long, but some find it to our liking. I was the spirit of a Colorado spring. By the time I was two hundred and thirty-nine, I'd had enough of John Denvering it and swam east. I ended up here and loved it.

"Some are born here. Central Park is home to several native New York fae. And that's where most of the visiting fae stay. There are some nice hotels set up there, and hostels in the trees in Brooklyn."

"And as you don't really feed off humans, the fae don't get into a lot of trouble?"

Morgen stilled. She dipped her finger into the glass and it disappeared. Her face filled out a bit, although Zoë hadn't noticed that she had gotten thinner. She pulled her finger—whole again—out of the glass and regarded Zoë. "John and I are a lot alike. I commune with and feed off water. Succubi and incubi commune with and feed off sex energy. And there's a little-known race of fae called the anemofae—blood sprites. They are parasitic to humans like vampires are. Instead of being born from something natural, we believe they have demonic origin, as they don't spawn from humans. But they do attach themselves and begin feeding off the host. Unlike vampires, these have to have an actual human host; they can't make deals with hospitals and blood banks. Public Works hunts them, and dislikes our connection to them. So we steer clear of them, even though we don't harm humans or the human way of life."

She took another bizarre sip of her drink, then shook her head as if removing a bad thought. Then she pulled out her phone, glared at it, and said, "Stay here. I'm going outside to call Phil again."

"Alone at last," John said. Zoë rolled her eyes, but she could feel the heat rising in her cheeks.

John began tracing little designs on her knee under the table, a touch firm enough to feel through her pants, but still light enough to tickle. A thrill ran up her leg at his touch. She gritted her teeth and pushed his hand away. She was about to say something about inappropriateness and sexual harassment, but he caught her pushing hand in his own and held it tightly. The skin-to-skin contact of just their hands was maddening. She wanted to remove all her clothes and rub up against him.

That would have been unprofessional, though.

She put forth monumental willpower and pulled her hand away. "I know there are no sexual harassment laws in the coterie world, but dude, you've got to lay off. It's not going to happen. It's too bad of a thing to happen. You're having your intended effect on me, and I suspect you know this. But I've fucked a coworker before and it landed me in a pit of shit."

He smiled at her vulgarity. *Uh oh.* She'd been hoping to turn him off. That obviously hadn't worked.

Morgen interrupted them by stomping back to the table, an impressive feat for a sprite. She plopped down in her chair in a most ungraceful manner. "Phil is livid. This is, to quote him, the stupidest thing they could have done. He thinks someone is messing with them, though. This wasn't a mistake."

The waiter wafted over with their food, and Zoë began shoveling scallops into her mouth without tasting them. "People steal food in break rooms all the time," Zoë said around a mouthful of sea creature. "Why do the zombies freak out about it?"

The sprite twirled a wet piece of kelp around her fork and stuffed it in her mouth. She thought as she swallowed, then wiped her mouth. "Humans steal each other's food? In coterie circles, it's taboo. For one thing, for so many of us food is hard to come by. Secondly, we have such different diets that it's pointless for me to steal Opal's blood stash, for example. It would simply be for spite and seen as hostility. And zombies wouldn't steal from each other; they're a communal species. It's against their nature to steal and hoard.

"Here's the deal," she continued, leaning forward. "Someone is messing with the zombies, and they're doing it inside Phil's office, which pisses Phil off. Public Works chasing after Rodrigo is a secondary concern; we deal with them all the time. No, the real problem is what, or who, is behind this meddling."

Zoë watched John give three bright red bills—hell notes—to the wispy waiter and motion for her to get up. Morgen led her to the bathroom and placed her in front of the mirror.

Surrounded by thin, wispy, otherworldly people, Zoë felt stocky and solid and utterly ridiculous. Morgen assessed her in the mirror. "You've seen where the fae eat, next we're heading to a club where the 'bus culture feeds. You"—she turned to look full-on at Zoë, with her sensible fall wardrobe, and made a face—"won't do."

"Oh, come on," Zoë said, shaking her head. "I'm not going home to get changed. If I go home, I'll be collapsing into sweats and a reality show. In fact, that sounds pretty good."

"No, Zoë. We're out, let's take advantage of it."

She frowned at the mirror. "Will I stand out that much?"

"It's a bondage club."

"Oh. You're taking me to a bondage club. Where incubi feed? And we have an incubus with us? Someone I'm having a great deal of trouble resisting? Am I the only one who thinks this is a terrible idea?"

Morgen grinned as she futzed with Zoë's hair. "You think he'd miss this trip? Besides, he's latched on to you because you're right here. It's not easy for an incubus to be with the same humans day in and day out, without getting caught stalking. But if we take him to a club, where there will be tons of humans begging him for attention, it'll be like you're a hamburger among steaks." She tweaked Zoë's nose affectionately. "I'm not saying you're not utterly adorable, I just mean the women there won't be wearing bulky cotton blends."

Zoë made a face. "Thanks. I think."

"You'll be OK, I've already told John you're going as *my* date. You're my new girlfriend and we're dabbling in the dom/sub culture. You're new to sub life, and we're taking it slow. The deal is"—she grinned, her eyes switching to green in the bright bathroom light—"you have to do everything I say. If you don't, the other doms in the club may punish you."

Zoë swallowed. "And if I'm a good girl?"

"You'll be protected from any 'bus in the place. Think you can handle that?"

Zoë looked at herself in the mirror again, and sighed. "This is to get me back for you helping me with the interviews last week, isn't it?"

"Oh, absolutely."

The Shambling Guide to New York City

QUEENS:
Hotels

The fae have several choices when it comes to the city. The elemental fae can take residence in any of the parks that have woods or ponds. For those who want a more structured visit, though, many of the best places to go serve as bed-and-breakfasts. The Last Petal is one of the best hotels in Queens for the fae, and it offers an intricate upstairs of pools, a greenhouse of exotic plants, perfumed air, and even a room with three feet of packed dirt, for the earth sprites who wish to sleep in complete safety. ■

CHAPTER FOURTEEN

Anything you want to do, you ask permission, understand?"
Morgen lectured her as they walked toward the club. "You
want a drink, you want to go to the bathroom, you want to talk
to someone, you ask me. You won't be able to write anything in
your little notebook unless you're hidden, and a dom wouldn't
let her new sub out of her sight anyway."

Zoë nodded, trying to keep it all in perspective. Pretending to
be a sex slave for a coworker had not been on her list of things to
do, but it was no weirder than the other stuff she'd encountered
already.

Well, maybe a *little* weirder, but less violent, surely.

She glanced at John, who just watched them, amusement
scrawled on his face.

They arrived and Morgen walked to the front of the line of
leather- and latex-clad attendees—many on leashes, Zoë realized
with discomfort—and nodded to the bouncer. Zoë recognized
him as a vampire; it was simply the very still way he stood, the
slightly reddish cast to his eyes, and the way he looked at the
humans in line—they were meat, not patrons.

He nodded to Morgen and John to come to the head of
the line. He cast a suspicious eye at Zoë, but pulled the barrier
aside when he saw her choker.

"New pet, Morgen?" he asked as the water sprite passed him
a hell note.

"Oh yes, Howard. Isn't she yummy?"

"I didn't know you went for the females," he said, looking at Zoë as if he wondered if she'd get caught in his teeth, or go down smoothly. She fought the desire to return his stare and remembered to look at the ground like a proper sub.

"I'll try anything once," Morgen replied breezily. "Twice, if I like it."

"Best keep her away from the incubi. There are some hungry ones here tonight. Like this one." He poked John in the arm in a way that was either joking or threatening, Zoë couldn't tell. John smiled at him and passed him a hell note, and they went inside.

Zoë had thought herself liberal in sexual views and sometimes even practices. Godfrey had tied her up a couple of times, and it had been fun. But clearly that was dipping a toe into an ocean. Here, women and men danced in cages in nothing but a suggestion of an attempt to cover themselves, which was more obscene than if they'd just gone nude. A woman was chained face-first to the wall, her latex skirt raised to her waist, a man whipping her naked, red, lined backside. She made noises of pain and ecstasy as he asked her if she had been a naughty girl.

A bartender, wearing a full latex bodysuit and cheekbones so high that Zoë decided he couldn't be human, leaned across the bar and asked Morgen, "What do you two want?" The "two" were John and Morgen.

John ordered red wine again, although he'd finished the bottle himself at the restaurant.

Morgen frowned. "Do you have any Red Sea?"

"What century?"

"Anything post-Moses, pre-pollution," she replied.

The man put a clear bottle on the bar and motioned again to Zoë. "Does it want anything?"

"She hasn't earned the right to alcohol yet," Morgen replied.

She reached over and pinched Zoë's cheek—hard—and winked at her. "We're breaking her in slowly. Ginger ale will do nicely."

The bartender accepted Morgen's hell note and handed Zoë a ginger ale. He looked Zoë in the eye for the first time. "Keep her close, Morgen," he said. "The 'buses won't be real happy with you parading food in front of them."

"Fuck 'em," Morgen said, "She's mine. I think the 'buses can get their own."

John made a low noise, and Zoë couldn't tell if he was protesting, or amused, or just hungry.

A heavy industrial track came blaring over the loudspeakers then, and the bartender's response was lost. He turned his attention to some vampires who had arrived at the bar, laughing and showing elongated teeth. Morgen motioned Zoë and John over to a table near the wall.

To avoid looking at the leather-clad, masked man dancing in the cage right above their table, Zoë focused on Morgen. "So is that seawater you're drinking?"

"Mmmm. Yeah. This stuff is intoxicating to freshwater sprites." She took a swig of the bottle and grinned. "Eighteen hundreds. Excellent."

Zoë shook her head. "So why does everyone tell you to be careful with me?"

"I don't feed off of humans, and they know it. I don't take their death energy like Gwen, nor their blood like a vampire, nor their sexual energy like a 'bus. I just like hanging around those coterie. And me parading a meal in front of them, that I'm not going to eat, but won't let them taste, is rude."

"Quite rude," John agreed, staring at Zoë. "But having me here will give at least a little bit of credibility to the ruse. I can't imagine what you thought you'd get away with, bringing her here alone, Morgen. I'm glad I came along."

Morgen looked at him with dislike. "I bet you are. But you're looking hungry, why don't you go get some food?"

Zoë fought the urge to protest. His eyes never left her as he said, "No, I'm fine. Besides, she needs to do research, right? Who better to ask than me?"

He scooted closer, sitting too close to Zoë, presumably so he could talk over the music. She could feel his heat through her sweater, and her skin prickled. "Do you have any questions for me?"

"OK, what's going on here from your point of view?"

"I thought you'd never ask," he said. "Let's go see the feeding rooms."

Morgen looked as if she was about to protest. Zoë shrugged at her and said, "I do need to learn."

Morgen sighed. "All right. Lead on, but I'm coming with you. And remember, we need to keep her safe."

"No one will lay a hand on her tonight," he agreed, rising. He looked down at Zoë and brushed his finger across her cheek and she shivered. "Unless she wishes it."

He led them through the tables and around a dance floor where bodies writhed together. Squinting into the mass of sweaty bodies, Zoë could clearly tell who the coterie were, their eyes focused as they devoured their victims' sexual energy, driving humans to extreme sexual pleasure by only the power of a couple of well-placed hands.

"Those are the succubi and incubi who gorge—they will just grab someone, use them, then grab someone else," John explained, his mouth close, his lips brushing her ear. "While the ones in the back rooms prefer one meal that they can linger over all night. Incidentally, that's how I feed." His lips were gone suddenly, and he was glaring at Morgen, who had pulled him away.

Zoë winked at Morgen.

They continued past the dance floor and into a corridor lined with smoky windows—one-way mirrors?—each of which looked into a room with a bed. Zoë's face became hot as they paused at the first room, where a woman writhed, tied spread-eagled to a bed, as a naked man crawled over her, licking every inch. Although the man seemed to be in control, his movements were a little too eager, not hungry enough, to indicate he was an incubus. He didn't turn her on the way John did.

She blinked. "Why would a succubus allow herself to be tied up?"

John's mouth was at her ear again, his body close behind her. "She's in total control. She's giving him what he wants—the more pleasure he gets out of it, the more energy he gives her to feed on. All we want is the pleasure of our partners." He moved her hair aside and bent to kiss her neck, a hot, lingering brand. She gasped. She opened her eyes without realizing she'd closed them and looked around frantically for Morgen. Where had she gone?

She caught sight of pink hair, bending down over a phone, hastily leaving the club to take a phone call.

Oh no.

John nibbled his way down her neck, moaning appreciatively as he tasted her. His fingers danced lightly at her waist until they found their way under her sweater and stroked her belly.

He pulled her closer, pressing her against his front, and she felt his hardness against her.

She forced herself to look away at what the man was doing to the succubus, forced herself not to wish she were having that done to her, forced herself not to realize that she could easily have that, right here, right now. She thought, instead, of the last time she had participated in said act, with Godfrey between her legs bringing her to a screaming orgasm. And then what that sexual encounter had led to.

The cold reality of Lucy and the loss of her job and the move to New York failed to squash the heat that rose in her body as John bit down lightly on her neck. She responded, gasping, and she could feel his lips curl into a smile as he bit harder.

"You like that," he said. It was not a question. Zoë moaned.

Then he stepped away from her, the chasm between them suddenly very cold. He kept his hands on her middle, sliding around to her back, to show her another room.

Her eyes widened. A naked succubus, clad only in red thigh-high boots, whipped two men's backs as one sobbed and the other watched the first, silently taking the lash.

A third room, with an incubus on a bed, groaning as two naked women pleasured him, licking and sucking, sometimes pushing each other away, but more often sharing, their lips and tongues meeting around him.

"It is rare we can find a woman who gets actual pleasure from that aspect of sex. My colleague there has found two." John bit her earlobe and breathed heavily in her ear.

Zoë stared at the scene. "What happens when he's... done?" she managed to ask.

"He won't be done until he's eaten his fill. So he will end up having both of them. We can live off of play, as hands groping and lips sucking and the soft sighs of a lover are definitely sustaining, but we haven't really eaten until there's been penetration."

He pulled her around and kissed her again, catching her lip in his teeth and sucking on it, and ah God, it was better than before, stronger than before. Better than it had ever been with Godfrey.

I need this, I need to erase the taint of him, overwrite him. Just once, just let me have him once.

Her hands were on him now, and he was lifting her, still kissing, still taking her somewhere—to a corner, a room, a bed?—

she didn't care. She groaned when his hand trailed over her bra, seeking a convenient place to slide inside.

She didn't care where she was, who could see. She didn't care what her morning would be like, what he would take from her. His hot fingers unsnapped her bra, and she was placed on a bed, her sweater torn from her torso, bra discarded.

She opened her eyes: the room had a large bed with clean silk sheets, three red walls, and one mirrored wall. He took his hands off her and stood next to the bed. He watched her, his brown eyes never leaving her face, as he unbuttoned his shirt with agonizing slowness.

His body was a sculpture of flesh and muscle, nipples begging to be licked, back ready to be scratched to ribbons. He put his hands on his belt, and then smiled tenderly.

"No. I'm going to savor you, Zoë, for as long as you'll let me. When you're ready to beg for it, then I'll give it to you."

He got back on the bed and finished undressing her, hand trailing lazily over her breasts. She knew nothing else but being here, with him, needing him.

(Not man.)

He caressed her breasts, rolling her nipples between his fingers, scratching his nails lightly over the sensitive skin on the undersides. She gasped and grabbed his hand, dragging it southward.

"Eager," he murmured into her ear. The bass of the club outside thumped in time to her heartbeat, and John hissed with pleasure when he felt her, felt how ready she was.

"Have you been like this all night?" he asked, sliding a finger in.

"Since you kissed me," she said, starting to writhe.

"Glorious. I must have a taste," he said.

(*Not a man. Incubus.*) The thought was so faint it might as well have been a memory.

He began kissing down her neck, pausing to suck on each of her nipples, spending almost too much time there, until she moaned impatiently. He was positioned between her legs, his eyes still watching her face, when there was a banging on the mirrored wall. Zoë remembered people were likely watching, and the thought only thrilled her more.

John raised his head before he took a taste. "Oh, I'm sorry, Zoë. The crowd will want something rougher. I think we may have to tie you up. Possibly blindfold you."

He dipped his head down and licked her with a quick flick of the tongue. She cried out, nearly there.

"May I tie you up?" he asked again, then wrapped his lips around her clit and sucked.

Zoë moaned, sweat beading on her skin, gasping. She needed something, needed him to do more, to stop holding back. She needed him inside her.

"Yes, please, anything, please, fuck me, I need it," she said, gasping and babbling so fast she didn't know if he heard her.

He smiled at her, lips glistening with her juices, and moved to get the restraints already attached to the headboard. He nearly had her hand through a handcuff when the door opened.

"This is a rented room!" John said, whirling around.

Morgen stood there, looking shocked and uncertain as Granny Good Mae, eyes blazing, pushed past her. "You don't get to have her," Granny Good Mae said, pointing at John.

"I certainly do," John said. "She's consented."

"Yes, yes, I consent, please, anything," Zoë said, nearly sobbing at the interruption.

The woman walked forward, her overcoat flapping behind her, and picked up Zoë's sweater and threw it on her.

"Get dressed."

"What the fuck are you doing here?" John asked, clearly shocked at this woman's audacity. "Who are—Wait, I know you. You're that Granny lady. How did you get in? Public Works isn't allowed in here."

"Granny Good Mae is not here on business. And I go where I want."

Ah God, Granny Good Mae. Her watching, seeing Zoë spread-eagled, waiting for an incubus, wasn't hot. It was shameful. Her hand closed on Zoë's wrist, and with the touch Zoë gained clarity. She was naked, in a bondage club, with an audience.

With a *coworker*.

"Dammit!" she said. "What am I doing? Morgen, where did you go?" She turned her head to look at John. "What do you think you're doing?"

John deflated. "I—You wanted—You were ready."

Zoë pulled her sweater over her head and found her pants at the foot of the bed. She stood up and began pulling them on. "Listen, asshole, when I want to fuck on a first date, I'm going to hope that there's actually a date involved, there's a private room, and he will preferably be human!"

"Out of all the humans in the city, you had to go for our new editor," Morgen said. "I turned my back for one second. You're unbelievable!"

Panting, Zoë became aware of the various club inhabitants staring at her. Granny Good Mae stood between her and John. She looked at Morgen.

The water sprite came up, took her hand, and led her from the room.

She walked, stunned, through the crowd of interested bystanders, out of the club, past the vampire bouncer nursing a broken nose with murder in his eyes, and down the street.

Once they'd turned the corner, Morgen stopped and took a deep breath. "Damn him anyway. Are you all right?"

"Yeah, I think so," Zoë said, shaking her head to clear it. "I thought I could handle him."

"My little air bubble, you're strong for a human, but you're still human. Never forget that when you're dealing with coterie. I'm sorry I let him wander off with you. I honestly thought he'd go for one of the other clubbers."

"What happened in there? Where did you go?"

"Phil called, I had to go outside to answer," Morgen said, her face grim. "Public Works got Paul, and Rodrigo's missing."

Zoë stared out the window of the cab that took them back to her apartment. Her headache had returned.

"So why did Granny Good Mae take an interest in you?" Morgen asked suddenly.

Zoë pursed her lips. She had been hoping Morgen would forget that in the excitement. "I bought her tea a couple of weeks ago. Maybe she remembered me."

"But how did she know where you were and that you needed help?"

"I have absolutely no idea," Zoë said honestly. On the way out, Granny Good Mae had whispered to her that she'd missed their workout that afternoon, and they would deal with that tomorrow. But Zoë still didn't know how she had figured out where Zoë was.

Morgen shrugged. "Weird shit seems to happen around you, Zoë. Let's get you home so nothing else can happen."

As the adrenaline wore off, Zoë sagged, feeling as if she had just given blood. She leaned on Morgen as the cab headed to Brooklyn. She was dimly aware of the cab stopping at the corner, of Morgen rooting around inside Zoë's purse for cash to pay the cabbie, and of Morgan helping her get out and scale the suddenly gargantuan curb.

"You'll need to tell Phil about this tomorrow. He might need to put a better guard on you than me," Morgen said, catching her after she stumbled over a particularly massive crack in the sidewalk.

"Oh sure, then he'll know how easy I am when it comes to you coterie types. God. Do you know the day I've had?" Zoë said, her head reeling.

"Yes, I've been with you the whole time." They stopped outside Zoë's apartment building. "Do you need me to help you up?"

"No. I c'n make it," Zoë said, and promptly fell down.

Morgen groaned and pulled her to her feet. Zoë hadn't thought the day could get worse, but Morgen began lecturing her. "You thought you could handle the job, and it's beating you. You thought you could handle the incubus, and he nearly fucked you. I was hoping you'd be stronger, Zoë."

Oh. That hurt. "Last month I knew nothing about all of this. Today I kept my shit together while having a meeting with vampires. I work with the dead head of my ex-boyfriend. I saw a man get eaten by a zombie. I nearly had mind-blowing sex that somehow has drained me of my life force. I think, all things considered, I'm doing pretty goddamn good."

"There is no relative in this world, babe. You survive or you don't. The incubi aren't going to hold off from seducing you because you had a bad day with vampires and the vampires aren't going to take it easy on you because you saw a zombie attack. You have to be strong all the time. And if you feel that drained now, think of what would have happened if you had actually had sex with him."

They arrived at Zoë's door. She fumbled for her keys, dropped them, and then swore when the door opened.

The bare feet were large, the sweatpants were clean, and,

when she looked up, the long-sleeved T-shirt was filled out very, very well. She stood up and faced the man inside the T-shirt, this man in her apartment, this very hot man, with brown skin, short hair, and gorgeous eyes behind small glasses. He had also apparently replaced everything in her apartment with his own stuff, and Zoë opened her mouth to accuse him of breaking, entering, stealing, and possibly the Bush administration.

Before Zoë could speak, Morgen said, "Zoë, what's your apartment number again?"

"Twenty-seven A, I told you that."

"Then why are you trying to open apartment twenty-seven B?"

Zoë squinted at the door. "Hell. Right. You. You're my hot neighbor. Alvin or something."

He looked from Zoë to Morgen and back to Zoë. "Arthur Anthony. We met last month."

Zoë frowned. "And you're never home. What's up with that? I even came over to borrow some sugar. Don't you want to give me some sugar? Some brown sugar, perhaps?"

Morgen groaned and tugged at Zoë's arm. "Come on, hon. Let's find the right apartment before you add to the list of things you've messed up today." To Arthur she said, "Sorry about that. She's had a little bit too much to drink; you really should meet her when she's in a better frame of mind."

Arthur frowned. "You sure she's OK?"

"Sure, we just had a hard day at work, and we went out to blow off steam." Morgen dragged Zoë, still clutching her keys, one more door down.

"He's hot," said Zoë in a stage whisper.

"No, Zoë."

"I think he's single."

"No, Zoë."

"I wonder if he's doing anything tonight. Or anyone."

"It's after midnight. You have work tomorrow. And this is only John's influence still on you. Go sleep it off. Do you have a vibrator?"

"Morgen! Well, yes, but it's none of your business."

Morgen unlocked her door. "But talking about fucking your neighbor—who's still standing right there, by the way—*is* my business?"

Despair flooded her. Zoë walked to the middle of her apartment and dropped her coat on the floor. "What am I doing, Morgen?"

"I don't really know."

"Call me tomorrow. Make sure I get to the office, OK?"

"Sure."

"Thanks for taking care of me."

Morgen hugged her tightly. "You're cool, for a human. Go to bed."

The moment the sprite closed the door behind her, Zoë staggered to the couch and collapsed. She didn't stir until the pounding on the door woke her at six a.m.

Her limbs wouldn't move. The knocking at the door was not hesitant, like that of someone who wanted her to answer the door only if she was already awake. It was insistent, not taking no for an answer. Like the police, or an angry neighbor with nothing better to do. Too bad Zoë couldn't move.

Was her door open? Had she locked it? *Sloppy security, Zoë.*

"C'min," she said, unsure if she was audible. Unsure if she was just inviting a robber, a rapist, or another incubus into her home.

The figure came in. She tried to open her eyes and saw only haze. Panic gripped her, or would have, if she could have gotten enough strength up. She made a sound that was meant to be a question, but even she had to admit she didn't know what she was saying.

She faded out again.

She woke when a spoon was forced past her lips. She felt a thick goo dribble down her chin. She gave a mammoth effort and opened her eyes.

Granny Good Mae came into focus, her sharp face frowning down on Zoë. "You're alive. I thought you were dead."

"No. Just robbed of all will to live," Zoë mumbled, and wiped a hand down her chin. "Why are you feeding me baby food? What happened?"

"You had a brush with an incubus." The woman spooned more of the goo, tasting of strawberries and molasses, into Zoë's mouth. "This is called sugar monk's blood. It will counteract his effect on you."

"What's a sugar monk?" Zoë asked. Granny Good Mae didn't answer, and just shoveled another spoonful into her mouth.

"I thought incubi didn't kill," Zoë mumbled past the spoon. "So why do I want to die right now?"

"They take your life force," Granny Good Mae said. "You stumble around, get hit by delivery truck, forget to eat, die of starvation."

"I didn't know it would be like this," Zoë moaned. Her energy returned slowly, like a rabbit checking to see if the circling hawk has left. She struggled to sit up. "What are you doing here? How did you know I needed help?"

"I'm here because I knew you would need help after last night."

Memories of nearly being publicly devoured the night before flooded her, and she groaned and closed her eyes. "God. How am I going to go back to work?"

168

"You take subway, walk a couple of blocks. Work for a few hours, go to the Jade Crane for lunch. You buy me some twice-cooked pork and jasmine tea for lunch. You can have some too. Then you feel better." Granny Good Mae put the medicine bowl into Zoë's hands. "But you start with shower."

"Thanks," she mumbled, not having wanted a step-by-step literal description. Morgen and John had seen her naked, begging for sex. That was more embarrassing than Godfrey. And she'd been with John to erase Godfrey. It seemed she'd thought she could erase a pen stain with a bucket of paint . . .

She put the bowl on the floor and held her head in her hands. "I'm such an idiot."

Granny Good Mae looked down at her. "It's OK. We haven't covered incubi. That's lesson fifteen."

Zoë looked up at her, unable to tell if she was kidding. "Good timing, then."

"Shower. Work. Meet me at lunch. You learn to fight more tomorrow. Today you get break." Granny Good Mae picked up her backpack and left as abruptly as she had arrived.

Zoë felt broken. She sighed and wondered why the old homeless woman cared about her. Then she realized she'd forgotten to ask Granny Good Mae how she'd known how to locate Zoë in a city of millions.

Something to discuss at lunch, I guess. If I make it that long.

She got up and trudged to the shower.

The Shambling Guide to New York City

BRONX:
Attractions

The Bronx Zoo is run covertly by Public Works, many of the "animals" on display being captured animal spirits. The Coterie Council has petitioned for this cruel and illegal prison to be shut down, but Public Works doesn't budge. It is assumed that the great trickster god Coyote is imprisoned there, but the Coterie Council has not been able to confirm this.

We list it here to encourage you to visit not the hideous prison, but instead the small café nearby, Petey's, in order to read about the history of the zoo and sign the petition against its existence. ■

CHAPTER FIFTEEN

When she got out of the shower, her phone was blinking. The call had come, as Zoë had suspected, from Morgen.

"Hey, human, just checking to see if you're still with us. I hope you didn't go to Arthur's apartment after I left. I know John injected enough of his juju into you to make you a little bit of a sex kitten. I mean, he didn't *inject* you. You'd likely be a lot worse off if he had. Anyway, it's eight thirty, and I thought you might like to know you should be here by now." She paused. "John's here. He looks like he ate last night, so he might leave you alone for a bit. Phil is pretty pissed with him. I think the only thing saving him is the fact that the situation with the zombies is so much worse than John behaving badly."

"Thank God for small favors," Zoë grumbled. She dressed quickly and grabbed a bagel to eat on the way to work. On her way to the train station, she dialed Morgen's direct number.

"Underground Publishing, Morgen speaking."

Zoë chuckled. "You sound so professional. I'm impressed."

Morgen snorted. "Hey, marketing's gotta wear a mask. Where the hell are you?"

"On my way to the train."

"Catch a coterie cab; you'll get here a lot faster."

Zoë squinted down the street at the many cabs. "I don't know how, and I don't have any hell notes, remember?"

"Coterie cabs take either denomination. When you hail, just hold up your talisman."

Zoë shrugged and said good-bye. She pulled the hated choker off her neck and held it up, feeling ridiculous.

A cab screeched to a stop in front of her, patchouli drifting out of the windows in a choking haze. Zoë hesitated for a moment, then got in. Now that she was getting used to coterie, she could tell immediately that the driver was a demon of some kind, disguised by an ugly checkered coat and a pulled-low ball cap. He—she assumed it was a he—grunted at her, and she gave the address for Underground Publishing.

"I heard of that last week. Humans work there, huh?" he asked as he floored it. His voice was surprisingly light, and he reminded Zoë of Mike Tyson.

"Yeah, I'm the only one. Mostly vampires, zombies, fae, a death goddess, and some others." She purposefully didn't mention John.

The cabbie grunted again. "It's about time someone started that up. We sure could use some maps to the city."

"Oh?" Zoë asked. "Human maps aren't sufficient?"

He focused his yellow eyes on the rearview mirror to stare at her. "Naw. Coterie have their own way of moving around town. You didn't know this?"

"No, actually, I'm new to the coterie way of life," she replied. "Been getting a crash course over the last month, so to speak. I'm taking notes for a guide to the city. So you think we need someone to map the area?"

"Sure. Else how is someone going to know about this short-cut?" he asked, and took an abrupt right turn. Zoë bit her tongue to avoid screaming as the cab careened straight for a wrought-iron fence, but before they hit, it dropped down through an unseen opening and then they were trundling along a tunnel paved with cobblestones.

She gasped and peered out the windows as they passed numerous branching tunnels occupied by coterie traveling by foot and in cars. She saw what she assumed to be several vampires in one thin tunnel, but then the cab turned left and she lost them.

"How far does this system of tunnels go?" she asked, scribbling in her book.

"This is the Rat's Nest—it goes pretty much everywhere the subway doesn't. Under the East River. And it's a lot faster."

Zoë couldn't see road signs or traffic lights and she secured her seat belt. "Are there many accidents?"

"Naw, we always know where we are. It's a coterie thing; you wouldn't understand."

Zoë stifled the snicker and kept making notes. "So why call it the Rat's Nest?"

"As I understand it, the rats had mapped out their own system well below the city. They have their own city about fifty feet below this. When the humans were building their subways, some coterie connected with some rats and had them design this for us."

"Rats," Zoë muttered. Were they coterie or did coterie just communicate with them? Another thing to investigate.

"And is it mapped?" she continued.

"Naw, which is why nonnatives have to hail cabs. You come down here without knowing where you're going, you'll get lost forever. There are some..." He paused. "Well, best I can describe it is pockets. Some demons set them up, they go places. One of them goes nowhere. If you don't know where you're going, you shouldn't go exploring."

Zoë was so busy scribbling that when daylight returned she barely looked up. "What keeps the humans from finding out about the Rat's Nest?"

"Illusions cover the entrance holes. Usually large trees. We had a master wizard from Chicago visit us back in, oh, 1930 or so and helped us set up the whole system, including the camo." The cab screeched to a stop on Fifty-First Street. "We're here. That'll be one finger."

Her breath caught in her throat, but she kept her voice calm. "I was under the impression you took either hell notes or human currency."

"I'm just fuckin' with you. You're pretty cool for a human." He grinned at her, displaying a number of teeth that shouldn't have fit into his mouth. "I'll take ten human bucks and we'll be golden."

She handed over fifteen and he tipped his hat to her.

"Thanks, uh," she said, pausing.

"Max. You wave that talisman and think my name any time you need a ride. Most humans are either too much in thrall or batshit insane. I like you."

"Thanks, Max." She grinned back at him and exited the cab.

He raced off and in an instant his cab had disappeared. Zoë shook her head. How had humans not noticed these beings around them? Now that she knew they existed, she saw the city in a completely different light. Although she'd seen proof that humans did seem to be able to fool themselves quite well.

She hurried inside, preparing her excuses for being late to Montel, trying to figure out a way to leave the embarrassing incident with John out of the picture. Phil and Montel stood inside the writing room, talking in low voices.

Then she realized that everyone was quiet, and it wasn't a busy quiet, it was a tense quiet. A somber cloud hung over the office, which was a feat since most of her coworkers were already dead. Gwen, a teacup in her hand, caught sight of Zoë and hurried up to her. "Your office. Now," she whispered, and took Zoë by the elbow.

Zoë allowed herself to be dragged through the office by the death goddess, confusion making any question difficult to voice.

Morgen met them there, a frown on her usually mischievous face. "We've got a situation, Zoë."

"What's going on?"

Gwen closed the door behind them. "You heard Paul was returned to second death last night?"

Zoë nodded.

"Montel lost him after the attack. Paul said he had a job to do. Montel told him he needed to eat first, and apparently Paul attacked a jogger in Central Park. Public Works caught him soon after."

Zoë flopped into her chair. She'd liked Paul. "Did he...turn someone?"

Morgen rolled her eyes. "If Public Works got there, it doesn't matter; they'd both be dead."

Zoë rubbed her face. "But Montel is OK? Did he eat?"

Gwen glared at Morgen. "She needs to know more about our world."

"She's already gotten a crash course, you emo witch," Morgen snapped. "I told her what I could last night about the morgues, but John pretty much erased anything she learned." She focused on Zoë. "Montel is fine. All zombies keep food at home, which makes it doubly strange that the zombies would go mad with hunger at work."

Zoë had a bad feeling about Paul. "Who witnessed the attack?"

"Who knows?" Gwen said. "Public Works have agents everywhere."

"How do you feel about Public Works?" Zoë asked.

Gwen thought, apparently not having anticipated the question. "Some coterie, like Phil, try to work with them, others say they're fascists who just try to hold us back from our honest right to food. But Phil is right, if we could eat freely, then we'd run short of humans, and too many coterie means the balance shifts, and eventually we run out of food. Not to mention, if a city the size of New York falls, the rest of the world will discover the truth about coterie, which will encourage hunting of coterie in other cities."

Morgen piped up. "Some people believe that would be a good thing, that if an outright war started, we could finally take over."

"What about food?" Zoë asked, uncomfortable with the line of discussion.

Morgen shrugged. "There are some vampire sects who talk about 'humane farming' of humans for a sustainable food supply, but most coterie write them off as insane."

"Which makes them more dangerous," Zoë guessed. "Do you guys know anyone like that?"

They both shook their heads.

Zoë nodded. "OK, I think I get it. So last night the zombies went crazy and hunted. And we don't know why. Is that what Phil and Montel are trying to figure out?"

Gwen shrugged, her black hair rippling. "Sort of. A brain shortage is a dire situation in a city with a large zombie population. Most zombies keep a supplier in town; it makes things safe. The supplier is protected by laws that the coterie and Public Works came up with. Which means the morgue workers are untouchable, so that man's murder was doubly bad, like a diplomatic incident. Then Paul's extra meal, the jogger, was just insult to injury. So the problem is twofold: find out why the brains are missing and find Rodrigo before Public Works does."

Although she liked her coworkers as much as she could, considering the new and frightening world she lived in, Zoë wanted to ask *why* they needed to find him before the law did, but she

176

didn't figure these women would look at it from a human's point of view.

Zoë got the rest of the story from her coworkers: apparently the jogger that Paul had eaten had had a brain tumor, and Paul had eaten it. This gave him an upset stomach, and he wasn't able to lurch as fast as the other zombies, and Public Works caught him.

Zoë tapped a pen on her desk. "What if whoever took the brains is aiming for a zombie uprising?"

Morgen whistled. "Wow. Conspiracy theory, meet Zoë; Zoë, meet conspiracy theory."

Zoë shrugged. "You tell me another reason to steal a zombie's brains. Tell me why you think all of this is happening."

Morgen snapped her fingers, interrupting Zoë. "Didn't you tell me that Paul was supposed to tail Wesley last night? And he didn't do it because he got hungry. You think it could be connected?"

Gwen gnawed at her bottom lip in a very non-goddess-like gesture. "I don't know. It's terribly far-fetched."

"I can't think of any other reason for what is going on," Zoë said. "You come up with an explanation, let me know. For now I will work with my door closed and I'd appreciate not seeing Wesley without someone to back me up. Or John. And, uh, you did say Montel ate last night, right?" she added as an afterthought.

Gwen nodded. "He went home to his personal stash."

Zoë sighed with relief. "All right. I'll see him, then, if he wants."

Gwen and Morgen left Zoë alone to work, but her head was too much of a whirlwind with what was going on. She wondered

if there was a way to leave the world of the coterie once introduced to it. She fingered the talisman around her neck.

A knock came at her door and she looked up. Phil opened the
door, a hard look on his pleasant, round face.

"Hi, boss," she said.

"Zoë. We need to talk."

"Is this about the zombie thing last night?" she asked.

He waved his hand at her. "There are other things to discuss,
which is why I want privacy." He closed the door behind him.
"How are you holding up?"

Her first instinct was to say, "I'm great!" but she stopped herself. After a pause, she said, "Honestly, boss, I'm not holding
up. I'm a little overwhelmed right now. Last night was pretty
intense—I am guessing you heard?" She blushed and didn't look
at him.

"Morgen told me about your evening, yes." His voice was
even.

"Anyway, I've still got a bit of a hangover, or whatever you
call the day after being with an incubus." Phil nodded. "And
now there's the thing with the zombies, and Morgen and Gwen
are talking about war, and I don't know whether I should look
at Public Works as good guys for protecting me or bad guys for
killing Paul, who I liked. I'm supposed to be planning a book
here, but suddenly that seems very low-priority."

"I have had time in the past weeks to regret giving you a
chance at this job. But still think you're in the right place. I
have Morgen's and Montel's accounts of what happened last
night. I wanted to get your story."

Zoë nodded. She told Phil about her day, with the zombies,
the devouring of Jorge, the dinner at the fae restaurant, and then
the fetish club. She glossed over the details after they arrived
at the club, her face hot, refusing to meet his eyes.

"And then I went home and passed out. Felt like crap this morning."

Phil glared at her. "I don't know why you and Morgen went to the fetish club. One of many stupid things done by my employees last night."

"Morgen's a risk-taker," Zoë said. "And I thought you wanted me to do field research. So what have you figured out about last night?"

Phil sighed and took a flask from his pocket, took a long pull, and replaced it with a shudder. When he caught Zoë's raised eyebrow, he dabbed his mouth with a handkerchief. "Hobo blood. It's soaked in alcohol. The closest my kind can come to drinking."

"Gotcha," she said.

"It's a mess. And considering Paul and Rodrigo worked for me, it casts our publishing company in a bad light before we can even begin to do the coterie community any good. We're going to attract the ire of Public Works, which is going to accuse us of protecting Montel and Rodrigo."

"Are we protecting Rodrigo?"

"They will think we are," he said grimly.

"OK, this is perhaps an extremely selfish question, but what does all of this have to do with me?" Zoë asked. "I agree that having monster hunters watching the offices is bad, but I really don't know what I can do for you. I've got a book to write, an incubus to avoid, and a construct made of an ex-boyfriend that seems to hate me."

Phil was silent for a moment, as if he was considering something. "That last one is still an issue, especially with Paul gone now. I don't know if he found out anything about Wesley." He tapped his fingers on the desk, then brightened. "We want to know how much Public Works know about Rodrigo. You want to know about the movements of zoëtists in the city. Zoëtists are supposed to register with Public Works. As a human, you would be our best liaison with them. I want you to approach Public Works, find out if they know anything about either issue. This will help the book as well, as they will accept us more if they know a human is managing editor of our biggest titles."

"How am I going to have time for that? That book you just mentioned isn't going to design itself."

"More money? I'll throw in hell notes with your first paycheck to cover the extra hours."

"How can you afford that when we haven't even put out a book?" she asked, frowning.

Phil grinned, his teeth elongating and reminding her what he was. "I'm immortal, Zoë. Compound interest was created by vampires, you know."

She paused. For the second time in the past year, she discovered she had a price. It wasn't a good feeling.

"Fine. I'm in."

John came to see her after lunch.

The Jade Crane's twice-cooked pork was, indeed, quite restorative and Zoë felt better than she had in days. Granny Good Mae had given her some hints about dealing with incubi, most of which included the simple act of not looking them in the eye or touching them.

"That's fucking obvious," Zoë muttered, mad she hadn't thought of it.

She tried to ask Granny Good Mae how she should approach Public Works, but the old woman didn't seem interested in that problem. She just kept shoveling food into her face. She also refused to explain how she had located Zoë the night before.

When John appeared in Zoë's doorway, drab, portly, and lugubrious as before, she began to understand.

"John." It was less of a greeting and more of a realization. She looked at his protruding belly, and not his eyes.

He smiled, cocksure as always. "Zoë. You're looking quite well."

"So this," she waved her hand, indicating his appearance, "is what an incubus looks like after feeding?"

He looked surprised. "How did you know I'd fed?"

Zoë smiled, lips tight. "First, Morgen told me, second, I figure your sex appeal wanes when you're not actively hungry. So who was the lucky girl?"

"She was a consenting club patron."

"I doubt that."

"I had tasted her before. She came back," John said, his voice low and tight.

"Good. Then you're full, and you don't need to come here." Zoë looked down, ignoring him.

"Zoë," he said. She finally looked up, her eyes stopping at his throat. "It is not in my kind's nature to apologize to—"

"Your food?" she interrupted.

He sighed. "You consented to it."

"Yeah. I read up on you guys this morning. Your pheromones are intoxicating, and it's nearly impossible to resist you. You're basically a big bottle of gin that walks and talks. That argument won't stand."

He smiled. "We'll see what you say when I'm hungry again."

"Yeah, I'm not holding my breath." She switched her focus to her computer.

He left, and she let out a big, shaky breath.

She honestly didn't know which she dreaded more: finding out Wesley's origins, or John's returning hunger.

The Shambling Guide to New York City

MIDTOWN:
Architecture

While the humans will be checking out the Apple Store for expensive computers and gadgets, we encourage any visiting coterie to stop and admire its all-glass structure. It is actually crystal, and was built by a race of apini demons native to the southern US. Their knowledge of building sturdy, blocky constructions moved Steve Jobs to hire them to work with crystal and design a unique store.

Some of the apini demons decided to stay in the city, and reside mostly in Brooklyn or the many parks, anywhere they have access to flowers. Some coterie architecture schools invite the demons to speak, and, embracing the hive mentality, they always insist the lectures be free and open to the public. ■

CHAPTER SIXTEEN

The next week and a half were, amazingly enough, uneventful. John kept out of her way, even when he became hungrier and therefore sexier. She found that when she didn't make eye contact, she really wasn't as attracted to him.

She made headway on the book, and got some good training in with Granny Good Mae. The training became more sporadic, however, as sometimes the old woman wouldn't show up, and then refused to tell Zoë where she had been.

Without giving too much identifying information, Zoë contacted Public Works, but wasn't able to make an appointment with its media relations until the next week. She said only that she was working on a book about the city.

Phil sequestered Montel in the office, waiting for the furor to die down. Rodrigo remained missing, which meant Phil had to put up "Help Wanted" signs for his position as well as Paul's. Zoë wondered if they could get the health goddess to come back in. Suddenly having a magical healing lady on their side, even one who was quick to offend, sounded pretty good.

Wesley quit. Phil had e-mailed a picture of the construct to the zoëtist Benjamin, but hadn't heard back. Phil had also put Kevin the vampire on the job of tailing him, but Kevin said Wesley didn't leave his apartment. Soon after, the construct e-mailed his resignation.

Phil thought that was the end of things, and asked Montel to start looking for a new CR representative. Zoë wasn't so sure.

And Zoë ran into Arthur again.

Before "The Night with the Incubus," as she had begun thinking about it (as that was better than "The Night I Was Fucking Insane"), she had been of the opinion that the difference between their schedules was a shame, since she never saw him. Now she was glad to avoid him, not wanting to admit that she had hit on him blatantly while under the influence of—well, it didn't matter whether it was alcohol or drugs or an otherworldly creature, it certainly didn't make her look good.

She headed home early, since Phil had said he wanted her to accompany him that evening to visit Rodrigo's apartment and look for signs of the zombie. When she had balked, he mentioned he thought it would be good for Zoë to see where zombies lived. She couldn't argue that, but insisted on going home early to prepare. She got home around three in the afternoon, and ran into Arthur leaving his apartment.

She briefly thought she should run pell-mell into her apartment, since acting like a six-year-old seemed to be a good course of action, but decided to be a grown-up. She firmly put a smile on her face and met his eyes.

She nearly swore out loud when she saw his uniform. Brown coveralls with a blue badge on the sleeve, a hard hat, and a heavy cotton bag that clanked as if tools were inside. She froze as everything fell into place.

He smiled when he saw her. "Hi, Zoë, home early?"

She just stared at him.

His smile faltered and he shrugged a little. "You all right?"

She snapped out of her shock. "Oh! Yes, I'm fine. I didn't realize you, ah, worked second shift. That's why I never see you around, I guess."

He hefted his bag on his shoulder. "Someone's got to keep the sewers and water lines working even after everyone else goes home."

"So you're like a doctor for the city, always on call?" she asked, realizing she sounded ridiculous.

Arthur frowned, and she realized he thought she was mocking him. "Something like that. Listen, I gotta go. Have a good night."

She watched his lovely back as he left and she smacked herself in the head. She was supposed to research Public Works, which she had been doing, and then meet someone to gain his trust, which she hadn't. She didn't know how to just approach a street crew who were secret monster hunters and begin interviewing them, and had made it only as far as scheduling an interview for the next week. Now, with someone dropped in her lap, she was completely flummoxed.

She reached for the feminine wiles, skills she had never fine-tuned. "I, uh, was just startled at the fact that you make Public Work coveralls look good," she said, but the door closed between them.

"That was not my best encounter," she mumbled to herself, and unlocked her door.

When she got into her apartment, she leaned against the door and put her head in her hands. She tried to blame her inability to flirt on John, trying to believe that he had broken something inside her, but knew the failed conversation was all her responsibility.

She relaxed on the couch and ate some self-loathing ice cream while watching mindless television, hoping she wouldn't panic about whatever Phil had planned for that night. Soon after sundown, her cell phone rang.

It was Phil, who made little preamble. "Rodrigo's apartment.

Zombies always have a supply of brains on hand, and I want to know what drove him to hunt again."

"Do you not think he'll be there?"

"If he is then we can talk to him. I have tried everywhere else, and my sources say Public Works hasn't caught him yet."

She shrugged. "What the hell. Tell me where to meet you."

"I'm outside your apartment now."

Zoë parted her curtains and, indeed, the vampire was standing under her window with his cell phone pressed to his ear. "You're creepy sometimes, Phil. Did you know that?"

"I'm a vampire, Zoë."

"You're not making a good case for me to go gallivanting with you tonight."

"You're safest when you're with me." His voice had a nononsense quality that both comforted and irritated Zoë.

She sighed loudly into the phone. "I'll be right down."

Zoë had had her first payday recently; she had purchased some restorative herbs and teas from the Jade Crane, instructed on which to purchase by Granny Good Mae. She had also bought a silver blade that was frighteningly sharp, good for fighting werewolves or cutting the heads of zombies. She strapped it to her forearm, slipped her coat on over it, and felt monumentally ridiculous. She had worked only with sticks and other fake weaponry; she'd never really used a weapon. But this seemed like the night to carry one.

Phil was waiting by an idling cab. "So tell me why I'm needed instead of someone like Montel," she said without greeting him.

"You're the one who is keeping track of all this. You're in the middle of it. I don't want to split my efforts. And anyway, an outsider's viewpoint might give me what I need to figure this out."

"Or else you're just trying to get me eaten," Zoë said.

Phil looked startled. "Zoë, if I wanted you eaten, I would have done the job myself. Setting up an elaborate plan to get you eaten is way more work than I would prefer to expend."

"Someday you'll get a sense of humor. Let's go," she said.

Rodrigo lived in a shoddy apartment building in Brooklyn. It leaned slightly to the right, its third and top stories looking decidedly dangerous.

Zoë squinted up at it as they exited the cab. "This looks condemned."

Phil started up the stairs, kicking aside trash and empty beer cans. "It is condemned. You think it's easy for zombies to find an apartment in the city?"

Zoë choked back a laugh. "Phil, only a couple of months ago I didn't think zombies existed. Now that I know they do, why shouldn't I think they'd be able to get a penthouse? They can hold down jobs and think for themselves and make deals with local morticians—or eat the morticians—why not get a good apartment?"

Phil pulled on the front door hard, forcing it open. The frame had warped, making this difficult, and Zoë tried not to think about what she would do if she had to leave the building in a hurry. She followed Phil inside.

"Good point," he said, "but now that you know they exist, the commonsense rules apply. I can't go to the noon opening of the new Apple Store, and zombies can't apply for Manhattan penthouses. They usually live in condemned buildings or, in a pinch, outdoors, but no zombie really likes that. Too many fae in the woods. Also, rain is best avoided."

Zoë made a face at the thought of waterlogged, rotting zombies.

"So is this a zombie-only building?" she asked, stepping over what she would have previously assumed was a sleeping bum, but now clearly identified as a zombie dozing in the hallway.

"I think so," Phil said. "I've never been here."

Rodrigo's door, 3A, was unlocked. Phil opened it and Zoë looked in after him with interest.

Whatever she had imagined—ropy entrails hanging from the walls, beds made from squishy viscera, or embalmed brains sitting in well-lit jars on shelves—it hadn't included pictures of Kate Hudson on the wall.

Some were cutouts from gossip magazines, some were teen posters ready for hanging on the wall, depicting her in that action movie she had been in. One was a very blurry picture from a tabloid, of her exiting a car.

Other than Hudson, the small apartment sported a thread-bare chair in the corner, a surprisingly high-tech DVD-and-television setup (with a complete catalog of Hudson movies, including several Zoë had never heard of, like *Walking in My Pants* and *Twelve Librarians, One Bottle of Rum*).

"How do they get electricity to run this stuff?" she asked.

"Generators," Phil said from the bedroom. He came out, fangs extended, frowning. "He's not here."

"Uhhh," she said, looking closely at one gossip magazine clipping that appeared to have had Hudson's date for the evening chewed away. "What's with the Hudson obsession?"

"Most zombies attach themselves to one celebrity or another," Phil said. "It's one of the downsides of returning to sentient living. They seem to always have the hearts of love-struck teenagers. You should see the security detail that Public Works has to put on Justin Bieber. The thing is, unlike teens, zombies never mature, so their obsessions grow and grow. Very few zombies are allowed into LA because of it—it would just be too dangerous. Rodrigo liked Kate Hudson."

"No kidding," Zoë said, fingering another clipping. "Do they try to eat their obsessions?"

"Some do. Some don't." Phil stepped over a discarded copy of *Us Weekly* and walked to the kitchen. "Good for the humans to be on their toes, though."

"But most of the humans don't know about zombies, do they?" asked Zoë, following him.

Phil opened the fridge. "Well, no. But Public Works of the cities do, and they watch over the celebrities."

He swore softly in a language Zoë was pretty sure wasn't English. "I was right. There aren't any brains in here."

Zoë breathed a quiet sigh of relief that she wouldn't have to look at body parts and ventured a look over his shoulder. A neat line of condiments sat in the door, including horseradish, chutney, and ketchup, but the fridge was otherwise empty.

Phil got out an unlabeled bottle of something that looked like hot sauce. He uncapped it and sniffed, then held it out for Zoë. "Tell me what you smell."

Her nose hairs nearly curled as the odor assaulted her. She winced but inhaled deeply. "Tabasco. Mustard. Thai spices. And something else… I can't place it."

Phil put the cap back on the bottle and slipped it into his pocket. He looked grimmer than usual. "That extra something is formaldehyde. It's very bad for zombies. If they eat an embalmed brain, it freezes their higher thinking functions. Any zombie who eats this will revert back to mindless hunger even if he's just eaten."

"Like our zombies did last week."

"Exactly."

"So this means..."

"Someone is polluting zombies' condiments, which encourages them to hunt even if they have food. I bet if we checked other apartments we'd find formaldehyde lurking in some condiment or other." Phil closed the fridge as someone groaned outside in the hallway.

"Or maybe we could just wait until someone proves it for us," Zoë said, peeking into the living room as the apartment door opened. The zombie from the hallway shambled in, eyes fixed on Zoë. She was suddenly very aware of the heavy, edible organ she carried around in her cranium, and also very aware of how much it meant to her. She took a step back as Phil stepped in front of her.

"Back. This one is mine," he hissed.

"Are you talking to him, or me?" Zoë asked, her voice shaking.

"Hungry..." the zombie moaned. "Been so long..."

The zombie did not stop its forward motion, still fixated on the meal in front of him. Phil snarled and leaped forward, knocking the zombie back. They struggled on the floor, Phil's vampire strength tearing the zombie's limbs from his body, and as Zoë stumbled backward out of their way, into the kitchen, another zombie appeared at the door. More moans echoed from down the hall.

Zoë pulled the silver knife from its sheath and looked at it briefly. "It will be a miracle if I don't do myself in with this thing before the zombies can even get to me."

Zoë found that her training with Granny Good Mae was useful—the rules about zombies were to stay away from them, which she did her best to do. Word must have spread about the visiting human, though, and they began crowding the doorway. The ones Phil didn't engage came straight for her.

The vampire was impressive. It was odd seeing this business-oriented, kinda dumpy, friendly-faced guy move faster than even Granny Good Mae as he attacked the zombies, pulling off limbs and knocking them down. At first she wondered why he did that, considering that didn't stop them, but it did unbalance them, and they no longer had hands to grab with.

The first zombie to reach her had only one arm, which was good, since she had fewer limbs to avoid. As Granny Good Mae had taught her, she avoided the grasping arm and danced out of the way. She went around the kitchen table, but another zombie had cut her off. This one was a woman, also one-armed.

"Dammit, Phil, can you stop tearing their arms off and do something about their heads?"

The vampire struggled under three zombies and failed to come to her aid.

"All right, then. Here's where I go down fighting, I guess," she muttered, and held her knife at the ready. The male zombie was closer, and she paused a millisecond to get her bearings as he shuffled closer.

Parry the arm, avoid the fingers. Go inside. Slice.

She made a purposeful move forward, and promptly tripped on a cockeyed kitchen chair. She fell forward onto the zombie and they toppled down together, Zoë on top of the zombie, his mouth at her throat.

But he wasn't moving at all. She stumbled to her feet and realized she'd stuck her knife under his chin and into his brain.

"Luck," she said grimly, and looked around for the next threat.

A short, thin zombie had her back to Zoë and was trying to pummel Phil while groaning what sounded like the tune of "The Ride of the Valkyries." Zoë took her by the shoulder with one hand and cut at her neck with the knife.

Zoë didn't know what to expect. She knew there would be no

blood when she cut, and she was seriously aware that the zombie could bite her. What she didn't expect was for the knife to slice through the zombie's neck as if it were papier-mâché.

The head toppled from the body and bounced on the floor, rolling slightly to come to rest on a Kate Hudson clipping.

"Huh. That was too easy," she said. She looked up to find her initial one-armed female zombie, and three males, shambling toward her.

"Uh-oh," she said.

"Public Works. Stand down!" The voice came from the hallway. More angry voices, moaning, and a yelling human.

Another zombie head bounced into the room, followed by the words, "By order of Public Works"—Zoë could see a Public Works uniform, with a strong arm wielding a wrench—"I am ordering you to"—another head knocked off—"stand down!"

After four zombies fell, the others in the room finally took note of his presence and turned on him. Zoë stood there dumbly and watched as his targets became the ones who came for him. It became a fight of self-preservation, the man dodging the snapping, sluggish jaws, the grasping hands, all the while shouting commands to stand down.

Zoë looked at Phil, who looked as startled as she did, and— Was that fear? Zoë realized that if Public Works came in killing zombies, Phil might be a target as well.

Phil stopped fighting and simply watched. Zoë swore at him and went in to help her fellow human. She'd protect Phil if she had to, but she definitely wasn't going to watch this human get ripped apart.

Fighting zombies from the rear was, as Granny Good Mae had said, much easier. Zoë had to be careful not to cut the man, as her knife decapitated zombies with no problem and she could easily lose her control, but she and Public Works guy cleared the room shortly.

Panting and shaking, Zoë looked at the guy.

His mouth was open. "Zoë?"

She glanced at him, took a moment to assess him, his clothing, and his weaponry, and then said, "Oh. Hi, Arthur. Thanks for having our backs."

He opened his mouth to reply, but another zombie came in behind him.

"Behind you!" she yelled.

Arthur whirled around, taking off the zombie's head with his wrench.

"Nice reflexes," she said. She tried not to stare at him. He looked like a freaking action hero. Her eyes flicked to Phil, rumpled and grimy, who was staring at them.

Arthur looked from Zoë to Phil and back to Zoë, then down at the pile of bodies around him. "You want to tell me what's going on here?"

"It's a long story," Zoë said, looking at Phil. He hissed, his fangs coming out again, and he ran at Arthur.

"Phil, don't!" she yelled. Arthur raised his wrench, opening his mouth to say something, but the vampire didn't slow down. Arthur stepped backward, taking a defensive stance, but stopped when he bumped into a body behind him.

Rodrigo had come home. The much shorter zombie bit deeply into Arthur's arm before Phil could reach him, the vampire's white fingers outstretched to rip the zombie apart.

The Shambling Guide to New York City

APPENDIX:
Famous Faces

Until recently, Heather Welliver was the leader of the zombies in New York City. She was a police officer, having attained the rank of captain, and a native of the city. She was turned in her fifties during a doughnut run for her precinct.

Welliver brought the discipline she used in raising a family of five and running a police station into the coterie world, quickly whipping the city's zombies into some semblance of shape and making them the second-most dominant coterie in the city. She was a diplomat, forging a tight truce with Public Works and working tirelessly to maintain the balance in the city. She worked to get contacts in the major hospitals in all the boroughs and lowered the necessity to hunt.

Of course, she did allow her people to hunt; she wasn't a complete human sympathizer. She let her monstrous part run this aspect of her being, and by *monstrous* we refer to her desire as a police officer to make the city better without the pesky tie-ups of court. Welliver had her list of criminals who had gotten off due to connections, lack of evidence, an abundance of money, or just sloppy work on the judge's part. And she went after all of them. After her zombies completed her vigilante justice, many of the criminals rose again to join her, former criminals turned vigilantes. She ruled over zombified gang members, drug lords, mob bosses, and one rich boy who was a suspected rapist.

Having been well loved and respected, Welliver is honestly mourned by the few remaining zombies in New York City, as she died on 12/8/15. ∎

CHAPTER SEVENTEEN

S o many things happened at once.

While Rodrigo gnawed on the screaming Arthur, Phil easily tore through his neck with his bare hands. He had to pry the zombie's head from Arthur's arm, as it had attached itself like a tick.

Blood gushed forth and Arthur sank to his knees, grabbing his arm. His dark skin paled considerably. He looked up at Zoë's stricken face. "Kill me, please."

Zoë looked at Phil, then back at him. "What do we do?"

"You hang with them but you don't realize what's about to happen to me?" Arthur shouted, his eyes bulging. "Kill me, now, before I turn into one of them!"

Zoë glared at him. "Hey, just calm down, Boy Scout. Let me talk to Phil."

"Why should we do anything?" Phil asked. "He's Public Works. He waded into a zombie fight. This is a risk he accepted when he took the job."

Zoë gritted her teeth and took a step forward, hand tightening on the knife. She was tired, covered in flaky zombie bits, and lacking in patience as she stared up at the vampire.

"We were losing. And he showed up and saved our asses. I know the zombies couldn't hurt you much, but they could certainly have turned me into undead sausage. I'm rather appreciative. If you're just going to let him die, that means you devalue humans who help you. And if that's the case, then I'm not sure our little arrangement will work out."

The vampire was silent. Arthur closed his eyes. "You know, you could stop arguing and kill me, which would solve everyone's problems."

"He has a point," Phil said.

"Can a zombie bite be cured?" she asked.

He shifted behind Arthur. "Not...as such. A strong zoëtist might be able to do something about it. It won't be cheap."

"Do it."

Phil paused. Zoë wanted to shout at him, but remained patient while he did whatever mysterious thinking he was doing. "He'll need watching," the vampire finally said. "If he begins to turn before I get back, it will be too late."

She held up her wicked blade. "I'm ready. Just go. Call me when you find the right person. I'll get him back to my apartment."

The vampire was gone then. Zoë sheathed her weapon carefully against her forearm and went to help Arthur up.

"Kill me," he moaned. "Or give me your weapon so I can kill myself."

"Nah," she said, hauling him to his feet. "You've got some time left. You up for a little walk?"

"No."

"Good. We're going just a few blocks."

"Zoë—"

She looked at him then, her expression stopping his protests. "Look. Can you trust me?"

"I barely know you. You fraternize with vampires. You willingly walked into a zombie nest. Why in the world would I trust you?"

"I'm the only one left who can help you? I could leave you my knife and you could kill yourself now, or you could let me and

Phil try to save you, and if we can't, one of us can kill you later. With my way you at least have a chance."

"How do I know you won't just let me turn and then have me join him and you in whatever activity you're doing?"

Zoë snorted. "All you know that we do is kill zombies." She tried to keep hysterical laughter from her voice at the thought of her, the mighty zombie slayer. "Why would we want you turned just to make more of them?"

He finally nodded. "Whatever. Just get me somewhere where I can lie down."

"Sure," Zoë said.

She wedged herself under his good arm and headed out of the building, her knife at the ready for any more attacks.

She assumed they'd killed all the zombies, as they left unmolested. She got to street level and futzed at her neck for her coterie talisman, thinking about Max.

(Left left left left ware left!)

"What did you—?" Zoë started to say, turning her head to the left. She gasped and stepped backward, dragging Arthur with her, narrowly dodging the knife that swooped down.

No one stabs like that, not if you know how to use a knife, she thought, her training kicking in even through her exhaustion. She grabbed the hand, a woman's hand, and twisted it sharply, making the assailant drop the knife, but not before it sliced over her right forearm.

"Damn," she said. She was still under Arthur's weight and unable to do much more, so she failed to evade when another hand, a man's hand, swung up and punched her in the jaw. Stars bloomed in her vision as she reeled, and she dimly heard Arthur shouting, his good arm grasping her to keep her from falling.

Wesley, woman's hand, man's hand, it's Wesley—She managed to process this thought before a garbled war cry came from the shadows and the construct fell under the weight of a flurry of overcoat and arms.

The new attacker pulled out a knife, as wicked as Zoë's, and began slicing through Wesley's clothing, carving away at the body parts underneath. Zoë winced, expecting to see blood, but nothing spurted as the construct's skin opened obscenely. Wesley floundered, getting weaker, calling feebly for help, until he stilled.

"There it is, crafty bitch hid it under his arm, I knew it was there, *she* told me, yes *she* did, Granny Good Mae always listens," the woman was saying, sheathing her clean knife and wiping her hands off as if she had touched something dirty, although there was no blood on her hands.

"Holy shit," Zoë said, rubbing her jaw.

"That one didn't like you," Granny Good Mae said.

"Yeah, no kidding." Zoë steadied herself and tried to shake off the shock from the punch. Her jaw throbbed. "Don't you live in Manhattan? And how the hell do you always know when I'm in trouble?"

"You know Granny Good Mae?" Arthur asked, amazement coloring his voice.

She ignored him and pointed to the body that Granny Good Mae was dragging, in pieces, into an alley.

"What do you know about Wesley?" Zoë asked.

"He wanted to rile the zombies up, to keep these guys busy," Granny Good Mae said, pointing at Arthur. "He hoped to do you in as well. He was a busy boy." She rooted around in Wesley's pocket. She pulled out a little bottle and held it up to them. "Formaldehyde. Turns their brains off."

"Granny Good Mae, thank you," said Arthur.

"Wait, how do *you* know her?" Zoë asked. Then she grimaced. Of course he did. Like a lot of homeless, she freelanced for Public Works. Assassin.

"How did you know where his word was?" Arthur asked, ignoring Zoë.

"*She* told me. It was under his arm. Zoëtists hide them better now, used to be they'd put it on the construct's forehead, then wonder why their armies would fall when someone wiped the mark off."

"Zoë told you where his word was?" Arthur asked, shaking his head.

The old woman looked at him as if he were mad. "No," she said slowly, as if explaining to a child. "*SHE* told me. *She* has interest in Life. Keep her safe, *she* said. Keep her from getting eaten." She looked at Zoë fondly.

Arthur met Zoë's eyes and she shrugged. "I have no idea what she's talking about. I mean, I know Granny Good Mae, but I don't know about this *she* person."

Granny Good Mae cackled. "Just listen. You'll know."

She turned and ran, ducking into the alley behind the building.

Zoë picked up the formaldehyde. She shrugged. "Let's go home."

Luckily, the cabbie Max didn't care about human blood on his cab seat. On the contrary, he said, it made the ride more attractive to some of his customers.

"I don't know what your vampire thinks he can do to save me. I've got thirty-six hours, tops," Arthur said as Zoë tried to wrap her coat around his bleeding arm. She tried to ignore the cut on her own arm that throbbed and leaked blood slowly, making her hand tacky with it. *Zombie bite worse than a simple cut*, she thought firmly.

"Oh really?" she asked, mostly to keep him talking. "Tell me what happens."

Arthur's voice took on an academic quality. "First the wound will fester despite any attempts to keep it clean and infection-free. Within a day high fever sets in to kill higher brain functions. My consciousness checks out fully after thirty-six hours, and my body will die. Then I'll reanimate, hungry. If I can manage to find food in a legal way, I may gain some of my old personality back. Zombies usually take care of their own. If I just kill, then Public Works will find me soon enough. That is, if you don't do what you promised and kill me when it's necessary."

She poked him gently in the ribs. "Let's keep the passive-aggressive barbs away from the woman who's trying to save you, OK?"

They stopped in front of their apartment building. Arthur was able to walk, but seemed too woozy to speak. Zoë got him into her apartment and onto her couch. Then she went to get her first-aid kit.

Granny Good Mae had helped her buy proper things for coterie attacks. Besides gauze and tape and antibiotic cream, she also had bottles of holy water, herbs, and tea. She had no idea what to do with a zombie bite, but she knew that rinsing with holy water was a good step, and then some tea. It wouldn't help the zombie curse, but it would keep him calm and help the skin heal.

Arthur closed his eyes as Zoë examined his arm. She took some scissors from her first-aid kit and sliced through his coveralls and shirt, leaving it under him. She tried not to wince at the bite, but noticed it didn't look beyond her skills. There was nothing to stitch up, at least.

Arthur gasped as she poured cold water on him from a bottle. "What is bottled water going to do?"

"Holy water," she said. "Can't hurt. May help."

He hissed as she poured something new on his arm, and it bubbled in the wound. "Peroxide, for germs. Holy water won't help that."

Arthur set his teeth as Zoë smeared a warm salve over his wound and packed it tightly with gauze. She wrapped it up and taped it.

"You're pretty handy," he said. He started to shiver. "Do you have anything for the pain?"

Zoë plugged her electric kettle into the socket in the living room, made some tea, then helped prop him up to drink. The pinched, pained look in his face eased immediately.

"What is that?" he asked, his voice far away. He dozed off before she could answer.

"Get some sleep. Phil will be back soon," she said.

I hope, she added mentally.

Zoë sat on the floor, back to the sofa, shock and exhaustion finally hitting her. She sat for a while to calm herself, then went to change clothes and clean herself up.

"How do you get yourself into these things?" she asked the bathroom mirror, which didn't answer.

All things considered, that comforted her.

And she realized that none of this was as bad as the night after Godfrey's wife found out about their affair. The memory came, as always, unbidden, flashes of the bulky feet stomping inside her house, her quietly dry-heaving in the chest in her bedroom. She couldn't call the police; Lucy was chief. No one would believe her. And even if they did, she knew enough to know that the cops would take care of their own. Lucy was the victim here. Zoë was the other woman.

No. Not anymore.

Zoë pushed the memories down, washed her face and hands, and put a bandage on her arm.

That's not me anymore. She looked at herself in the mirror again and was surprised that her eyes were not wide with fear and uncertainty. Tired, yes. Apprehensive. But she was sure of herself for perhaps the first time ever.

She went to sit on the floor beside Arthur and wait for Phil.

The moonlight played on Arthur's face, which was slack and relaxed, and she admired it as he slept. He frowned, and began to shift around, moaning. Worried he'd injure himself, she took his good arm and shook it gently.

"Wha'?" Arthur woke up with a start, staring at her in fear.

"You're safe. It's Zoë, you're in my apartment, you had a bad dream."

"Was the dream that I got bit by a zombie?"

"Uh. No. That was real."

"Interesting use of the word 'safe,' then."

"Well there are no zombies here now, are there?"

"Isn't a vampire coming over soon?"

Zoë didn't answer. Under her hand his body vibrated, as if he were prepared to lash out at any moment.

"Are you saving me to make sure I turn?" he asked. His eyes were closed, as if he feared the answer. "Are you trying to help your boss make more coterie? Replace the zombies we exterminated?"

She ran her hand through her hair, smiling weakly. "No, Arthur. We're not. And you're not going to turn. Do you not remember?"

"What kind of lies are you accepting from them? If a zombie bites you, you turn into one. It's that simple. I have about a day left before I die and then reanimate. I'm begging you to kill me. Hell, go to my apartment and bring me my gun—I'll do it myself."

Zoë snorted. "Sure. I'll get right on that. 'I'm sorry, Officer, I have no idea how my neighbor ended up on my couch with a bullet in his head.' Now will you let me explain?"

He nodded.

"Good." She pulled the still-warm electric kettle off her end table and poured hot water into a cup. She helped him sit up, propped him up on pillows, and handed him some bright-yellow tea that looked like Easter egg dye.

"What's this?"

"It's a restorative, you drank it more concentrated before. I got it from a Chinese herbalist."

He sipped it and grimaced. "It tastes like cough syrup." He breathed deeply and relaxed back on his pillow. "Amazing. What's in this?"

"I'm surprised you don't know about it. But we can talk about that later. For now, trust me." She stared into his eyes, unblinking. "You are not going to die or become a zombie."

He drained the rest of the tea. "Tell me why."

"Because Phil will be here soon with a zoëtist he knows. He says the right zoëtist can help this." She took the empty cup from him, praying what she told him was true.

"I can't believe this. Zoëtists make zombies, but nothing can reverse the curse."

She sat down. "You don't know everything about coterie, do you?"

He tried to shrug but winced as his arm moved. "I suppose

you're right. But this is one of those basic things you'd think we would have found out about, like how vampires don't like the sun."

She watched him for a moment, then said, "Phil is going to ask something from you, you know."

"If he can save me from this, he can have it." He paused. "Within reason," he amended. "Although it's pretty amazing how priorities shift when you have a festering zombie wound. So can you tell me what the hell was going on? I don't often find zombies attacking vampires and their thralls."

"OK, first, I'm not a thrall," she said, offended. "I'm an employee. We were looking for information on a coworker who had disappeared. The zombies who have been attacking people shouldn't have needed to, they should have had enough food from his contacts in the city. So we went to see if he had food in his apartment, and that's when the others attacked us." She paused, then sighed. "Phil thinks someone is messing with the zombies to take their food and make them revert to shambling monsters. Which is what we saw last night. And from what Granny Good Mae said, I guess that was Wesley."

"Who's Wesley?"

"A construct who was created from my ex-boyfriend. It's a whole thing." She waved her hand, dismissing the details.

Arthur took a deep breath. "So what do you do with vampires that has you breaking into a zombie's apartment at night?"

"I'm a managing editor at a publishing company. We're writing travel guides." She laughed, a short, bitter sound. "I've been on the job since November second. It's been a little more than I expected, and I expected a lot from working with people who would just as soon eat me."

"So how's the book going?"

She frowned. "I've been spending my time trying to learn the coterie lifestyle—*all* the different coterie lifestyles—and then I find out the CR representative in the company is a construct that hates me—and then the zombies start just eating people, which my coworkers say is somewhat odd for them in this civilized age. But believe it or not, the book is moving along nicely."

Arthur dozed off again, allowing Zoë to nap, sitting up on the floor, back to the couch. She sat bolt upright when the doorbell rang, and she ran to let Phil in. He brought with him a thin white man with slick hair, glasses, and a bow tie.

"This is Benjamin Rosenberg," Phil said. The man shook Zoë's hand and smiled. "Internal medicine and zoëtism, whatever you need. Now where is our patient?"

She led them to her sofa, where Ben tut-tutted over the mess, but made appreciative noises at how Zoë had wrapped the wound. He expertly unwrapped it without waking Arthur and examined it.

"Can you heal him?" Zoë asked.

"Oh, my dear," Ben said without looking up. "One cannot *heal* a zombie bite. But medicine and magic have evolved to where we are able to keep a victim stable for decades, as long as he follows some of the basic instructions."

Zoë felt cold and relieved at the same time. Arthur would have known if there had been an easy fix to a zombie bite. Why didn't Public Works know about this? She said, "He won't like having to deal with the wound for the rest of his life, but it's better than death. Or undeath."

Phil raised an eyebrow to her, but she stood her ground. "What? It's true. If we wanted to be turned, we would throw ourselves at you."

Ben carried an old-fashioned doctor's bag and sat it on the floor by the couch.

205

"You're going to have to replace this couch. Or get a nice cover," Ben said.

"Right," she said, seeing for the first time that her couch cushion was soaked in blood, holy water, and peroxide. "Oh well," she said weakly.

She and Phil stood with the closed door behind them, watching Ben calmly fix herbs and tiny bones, arrange them all on Zoë's floor, and say some words over them. It was surreal to see a small Jewish man moan and chant like a hoodoo priestess, but he moaned and chanted with no self-consciousness, and Zoë glanced at Phil. He didn't look back over at her, his face stony.

At the end, Ben had a mortar filled with a gooey yellow sludge. He unwrapped Arthur's arm and smeared it on the wound with a gloved hand. Zoë glanced at Phil and noticed his nostrils flaring at the scent of blood.

Arthur's eyes opened as Ben was re-bandaging the wound. "You have some powerful friends, sir," Ben said. "You will survive. You might want to take some time off to let that arm heal. Change the dressings after three days. You have enough salve to last you three months, apply daily after the first three days, then come see me after three months. I'll give you some written instructions before I leave."

Arthur worked his mouth soundlessly, discovering that his tongue worked. "Did the zoëtist come? Where is she?"

Ben pursed his lips and straightened his tie again. "Zoëtists aren't all females, sir. I can create golems, constructs, and similar things, but I am also one of the few living zoëtists who can treat early forms of zombism."

"So...I'm not going to die and come back?"

The man smiled. "No, sir, as long as you follow my treatment plan."

206

"So I could still become a zombie," Arthur said, frowning.

Ben nodded. "If you don't do as I say. Just like if you don't follow the treatment plan of eating regularly, you will die of starvation, and if you don't follow the treatment plan of sleeping regularly, you will go mad. Our lives are full of routines that we must follow to stay alive. This is just one more for you."

Zoë accepted the written instructions for Arthur, who still pondered this.

Phil escorted the zoëtist to Zoë's hallway, where they chatted in low voices. The sleeping tea must have been wearing off, because Arthur managed to sit up. He looked at Zoë, who was smiling at him.

He stared at her for a moment, then sighed. "I can't figure you out, Zoë. Really."

She laughed. "Not many can. That's why I am still alive, I think. Now, do you think you can make it to your apartment or do you want to crash on my couch?"

"Bed," he said, almost longingly.

She helped him off the couch; he was weaker than either of them had expected. "Thank you," he said. "I mean it."

"You saved our lives. Or whatever Phil calls his life. Thanks for that," she replied.

"Part of the job," he said, then made a pained expression. "Which I have to call into. Man, am I going to be in trouble."

"For getting bitten?"

"For not following protocol. I should have had a partner. I should have let someone know where I was going. For all they know, I'm dead."

"Er, then yeah, call in."

"I'm going to have to tell them about the bite, and the zoëtist. I can't believe we didn't know they could do that."

"Well, Ben said not many could do it."

Ben and Phil entered the room then. Ben nodded at Arthur as he left, while Phil made no acknowledgment of him.

Arthur paused and touched Phil's shoulder with his good hand. Phil's eyes grew wide, but he made no threatening move.

"Thanks," Arthur said, and left without waiting for a response.

The Shambling Guide to New York City

MANHATTAN:
Places of Interest

Sponsored by Public Works and the city's coterie, the memorial to all who gave their lives on 12/8/15 is a large rock on the bank of the reservoir in Central Park. It looks like a graffiti magnet, but each tag references a name of someone who died during the events of New York City's darkest day since 9/11/01. The largest tag is the drawing of a long white braid, as the freelance assassin Granny Good Mae joined the coterie that day and saved the city. Smaller memorial shrines on the banks, where people leave boxes of Chinese food, still crop up in the winter. ■

CHAPTER EIGHTEEN

When she closed the door, Phil and Ben were in her kitchen, sitting at her table. Not her usual Saturday-morning guests. She approached them, but her cell phone rang.

Exhausted, she answered it without thinking, then winced when she belatedly saw that caller ID read GODFREY.

"I'm going to take this call and make some tea. I'll be right back," she told her guests, and then took the electric kettle to the sink to fill it.

"Hello, Godfrey."

"Hey, baby," he said, his voice muffled.

"Don't call me that, Godfrey," she said.

"What's the matter? Never mind, I don't have a lot of time here. Listen, Lucy has been called to the city on business, and I'm coming with her. We'll get there on Tuesday. I was wondering if I could see you."

She plugged in the kettle and put it on the counter, feeling pleased at her composure. "Doesn't she know I moved here? She'd be suspicious."

"Well, I didn't tell her," he said.

"Godfrey, she's a cop, do you think she's stupid? It was you underestimating her that got us caught in the first place! Oh, and lying to me about her existence."

"What's gotten into you? I thought you'd want to see me!" His voice took on a whiny quality.

Zoë felt exhaustion and rage that she'd kept under wraps for months begin to boil over. She went into the living room and whispered into the phone. "What's *wrong* with me? You're married. You seduced me. Your wife found out and threatened me. Sent thugs to my house to scare me. I was forced out of my job and had to *leave town*. And now you want to see me again, pretending I moved here for a completely different reason? You're a fucking coward. Don't call me again."

"Why are you whispering? Is someone there? Have you found someone else?"

Zoë nearly sputtered at his audacity. "'*Else*'? What do you mean 'else'? That implies I had someone to begin with. You were never mine. You were always hers."

"I...thought you loved me."

She refused to bite. "Honestly, so did I. Enjoy your trip to the city, Godfrey. Take your wife to a show or something. Nine million or so people between us isn't quite enough for me, but it'll have to do."

She turned off her cell phone with shaking hands. Tossing the phone onto the soiled couch, she returned to the kitchen. Her kettle was whistling, and she carefully made herself some green tea, refusing to look at the men who stared at her.

"Problems?" Ben asked.

"Not anymore," she said, taking a deep breath. She composed herself. "So did you see Wesley when you left the apartment building last night?"

Phil's gaze sharpened. "No. Why? Did you?"

Phil took his flask from his pocket and began sipping from it as he listened to Zoë tell her story. Again she downplayed Granny Good Mae's role, but she couldn't deny that the woman had been there. Or she was too tired to think of a quick lie.

She sipped her tea and felt the knot of anxiety between her shoulder blades slowly release.

"The Wesley problem is dealt with. That's good," Phil said.

Ben frowned. "Not necessarily. I took what you told me about this construct and narrowed it down to a handful of my colleagues."

Zoë blinked. "Really? You can do that?"

He smiled thinly. "There aren't that many of us practicing."

"And?"

"I wasn't sure who he was attached to, though, until what you just said about his holy word being under his left arm. That told me everything I need to know. I'm pretty sure I know who this construct's zoëtist is. And it's not good news."

He removed his glasses and rubbed his nose. "There was a student alongside me years ago when we studied in Cajun country. I didn't enjoy hoodoo, but she took to it quickly. We had a disagreement during an ethics lecture, and later that night she set a vampire on me. Orson rescued me." He smiled down at his wedding ring. "But I learned her calling cards. She's a dangerous one, likes to imagine a world with the cities out of balance. She, a human, wants coterie dominance more than any supernatural coterie I know."

"Why? Is she insane?" Zoë asked.

Ben shrugged. "More parts for her to play with. Dead, drained humans means more things she can build into soldiers. More power. More chaos. I didn't say she was logical."

"So she's messing with New York coterie. And me. Why?" Zoë asked.

Ben looked at her. "New York is a powerful city, with millions of people, thousands of coterie. It's a great place for the power-hungry. And I know she was into some questionable research. Making a construct to mess with the zombies to simply sow chaos and distract Public Works is a logical step for someone as messed up as her.

"But why she created the construct out of someone you know, to attack you, I don't know. Do you have any enemies?"

Zoë felt very cold. "What was this woman's name?"

"Lucille Haarden."

Phil wanted to talk more about Arthur, and Public Works, and what they owed the coterie, and future plans for dealing with the zoëtist now known to be Lucy Haarden.

Who had been stirring up the zombies in preparation for coming to town shortly.

The fear was in her throat, she could smell it in her own sweat, the same tangy, metallic scent that she had smelled when Lucy stalked her the first time. Phil's nostrils flared again.

"You're terrified," he said, his face softening with wonder. "Much more so than last night. How is this possible?"

"Lucy. Fucking Lucy Haarden is the zoëtist who's probably killed my ex, made a construct to annoy the shit out of me, and then set a bunch of zombies on me? Lucy is the one who killed that morgue worker, and that jogger, and all those zombies. And we're supposed to stop her? I'd sooner leave town!"

Phil waved his hand. "Now that we know, it's no problem. We'll get her. Besides, now it's clear she wanted to sow chaos in town, and when she found out that you were working with coterie, she just found it convenient to create a construct to bother you while it set the stage for her chaos. It's a mental game, Zoë, and she's clearly beating you."

Ben nodded. "We could just tell Public Works about her."

Phil grimaced slightly, but nodded. "She's coterie. They can stop her."

Zoë put her head in her hands. "I can't take this. I have to sleep. Just let me sleep, all weekend if possible. I'll function better when I wake up."

Phil stood. "Good work, Zoë. Have a good weekend, and I'll expect to see the outline for the book on my desk at the end of the day on Monday."

She stared at him through her tired eyes. "You unbelievable bastard."

He pulled his cell phone out of his pocket and dialed. As he waited, he said, "You've shown me you can work miracles. I believe you can get me a rough outline by then."

"Provided Crazy McKillerBitch doesn't come up with something else to threaten our lives."

Ben smiled. "Lucille is formidable, but now at least we know who she is and what she wants. I wouldn't worry." He handed her his card. "And if you ever need patching up, give me a call. I work for hell notes and I'm very discreet."

Zoë took the card. "I thought you stayed out of the coterie work for Orson's sake."

Ben drew himself up importantly. "I don't do a lot of zoëtist work these days, but I'm always a doctor, and I know how to treat many coterie-inflicted wounds."

He picked up his bag and, smiling, left Zoë's apartment.

Phil followed him as his call was picked up. "Yes, I need a UV-protected cab and escort to—" he was saying as he shut the door behind him and Ben.

Lucy's a fucking zoëtist. Oddly, that means a lot of shit makes sense, she said to herself.

Zoë paused, and then closed her eyes. Taking what she knew about coterie, she thought back to her time in North Carolina, how easily she had fallen for Godfrey, how quickly she'd believed his lies.

She wondered if Godfrey had been a construct, but she

remembered with a blush that she'd seen his entire body, and there had been no scars or Hebrew tattoos. She'd love to have blamed the affair on anything but her own idiocy, but it was time to move on.

She trudged to her bedroom, slipped into a pair of sweatpants, took a ratty old blanket from the closet, and put it over the couch. She sat down and turned the TV on. She stared at a *Twilight Zone* marathon until she fell asleep.

After twenty-four hours of sleep interrupted by meals and hot baths, Zoë woke up on Sunday sore, but alert and in decent spirits. She contemplated going back to bed again, but realized this was her first real day off after an incredibly stressful week and decided she was going to have some fun, dammit. Lucy and Godfrey wouldn't be in town for a couple of days. She didn't need to interact with any coterie until Monday. And the day was simply gorgeous.

It would be a grand day for shopping, watching television, and napping. She decided to have breakfast at a café down the street to start with.

The November sunlight cheered Zoë, her sore muscles loosening up during the walk. Inside the bakery, she ordered two croissants and two coffees to go.

Refusing to think too much about it, in case she lost her nerve, she carried them back to her apartment and knocked on Arthur's door.

He came out shirtless, with his arm in a sling. Zoë tried not to stare. When he'd been lying on her couch, dying, he hadn't seemed that attractive, but now, even injured, he was—

She mentally shook her head. "I bring breakfast!" she said, smiling. He didn't smile at her, but just stood at the door.

She frowned. "Should I just leave it here on the floor for you to get after I leave? I have coffee too. I took a chance on you liking sugar in your coffee. Come to mention, I took a chance on you liking coffee..." She trailed off. Arthur still stood motionless.

He finally stepped aside and silently allowed her in the apartment. She smiled through her discomfort and entered. It was the same size as hers, but seemed more spacious, as an apparently Spartan mind-set had decorated it. The white walls held little except for a small weapons rack near the door. The morning sun lit up the spacious living room, though, and it looked comfortable, if liable to cause echoes.

"So, Arthur, how are you feeling?"

"Like I've been bitten by a zombie."

"Ah." Zoë put the food on his coffee table. "So. How long have you lived in the city?"

"I was born in the Bronx."

"Cool." She tried not to be so stupidly monosyllabic. "So!" She failed.

She gestured to the bag and drink caddy on the coffee table. "I brought coffee and croissants. I hope you like caffeine and carbs."

Arthur watched her, saying nothing. She deflated. "All right. I'm trying here. Should I just leave?"

"Why are you here? Really?" he asked.

"Well, yesterday you were at death's door. Or undeath's. I was pretty sure you lived alone, so I thought I'd check on you. And since I was getting breakfast for myself, I figured I'd bring you some food."

"You're not spying for your boss?"

She folded her arms and glared at him. "No. My work with the coterie is still being established, but I haven't yet been asked

216

to betray my own race. And if you will remember, I made sure Phil got that zoëtist for you."

"I don't know any humans who work with them who aren't zoëtists or thralls. Whose side are you on, Zoë? Do you help him get blood? Does he feed off you? I can't trust you if I don't know that."

She sighed and sat down on his couch. "I just wanted a job. That's it. I seemed to fit in with Underground Publishing, believe it or not. Then it became a matter of pride as some of them didn't think I could do it. Then it was fighting back as someone clearly is fucking with me. Then it was just fighting as Rodrigo went insane and then the zombies attacked.

"I haven't told Phil about how Granny Good Mae is helping me. I mean, she's really teaching me about coterie, not just rescuing me when I do stupid shit. Although he may ask questions soon. I have to decide what to tell him."

She took a sip of her coffee, hoping Arthur would speak, but he stayed silent. "I am not trying to play two sides against each other. I just want to put out a book and figure out how to stop whatever's going on. They say there's a zoëtist coming to town to mess with the balance. It seems it's also someone from my past who has cause to dislike me greatly." She didn't look at him, instead focusing on his stark living room. "If you don't want me around I'll understand. But I guess I wanted someone, a human, to talk to who understands what I face every day."

Arthur still stood by the coffee table, looking down on her.

"All right," she said, putting her hands on her knees and getting up from the couch. "I'll go. I'm sorry to have intruded on your Sunday morning. Incidentally, you're looking a lot better. I'm glad you made it through the zombie scare." *Stop babbling and go!* she admonished herself, and headed for the door.

She didn't look at him as she slid past his half-naked body. She had opened the door and was halfway out, her face still burning, when he finally spoke. "Hey."

She stopped, but didn't turn around.

"If you go out again, I take my coffee black."

She smiled, said, "Noted," and closed the door behind her.

MANHATTAN:
Necessaries

If you find yourself running low on hell notes in the city, look to the ravens. These birds are the bankers, and will be happy to do an exchange of human money for hell notes, or dip into your existing account. Their bank is the most sophisticated in the world, connected to all the raven branches throughout the world.

If you do not normally bank with ravens, then they'll still allow you to make a withdrawal, but for a mutually agreed-upon negotiating price. It will be unique to your situation. And we definitely recommend opening an account with the ravens before travel to the city so you do not run into this problem.

Most any raven in the city will help you out with your banking needs; you can usually find them congregating near Wall Street. ■

CHAPTER NINETEEN

On Monday morning, Zoë got to work early and taped a sign to her office door.

CRISIS-FREE, FLIRT-FREE, DISTRACTION-FREE, THREAT-FREE ZONE.

I HAVE WEAPONS.

Come back tomorrow, I'll be happy to cope with anything. For today, I have to do my job.

This sign drew Morgen immediately, as Zoë had known it would. The water sprite tried the door and, when she found it looked, yelled at her to open up, or she would come in anyway.

"Look at the sign," Zoë called.

A wet sound came from the other side of the door, and a stream of water slid through the crack. Zoë had forgotten that part of Morgen's coterie skills. The sprite slid easily under the door as a puddle of water and re-formed in front of Zoë, her hands on her hips.

"Wonder Twin powers, activate," Zoë said. "What about the sign did you not understand?"

Morgen sat down on Zoë's guest chair and waved her hand

casually. "Oh, I don't pay attention to those. I wanted to hear about the zombie attack and that guy from Public Works!"

Zoë closed her browser. "Look, if you know that much about it, you already know the details. Phil probably can tell you more, being a vampire and all. The whole weekend was a blur and I'm glad it's over."

"But it was that cute guy that lives next to you, right? He's in Public Works?"

Zoë nodded. "Yeah. Awkward, huh? Even though I saved him from being undead he still doesn't trust me as far he can spit a dead rat."

"So no hopes of getting laid in the near future, huh?"

Zoë laughed, finally. "Yeah, you could say that. But seriously, between all this shit that's been going on outside the office, I still have a book to put together. Can you help me out here and let me work?"

Morgen stood. "Sure. I'll keep the bastards away from your door, too. But we're going to lunch, dammit. You're going to tell me whatever you're not telling me."

Zoë just stared at her. "I don't even know what that would be."

"That's what we'll figure out at lunch," she said, and melted again into water.

"You could have just opened the door from this side," Zoë said, leaning over the desk and watching the puddle slither under the door again. "Show-off."

Zoë noticed quickly that the sign on her door did more to attract curious coworkers than to repel them, and at ten in the morning she slammed her pen down on the desk and picked up her phone to dial Phil's extension.

"Yes?" he said smoothly.

"It's Zoë. Listen, if you want this book done I need to work from home, your office is driving me crazy. I'm heading home

221

and working from there. I'm turning off my phone right now to avoid distractions."

"Zoë—wait, I need to talk to you about—"

"No, Phil. You said you wanted this book done. It can wait till tomorrow. Whatever it is, it can wait until this project is done. You give me the deadline, you deal with me not being available to traipse around the city getting into coterie intrigue with you. Understand?"

"But—" her boss said, but she hung up on him.

Shutting the phone off, she felt a sense of freedom, and gathered her stuff.

Morgen came up behind her as she was leaving. "Now what?"

"Working from home," she said over her shoulder. "Don't call. I'll be back in tomorrow."

"But—" Morgen said, but Zoë shut the door behind her.

She paused when she got out on the street. Phil obviously couldn't get to her apartment until sundown, and he couldn't send any of the vampires or, likely, the zombies (*zombie*, Zoë mentally corrected herself, realizing Montel was the only one left) after her. But he could send Gwen or Morgen or—she gulped—John. She'd have to remember to lock her door.

Then she wondered if living beside someone from Public Works would make her coworkers less likely to visit her, or more. She wondered if living beside Arthur put him in danger. Then she remembered the weapons rack by his door and decided he could probably take care of himself.

She wondered for a moment if a weapons rack would keep Lucy away from her. Then, to remove the thought of the evil couple from her mind, she ducked into Bakery Under Starlight for a cup of coffee. Carl was checking out a guy who had bought a grocery-bagful of baked goods and two coffees. The customer backed up from the counter slowly, staring at Carl, who just smiled at him.

After the man stumbled out, splashing coffee on the door and window, Zoë laughed. "Let me guess. He came in for one coffee and a Danish?"

Carl smiled uncertainly. "Why?"

"Because you're an incubus."

The baker's face went slack with shock. "How did you know? Did John tell you?" He looked around quickly. The empty shop seemed innocent and friendly, but he looked as if he'd been cornered.

Zoë laughed at the big powerful incubus who seemed scared shitless of her. "Carl, calm down. I'm just learning to spot the signs. Part of the job."

"What gave me away?" he asked, breathing a little more regularly and shoving several croissants—her usual order—in a bag. He handed her the bag, heavy with baked goods, over the counter.

"Your bracelet. I've seen it before," Zoë said, pointing to his left wrist before she accepted the bag. Slim links interlocked around his wrist, held together with a tiny padlock. "Another incubus I know wears it."

His face was slack as he stared at her. "You're basing this on a bracelet?"

"Well, not just that. Your nails are perfectly manicured. You have scars on your wrists and neck. I just guessed you were a submissive incubus." She put her hands on her hips. "What I can't understand, though, is why I'm not madly attracted to you."

He looked at her as if she had just suggested they put on goggles and go to church together. He shook his head once and said, "I'm gay. My sexual energy is directed toward men. They love my pastries, and I feed on that love."

She smacked her forehead. "Of course, makes perfect sense!"

He finally grinned at her. "So for scaring the shit out of me, are you going to give me a write-up in that book I hear you are working on?"

"Of course! And I'll take two large coffees, no sexual energy on the side, please." Zoë paid him (he didn't charge her for the croissants; hush pastries, she assumed) took her bag and drink caddy. "Thanks a lot. And don't worry, I'll keep your secret."

"Don't keep it secret from your coterie friends, though! I give discounts!" he called as she left the shop. Zoë looked up at the sign above the door. "Bakery Under Starlight"—or "BUS." She needed to pay attention more often.

Arthur wasn't home. Zoë left the coffee outside his door and returned to her apartment, where she promptly took the phone off the hook.

She got out her laptop and toyed with the idea of checking her e-mail, but shut off the Wi-Fi with a firm resolve—she was here to work and she didn't need distractions. Besides, Godfrey might be online, and she kept forgetting to block him on her IM programs.

Here at home, the work was surprisingly easy. She had worried about how well she would be able to lay out a book based on a people she had known about for only a few weeks, but quickly the problems coterie might face seemed just like the problems humans would: where to get food, where to stay, what would be interesting to see. It made sense to cover dangerous parts of the city as well, as she'd seen some of the more progressive rival guides do in their chapters focused toward gay travelers.

She got into the groove, setting a rough outline for the book and assigning writers to each area. She decided to make sure each section had a diurnal and a nocturnal writer covering. Ideally, she wanted to have one of each major coterie group—vampires, zombies, fae, and demons? Where did the succubi and incubi fall? She'd have to check—covering each section of the book, but for now she'd settle for two writers per project.

Once the book was planned, she made a list of her current writers, assigning them to food, nightlife, sightseeing, lodging, and other areas, and then she made a list of what she'd need in staffing, in terms of both writing ability and race.

No affirmative action in the coterie world, she guessed. Remembering there was still a good deal she needed to learn, with just what races existed in the coterie at the top of the list, she began to jot down notes that she would need to follow up on.

Her hands began to ache from typing, and she looked up with a sudden full feeling in her bladder and an empty feeling in her stomach. She squinted at her watch—three p.m. She'd completely blown off lunch. Still, she'd gotten the thing laid out and outlined. It did have several question marks and notes where she would have to research more, but it was a solid outline she could present to Montel and Phil with confidence.

She rubbed her tired eyes and got up from her desk to deal with her various bodily needs. As she was cutting a ham sandwich in half, a knock sounded at her door.

She sighed. Arthur would be good. Anyone from work would be bad. John would be very very bad. The sky through the kitchen window over her sink darkened as a shadow crossed. Zoë blinked.

Ah.

She put the knife down (she'd planned on answering the door with it in hand in case of a threatening coworker) and went to greet Gwen, the death goddess. Unfortunately John was with her. And from the looks of him, he was very, very hungry.

"Hey guys, come in, I guess. I'm mostly done with my out-line, or I wouldn't have—"

The death goddess barged past her into her apartment. "You have been impossible to get in touch with."

John followed more sedately, moving like a panther. He tried to slide past Zoë, close, but she stepped out of the way so she wouldn't touch him. She shut the door calmly. "I said I would be. I was actually hired to do a job within the office, not wander around getting attacked by incubi and zombies." She glared at John, who merely grinned at her.

"When the coterie know of your existence, and know that you know of theirs, you are in greater danger than normal people. You should have been accessible."

Zoë tried not to flinch. Gwen's presence filled the living room, her black cloak seeming to billow in the still air. Outside it grew darker as more sparrows perched near the windows.

"Well, you can taste how far away I am from death. Did this afternoon mess that up?"

She didn't blink. "Yes."

Zoë looked at her with a steady gaze. "Is there anything I can do to reverse that?"

"Possibly."

"Are you going to give me more information, or did you just come here to stand there like a goth princess, intimidate me, and deliver bad but vague news I'll never be able to prove right or wrong?"

The goddess's cloak stopped billowing and she gave an unex-pected, rueful laugh. "Yes, I suppose I can do that."

The tension in Zoë's chest loosened, but she was careful not to look visibly relieved. "Then why not have a seat?"

Gwen sat down primly on the old blanket (Zoë had washed it and the cushion cover, but the blanket looked better than the bloodstained cushion), looking again like nothing more than a goth chick. Zoë sat in the armchair to keep John from trying to sit beside her, but he just sat on the arm. She still refused to meet his eyes.

"The zombies continue to cause problems," Gwen said. "Even after Wesley's death. Public Works is stressed to the limit. That's what Phil and Morgen were trying to tell you before you left."

"How did Wesley get to them? He's dead," Zoë began, but at that moment her door burst open and Arthur ran in, holding a sword in his good hand.

He saw them sitting there and stopped. They gaped at him, Zoë finding that despite her shock, a small part of her was disappointed he'd put on a shirt. A moment passed.

"Hi, Arthur," Zoë finally said, and the point of his sword wavered, then dropped.

"I—" He swallowed. "The outside of your window is covered in sparrows. That's a bad sign."

"Oh, don't worry. Gwen, meet Arthur. Gwen is a death goddess, Arthur. Gwen, Arthur is with Public Works and my next-door neighbor."

Gwen eyed his sword, an amused look on her face. She stood and reached around the sword to grasp and gently shake the hand confined in the sling. "Pleased to meet you. I am not here to kill Zoë, don't worry. I needed to carry a message from work. Those"—she gestured to the window—"are merely my heralds."

Arthur eyed Gwen carefully. "Ah. Well. Sorry to interrupt."

"Don't be," Gwen said quickly. "I'm pleased she has someone nearby ready to defend her."

John had stood up beside her chair and looked at Arthur. "Zoë, I haven't had the pleasure."

Zoë rolled her eyes. "And Arthur, this is John. I also, uh, work with him."

The two men did not shake hands. John looked at Arthur calmly, his short, muscular build nearly the opposite of Arthur's trim build.

"And Zoë," John said, tensing slightly. "Have *you* had the pleasure?"

She glared at him. "What are you talking about, John? Are you seriously asking what I think you're asking?"

He spread his hands innocently. "I can't imagine what you mean."

She stood and turned her back to him, cold with anger. "Listen, John. My life is none of your business. None. If you're going to treat my friends badly, or treat me badly, just leave now."

She could feel him then, as if he had turned his pheromones up to eleven. Her mouth nearly watered at the thought of licking one small bead of sweat on his neck. "Are you sure, Zoë? I could take care of every need you have. I could taste you"—he glanced at Arthur and smirked—"again."

Zoë closed her eyes against the lust and shame that blossomed in her. She didn't want to look at Arthur, see his face, his revulsion. She looked at the floor and turned back toward the men. Eyes still down, she reached out and put her hand on John's chest, feeling the tight muscles underneath. Then she pushed.

He stumbled backward, surprised by her attack. She looked at the ground. "Just go. Get out. Now. Try this again, come to my home again, and—"

He interrupted her, laughing. "You'll what? Call Public Works on me? Get your knight here to save you?"

She looked at Arthur, who looked shocked at her aggression. She held out her hand, and comprehension dawned on his face. He handed her the sword, and she lifted it, trying not to show how heavy it was for her.

"No, I'm not calling for help. I'll gut you myself."

He opened his mouth once, then closed it. He glared at Gwen, then at Arthur, then stormed out.

Zoë handed the sword back to Arthur, afraid to look him in the face. She sat down beside Gwen and put her face in her hands, feeling soiled. "Thanks for coming by, Arthur, but I'm fine. You can go now. I'd rather you not see me right now."

No one moved. Zoë looked up at Gwen, who was looking at Arthur. "No," Gwen said, slowly. "He needs to stay. He needs to hear this too."

"Why?" Arthur and Zoë asked at the same time.

Gwen's eyes had gone completely black. "Because the odds of your impending doom dropped considerably when he came into the room."

The Shambling Guide to New York City

MANHATTAN:
Notable Tourist Spots

One of the biggest spots for visiting coterie, and resident coterie of Scandinavian descent, is Rockefeller Center. Funded by a descendant of Odin, Lore Burnaby, the center was blessed with one of the few seeds of the ancient tree of life, the Yggdrasil. The tree grows to full height every year around the Solstice; it is a common reminder of rebirth out of winter.

Of course, the humans have determined their own meaning for the tree, but as long as they don't pervert the tree itself, Burnaby allows their celebrations. ∎

CHAPTER TWENTY

Her impending doom. She'd forgotten about that.

"I kinda hoped my doom was John's proximity, actually," she said, grinning slightly.

"What are you talking about?" Arthur asked, raising his sword toward Gwen again.

Zoë sighed. "She's OK, Arthur. Put that thing down. You're going to cause a scene."

He finally lowered the sword and propped it against the door as if it were an umbrella, and awkwardly joined Zoë on the couch.

"To explain," Zoë said, "Gwen is a death goddess: not only does she get followed by a flock of sparrows, but she can see someone's death. Apparently my future has been fluctuating today. And apparently I'll never get my damn deadline met. So what else is up, Gwen? Why did you come here, really? And why'd you bring John?"

Gwen sat on the couch. "John's desire to be here was obvious. Phil told him not to come, but I think he's become fixated on you. I am here to tell you about the zombie uprisings, and to remind you that Phil wants you to check out Public Works. They need to know about the coming zoëtist." She looked at Arthur. "It seems you've already done that."

Arthur looked at Zoë but she didn't meet his eyes. "Your mission was to get to know me?"

"Yes, well, no. I mean, I wanted to get to know you before I found you were Public Works. And yes, I needed to approach someone at Public Works on a professional level. There's that zoëtist I mentioned coming to town tomorrow. She's behind the zombie attacks on the city. And behind that construct that attacked us last weekend."

"When were you going to tell me this?"

"I told you! But it was the day after your attack, so I think you weren't at your clearest. Christ, Arthur, I didn't deceive you. I never hid what I was from you. We haven't had any chances to talk about work life yet, for either of us. We've been too busy fighting or bleeding to really think about it!"

She finally met his eyes. He frowned at her, tension in his shoulders conveying his anger. "I have to tell my superior officers about this."

Gwen didn't blink. "We were counting on it. But remember you owe Phil a rather large favor. And that's going to be repaid now."

Arthur swallowed but his gaze didn't waver. "I'm listening."

"You're to take Zoë with you to Public Works."

Zoë and Arthur stared at Gwen. Then they stared at each other. Then they spoke at the same time.

"You've got to be kidding me."

"My bosses will never go for me bringing a coterie spy into the organization."

"Wait, *spy?*"

"I could lose my job."

"Does my job as an editor matter at all?"

"I shouldn't even go in today."

"Did Phil take into account my current mental state?"

232

"I don't know why you work with them in the first place. They eat people, Zoë."

"Oh, what the hell do you know?"

Even as she squabbled in a slight panic, she caught the look of tired bemusement on Gwen's face, like that of a parent watching teens fight. She subsided in mid-insult and took a deep breath.

"Gwen, I think that's a terrible idea. They would never agree to it, and I'm a book editor, not a diplomat." She flopped back on the couch and tried to relax the muscles around her spine.

"You were open to it when you spoke with Phil earlier about it," Gwen said.

"You what?" Arthur said, whirling to face her.

"Stuff has changed since then, Gwen, I don't think I can do it," Zoë said. She didn't know how much Gwen knew about Lucy, and didn't want to talk about it in front of Arthur.

"She's right. She has no experience, she would be a liability," Arthur said.

Zoë prickled again at his immediate dismissal of her. "Now wait, I charmed myself into a job with coterie, what makes you think I can't talk to humans? I am not the dead weight that you're implying." She turned toward the death goddess. "Gwen, what's the point of all this? Phil had to know that Arthur wouldn't go for this. How did he expect Arthur to get me in there, anyway?"

"The answer is very simple, Zoë," Gwen said, relaxing back in her seat. "Tell them the truth. You're writing a book about New York City and you want to do some research about the underbelly of the city. And you have some information about some danger coming into the city. None of that is a lie."

"What do you know about this zoëtist?" Arthur asked her.

"Like I told you," she said pointedly, closing her eyes and sighing. "We found out someone big is coming to town, and she's probably behind all the zombie problems."

"Children." Gwen said it softly but it silenced them both. "We need to deal with something bigger than you two." She leaned forward and looked at Arthur. "This is what Phil is asking of you. Now, did you think that repaying a vampire's debt would be so minor as to take a woman to work with you?"

Arthur nodded slowly. "I don't have a choice, do I?"

Gwen smiled. "You're coming around; that's good. Yes, Phil has put a geas on you. If you don't take Zoë to work with you tonight, then you'll start to suffer a great deal of pain."

"Wait a second," said Zoë. "What if I refuse to go? Why can't he send someone else?"

"He wants a human to be a bridge. And if you don't go, then Arthur will still suffer great pain, only it will be your fault."

She whistled long and low. "Vampires really are bastards, aren't they?"

"What was your first clue?" Arthur asked dryly.

Zoë put her hand on the closed front door, after Arthur had slammed it to go get dressed. "Gwen, I'm not terribly happy with this."

The woman leaned back and looked at Zoë for a lengthy time, long enough to make it uncomfortable for her. "What?" Zoë finally asked, exasperated.

"You work for a vampire, Zoë. You conspire with zombies, gods, undead, and other beings that most humans consider the stuff of nightmares. And you're surprised when you're put in a position that makes you uncomfortable?"

"It's not that," Zoë said. "I did everything else of my own free will. Now, for the sake of Arthur's geese thing, I'm forced into something. I have no choice. Before, I could have told Phil no.

I went with him to the zombie apartment complex, for God's sake, of my own free will. But now, I have nothing."

"Again. Why are you surprised?"

Zoë frowned. "I just..." She chewed her lip. "I guess I felt like Phil and I were—fuck it. Never mind."

Gwen smiled. Her eyes glittered. "Friends? Peers?"

Zoë gritted her teeth, staring at the floor. "I said never mind."

"We are very different beings, Zoë."

"I am starting to realize that. Thank you." Zoë kept her hand on the front door, pressing on it until her hand went white.

"Would you like me to go?"

"Far be it from me to kick a death goddess out of my apartment," Zoë said. She went into her bedroom and changed into old jeans and a sweatshirt. She went to the kitchen, where she picked up her collection of herbs. She walked back into the living room, ignoring Gwen, who watched her with interest. She strapped her knife to her forearm and threw her leather jacket on top of her sweatshirt. The herbs went into her pocket, which she then zipped.

"There's tea in the kitchen, as well as wine. I don't know what, if anything, you drink. I don't know much of anything anymore," Zoë said, still not looking at Gwen as she checked to make sure she could draw her knife without damaging her jacket. *Priorities and all.*

"I am leaving, Zoë," Gwen said, standing up.

"Oh really? That's cool. I apparently have to go talk to people who will hate me in order to save a guy from a lot of pain. Or a bunch of waterfowl. I never know with you people. And I don't even think he likes me very much."

"And save the city," Gwen reminded her, brushing past her toward the door. "Cheer up. It could be worse."

235

"Really?"

"Could be raining."

Zoë glanced outside at the sunny day, then thought of spending time in the sewer with the runoff of the grimy New York streets pouring down on her head. She finally had to laugh. "Fair enough. Here." She pulled a thumb drive from her computer and tossed it to the death goddess. "That's the book outline. Give it to Phil. If I don't live through this, then promote Morgen to take my place. She may not seem like she's got the skills, but I think she could carry this."

"Understood," Gwen said. "Good luck."

"Save it," Zoë said. "I am not really in the mood. I'll see you tomorrow at work, if I survive this."

"This is why he hired you, Zoë."

"No, not this part. I'm pretty sure he didn't hire me for this," she said without much venom, and let the death goddess out of the apartment. She followed her, locked her door, and as Gwen headed out, took a deep breath and went to knock on Arthur's door.

"I don't even know how I'm supposed to pass you off," Arthur said, casting an appraising eye at Zoë. He had put on his stained Public Works coveralls and tossed some weapons into a duffel bag. He had taken off his sling and tossed it inside the bag as well.

"Don't you need that?"

He flexed his arm and winced slightly. "It still hurts, but it's healing fast. I think whatever that Chinese stuff was helped, and the zoëtist did the rest of the work. It's impressive, I will admit."

"Anyway, let me worry about passing me off. I'll just introduce myself and be honest," she said, crossing her arms and leaning against the doorjamb.

236

He zipped the bag and sighed. "I can't think of any way that this is going to go well."

"Well, I don't know a lot about, uh, geases? Geeses?"

"Geasa," Arthur said absently.

"Sure, geasa. Whatever. I don't know much about them, but it sounded pretty serious."

He hefted the shoulder bag. "It is. I'm magically obligated to do what he tells me to, and I'm free once I'm done. And you heard what happens if I don't." He didn't look at her as he opened the door and waited for her to exit.

Their shoes echoed in the hall, a sound that always made Zoë think that she was being followed. "So what is the plan?"

"We have to go to the Department of Public Works first, and get a briefing and assignment for the day. With luck it'll be plain old sewer problems and not monster movement. I'll introduce you to my boss and my team. We'll drop the information about the zoëtist. If I'm not fired and you're not kicked out, we'll talk some more. I might get called away to take care of something, but hopefully it'll be a quiet night."

He didn't sound convinced.

APPENDIX:
Alternate Lifestyles

It's already hard to exist in the city as the most hated minority of all, so one would expect the auto-sexual, homosexual, pansexual, and budding coterie to have an even tougher time of it. But many humans may find it surprising that there's very little prejudice in New York. The coterie work hard to maintain balance in their associations with the humans, so much so that the sexuality of coterie rarely enters into any equation.

If you're looking to hook up or meet people, do what anyone would do, be polite, flirt, flash your colors, drool, or moan at your intended before engaging in any aggressive courtship. Unless your species is into aggressive courtship, that is. If they're into you, you'll know. If not, then move on. No one wants unwelcome advances. That's why they're unwelcome.

Please know that New York is rare in this respect. Places such as Columbia, SC, are completely intolerant to any coterie but the heterosexual, and on the flip side, Las Vegas, NV, and Celebration, FL, will accept only gay coterie. Alternatively, Santa Monica, CA, will accept only fae who bud, and the town forbids coterie sex entirely. ■

CHAPTER TWENTY-ONE

When they got to street level, Arthur swore and checked his watch.

"What?" Zoë asked.

"That argument made me lose track of time. I'll be late if I catch the bus."

"No problem," Zoë said. She stripped the choker from her neck and stepped around Arthur and raised it, trying not to grin when the cab screeched to a halt in front of her, incense wafting from the cracked windows.

"What...is that driving the cab?" he asked.

"That's Max. He's a demon. He helped us the other night, but you probably don't remember." She peered through the haze at the grinning demon. "Max, can you get us to the Department of Public Works?"

"Taking humans to Public Works? That'll cost you two fingers!" he said, glaring at Arthur's coveralls. Zoë just laughed and opened the door to the backseat.

"We're on a diplomatic mission. It's cool. I promise."

Max jabbed a taloned thumb at Arthur. "That one is diplomatic, you're telling me?"

Arthur raised his empty hands. "You obey the law and I'm just a passenger. Agreed?"

Max grunted, but allowed Arthur to climb in beside Zoë.

Zoë jerked backward as Max accelerated quickly, and grabbed

on to the door handle. "I'll vouch for him, Max. My boss needs me to deliver some information to his boss. If you eat him, then his boss probably won't be open to talking to me. And you might get your cab license taken away." She ignored the panicked look Arthur gave her.

"What's going on?" Max asked, perking up at the promise of gossip.

Zoë glanced at Arthur, who shrugged. "There's . . . apparently something big coming to town that could stir things up for both humans and coterie. My boss thinks that if we cooperate with Public Works, we can stop the threat."

"Man, I fuckin' hate Public Works," Max grumbled.

"Aw, just think of them like police. They just want to keep the peace," Zoë said.

"I fuckin' hate the police, too," Max said.

Max jerked the cab to the right and Arthur swore as the city disappeared. Zoë patted his arm awkwardly.

"I guess you didn't know about the Rat's Nest?"

Arthur ignored her. He pressed his face to the window as Max zipped through the tunnel, mumbling to himself. "How did they build this without us knowing? Are we above or below the sewer system? This is amazing!"

"There are spells hiding it from humans," Zoë said. "It has something to do with the rats. I'll be researching it for the book, incidentally."

They popped out of the Rat's Nest and Arthur made a disappointed noise as the cab tore down the street toward Public Works. It stopped on the corner with a lurch.

"This is as far as I go," announced Max.

"Thanks a ton, Max, I owe you," Zoë said. "Actually, how much *do* I owe you?"

His red eyes slid along the mirror to stare at Arthur, and Zoë realized that she was going to have to pay more for bringing an enemy into the car. She groaned inwardly.

"Twenty. And a write-up in your book."

She exhaled slowly. She'd been sure he'd ask for a finger again, only mean it this time. "Of course. No problem. I'll take care of it. Thanks a lot, Max."

The demon grunted as they climbed out. The cab peeled out, did a U-turn that nearly caused a bus to ram into a light pole, and disappeared in a cloud of smoke.

Arthur's eyes were still wide and dazed. Zoë punched him in his good arm. "Hey, wake up. We have a job ahead of us."

He shook his head and finally focused on her. "You don't understand. We know a lot about their culture, but we'll be the first to admit that we don't know half of what we should. There's over six thousand miles of sewers and tunnels in the city, and I know we can't watch all of it all the time, but I didn't know there were whole systems we didn't even know about."

"Well, they're designed for you to miss. Don't be so hard on yourself."

They headed up the grand steps of the Department of Public Works. Zoë eyed the tall marble pillars that seemed to loom in the afternoon sun. "I feel very small."

"You get used to it," Arthur said, heaving the massive brass and wood door open for her.

Zoë wondered if Arthur knew that his boss was coterie.

Ms. Fanny Hogbottom would have had a funny name, if you'd dared to laugh at her. She was six feet of solid muscle and curves that reminded Zoë not of a woman, but of an automobile. Zoë didn't know what she was, goddess or demon, but she was pretty sure the woman had an otherworldly quality. Her skin was dark black and her hair snaked around her head in cornrows that formed an intricate pattern. Her brown eyes were very wide and they did not blink.

Fanny crossed her arms under her massive breasts and stared at Zoë. She'd brought Arthur and Zoë into the office when Arthur had mentioned that Zoë had some news of a diplomatic nature. She closed the door behind them and cocked an eyebrow. "Why are you really here?" she asked, a hint of an accent on her tongue.

Zoë loosened her scarf to show her coterie pendant. "I assume you know what this is?"

Fanny nodded without changing her expression.

"I work for a publishing company that puts out travel books for visiting coterie. We want New York City to be a safe place for the coterie who visit as well as the resident humans."

"I still don't understand why you, a human, would spy on Public Works." Her voice was hard, and Zoë's hands started to sweat.

"This is not spying. This is being completely up front about my intentions," she said, hoping her voice didn't sound shrill. "I am doing research on Public Works, yes, partly to continue my own education in the coterie world, but also my boss, Phil Rand, a vampire, sent me here with a message for you."

Fanny sat down in a brown leather desk chair that squeaked ominously, as if warning that this was the last time it would stand for that kind of abuse. "A message from a vampire. I await this with considerable interest."

"I'm a human, so I've been trying to learn as much about the coterie as I can in the past few weeks. In that time I've uncovered things my boss says are signs of some bad stuff happening and he thinks you should know about it."

" 'Bad stuff,' " Fanny repeated.

God, did she ever blink? Zoë tried to drop the feeling of being in the principal's office, and soldiered on. "Apparently a high-level zoëtist is coming to town to stir things up."

Finally the woman blinked. "That's impossible. The balance has been maintained for a good forty years. How can one zoëtist cause such a stir?"

Zoë shrugged. "Like I said, I'm still learning about all this. I'm not even sure what zoëtists do. This woman" (she was loath to mention she knew Lucy) "is allegedly behind the spiking of zombie food with formaldehyde."

She waited, watching Fanny, but the woman didn't ask what that meant, so she continued. "A construct stole brains from the zombies at work, and we found out he had already been spiking the brains they did eat. Hunger and formaldehyde were behind the attack of the morgue worker and the jogger. We think. All I know is that I am to tell you to be on your guard for an increase in coterie activity when she gets here."

Fanny's eyes narrowed. "We are always on our guard. Do you know when she'll arrive?"

Zoë swallowed. "Tomorrow."

"And why should we trust you?"

Arthur leaned forward. "Ms. Hogbottom, I encountered Zoë when she was in the middle of the zombie uprising I reported last weekend. She fought bravely. She could have killed me any-time during that fight. Hell, she could have just let the zombies get me."

Fanny fixed her shiny eyes on Arthur. "And this boss? You've met the vampire?"

Arthur nodded. "He seems dedicated to keeping the balance of the city. And the fact that he's employed Zoë—who's there of her own free will, I'm certain she's not enthralled—is also a sign that makes me, if not trust him, respect him."

"When were you going to tell me that you had been speaking with a vampire?"

He didn't drop his gaze. "I just did."

"Wait in the hall, Arthur. I want to talk to this woman alone."

Arthur looked at Zoë, eyebrows raised, and she nodded. She had a feeling she knew what was coming.

"I'll be right outside," he said.

When the door latched behind them, Fanny relaxed visibly. Her head became rounder and her breasts swelled to become even larger. Her girth also increased, making her appear less strong and much more obese. She smiled at Zoë, her fat cheeks lifting. "That's better. Holding that shape all day isn't easy."

Zoë nodded slowly. "Please forgive my rudeness. I feel I should know you, but I am not sure who you are."

Fanny reached into a desk drawer and pulled out a pomegranate. She split it in half easily by twisting it. The juice ran down her wrists. "Few know my name anymore. And yet I'm worshipped more worldwide than nearly any other god these days." Her tongue snaked up her arm, slurping at the juice. "The only people who pray more than men in foxholes are women in labor. Or women trying to get pregnant."

"Then why are you heading up Public Works? Why aren't you an ob-gyn or something? You're a fertility goddess, right?"

"*The* fertility goddess, my little pomegranate. I been those. I been everything that creates. I got bored. People are comfortable around new life. It brings them the hope. So who better to infiltrate the humans' biggest coterie control organization than someone who puts them at ease?"

Zoë glanced at the door and laughed. "Arthur didn't seem comfortable around you."

Fanny laughed too, a booming, lovely sound. Zoë wanted to crawl into her lap and ask for a story. "Oh, the underlings don't need to be comfortable. Still, they're the best-trained humans to keep coterie under wraps, and when they look at me, they don't see me. That's the comfort I'm speaking of. I been in the maternity wards. Fertility clinics. Even television—the Learning Channel shows *A Baby Story* and *A Wedding Story* were my ideas. But I think mothering two children, humans and coterie, that hate each other is also a part of my job, and managing Public Works fits that well."

Zoë frowned, thinking of everything that had surprised Arthur in the past several days. "But shouldn't Public Works know everything about the coterie if you're leading them? Arthur didn't know much about zoëtists or the Rat's Nest."

Fanny laughed again. "They know what they need to know. When we need to discover the Rat's Nest, we will. I assume by the way Arthur was holding his arm that he got a zombie bite the other night? And he's doing all right now?"

Zoë's mouth fell open. "Yes, but—well, if you know a zoëtist can hold off the zombie curse, then why doesn't the rest of Public Works know it?"

Fanny frowned. "There are many reasons, my ripe orange. It's expensive. Not many can do it, not well, anyway. But mostly, when someone is bitten, they're usually devoured. There are very few simple zombie bites."

"Why don't you have a zoëtist on staff?"

"We have to police them too, and they don't want to be part of that. They'd be a pariah to their own kind."

Zoë sat back, feeling a little ill at the thought that people were dying because of money and the availability of health care. She guessed that problem was everywhere.

She focused on the matter at hand. "So do you believe me about the zoëtist coming to town? Will you do something about her?"

Fanny nodded slowly. "I believe you believe there's a problem. I also know that you're not as experienced with coterie as you'd like to think you are. You fear this woman on a level that you do not fear even your boss. I can smell it on you." Her nostrils flared and she inhaled with gusto. "You'd pee yourself if you got any more frightened. You're afraid of her for your own sake, not the city's."

Zoë's face flushed in anger and embarrassment. "I won't deny that, but my boss thinks it's a danger too. She's been messing with the zombies of the city. She made a construct specifically to antagonize me. People are dying, and zombies are dying, uh, again, because of it. She is dangerous."

Fanny stretched, her chair creaking loudly. "I understand that. Most of us are dangerous. We'll watch the usual zoëtist haunts: cemeteries, power stations. I'd put someone watching the airports, but is she coming into JFK or LaGuardia or Newark? What time is she coming in? Does she suspect we know she's coming and will therefore drive into the city instead?"

Zoë blanched. "I—I don't know." She could call Godfrey, but that was dangerous, because he might be with Lucy. And the idiot might still have Zoë's name programmed into his cell.

"Then we likely will have to wait and see. It is probably nothing. The city hasn't been threatened on a major level for—" Fanny stopped talking, and tilted her head as if she was listening.

"What's wrong?" Zoë asked.

She stood with a fluid motion, her body contracting, become smaller and more muscular. The lights flickered once, then twice, and the ubiquitous building hum that indicated air units and electric devices and computers stopped, and shouts of alarm came up in the hall.

"What's wrong?" Zoë repeated. "It's just a power flicker."

"Public Works doesn't get power flickers. If it happens to us, then something is wrong. Arthur!" The last part was a barking command, and Arthur ran inside the room.

"Get your friend to safety. Then get down the Blue Tunnel to watch the sewers. Send any team leads you come across in the halls to me. We are likely under attack."

He nodded once and grabbed Zoë's hand, pulling her out of the room.

"What's going on?" she asked as he pulled her down the hall, pausing to stop people and give them orders. Emergency lights illuminated the dark hallway as they ran forward.

"Something's messing with the electricity. Probably something in the sewers. I need to turn off the water to the building before they attack that, and see what's going on."

"I'm going with you."

He didn't even bother to stop and argue. He just kept pulling her. She tried to resist. "Arthur, you know I can handle myself, I can help you, let me go with you."

He ignored her until they were in front of the massive doors. He opened one of them, picked her up, and deposited her outside. "Go home. Be safe. I can't worry about you right now."

With that, he slammed the door in her face. She blinked, outraged. Outside, dusk was falling, and the city bustled along, completely ignorant of the panic going on inside the walls. Zoë shrugged and wrestled open the door, heading back into the chaos that was Public Works.

It was surprisingly easy to find the Blue Tunnel. She decided to find a sympathetic woman who had experience with male-dominated jobs. All it took was finding a low-level female employee and complaining that it was her first day and her team wouldn't let her follow them into the sewers, even though Ms. Hogbottom had ordered Zoë to shadow Arthur.

Fanny's word was law, and the woman, a young Korean desk clerk, could appreciate the implied sexism. After showing Zoë where she could get a new pair of coveralls, she pointed down a hall and instructed her to take the stairs down, and the third door on the right. Zoë nodded, thanked her, and followed her instructions at a run.

As she was counting the doors, Zoë shook her head. *Weapons cupboard*, a voice whispered, and she looked around in alarm. She was alone, but at the end of the hall stood a closed cupboard. She ran to it and opened it.

Hanging inside were an assortment of knives, swords, police batons, crossbows, and even a few guns. She wondered why they didn't use guns more often, but now wasn't the time to wonder about that. She grabbed a belt with two sheathed knives and strapped it to her waist. Three knives should be enough, she figured.

Someday I'm going to have to find out what that voice is, or if I'm going mad, she thought. *But not right now.*

Zoë had steeled herself for the sewers not to be wide, well lit from unknown sources, and clean, with some clear water cascading down the walls, as she'd seen on television. Television made the sewer look like an underground grotto that was a nice place to visit. But she was surprised by what she did find.

The tunnel was dry, clearly disused. Rusted rails lined the floor and she realized it was an old subway tunnel. She looked right and left and found Arthur and two other men spreading out across the tunnel, Arthur in the center, their backs to her.

One rat scrabbled softly past the men, stopping to sit on its haunches and regard her, then going back to all fours and running past her into the darkness. She turned and took a step, wondering if it wanted her to follow.

"So is it everything you dreamed of and more?" Arthur said from behind her.

Zoë bit her lip hard against yelling in surprise, which would just reward him. She turned slowly and smiled. "Well, it's dark and drier than expected. Throw in an uncomfortable backseat and you have my first sexual experience."

Arthur choked back laughter. "Seriously, Zoë, you shouldn't be here. I can't be responsible for you."

"No one asked you to be. I can handle myself," she said.

Arthur screwed up his face and put his hands on her shoulders and leaned in. "No. You don't understand. I am responsible for you. Phil put the geas on me. I can't have you injured; if so, the geas might activate."

"Oh."

"Yeah. 'Oh.'" He waved his hand, keeping his headlamp to the right so he didn't blind her. "I owe Phil my life. This is really a minor way to pay him back. Or it would be if Public Works hadn't fallen apart the minute you stepped inside." His eyes flicked to her, and she could tell he didn't trust her anymore. "So, seriously, for my sake will you go back up the stairs?"

One of the men called back to Arthur. "Hey boss, I think we got a leak down the bend."

"Hang on, Mel," he said over his shoulder, then focused his brown eyes on Zoë again. "Go," he repeated, and moved past her to his man. He stopped and Zoë couldn't resist stopping on the steps to watch them. From what she could hear, there actually was a leak. The men's lights played over several large water pipes stretching over their heads, one of them dripping water.

"Someone let a pet loose in the sewers again," Mel said, sounding relieved. "It's just a snake."

Zoë caught sight of it. "Snake" was an understatement. The beast was at least forty feet long and twined tightly around the pipe. It constricted, moved, and constricted again. Every time it squeezed, more water came out of the pipe as the stress fracture it had caused grew a little bit.

"You idiot, that's a water demon," Arthur said. "Don't touch it; part of it is wrapped in the power lines and it's constricting to split the pipe under it."

"Water and electricity. This could get ugly," said the second man.

"Only if it damages the wires. But you shouldn't touch it, to be safe," Arthur said. He turned around, and Zoë ran up the stairs before he could see her.

Back in the basement, she could hear the chaos above her, but the hallway was clear. She pulled out her cell phone and dialed Phil.

"Yes, Zoë?"

"I'm at Public Works. They're under attack by some big water demon, a snake thing, yellow. It's wrapped in the power lines and is breaking the water line."

"And?"

She sighed in frustration. "What is it?"

"Ah. I may have some idea. Tell me, which way is the demon heading?"

"What? How should I know?"

"Which way was its head pointing?" Phil asked patiently.

"Oh," she said, thinking. "North."

"And it's yellow and a water demon?"

"That's what they said."

He paused. "Without seeing it, I'd say that it's the demon Apep. Which isn't good."

A panicked shout came from under Zoë's feet, and she grimaced. "Yeah, I'm hearing that. It's attacking them. How do I stop it?"

"No, Zoë, it's not bad because it's dangerous. It's bad because it's a demon attracted to chaos. It's heading north to LaGuardia. It's going to be there when the zoëtist gets here."

"You know all of this?"

"Educated guess. There aren't a lot of yellow snake water demons. And we do have some chaos going on in the city. Just leave it alone, it just wants to watch the chaos."

From the sound below her, that wasn't an option anymore. "Phil, it's attacking the guys from Public Works. Or they're attacking it. How can I help?"

"They attacked first, I'm sure."

"Phil!"

He paused for a long time. She made an exasperated sound. "Fine," he said. "If you stab him with steel and leave it in him, it'll incapacitate him. But I can't promise what will happen when you take the knife out."

"Gotcha," she said, and hung up.

She took a deep breath, then headed for the door again.

The Shambling Guide to New York City

MANHATTAN:
Hotels

The sewers of New York are famous for housing everything from alligators to homeless. They also house the runoff water, and the dirt, grime, and sewage of the city. And New York is a big, dirty city.

This makes the sewers prime tourist areas for demons of all kinds, especially those who thrive on either human waste or just plain filth. Under Tenth Avenue you can find Mama Bloodstone's Hostel, a series of carved-out rooms run by a blood demon. But don't let her fool you, she's developed a taste for the sewers and not only is an excellent hostess, but also provides excellent suggestions for the best places for demons to visit in the city.

Corrupted river sprites have different sewer areas that they consider their territory, and will require a toll to move through them. Public Works tries to cut down on such bullying, but it's tough to maintain the peace underground.

Speaking of Public Works, they are frequent visitors underground, so if you encounter one, stay calm, stay peaceful, and don't be the one who attacks first. ■

CHAPTER TWENTY-TWO

Her first thought as she was running clumsily down the spiral stairs was that maybe she ought to tell Fanny. Then a roar shook the walls around her and Zoë dropped to her knees in a puddle at the bottom of the stairs, hands clasped to her head in agony. The roar seemed to go on and on, and ceramic tiles fell around her, a couple striking her shoulders. At that point she figured Fanny must already know.

The lights from the men's hard hats bobbed frantically as they fought in the increasingly wet corridor of the tunnel.

When the noise stopped, she got to her feet, dripping dirty water, and ran on toward the noise, albeit somewhat shakily. Her ears rang with punk concert–like abuse. The sound of her splashing feet seemed muffled and far away, as did the cries of Arthur and the other men.

When she reached where they had first seen the demon, it reminded her of the one time she'd taken LSD and gone out to a club. The demon had split the water line it had coiled around, causing a spray of water between her and the battle. The lights from the men's helmets danced around, causing a strobe effect, not staying still on anything long enough for Zoë to figure out what was going on. The only thing she could ascertain from the panicked shouts was that things were going very badly.

Briefly thankful that her nose confirmed that the water main that had split was a freshwater main instead of a sewer, Zoë ran through the torrent and focused on the scene in front of her.

A small part of her wished that she'd stayed up top to tell Fanny. This was not her fight.

Apep had captured one of the men in its coils and, from the pained look on his face, constricted tightly around him. Its tail whipped around to knock another to the ground, but he leaped out of the way.

Arthur battled the head, the short sword he'd taken from his abandoned duffel bag looking minuscule next to the snakelike demon's yard-long fangs, which it bared as it danced around, looking for a proper place to strike.

The demon's body bled in several places where the men had managed to wound it, but it seemed not to notice the cuts. Arthur's injured arm hung awkwardly at his side, and his sleeve was dark. Zoë hoped it was from the water in the sewer and not blood, but the light wouldn't help her identify it.

The men still hadn't noticed her. Zoë realized belatedly that they probably couldn't hear her, as they had been much closer to the demon when it had roared. Their hearing would be greatly muffled now.

The man in the demon's coils cried out again as the thing constricted, and Zoë took a deep breath and dashed into the fray.

The snake, thrashing as it handled three assailants, reminded her of a rickety carnival ride: exciting, unpredictable, and completely life-threatening. It had yet to notice her, and she ducked the tail and rolled as it whipped around for one of the men again, gritting her teeth at the pool of dirty water soaking her further. She came up on her knees, slicing her right shoulder on a dropped sword.

"Oh that was just smooth," she muttered.

"Goddammit, Zoë, get out of here!" Arthur had noticed her. His distraction nearly killed him, as the demon struck again, and he stumbled backward, falling into the water.

"You can't battle this thing!" Zoë said, aiming for the demon's midriff. Her attempt failed—it constricted again and her jab went into the water. The man groaned and slumped over—unconscious, Zoë hoped.

"What?" screamed Arthur, and Zoë remembered his ears had to be worse off than hers. She waved her hand at the snake hoping he'd understand that he had a bigger problem than taking care of her.

The tail whipped again, this time catching the third man and knocking him against the wall. He fell to the ground and didn't move.

"Well, that's just great," Zoë said. The massive demon had turned to fix her with its gaze now, and Arthur jumped forward, sword raised.

"No, wait!" she yelled, but he didn't hear her, or didn't care, and as he brought his sword down, the head whirled around and knocked him over. He tumbled, dropping his sword, and Zoë held her breath. He writhed in the water, and she allowed herself a moment of relief that he was still alive. She focused on the issue at hand and remembered what Phil had said. As the demon came around to face her again, she leaped onto one of its coils and immediately drove her knife deep into its body.

The demon hissed loudly, clearly enraged, but its body relaxed. The man it held fell out of its coils and slumped on the ground. Zoë let go of the hilt, leaving the blade in the body, and ran to the demon's head, which now lay flat on the ground, feet from where Arthur still groaned.

Zoë pulled off her necklace and put it in front of the demon's face. "Apep, do you recognize this?"

It hissed again, its paralyzed body lax.

"You don't speak English?"

It hissed again.

"Shit."

She looked at the demon again. Sudden uncertainty washed over her. "You are Apep, right?"

It hissed again. She wasn't sure what that meant, but she took it as a yes. It seemed completely relaxed. She ran over to where Arthur had just sat up, looking at her. He held his head in one hand, stemming the flow of blood from his forehead.

His helmet was beside him, the light illuminating the six-inch-deep water. Zoë put it on her own soaked head and removed his hand to get a look at his injury. "Looks like a nasty bump, but a shallow cut. You'll live."

He squinted his eyes and cocked his head. "What?"

"Jesus," she muttered. She raised her voice, "Can you hear me?"

"Barely," he said, his own voice raised.

"You're going to be OK. I'm going to check on the other guys," she yelled.

He looked around blearily. "Why are you here? I told you to get out."

"I'm not going to argue about this when I have to yell to communicate. We can argue when your hearing comes back."

"What?"

Zoë groaned and went to check on the other men, unconscious but alive, slumped near the lax coils of Apep. She finally let out the breath she'd been holding and wondered how many ribs—or other bones—they'd broken.

"Are they OK?" Arthur shouted, getting to his feet and lumbering over to her.

"Yes," she called, then gave a thumbs-up. "Well, they're alive, both knocked out."

Arthur bent over the demon's head. "What did you do to it?"

She moved close to his ear again. "This is the chaos demon Apep. Cutting him does no good, you have to actually stab him and leave the weapon in him. That paralyzes him."

He stared at her. "How in the hell did you know that?"

She shrugged. "I work with coterie. I think Apep understands that I'm trying to communicate, but I can't understand his hisses."

"Why would you want to communicate with it?" he asked, staring at her.

"Because I want to know what he's doing here."

"It was attacking Public Works!"

"Well, yeah, but Public Works isn't a bastion of chaos. Phil thinks it's here because the zoëtist is coming to do something bad."

"What's going on is attracting an Egyptian chaos demon? Jesus, that's big," he said. "We need to finish it off and then get some paramedics down here. How do we kill it?"

"Uh, all I know is you stab it to incapacitate it," she said. "Phil didn't tell me how to kill it."

"I don't suppose he would," Arthur said. "I don't know any snake who can survive being cut in half."

"No, wait, Arthur!" Zoë yelled, but it was too late. He raised his sword with his good hand and dug it deep into the demon's skin, cutting through and sawing. Apep, still incapacitated, hissed, but didn't move, making it simple for Arthur to have at it, hacking and sawing, making the black ichor fly, and finally making it through.

Zoë backed up. She didn't know what would happen, but she'd read enough mythology to guess. When Arthur had severed the two halves of the snake, the back half writhed in a way that turned Zoë's stomach over; it was the agonized writhing of the earthworms and garden snakes her grandmother used to attack with a hoe. But unlike those, this one didn't eventually stop.

"Arthur. Get out of the way!" But either he didn't hear her because of his ringing ears, or he chose not to hear the warning. He stood triumphant, covered in gore, watching the other half writhe. It was still dark, the haphazard light thrown off from the discarded hard hats casting bizarre shadows, but Zoë was pretty sure that Apep's other half was, like an earthworm, going to be just fine.

Admit defeat, go off into the shadows, Zoë thought as the headlamps played off an elongating snout, forming from the stump that had stopped streaming ichor. She ran forward and grabbed Arthur's sword arm. "We have to get out of here," she shouted, and saw his eyes were wide with shock.

Again, she thought of the people aboveground, and wondered why reinforcements hadn't arrived. She could go get them, but didn't want to leave the men. Arthur was the only one able— and he wasn't very much so.

"It's—" he said.

"Yes, you cut it in half and you made two fully functioning demons. You should try that with a cheesecake," she said, dragging him away. "We need to get the others out of here. It's going to be pissed."

"No. I'm finishing this," he said, and stepped forward.

She held him back. "How the hell do you plan on doing that? What if it's a god, what if it can't be killed, just pissed off more and more? You can incapacitate it indefinitely, but how will you kill it?"

He shook her off. "Then what do you suggest we do? We can't leave, we can't stay and fight, what can we—"

She didn't hear the rest of what he said, because the new Apep roared at them, and charged, slithering out of the shadows and rearing back like a cobra. He struck downward then, and Zoë pushed Arthur out of the way. The head knocked into her, and she felt as if she'd been hit by a car. She flew through the air and landed on something soft—quite soft—and bounced off, hitting the wall. She struggled to stand up, woozy from the fall, and realized she had bounced off the part of Apep that had been incapacitated.

Only now it seemed like a squashy Apap beanbag, and getting squashier as she watched it. She staggered around to the head, and saw the black eyes had lost their shine and had gone milky white. Was it dead, reincarnated in the new body? Her vision blurred; she must have hit her head pretty hard. She blinked and reached over to pull out the knife she'd stuck in the demon.

Not dead, the voice whispered, and she paused, wondering if she was going mad or if she had just hit her head too many times. She grasped the knife, but then Arthur's yell cut through the fuzzy feeling in her ears. She couldn't hear what he said, but she pulled the knife out and ran to him.

The new Apep lay, stabbed in the side, beside a panting Arthur.

When Zoë approached, he surprised her by putting his arms around her. "Are you OK?" he asked into her hair, and she was very aware of how dirty she was.

"I hit my head, but I think I'm OK," she said. "Are you?"

"Yeah, I got it after it hit you. We need to get someone down here to deal with this."

"And paramedics," she said, reaching up and gingerly touching the bump on his forehead again.

"So you don't listen at all, do you?" he asked, but for once didn't sound angry with her.

She shrugged. "I figured you needed the help."

"You dying down here would be...very bad," he said.

She laughed. "I can imagine. Tons of red tape for Public Works, and the fruition of whatever geas my boss has on you."

He frowned, not upset, but more studying her. He touched her cheek lightly. "Yeah. Red tape. That's the problem here."

Her heart hammered as he distinctly was not letting her go. His arms felt different from Godfrey's, and different from John's.

"Um," she said, cursing her awkwardness. She should have been smoother, but she had never before stood in a sewer, dirty and bloodied, covered in demon gore, and attempted a first kiss. She didn't know the etiquette.

"I can't figure you out, Zoë," he said, his voice soft. "You work for vampires, had an encounter with an incubus, and yet you're here trying to save us from a demon."

She blushed and looked away at the mention of John. "I just am trying to do my job and do the right thing at the same time. I can't help who my coworkers are, and my workplace doesn't have sexual harassment laws."

He grinned and took her chin to make her look at him again. "You think I never had an encounter with a succubus? They're dreadfully hard to fight when you treat them as a hostile. I can't imagine what it would be like to work with one."

"You don't want to," she said, shuddering.

"Let's get patched up and cleaned up. Then I would like an opportunity to figure you out," he said.

Was he asking her out? His grip did not relax. She smiled at him. "That works."

The door to the basement opened then, and he let her go. "Dammit," he murmured, but went to greet his coworkers.

"We need paramedics down here," Arthur reported.

"We had a zombie attack! Midday!" the man said. "I don't know what's going on anymore. And what the fuck happened down here?" He stared at the two demons, the broken water main, and the bodies of his coworkers.

"Immortal, regenerating water demon, near as I can tell," Arthur said. "Need to keep it impaled to incapacitate."

Zoë left him to do his report and went back to examine the first Apep. Had he sent his life force to his other half?

It seemed a little farther away than before, its ragged end still oozing where Arthur had cleaved it in two. She reached the head, which lay in the shadows. She had no chance to react when it moved quickly, its mouth opening and opening, and then closing over her.

Gross.

She couldn't breathe. The demon moved: she couldn't tell if it was moving quickly, but she could feel its muscles contract around her. She could barely move, stuck in the beast's esophageal tract. Its muscle constricted as it swallowed, and she groaned as she was crushed. Then it relaxed a bit, and she was able to move. Was she in its stomach? Was she being digested?

Did Arthur notice she'd been eaten? Was he fighting to stop this monster again, or was he worried about making a third incarnation?

She realized her hands were empty; she must have dropped her knife when it attacked her. She couldn't reach the knives at her belt. She struggled a bit, realizing that this was very bad. Her lungs began to burn.

One hand was stretched above her head, one down by her waist. The muscles around her constricted and she struggled in earnest now, moving farther down its gullet.

Her fingers brushed against the hilt of the second knife at her side. It was something. She threw her strength into slightly bending her wrist away from her so she could pull the knife free, and the blade slid along her leg, parting her jeans and cutting her. She paid no attention to the pain, focusing instead on using the knife before she passed out. Red blooms appeared behind her eyelids. Apep's muscles closed again, and she slid farther.

This time her hand felt cold air instead of hot snake. It hadn't healed fully; it was still open at one end. She finally maneuvered the blade away from where it dug into her left hip and sank it deeply into the snake's esophagus.

It relaxed around her. She had wiggle room now, and flailed her hand about in the air, trying to grasp onto anything to gain purchase to pull herself out. But even with the snake incapacitated, she still couldn't move easily, and she was starting to feel dizzy now, the need to breathe in starting to overwhelm her.

So close, she thought, trying to wiggle down the tight, slimy tube. The pounding of her head combined with the lack of oxygen won out, though, and as she was birthed in a disgusting wash of blood and bile, she hit the floor and passed out.

Safe to wake, now.

Zoë's eyes opened. She was lying on a pile of pillows, caked with goo and blood, and she smelled something oddly familiar.

"Coffee? I hear the kids like coffee these days. I get my tea from a nice gay incubus up top," the voice said. "Of course, he and his customers hate me. I think it's because sometimes I kill coterie for the Public Works. But I'd never kill a man who gave me good tea. Once he stopped giving me garbage tea in bags, we got along quite well."

Zoë blinked and focused on the overcoat and boots and little wrinkled face of Granny Good Mae.

"You saved me again," Zoë croaked.

"Well, I didn't save you so much as pick you up from your unique automobile. Very clever to have a demon bring you to the sewers, but I would have chosen one with a roomier interior," Granny Good Mae said.

"What happened?"

"You stopped your demon car in the sewers and I came across it when I was coming home. There was a hand waving at me, so I waved back, and then it waved again, and I thought to myself, I thought, 'Granny Good Mae, you don't wave twice at someone unless you're under the age of five, or you need help. And that's a woman's hand.' So I looked closer and then saw you come out of the demon. I carried you home." She looked appraisingly at Zoë. "You have some snake on you. But I don't mind. I'm just lucky I bought a coffee along with my tea. She told me to buy it, you know."

"Granny Good Mae?" Zoë asked dumbly. "Are you all right?"

Her brown eyes were wide. "Of course, poppet. Why?"

"You just don't sound like yourself, you're not as...coherent. Actually you sound like you did when I first met you."

"That could be because you have demon in your ears. Or it could be because I can relax more at home. Or because it's Thursday."

"It's Monday. Or Tuesday. I think," she said, trying to think. Right now, oxygen was her favorite thing in the world.

Granny Good Mae nodded. "She told me where you were and that I should find you. She likes you a lot. You're Life." She took out an ancient china set from a cardboard box and took the plastic lids off the coffee cups. She daintily poured some coffee into two little cups and handed one to Zoë.

Zoë struggled to sit up and accept the cup. "Where are we?"

"My home, honey!" Granny Good Mae looked surprised at the question.

They were in a small series of rooms lined with lightbulbs on cords, pillows on the floor, chests, a low table, a hot plate, and what looked like a sink from a workshop with a deep basin and U-shaped faucet. Some of the wall coverings were kitschy quilts, but others were fine silk. The place looked as if it had been decorated by several different ladies at once, or just one lady with several places to Dumpster-dive.

"We're still in the sewers?"

Granny Good Mae snorted. "I'd appreciate it if you referred to them as tunnels. Shit hasn't flowed through here in years." She covered her mouth and giggled like a girl who'd sworn without her parents around.

Zoë sipped her coffee. It tasted good, a mouthful of normal in the bizarre and painful hell that had dumped her, shat from a demon, injured in various places, into a homeless woman's quite cozy home, covered in blood and snake goo, drinking coffee from a cup that demanded her pinkie finger be raised in a ladylike way. She felt as if she were having a tea party with a girlfriend, considering how ragged they both were. It felt like a surreal game of pretend.

"Why do you keep rescuing me?" she asked. "I mean, I appreciate it and all, but every time I get into trouble, you're there. What's up with that?"

The older woman's eyes widened. "I rescue you because you need rescuing. Perhaps the question is why do you need rescuing?"

"Because I'm getting involved with coterie," she said, running her hand through her stiffening hair. She grimaced and wondered how soon she could get to a shower.

"And why did you get involved with them?"

Zoë snorted. "I needed a job."

"And why did you need a job?"

Zoë bit her lip. "I lost my job."

"And why did you lose your job?"

Granny Good Mae's eyes were wide with innocence. Zoë frowned. "How much do you know?"

"Just what *she* told me."

"Who is 'she'?" Zoë shouted, spilling her coffee on her pants. Her outburst surprised her.

Granny Good Mae looked sad. "I'm trying to keep you safe. She wants me to. I want me to. You're in a lot of danger, all the time. She talks to me, I talk to me, and I think she'd talk to you too, if you'd listen. She's my special friend, but she really likes you, too."

The pronoun mystery was making Zoë's head spin. She held her cup out and Granny Good Mae poured more coffee. "All right. I'll listen to her. And I am grateful."

Granny Good Mae looked satisfied. "I do like you. It's been a lonely life. Most of the time I have only her to talk to. I've been here in the tunnels for so long."

"How long?"

Mae screwed up her face. "Reagan. He was president. I was studying his security detail for leaks. I learned some things. I went to the hospital. I broke out and came here. I like it here better than the CIA."

Zoë had forgotten the woman's spy background. "You were in the hospital?"

Mae nodded. "They thought I was crazy. Me!"

Zoë blinked and looked away. "Can't see how they could do that." She drained her dainty cup. "Not that you haven't been a delightful host, and a heroic savior—again—but I should probably go see a doctor. Can you direct me to the surface?"

Granny Good Mae jumped up. "Of course I can! It's nearly ten o'clock, and the urgent care is still open. I'll take you to my friend Ben. He can fix you right up, and"—her voice lowered—"he has a back door."

The thought of walking to Ben's or even her own apartment made her want to cry, but she nodded. "Right. Let's go."

The Shambling Guide to New York City

MANHATTAN:
Cafés

Bakery Under Starlight, owned by the incubus Carl Boatwright, is a small slice of magic on Fifty-First and Eighth. Carl does all his own baking and most often works the register as well so he can have constant contact with his customers. Carl is an odd incubus; he doesn't feed off of pure sexual energy, but the passion people have for baked goods; this of course fuels his talent for baking, which is substantial.

His food caters mostly to humans, but some pastry-loving coterie can find plenty to eat there. Go for the croissants, stay for a latte, and be sure to take some muffins home. The interior is bright and sunny, not the most welcoming to many coterie, but he does stay open until late for the photophobic. ■

CHAPTER TWENTY-THREE

After forty minutes in the shower, Zoë was finally clean. She wrapped some gauze around her still-oozing shoulder, rewrapped the cut on her forearm, and frowned at the hole she'd gouged in her hip. The cut was quite deep, and there was no way a wound received in the sewer would heal cleanly.

Granny Good Mae sat on her couch, waiting patiently for her.

"Did you see if Arthur was home?" Zoë asked.

"He's not," Granny Good Mae said. "He's still at Public Works. They're working on the Apep problem."

"I wonder if they found the one that I was, uh, in."

"Oh, I doubt it. But I can assure you they're looking for it. Shall we take you to the doctor?"

Zoë sighed and looked at her bed, mournfully. She'd rather lie there and bleed. "I guess so, yeah."

Benjamin Rosenberg was busy, but he waved at Zoë and sent a colleague in to see her.

The doctor, a harried woman from Tennessee ("My name's Dr. Morrison but everyone calls me Becca Sue!"), tried to get out of Zoë what she had been doing in the sewers and if she was going to try to sue the city, but Zoë gave evasive answers until Dr. Morrison let it slide. The gash in her right shoulder needed twenty-three stitches and she would have a handsome scar. The one on her left hip was tougher, being too wide to suture. Dr. Morrison carefully packed it with gauze and taped it securely.

Dr. Morrison insisted—after finding out if Zoë was pregnant or not—on a course of both Cipro (for water-loving bacteria) and clindamycin (for gangrene bugs) to counter whatever nastiness Zoë had encountered in the sewer, and then she was released with an admonition to return in two weeks, rest, and keep her injuries clean.

Also to watch for severe stomach problems as a side effect of the drugs. Great.

"Thanks, Becca Sue," Zoë said as she left.

It was one in the morning by the time she left the urgent care clinic. She wanted nothing more than her bed, but remembered she should check in with work, and possibly Public Works.

"Took you long enough," Phil said as he answered.

"Thanks, I'm fine. Don't be so worried, you're embarrassing me."

"What happened to Apep?"

"We incapacitated him. Then Arthur cut him in two. Then he turned into two demons, and Arthur had to fight the other one. I got eaten by the first one, but Granny Good Mae saved me. Then I passed out for a while. Both Apeps are still in the tunnels, as far as I know, if you're worried about him." Zoë's voice was light.

Phil ignored her snark. "Where are you?"

"Just left Benjamin's clinic. I'm going to head to my place by way of a pharmacy. I've had enough adventure for the fucking day. I'm not going back out." She hung up the phone, surprised at her own anger. What the hell was she doing working for vampires and letting demons loose on the city?

Lucy arrives tomorrow night.

She didn't know if it was her own thought, or something else's, but she ignored it. Let someone else deal.

She found an all-night pharmacy a couple of blocks from her apartment and sat under the glaringly painful fluorescent lights as she waited for her medicine. She thought about Becca Sue and wondered what a country house-call kind of doctor was doing in New York City. Did the coterie have anything to do with it? Perhaps she was simply paranoid and seeing coterie wherever she looked. But she hadn't guessed wrong yet...

She paid for her meds, completely sure the pharmacist was a human, and felt better about her instincts. Which made her wonder again about Dr. Becca Sue. Phil might know. But she was damned if she'd ask him—she was tired of his know-it-all mentality. Even if he did know it all.

When she got to her apartment, she was so tired she didn't even think to knock on Arthur's door to see if he was home, to tell him she was alive.

Inside, all the blinds were closed and Phil sat on her couch, waiting for her.

"Shit," she said.

The vampire wore a heavy gray cable-knit sweater, looking like a slightly rounder version of a J.Crew model and not quite the bloodsucking fiend she knew him to be.

"You look like hell," he said.

She stared at him blankly as she locked the door behind her.

"You're not angry with *me*, are you?" he asked.

"I think I have a right to be a little angry with you," she said. "I entered this job to work for a publisher. I wanted to make books. I was looking to start a new life in New York."

He smiled. "Well, you certainly did that."

She flopped on her couch, wishing he would look a little chagrined or nervous or uncomfortable. He was so damn sure of himself. "I got eaten by a snake tonight, Phil."

"You're doing a good job. On the book, I mean," he said. "You have a meeting with the writers this afternoon at three."

She glared at him, then glared at her watch. Three thirty a.m. "So I don't get a day off to recuperate?"

"I moved it from eleven a.m.," he said mildly, as if he had done her a favor. "Besides, you got a couple of cuts. You didn't lose a limb or get turned or—"

"Fine, fine," she interrupted. "So I'm peachy. I spent most of the night in a sewer, and I'm nearly dead after getting eaten by a snake, and I'm exhausted and sleep-deprived, but still peachy. And I have a meeting tomorrow. Today. Whatever. Why are you here?"

"We need to prepare for tonight," he said. "We discovered she's coming into LaGuardia. We can go to meet her."

Zoë deflated. "Why me? Why do I have to stop her?"

"Because you're a target. Because she's messed with you and you want revenge. Because you know her better than anyone here."

"She's cold and ruthless. She cares more about owning something than loving it. She sees her husband as her property. She doesn't love what she has, but she'll be damned if she's going to let anyone else have it. And her concept of revenge is overblown and intense and apparently never-ending. There. You know everything I do. I'm exhausted. And I'm hurt. I can't fight anymore, Phil."

She leaned her head back on the couch and her eyes fell shut.

She's threatening you. And your city.

"And I'm damn tired of whatever voice is in my head," she grumbled to herself. She took a deep breath and opened her eyes.

"All right. There's a deli on the corner. They open at six. I'm going to take my antibiotics and about ten ibuprofen, and make some tea. Then I'm going to lie down on my bed and get a nap. After the deli opens, you are going to call them and order me a Reuben with horseradish and a large coffee. I need food and caffeine to keep going. After I have eaten, we can head to the office and I will meet with your writers. And then we'll face Lucy."

"Why the change of heart?"

"Because I'm a fucking bridge," she said, exhaustion making her sound and feel drunk. "I needed to help Arthur fight Apep because he didn't understand the demon. And I have to help you fight Lucy because you don't understand her. You both need me. And I need the two of you like I need a punch in the throat. Christ, Arthur hasn't even checked to see if I'm dead or alive. Whatever. I'm going to go to sleep. Wake me when there's a sandwich."

She wondered if he'd balk at the orders, but he said, "Done."

She went to the kitchen and made herself some of the strong restorative tea Granny Good Mae had recommended, then took her medicine with the scalding tea, ignoring the pain in her mouth, since it was completely outclassed by the pain of her other injuries.

Her bed beckoned her, and she gratefully lay down on it, dozing off immediately. The food arrived all too soon, and she sluggishly ate her sandwich while Phil watched.

She downed the coffee, changed clothes, and got her coat, the knife from Public Works she had managed to keep, her painkillers, and her travel mug. Why did her days seem to mush together with pain and sleep deprivation?

She ushered Phil out, locking the door behind her. "How are we getting you to work?" she asked.

"I'll take the Rat's Nest," he said. "There's an entrance in the basement of your building." With that, he headed toward the stairs.

"How does he know...never mind," Zoë muttered, heading out into the December gray.

Before the writers' meeting, Zoë sat down in Phil's office.

"LaGuardia's not a small airport, you know," she said. "If you don't know where she's coming in, it's going to be hard to be in the right spot."

"We can narrow it down to flights from Raleigh."

"Or Richmond, or Charlotte, or Atlanta, or Philly," Zoë said. "Raleigh-Durham doesn't fly direct to a lot of places. Believe me, I've gone way north to go way south before. How did you figure out she was coming at ten, anyway?"

"Public Works keeps tabs on incoming coterie to the airport. But she's managed to stymie them, and they don't know her flight number. But they know she's coming in tonight, and besides, Gwen said there's going to be a lot of death at the airport tonight," Phil said. "Around ten."

"That's what you're going on? That's it? You don't think it's a terrorist plot, or a disgruntled worker?"

Phil cocked an eyebrow at her. She sighed. "Oh all right, believe the goth goddess. You've not been wrong yet. Dammit."

A rare smile crossed his lips. "Oh, I'm sure I'll make a bad decision at some time. I have in the past."

"I hope I'm there when it happens," she grumbled.

Phil and, for some reason, John attended the writers' meeting. Zoë felt herself nodding off during, and she pinched herself. She caught John looking at her, eyebrows arched, but he had fed recently and looked more like a nebbish and less like a Narcissus. She still got a definite sense that he would be quite happy to pinch her, or bite her, or whatever, but her desire sat in her stomach like a surly lump of coal.

It was an odd feeling, realizing he'd fed on someone else, inspired someone else to dizzying lust. She knew he was bad news, but still the feeling that he inspired that in all women, and would sleep with anything that would sustain him, was bitter. But also eye-opening.

He's no better than any other bad boy. Or bad publishing-house CEO. I need a nap. Then I need to get laid. Too bad all the men in my life are way too complicated.

She was grateful when it was her turn to speak so she could focus. She went through the book outline and was astonished to see the impressed and interested looks on her coworkers' faces. She covered the assignments and set up the timeline for the book, taking into account new hires. Phil nodded slowly as she presented, and when the meeting was over, asked her to stay.

"You've really done a good job," he said.

She didn't look up from gathering her notes. "Good, I'm glad you liked it."

"Why don't you take a nap in your office? We can head to the airport at seven."

"Sure, whatever."

Phil looked at her for a long moment, then left the conference room. She sighed, so tired she wanted to weep, and trudged to her office. She locked the door, spread out her coat on the floor, and lay down.

She had one moment to realize she was going to sleep with vampires, zombies, and 'buses on the other side of the door, but then realized she was too tired to care.

A couple of hours later, Morgen woke her up with a little splash of water. "Come on, sunshine. Man, you humans sleep a lot."

"Not enough," Zoë said, wiping her eyes. "Ugh. Where did that come from?"

Morgen grinned. "Not telling."

"What's going on?"

"Ben is here, he's going to help us with the airport."

" 'Us'?"

"Yes! I'm going too! It sounds like fun!"

Zoë groaned as she sat up. The pain meds had worn off. "Can you get me some water?" she asked. "Real water, I mean," she amended, and Morgen traipsed down the hall.

When she returned, Zoë took some more painkillers and then left her office to find Phil and Ben. They sat in the break room, talking in low voices.

"You guys realize you're on stage?" she asked. They looked up.

"We're going over our plans," Phil said.

Zoë shrugged, then winced as her stitches pulled. "Do we know what we're going to do?"

"I bought us tickets for a flight to Philadelphia to get us through security," Ben said. "We're each heading in with one carry-on."

"And that's where we keep the weapons? Good plan, they'll never suspect that," Zoë said.

Phil and Ben exchanged looks. "There are ways to get weapons in the airport," Phil said. "But I have my own abilities, as does Benjamin."

Zoë groaned. "And I'm bait."

The Shambling Guide to New York City

HARLEM:
Live Music

Dark, smoky bars are perfect for coterie who still enjoy a good single malt or a bit of live music. Bloomberg's ban back in 2003 killed a lot of establishments that were quietly coterie-friendly, but that's slowly eroding. The popular Play It, on Lennox Avenue, is currently a private club that allows only coterie as members. The cost to join is four blood tokens or 245 hell notes per year. Visiting coterie can buy a week's pass for twenty-five hell notes.

For those who enjoy live music, especially jazz, the open mic night on Thursdays is very popular with the musically inclined.

It should go without saying that these bars are not recommended for air sprites or any coterie who rely on pure air. ■

CHAPTER TWENTY-FOUR

Zoë and Morgen carried backpacks full of blankets, and Phil carried a briefcase. Ben lugged a full duffel bag and made it through security without incident. Once they had put their shoes back on, Phil went down the hall with long strides.

"Look, can you just slow down a second?" Zoë asked, putting her hand on Phil's shoulder. She might as well have tried to stop a truck rolling in neutral. He didn't pull away violently, it was just that he wasn't going to stop because of her hand alone.

She ran for a second to catch up, limping a little due to her hip. "We don't know where we're looking. We aren't armed to prepare for this. What are we going to do? Somehow force them to circle the city and not land, or close down all the shops selling 'I heart NY' shirts to foil their tourist attempts?"

Phil moved on with purpose, and Zoë swore and followed. He paused at the door of the American Airlines Gold Members' Club door, pulled out a card, and swiped it.

"You're going for exclusive peanuts and gin when we have a monster to catch?" she asked, following him. Phil paused inside the door and she ran into his back.

He turned swiftly and suddenly his head was by her ear. She hadn't seen him move. "I will remind you that word is offensive to my kind. It's also a misnomer, as you're hunting a human. Regardless, don't use it in here, or else you may regret it."

She nodded once. "I'm sorry," she managed to say, but he had

already moved away from her. Morgen looked at her sympathetically, and Ben just moved past them silently.

The room was like the lounges Zoë had seen through open
doors in airports, but much darker. A hulking demon stood
behind the bar, a highball glass jammed onto one giant red hand
as she dried it with a dish towel. Her skin was a reddish purple,
and spikes jutted from it around her eyes and mouth.

They were alone in the bar. Couches of all sizes lined the
walls, and Phil chose a table near the wall and leaned back as if
he didn't have a care in the world.

A wispy air sprite floated up to them. "Hello, can I get you
anything or did you bring your own?" He looked pointedly
at Zoë.

"God, are people always going to assume I'm your meal?" she
asked, giving the waiter what she hoped was a haughty look.

Ben and Zoë ordered coffees. Morgen ordered water. "Nile,
pre-pollution if you have it, please."

Phil placed a hell note on the table. "A negative, Irish descent,
please," he said to the waiter, and then, "and access to the vault."

The waiter's eyes sharpened. "Reason?"

"I have reason to believe a zoëtist is arriving in the next half
hour who is a real threat to the city. I need to stop her. I have no
intention to get on a plane; she's coming here."

"Are you willing to accept a geas placed on the weapons?" the
waiter asked.

"I am," Phil said without hesitation.

The waiter nodded once and turned to float toward the bar.
He whispered something to the barkeep, who pulled a thick glass
of blood for Phil and loaded a tray up with the other drinks. She
handed the tray and a key to the waiter, who drifted back to
where Phil, Morgen, Ben, and Zoë had seated themselves on a
couch.

"Each weapon holds a geas," the waiter said. "Taking a weapon on the plane or giving the weapon to a human will cause violent vomiting. This is only for protection within the airport."

Zoë's eyes widened. "Wait, does this mean I can't get a weapon?"

The waiter didn't look at her. "No humans can touch these. Well, except for the business end, of course."

Phil frowned. "This is my colleague. She's capable of holding her own."

Zoë appreciated that, even though she felt far from able to hold her own, or anyone else's.

"That's not my problem," the waiter said, and then added, "sir."

Zoë snorted at the title. "So what am I supposed to do? Can I have a bar stool to throw?"

The waiter finally deigned to look at her. "Furniture stays here."

She made a face. "I bet if I had a vacuum cleaner you wouldn't be so high and mighty."

Phil put a hand on her shoulder and she winced. "Relax. We will make do. Thank you for your help." He handed the waiter a hell note. The waiter nodded and floated away. Phil drained his glass and seemed to grow warmer next to Zoë. She held back a shudder.

"I'm ready. Let me get a weapon and we can go."

Morgen sat back in the plush seat. "Dang, I just got comfortable."

"Do you want a weapon, Morgen?" Phil asked.

The sprite shrugged. "Never been good at using them. I'll be fine."

Phil nodded and unlocked a door on the wall next to them.

"Do you know yet how we're going to find her?" Zoë asked.

Phil pulled out two ceramic daggers. "I think she will make herself known to us, Zoë. It won't be a worry." He stuck them into his belt and covered them with his sweater. He looked at Ben. "Are you ready for this?"

Ben shrugged, looking very small in a too-large overcoat. "I studied the mystic arts under Rabbi Dansky in Newark, I covered golem creation and some zombie raising and curing of the curse, but Dansky wanted me to be well-rounded, so he sent me to Louisiana." His eyes were far away. "It was rare I found someone to teach me; zoëtists of different schools didn't mix. Even though they usually respect one another, they each think their own school of thought is superior. It was hard getting training from another school's master, but I found a shaman who had been betrayed by her apprentice and decided to pass her secrets along to a willing Jew. She died before I got fully trained, murdered by her former apprentice. She came after me then, and that's how I met Lucy.

"She was ruthless and cold and frankly terrifying. She learned how to make horrific flesh golems out of body parts instead of good clean golems out of the elements. I don't know what else she's studied."

"That sounds like Lucy," Zoë said.

Phil checked his watch. "Let's go."

"So you can't sneak a weapon to me?" Zoë asked.

"No. You will stay out of the fighting this time."

"Sure, I'm the bait and everyone will respect your wishes, right?" She rolled her eyes and stepped through the Members' Club door back into the airport. "This is just turning out to be awesome."

"Isn't it? Are you getting information about the lounge for the book?" Morgen asked.

"Research? Now?" she asked incredulously.

"Always do research, Zoë. Always learn," Phil said as they started walking up the concourse.

When they got outside, Zoë froze. She tried to make herself very small and unobtrusive, even though she had no bags and no typical harried traveling face. Still, the couple didn't look her way as they walked past, and she let out a breath.

"What's wrong?" asked Morgen.

Zoë watched Godfrey and his horrid wife walk away, and took another deep breath.

"They're here," she said.

"How are we going to stop them? What's your grand plan?" Zoë asked. Ben answered her by walking to the center of the concourse and dropping his duffel bag by his feet. He unzipped it and held his hand over it like a puppeteer holding a marionette whose strings have just been cut.

Lucy, her back ramrod-straight, five eight without heels, hair sleek and brown, stopped, then turned around. She stared at Ben, who suddenly seemed to be a small milquetoast of a man with glasses, drab brown hair and a *bow tie*, for God's sake. Recognition and loathing were scrawled on her face, and Zoë felt the desire to hide behind Phil. She stood off to the side, but Lucy didn't acknowledge her.

Next to her was Godfrey, trim and as sleek as she was, sharing in the aura of money and power around them. But he always seemed a bit diminished next to her. He looked at her, frowning, then at Ben.

"What's wrong? Who is that, Lucy?" Godfrey asked.

"Stay out of this," she said, and then her manner melted and she got the syrupy sweetness that frightened Zoë more than her wrath. "Benjamin," she said, "it's so good to see you. It's been a long time. What was it, Louisiana, 1996?"

"Something like that," Ben said. "Why are you here, Lucy?"

"I'm here with my husband on business." She smiled, showing all of her teeth. "Are you on your way out of town, or arriving?"

He ignored the question and kept waving his hand at the duffel. "Business. I figured. You do know you're not welcome here, right?"

Godfrey looked completely lost, but showed relief at finally having something he understood: an insult to respond to. "Now wait a minute. We were invited. Who is this prick, Lucy? Do you know him from college or something?"

"Something," said Ben, and grinned. "He doesn't know, does he, Lucy?"

"He's not that bright," she said, as if Godfrey weren't there.

"What the hell does that mean?" Godfrey asked, stepping away from her, the hurt plain on his face.

"Just turn around and go back to Raleigh," Benjamin said. "Whatever you have planned here can't happen."

She laughed. "You're going to stop me with your little Jew men made of Hebrew mud?"

"Lucy!" Godfrey said, clearly shocked that his wife could say something bigoted.

"If I have to," he said.

Zoë glanced around. A couple of people were glancing sidelong at them in a clear "frightened but don't want to get involved" manner. A desk clerk stared at them as she talked rapidly into a phone.

Airports are different, she reminded herself. *People are programmed to ignore coterie, but also programmed to spot anything weird in airports.*

Godfrey took Lucy's elbow. "Look, I don't know what's going on here, but an airport is not where you want to have an argument. Let's just get out of here."

She shook him off. "Stay out of this."

"Are you leaving this city or not?" Ben asked, his voice high and impatient.

She took a step closer to him. "No. I plan on making this city mine, Benjamin. You can have New Jersey if you turn around right now and don't mess with me. Tuck your tail between your legs and go if you want to live."

Ben took a small pad of paper out of his pocket. He scribbled something on the top sheet.

Lucy laughed again. "We're really going to do this? Here? You're challenging me?"

He nodded. "I can't let you out of the airport, Lucy. Turn around, or face my golem."

"Golem? What the fuck is a golem?" Godfrey asked.

Lucy waited, a small smile on her face, as Benjamin took a water bottle from a pocket of his duffel and upended it into the main pocket. He then dropped a yellow sticky note into the bag. A small cloud of dust puffed out, and despite his confusion, Godfrey leaned forward and looked at a little puddle of mud in the middle of a large collection of dust.

"I'm getting security. That might be a chemical weapon," he said. "Let's get out of here, Lucy."

He took her elbow again and tugged, but she didn't move. She looked as if she were made of iron: every muscle tensed, sweat broke out on her upper lip, and she kept that same serene smile. He tugged again and she stayed rooted to her spot.

"Luce?" Godfrey asked in a small voice.

Ben said something then in a different language—Hebrew, Zoë guessed—and the mud inside his bag began to move. Tendrils that quickly formed into digits grasped the zippered opening of the bag, pulling it wide to allow a much larger lump, a head, to rise out. It twisted briefly to birth its shoulders, then rose faster. The piece of paper stuck to its forehead fluttered as it took full form, finally a rough, sexless human shape. Benjamin held his hand out, guiding it, and it stepped out of the bag.

Zoë took a step back into Phil, who watched with what appeared to be distracted interest. Someone screamed behind them. A couple of people had caught sight of the mud man and were backing away.

More screams came from their left; a US Airways representative was running away from the check-in desk, which had begun to shift as if a great hand had grasped it and was working it free like a loose tooth. It shifted to the left, then the right, and then the whole thing moved. It turned on its side, spraying pens and papers and two computer terminals onto the ground. Four chairs uprooted themselves from the floor and slid over to the desk, where they attached themselves—two at the bottom corners, two on the sides. The bottom chairs worked their way under the desk until they supported the mass of it on their eight legs, and then began to lurch forward like a child's design made with white glue and whatever could be found.

It looked like a bizarre man with chairs for legs and arms. It reached out with the chair legs and wrapped them around a computer monitor on the undamaged desk behind it—the monitor showed one large symbol that looked Hebrew—and placed it on its "shoulders," completing the grotesque golem.

Godfrey had nearly lost his mind. Gibbering, he backed away from his wife. People around him screamed and ran, and a smudge of blue—security uniforms—dashed toward them. Someone slammed into Godfrey and he fell, raising his arms to shield himself from the stampede.

"Hell," Zoë said, and ran over to him. She elbowed several people out of the way with her good arm and provided a shield so Godfrey could take her hand and get to his feet. She pulled him out of the stampede, running into people as she wrestled him back to the calm corner where Phil stood.

She put her hands on her hips. "I thought your wife was just controlling and demeaning, Godfrey. You didn't tell me she was a zoëtist."

He gaped at her. "Zoë?" His eyes fell on Phil, who watched the action with no surprise, but with great interest. "Who's that guy?"

APPENDIX:
Travel

Perhaps the strongest spell in New York City is the one governing air travel. Before computers, the spell merely forced all airplanes containing coterie to stop at the same terminal in LaGuardia, but after computers, gremlins had to be hired by Public Works to get into the ticketing and air traffic software to track incoming coterie. It usually works, but isn't 100 percent accurate; it mostly keeps the city in balance.

Public Works, of course, doesn't trust the job the gremlins did, considering that, well, they're gremlins, but the software and spell have worked well thus far, so there's little they can do to investigate. The software is tested frequently.

With the new software, coterie have more options, including the previously closed JFK and Newark airports, but many still use LaGuardia because it's best equipped to deal with coterie eccentricities.

That said, enjoy LaGuardia when you arrive, and know you're surrounded by your fellows. ∎

CHAPTER TWENTY-FIVE

In a way it was gratifying, learning that the ultimate evil that threatened New York was also the ultimate evil in her life. It made things feel *tidy*, somehow. It wasn't gratifying or tidy to have to save Godfrey's ass, though.

And the airport terminal was anything but tidy.

Godfrey looked confused to see her, and there was even an element of hurt outrage in the way he demanded to know who Phil was.

"Now really isn't the time to explain," Zoë said. "We need to get out of the way of the zoëtists."

"The what?" Godfrey said.

She took a deep breath and pointed to the action. "Just watch."

While Godfrey made confused noises, Zoë stared, transfixed, at the massive golem, now fully animated, that had reached Benjamin's mud golem. It reared back with its chair arm and swung at the mud man. Benjamin's golem leaped aside, surprisingly nimble, and dodged the blow, which crashed into the wall.

The chair stuck in the wall, and the US Airways golem struggled. The mud golem took advantage and attacked. Zoë couldn't see how mud would beat metal and plastic, but he grew larger and engulfed the other golem, seeping into the fabricated joints and expanding. The golem's free arm flew off, finally forced away from its body.

"Stupid move," Morgen said to Phil. "She can just reattach

it. I thought you said this guy is a good zoëtist?" The vampire shrugged.

"Zoë, can you tell me what the hell is going on here?" Godfrey asked, hysteria making his voice rise to near-screeching levels.

"Your wife is a zoëtist, Godfrey. She can make life where there was none. She can raise zombies, create golems out of inanimate objects, stuff like that. She's here for some sort of big mayhem, and that guy, Benjamin, is also a zoëtist, and is trying to stop her. Incidentally, so are we. And—" She cut herself off as a tall, striking man with glasses caught her eye and she swore as she saw Arthur calmly searching through weapons in his backpack.

And security was getting closer, fighting against the rapids of panicked travelers.

"What are we going to do?" she asked Phil, who watched the battle closely. "We can't really fight those golems."

"It's a golem battle, like a cockfight! It's awesome," Morgen said lightly.

"But this is not what she came to do," Phil said, finally appearing to join Zoë in her concern. "This is minor chaos. We need to find out what she's really here for. Right now we're just in her way."

"My wife is here for a meeting with the NYPD. And who the hell are you?" Godfrey asked.

Phil ignored him.

The US Airways golem had freed its remaining arm from the wall and was beating its own chest, removing mud but not doing much to stop the mud from expanding within it. Its metal-and-plastic body began to crack in places, spewing mud like water from a breaking dam.

Zoë frowned. Benjamin watched the battle from several feet back, clearly concentrating on it, but at nowhere near the level of stress and concentration Lucy exhibited. She was absolutely still, sweat streaming down her face and making runs through her makeup, and her hands were fashioned into claws that shook very slightly. She looked as if you could hit her with a baseball bat and she wouldn't even stumble.

"Phil, why is she—" she began, but at that point, the US Airways golem's hollow plastic chair arm exploded, sending mud and plastic and metal shrapnel in all directions. The screaming began anew as injured people fell, and Zoë saw Arthur go down.

Without thinking about it, she ran out into the throng of people, dodging and pushing to get to Arthur. She dropped to her knees beside him.

A large piece of mud-covered plastic was imbedded in his left shoulder, several inches from his heart, she was glad to notice. His face was screwed up in pain.

"OK, you've got a rather large piece of plastic stuck in your shoulder. Are you hurt anywhere else? And what the hell are you doing here?" she asked, running her hands lightly over his arms and legs, trying to detect more injuries.

"Zoë?" he gasped. "I thought you were—"

"Hush. I'm fine, just got eaten for a little while last night. I preferred it when the incubus did it, frankly."

His pain-filled eyes focused beyond her. "Behind you," he whispered.

She turned, confused, in time to catch the full force of the golem's kick with its chair leg. She tumbled backward, landing on her left arm. Something snapped, and pain flared, bright and beautiful.

"Bitch!" screamed Lucy.

I guess she finally noticed me. Zoë propped herself up on her right elbow from where she had fallen. Arthur's eyes had closed.

"Arthur!" Zoë's yell brought him out of his daze. "Dammit, Arthur, wake up!"

The golem was moving more slowly, its insides still filling with the muck. Ben was trying to conjure up another mud golem, but was having trouble collecting the scattered mud.

"Arthur, how do I kill this thing?"

"Get rid of the character on its head! Wipe it off!"

"What?" she said in confusion.

"On its head should be a Hebrew character! You have to get rid of that, that's where the power is coming from!"

She looked up and saw the character on the monitor head, written in ASCII. It wasn't really something she could rub off.

She was about to ask Arthur for more info, but he was surrounded by three Homeland Security agents, one man pointing his gun at him, the other two demanding the golems stand down. *They really can't even comprehend those aren't people. Or even alive.* Other agents had Ben and (she sighed in relief) Lucy, in their sights, demanding they lie down on the ground. Phil, Morgen, and Godfrey blended into the crowd, safe for now.

But as one, nearly all the people looked up as the shriek of bending and tearing metal and falling roof tiles distracted them. Part of the ceiling was ripped away, revealing the chilly December evening. A gargantuan hand reached through the hole, fashioned apparently from several baggage carts that looked like motorized rooms that zipped from plane to plane. It was followed by the apparent head, fashioned from an Embraer E-Jet, which peered in at them, the windshield and cockpit achieving the characteristics of a face.

Zoë squinted and could just make out a Hebrew character on the plane's windshield, written in blood.

The immediate threat, beyond the guns and the giant golem tearing up the ceiling, was the smaller golem that still menaced her. How was she going to wipe computer characters from a screen?

Arthur was useless to her; security officials surrounded him. The trudging golem drew back for another kick. Then it paused as the huge mama golem of this little baby brought its arm closer. The security that surrounded Arthur yelled in alarm. One cut and ran, two more raised their guns and began firing at the airplane.

"Zoë!" Arthur shouted and with strength she hadn't known he had, he tossed her a short sword. It landed about five feet from her and skittered across the floor to rest beside her. She hissed as she tried to sit up—her left forearm lay useless and she was pretty sure she'd torn some of her new stitches—but the sword slid out of her reach.

Zoë flinched as the kick came forward, but opened her eyes when as a gush of water hit the golem's head at fire-hose force. It staggered back, but the water didn't drip off like normal water; it slipped between the cracks and then the monitor screen showing the ASCII art blew outward, extinguishing the letter that gave the golem life force.

It fell apart with no ceremony, and Zoë twisted awkwardly to avoid the falling chairs and monitor. The water streamed from the monitor and formed itself into a very satisfied Morgen.

"That was fun," she said, helping Zoë to her feet.

"I owe you one," Zoë said, and then stumbled over to where Arthur lay. She pulled him, wincing, upright. The security agents had backed up and taken cover behind another ticketing desk and were still firing at the airplane.

"You OK?" asked Arthur.

"Nope. You?" she replied.

He laughed weakly. "Nope. What the hell is that thing?"

"That is what happens when a master zoëtist gets mad, I think."

The plane reached its baggage-cart arm inside the airport and casually brushed the people firing at it aside. They flew back as if hit by a truck. It moved its arm more slowly toward its master, Lucy, who had finally relaxed. Zoë realized that the first golem had been a distraction while she constructed the bigger one outside. She must have had a minion in the airport who killed the pilot for her.

Shit. She planned this. This is her first step in fucking with the balance. It has nothing to do with us.

Lucy moved to get into the baggage area of one of the carts.

A movement caught Zoë's eye—Phil had emerged from the bathroom, knife in his hand. He lifted his arm to throw it at Lucy, but Godfrey ran up and plowed into him.

"That's my wife!" screamed Godfrey, and Phil's throw went wide, but only by inches. The knife twirled across the concourse and buried itself to the hilt in her upper arm.

She hissed, which scared Zoë more than anything else—the knife in her arm made her angry, not frightened or worried. She didn't even show pain. She threw herself into the baggage cart, and the golem lifted her—bullets pinging off its metal skin—and trudged away.

"The plane. It was full of people," whispered Arthur.

The horror of the situation was interrupted by the swift movement of Phil as he snarled and sank his teeth into Godfrey's neck.

The Shambling Guide to New York City

APPENDIX:
Getting Around

The Coterie Council offers shambling tours of the city, one in each borough, and you can find out more when you register your trip with the city.

Coterie taxis will stop for anyone and travel the Rat's Nest, a labyrinth under the city, making for a quick journey. Limited paths within the Rat's Nest are open to walking tours; most are accessible through building basements.

Buses are not recommended for anyone but the most human-looking coterie.

And creating golems for transport, or war, is strictly against the law. ■

CHAPTER TWENTY-SIX

Zoë ran, holding her broken arm to her side, fighting the nausea the pain caused. She grabbed the vampire by the ear and yanked hard.

Granny Good Mae had taught her that. The smallest parts of the body can cause extreme pain when pulled, tweaked, pinched, or just plain ripped. But Phil didn't budge; his drinking of Godfrey—clearly out of rage and spite—was zealous and unstoppable.

Zoë glanced about. The Homeland Security guys were still firing their weapons at Benjamin's golem, the departing plane golem, and the check-in desk that was once a golem, and Arthur was staggering on his feet. Morgen just watched, delighted at the excitement. Zoë didn't want to kill Phil, but she had to get him off Godfrey.

Something sparked in her memory—the geas on Phil's weapon—and she reached out to his belt and closed her hand on the hilt of the dagger sticking out—the forbidden dagger, the one she wasn't supposed to touch.

Phil staggered backward, vomiting forth a gout of blood. He fell to his hands and knees, retching, and Zoë jumped back to keep out of the mess. Vampires eat only one thing, after all, and Phil had eaten twice that night. Godfrey also fell, sprawling in the gore, his neck bleeding freely.

Zoë fought the rising bile in her throat and ran to his side, pulling off her scarf and pressing it to his neck.

He looked into her eyes with fright and confusion. "What's going on? Lucy..." and then he fainted.

His heart throbbed weakly under her pressure, but at least it throbbed.

She took his hand, and he tried to grasp it, but instead of holding it, she put it to his neck. "I don't think he hit the big artery. Just put pressure on it."

Godfrey made a strangled noise as she rose and approached her still-retching boss. She pressed the knife into his hand and let go.

He took a deep breath, instantly free of the dry heaves. He glared at her. "That was inadvisable."

Zoë shrugged. "You were going to kill him."

He looked at her for a long time, his eyes fading from red to hazel. "I think we all underestimated you." He stood wearily. Zoë didn't offer to help him.

He waved his hand at Godfrey, whose bleeding seemed to have slowed. "He possibly ruined everything. She's gotten away. We don't know where she's going. Or what her goal is."

"And she's got a ton of hostages. But she's in a massive *plane golem*, Phil. I think we can track her."

"It would be easiest with an aerial view," he said. "But none of us can fly."

Zoë pulled out her cell phone. "Gwen can."

Before she could even dial, though, a thousand wings descended through the hole in the airport ceiling. One of the small birds transformed into a very satisfied-looking Gwen as the others roosted around her. The goddess looked around at all the dead security officials and sighed happily.

"Did you think I would miss this?" she asked.

*　　　*　　　*

"With the initial security strike team gone, the next wave will come in three minutes," Arthur said, checking his watch as Gwen lovingly counted the dead.

"How are we going to do anything more to stop her? She has a plane. We are pretty beat up," Zoë said, cradling her broken arm and panting. Cold sweat had broken out on her forehead and she felt ill.

"We have to set your arm, get shrapnel out of my shoulder, Benjamin's probably concussed, and that guy will likely need a transfusion and maybe a tranquilizer," Arthur said. "The vampire and sprite seem fine, though."

Zoë shrugged. "They're coterie." Arthur grunted in agreement.

"Then again, we should also think about escape before any more guards get here," Zoë said. "How do you expect we'll get out of here?"

Phil smiled weakly, his red-tinged teeth back to their human form. "Terrorism?"

They were interrupted by the sound of running feet and clicking metal as guns were aimed and cocked. "Freeze! Hands on your head!" screamed a man. They turned as one to see a seven-man SWAT team staring at them.

"Yeah. And we're the terrorists," said Zoë.

No one complied with the guards. Zoë was tired enough to figure that if they shot her, Lucy would be someone else's problem. She and Arthur weren't capable of raising their injured arms. Benjamin and Godfrey were clearly too injured to worry about, and Phil just gave them a cool, easy look. Morgen looked delighted at the new arrivals.

"HANDS IN THE AIR!" the voice screamed again, then it dropped an octave and sounded unsure of itself. "Hold on a second. What the fuck? Arthur?"

One of the seven guns wavered and the SWAT team member stepped forward and raised the visor on his helmet. A round African-American face looked out and squinted. "Arthur? Is this a Public Works deal?"

Arthur relaxed visibly. "Chet. Man, it's good to see you."

"Who's Chet?" Zoë whispered. He ignored her.

"You here on"—Chet's voice lowered—"business?"

"Yeah, actually. Some pretty serious business. Not sanctioned by the home office, but it concerns them and I was about to call it in."

Chet nodded. He picked up a radio and said, "Alpha One to Gold Leader. Send query regarding Arthur Anthony to Black Phoenix."

"Copy Alpha One," came the scratchy reply.

"Can you vouch for the others?" Chet asked.

Arthur looked around, his gaze lingering on Phil. He caught Zoë's eye and she gave a slight nod. He turned back to Chet. "I can."

Zoë sighed softly. Now she was responsible for whatever her boss did to these humans. She had no doubt he could disable and possibly kill them all before a bullet hit him; even if a bullet did hit him, it wouldn't kill him.

"Good," Chet said.

They stood there uncomfortably while the six remaining guns on them didn't waver. "Arthur? Are they going to stop aiming at us?" Zoë whispered.

"They need to hear back from Public Works that we're legit."

" 'Black Phoenix'?"

"Exactly. Chet and I used to work together on zombie patrol in Manhattan, but he decided to go into SWAT after a couple of months under the sewers. Public Works likes to seed law enforcement with people who know what's really going on in the city, so they were fine to see him go. He's a good guy."

Chet's radio crackled again. "Gold Leader to Alpha One. Black Phoenix says Anthony checks out. Full clearance. He needs to report. Is the situation at LaGuardia what he feared?"

"One sec," Chet said, and raised his eyebrows to Arthur.

Arthur looked around. "What do you think?"

"Copy that. Gold Leader, it's far worse than anticipated."

"Stand down, Alpha One. Black Phoenix will handle this. Count the dead and report back, we'll let the PR guys spin it. Gold Leader out."

"Alpha One out." Chet put the radio back on his belt. He waved his hand and his team dropped their weapons. "Sorry about that, Arthur. But we don't take people blowing up airports lightly. This one is going to be a hell of a thing to explain. You wanna tell me what happened here?"

Phil stepped forward. "We don't have time. A zoëtist has escaped and we need to stop her."

Chet whistled. "Shit. You folks aren't going anywhere in that shape. That one is the only one who doesn't look like something chewed her up and spit her out," he said, pointing at Morgen, who blew a kiss at him.

"Can you help?" asked Arthur.

Chet grinned, his expression becoming even more light-hearted. "How many do you need to be battle-ready?"

Chet had sent back five of his team with orders that one return with a medic. A Black Phoenix medic, he'd specified, who arrived swiftly. The SWAT member who stayed with him was also former Public Works, a short stocky woman named Shirley Mahoney.

"You're fucking serious. A fucking *plane* golem?" she asked, peering at the hole in the roof.

Zoë gritted her teeth as the EMT set her arm and taped her ribs. "A plane golem and a US Airways ticketing desk golem. That woman does not like me."

"No fucking kidding," Shirley said, sucking at her teeth thoughtfully. "I've seen golems made of mud, sand, even water. But I ain't never seen a fucking plane golem." She sounded almost impressed.

Godfrey wasn't around to say why Lucy didn't like Zoë. He'd been proclaimed not battle-ready and taken off on a stretcher. Zoë hadn't been sorry to see him go.

Arthur had been more of a problem. Chet and the EMT had wanted him to go to the ER, but he'd refused. So the EMT had finally just removed the shrapnel, packed his wound with heavy gauze, and taped it. Zoë had tried again not to look at his bare chest as he was ministered to. *The man is injured and receiving medical treatment*, she told herself firmly. *This is not the time.*

Both Zoë and Arthur had been forced to take something for their pain, because the EMT and Chet would not let them go after Lucy otherwise. "Now, that Vicodin is going to make you a little tired, and possibly a little loopy," the EMT said.

"We're chasing after a giant walking airplane. We don't need drugs to be loopy," Zoë said, still grateful to have a cast and something to make the throbbing pain recede.

"I have to admit," said the EMT, a willowy man by the name of Michael Oh, who sported an eye patch ("There's a demon out there I have a date with" was his only explanation), "I don't approve of you continuing to fight with this. Lacerations and a broken arm? And you look like you could sleep for a week."

The mere mention of sleep made Zoë stagger a little. "I suppose the Vicodin will not help that drowsy feeling, will it?"

Michael laughed. "I doubt you'll be awake in thirty minutes. I will just say to find a safe place to sleep when you can't stay awake anymore. I have a feeling things are going to get worse before they get better."

"Is that experience talking?" she asked.

Michael winced. "No. Ever since this"—he indicated his scarred cheek under the eye patch—"I've had a twitchy feeling when there's a lot of demon activity. And tonight it's been going crazy."

Zoë looked at Phil, who watched impassively. "You know, I didn't think another sign pointing to the obvious would make me worry, but for some reason it is."

"Any idea where she's headed?" Michael asked.

"I have a couple of guesses," Phil said. "The power plant in south Queens is always attractive to zoëtists. There are the sporting arenas for space. And then there's Central Park for the relative obscuring of whatever she plans. We can't check them all."

Arthur closed his cell phone and said, "Public Works is nearly shut down. They're dealing with another zombie attack. They have increased patrols in the sewers and on the streets, and they've got the power plants locked down. So if she goes there, we've got her." He grimaced. "If we can stop a plane."

They both looked at Zoë. She threw up her hands. "I told her it would be big. She said she believed that I believed it would be big. But she thought I was more scared of Lucy on a personal level."

"That is not incorrect. But the threat is bigger than we could have imagined," Phil said.

Arthur looked at Phil. "I'm here to help, for what it's worth."

Phil paused. "This alliance is not one I expected."

Arthur shrugged, then winced. "We're trying to catch the same person. I don't think it matters how she's stopped. Just that she's stopped."

"So we have, what? Two humans who are injured and about

to be pretty damn high on painkillers, one water sprite, and one vampire?" Zoë asked. "How can we take her on?"

Benjamin looked up from where he had been sitting with his head between his knees. "I'm with you. I can't live with myself that she beat me. She matched me with a golem that she made on a whim, while she was making something much bigger."

Shame was apparent on his face. As were a swelling lump and a bandage where he'd hit the wall.

"Sir, you have a slight concussion," Michael said. "I can't let you go."

The zoëtist laughed bitterly. "But you're letting them go? No. They need all the help they can get."

Chet pulled out his radio. "Alpha One to Gold Leader. Permission to provide backup to Black Phoenix."

"Bullets won't work against the golem," Phil said.

"But they'll sure blow Lucy to bits, won't they?" asked Zoë.

"Fair enough," Phil said, raising his hands in surrender.

"We're all going to die, aren't we?" Zoë asked.

Phil shrugged. "It's not really a big deal, dying."

Zoë flexed her right arm, her shoulder still throbbing from the laceration. She might still be able to hold a weapon—if the Vidocin didn't put her out of her misery. "Sure, easy for you to say. I'm sure that's what the *Titanic* victims in the water said to those still on the deck."

Zoë winced as the flock of sparrows descended through the hole in the roof. "Actually, they didn't," Gwen's voice said as she appeared in a flurry of feathers. "They mostly screamed."

"You were there at the *Titanic*?" Zoë asked.

"Of course, many death gods were. Areas where many die are popular spots."

Zoë paused. "Does that mean that they will be in New York tonight?"

Gwen paused. "They're on their way, I think. With the airport massacre and the hostages in the plane, it'll be a busy time."

" 'Busy.' Sure. That describes it," Zoë said. "Will they be on our side?"

Gwen shrugged. "Depends on who shows. Some feed off of death, like me. Some are there to escort the souls to their final destination. Most will be indifferent. Spectators."

"So we can expect no help, but no trouble, either?" Zoë mused. "Back where we started. That's OK."

"I didn't say that," the death goddess said. "I am helping you, after all. I just said most will be indifferent. Death gods don't really interfere—everyone eventually dies, after all. We're a patient lot."

Zoë looked at her friend. "Then why are you helping us?"

Gwen shrugged. "Things got more interesting when you got here. When I got the job in the publishing house. I feed off of death energy, but I can enjoy other things too. And I find that living and working among humans allows for more interesting absorption of energy."

Zoë paused, then said, "Gwen? Am I—" She stopped and shook her head. "Never mind. I don't want to know."

Gwen smiled, then looked around for Phil. "She's hidden in the trees of Central Park. I lost sight of her, but my sparrows are tracking her still. She's stopped. I don't know what she's up to, but we should catch up while we can."

Phil nodded, then glanced around at their motley crew. "The goal is to stop her, people. We kill the zoëtist and we stop the threat."

"Wait," Zoë said. "Kill her? But she's a human. Shouldn't we arrest her or something?"

To Zoë's surprise, Arthur answered instead of Phil. "Not this time. When humans become coterie, they're governed by Public Works. I'm with Phil here. Kill her."

302

The Shambling Guide to New York City

APPENDIX:
New York for Human Coterie

Coterie humans, including zoëtists and vampire thralls, can obviously find existence in the city a little easier than most. This is beneficial to other coterie, who can usually find someone to do errands for them that they would not be able to do themselves. But these humans have needs within the city as well.

The thralls will find Lohan Memorial Hospital and Red Hook American Red Cross the most open to dealing in blood. What the humans assume are "expired" bags of blood are actually still quite sustaining to most vampires and other beings who feed on humans, and some establishments will sell the blood instead of destroying it. The going rate for blood fluctuates depending on demand, so try to stock up when you can. If you try to visit after a major accident or natural disaster, they'll turn you away—with Public Works backing them up.

These establishments are on neutral ground, by the way, and the person dealing with the coterie will always have connections with Public Works.

Zoëtists have found sympathetic humans—or, closer to the truth, humans who will accept hell notes—in Duke Power Station, and even have a separate room they can rent for their creations. Few cities cater to zoëtists, which makes New York a popular destination for a creator in need of some strong, reliable energy. This means, unfortunately, that the room is often booked months in advance. So if you're on your way to New York City to bring a new construct or two to life, remember to plan ahead!

The only resident practicing zoëtist in the city who is known to this publication is Karen Shea, who works within Duke Power Station. She is not a dominant figure and does not begrudge the presence of other zoëtists. ▪

CHAPTER TWENTY-SEVEN

Zoë wasn't sure how they fit everyone into the cab, but it was a coterie cab, after all, and she didn't question it too much. She was more concerned with the pain of Arthur's weight as he was forced to lean on her broken arm when the cab took a sharp turn on its way into the Rat's Nest.

The cabbie swore at the traffic, an oath in a strange language that made the hairs on the backs of Zoë's hands stand up and glow a faint red. She rubbed them absently.

Arthur shifted again, keeping an inch between Zoë and himself. "So what is our plan here?" he asked Phil. "You look to be leading this thing."

"I am not used to working with a team," Phil said.

"I am," Arthur said. "We have one zoëtist, one vampire, one water sprite, one death goddess, one SWAT, one Public Works employee, and—" He paused and looked at Zoë.

"And one book editor," she said, forcing a smile. "Who has a broken arm and no weapon. And who very likely got us into this whole thing."

Arthur frowned. "What do you mean?"

Zoë took a deep breath. "I have...a history with Lucy. The zoëtist. Or rather, I have a history with her husband." She blushed and looked down at her hand, the one that wasn't strapped tightly to her chest. "I didn't know he was married. So she doesn't like me very much."

"And you're the reason she's here?" Arthur asked incredulously.

"No." Benjamin replied softly as if coming out of a haze. "She's here for a much larger reason. She has planned this for years. Zoë returning to the city was just a convenience. She would have created a construct to poison the zombies anyway; with Zoë here, she could make that construct to disturb her as well. Two birds, one stone, if Gwen will pardon me the expression."

"Why did she just attack the zombies?" Zoë asked. "Why not the demons or vampires?"

"Zombies are the easiest to tamper with," Phil said. "Their humanity dies if they lose their higher brain functions. Mess with the food source and you have a shambling army. Since the zombies are still causing trouble, we can believe Wesley was not her only agent. He was just the one who was designed to tamper with Zoë. I'm sure she would be delighted if Zoë had died, but right now she's here for something bigger."

"So, plan?" Zoë prompted.

"Right," Arthur said. "I think we should send Benjamin's golems and Gwen's sparrows in for distraction. Then send the fighters in while the long-range people hold back."

"And me?" asked Zoë.

"You're really not in fighting shape," he said, not quite looking her in the eye.

"Neither are you."

"Touché," he said, and left it at that.

If only she felt like fighting. But her wounds still throbbed and the Vicodin was slowly making its way into her bloodstream, giving her exhausted body a full excuse to shut down.

Arthur was stiff beside her, body language making it clear he didn't like what he'd heard about Godfrey. But Zoë was exhausted and the Vicodin was taking hold, and she would much rather lean on someone mad at her than lean on a vampire.

She put her head on his good shoulder and allowed her eyelids to finally crash down.

She awoke not to a gentle shaking of her knee or her name being called, but a noxious smell that burned her nose hairs. She gagged and turned her head, and Granny Good Mae pulled back the horrible vial, satisfied.

Zoë was lying in the back of the cab with both doors open. "What the hell is that?" Zoë asked. "Wait, what are you doing here?"

"Smelling salts. Mixed with a couple more herbs. And she told me to come here. Said tonight would be big."

"Of course she did." Zoë's eyes focused on the little old lady in the woods, who stood shifting from foot to foot.

"She tells me what to do, and Granny Good Mae follows, and she does what is asked. Yes. She always finds an emergency exit."

Confused at the switching of names and pronouns, Zoë wasn't sure who was doing what was asked. "You seem less... coherent than usual. Are you OK?"

"They found the bad zoëtist," Granny Good Mae said brightly, pulling Zoë out of the cab by her good arm. "Let's go see!"

Zoë looked around in confusion. "How did a cab make it into the woods?"

The driver grinned, showing two bright fangs and nothing else. Ah. A snake demon. "You'd be surprised where this thing can go. The underground tunnel system doesn't hurt either. Have fun!"

He roared off, dodging trees, and then, abruptly, his taillights disappeared.

Zoë took a deep breath. "So where are we?"

"Central Park. The goddess is trying to learn more about the woman."

"Where is Gwen?"

Granny Good Mae pointed at a light through the trees. The screech of metal and ensuing thumps told her the golem was still active, and the screams of the people inside the plane were faint but obvious.

"What part of the park?"

"Far north."

Zoë gasped as a cool hand slid over her mouth. She hadn't even noticed Phil was there. "She's coming closer. Silence." he whispered, his breath cool against her ear.

She pulled his hand off and glared at him, but stayed silent.

The golem tromped away and Zoë could finally make out the slight, torch-bearing form of Lucy. *A torch? What's wrong with a flashlight?* she wondered. But then Lucy put the torch to a pile of brush and twigs and set it aflame, then proceeded to the next one. She meticulously began making a small clearing, a tidy circle surrounded by her fires.

A thin, dark hand closed on Zoë's right arm and drew her gently backward, away from the bonfires. Gwen held Phil's arm in her other hand. "It's definitely a ritual of some kind. Benjamin says it's to provide power for more golems."

Phil eyed the airplane golem, pacing back and forth. "We'll have to put that golem out of commission."

"And be careful with the people inside," Zoë reminded him.

"That's not as important as killing the golem," Phil said.

"Phil, you have five humans working with you. You don't think we're just going to let those people die?"

"You realize this makes it more complicated, right?" he asked.

"What, it was going to be easy before?" she asked.

"Of course," Phil said. "Run in there and kill her. The golem falls apart. Easy."

Through the trees, Lucy sat on the ground as five bonfires raged around her. She was cross-legged and had dirt smudges on her face. Her eyes were closed.

"Gonna wake up, she's gonna wake up, I'm telling you, Amsterdam stirring," droned Granny Good Mae.

"Shut up!" whispered Zoë frantically, and Gwen pulled the other woman away from the clearing.

Benjamin looked at her sharply. "What was that? What was she saying about Amsterdam?"

Gwen returned, having left Granny Good Mae with Morgen. "Granny Good Mae says she can talk to the spirit of the city. She's been saying it's going to wake up, that it's stirring, you know," Gwen said, watching Lucy through the trees. "Complete madness. If the city were alive, I'd sense how close it was to death."

Phil shrugged and looked at the meditating Lucy again. "I'm going in. Zoë, stay here. Benjamin, can you send a golem in with me for backup?"

Benjamin had covered his mouth, his eyes wide with terror. He took a step backward. Zoë recognized his shuffling steps as stutters before a full-out panicked run. She put her arm out to stop him and led him away from the group.

She put her head close to his. "You have to keep it together. What's going on? If you have information, don't turn tail and run. Give it up."

With a shaking hand, Ben pointed to the babbling woman. "You said she's been talking about the city waking up?"

Zoë nodded. "I guess. I've never heard her talk about the city before. She usually talks about some sort of imaginary friend she calls 'she.' Granny's got some mental issues, so it's probably just that."

He shook his head violently. "No, no, it's not. She sounds like a citytalker."

"A what?" Zoë asked.

Ben nodded slowly. "I've heard about them, read about them in New Orleans. Never met one, though. They're rare. Always human. They talk directly to the cities."

"The city actually does have a literal spirit?" Zoë asked, wonder in her voice.

Benjamin nodded. "And there are some older texts that most zoëtists don't talk about, but my master had a copy of one. It's about imprisoning a living spirit within a golem. Giving it a body, but forcing it to do your bidding."

"And a city has got to be the biggest spirit there is," Zoë said, comprehension making her dizzy. "All the times she knew things she shouldn't, all the time Granny Good Mae said 'she' told her things. She was talking to the city? And it was talking back?"

Yes.

The ground shook as the plane golem neared them, and Benjamin took the moment to run into the trees. Zoë stumbled forward into Arthur, who tried to hold her up with his one arm.

Phil dashed into the clearing, heading straight for Lucy, who still had her eyes closed. A weeping cherry tree near her uprooted itself with no effort and slapped Phil aside as if he were an annoying mosquito. He went flying into the woods.

"This is very bad," Zoë said.

Chet hefted his rifle to his shoulder and took aim. Before he could fire, a crevasse opened in front of him and he tumbled into it, shouting. Zoë and Arthur stumbled backward, and Zoë could hear Granny Good Mae shout above the sound of the ground rumbling. And in her own head, Zoë heard a voice.

I am here. I am everywhere.

"She's awake! Good morning! Good morning!" Granny Good Mae sang.

New York City has a great deal of light pollution from the countless buildings and streetlights. The city that never sleeps is named thus simply because no city could sleep with that much light and noise.

But it was the night the city woke up that the blackout came. Zoë blinked in the dark, but the bonfires still allowed her to see what was happening. Lucy's golem came together slowly, with trees forming a rough skeleton, but then larger items came flying into the clearing, almost magnetically.

They ducked instinctively as taxis flew over their heads to crash in the clearing, sliding together to form the golem's legs. A city bus drove through the woods, mowing down trees and bushes, breaking an axle on a rock and continuing to be drawn forward by the will of the powerful woman still meditating.

At first Zoë thought the thing would be the size of the airplane golem, which still patrolled the periphery. Soon it was apparent that the city was too large to be kept within a golem the size of a mere airplane. People in nearby blocks screamed and horns honked as a small condemned building slid toward them, and Zoë's group scrambled as it lumbered through the woods like a clumsy, legless rhino.

Zoë ran into a thick, feathery body and felt human arms wrapped around her, keeping her up. "Gwen! What's going on?"

"The city is awake. We were right. Many will die tonight," she said. Her eyes glowed softly, and Zoë realized she'd never seen the death goddess look so powerful.

"What can we do?" Zoë asked, trying not to shrink back from her friend.

"Killing the city is not advisable," Phil said, stumbling through the trees toward them.

"Are you all right?" Zoë asked. The vampire's clothing was ripped and bloody.

He nodded absently and looked around. "Where is the woman? The citytalker. The assassin."

"I think she's still with the water sprite, both back there." Arthur motioned toward the dark woods behind them, where more elements of the city were flying and skittering and dragging themselves to flesh out the golem. Mailboxes and streetlights, cars and buses, a small shed and a trash can.

"Should we check on Chet?" Zoë asked. "A hole opened up."

Arthur shook his head. "You do it. I have to call in to work and find out about the power grid. Blackouts are prime coterie activity time."

"Right, I'll go," she said. She spied one of Arthur's swords where he'd dropped it, picked it up, and ran into the darkness.

It didn't take long for her to realize that running into the darkness, not sure where she was going, carrying a naked sword, with cars, small buildings, and—Jesus, was that a homeless man?—flying toward the rapidly growing golem, might not have been the best idea she'd ever had. She felt as if she were in some sort of wilderness instead of in the heart of the city, wondering what dangerous animal would come through the darkness to try to eat her.

Arthur's expensive sword became a cane for her, a means of avoiding the trees and rocks in her path, and by poking the ground in front of her, a means of avoiding the crevasse Chet had fallen into.

"Chet! Are you down there? Are you OK?" she called as loudly as she dared. She didn't know why she was cautious; the chaos around her with screaming people and blaring horns was enough to cover her. But since Lucy hated her, Zoë didn't want her sending an entire city after her.

Zoë heard a groan. "Chet! How deep is it? Can you climb up? Can you see me?"

"Dropped my gun," grumbled the man. "I never drop my gun."

"Chet, you've got to get out of there. There's a lot of shit going down." A crash sounded in the woods—too close—and she added, "Actually I think you may be safer down there."

Something caught her eye and she looked to the clearing. A grotesque head comprised of yellow cabs perched on a torso of a building (that Zoë was pretty sure had once been a small library) rose above the trees, catching the light of the moon. It howled then, myriad car horns, sirens, angry voices, and jackhammers.

The voice of the city. The very angry city.

Trapped.

That's when the mailbox hit her in the back, knocking her into the hole after Chet.

The red haze subsided, and Zoë came to in complete blackness.

"Shit. Am I blind? What's going on?" she mumbled.

Hands were on her then, strong hands that helped her sit up. "No. You're just in a damn dark hole. I thought you were going to help me out?" The voice was strong, concerned and yet mildly amused.

A hole. A broken arm. A guy named Chet. And she worked for a vampire.

"Hell. It's all real, isn't it?" she mumbled, rubbing her head. Her hair was matted with blood.

Chet chuckled and helped her to her feet. "The times I've said that, either after one of these adventures or after waking up next to a previously hot woman."

Zoë smiled. "So how are we getting out of this hole?"

"We're down about eight feet, as far as I can tell. You fell on your head, I'm surprised you didn't break your neck."

Zoë sighed, wincing at the pain in her back. "I feel like I broke just about everything else."

"Can you try to climb out?" he asked. "Maybe standing on my shoulders?"

Zoë rotated her good shoulder, testing the muscles. Everything around it shrieked and she groaned. "No. Sorry, dude. I'm not sure I could with two arms, much less one. I don't have any strength left."

They gingerly explored their hole. It was about seven feet wide at its narrowest, twelve at its widest, and made a scar in the ground about twenty feet long.

"How did she do this?" Zoë asked. "It's like she knew what you were doing."

"Zoëtists are the hardest coterie to study because they're humans," Chet said from her right. "There are also different schools and we're not sure the extent of their abilities. I can safely say we've never experienced anyone this strong. She's tuned into everything around her."

"Can she communicate with her golems?"

"Of course she can," he said. "A zoëtiest can lose control of their golem, but the communication is there until it dies."

A deep, rhythmic rumbling neared. "That's the smaller golem," Zoë said, then laughed suddenly to realize she was calling the plane a "smaller" golem.

Chet grabbed her good arm and pulled her and she followed. "What are you doing?"

"Wait," he said.

The golem appeared above them, looming. Zoë could see the people inside the plane, still screaming. Emergency lights in all the vehicles that made up the golem flickered in the night, and Chet hissed a very rude victorious oath as the golem stamped into the hole with its leg made of heavily damaged luggage trucks.

"Let's go," Chet said, and Zoë allowed herself to be dragged along to leap into the rising cart as the golem pulled its leg out of the hole.

"How did you know it was going to do that?"

"She wanted to finish off the job," he said. "This isn't safe, by the way. She's going to know we're still alive, so we need to get out of here as soon as the leg touches back down."

"Oh sure. It's not safe. Thanks for letting me know that." Zoë clutched the opening of the luggage cart as they sailed through the air, and grunted as the foot came down hard.

"Jump and run!" Chet shouted, and Zoë jumped and stumbled immediately. She went down to her knees and lost track of where Chet had run to. But she could see Lucy.

She did some rapid math in her head and realized that the one place the golem wouldn't attack was where Lucy was. So she ran into the clearing, dodging the airplane golem's stamping feet.

CONEY ISLAND:
Attractions

Water demons and sprites have many choices of lodging and things to do, but they are often limited to parks and rivers. The New York Aquarium is a welcoming place with discreet tanks of fresh and salt water for visiting coterie, as well as exotic meals you can't find anywhere else.

It's also the main postal office for any water-based coterie, intercepting messages carried by sea creatures. If family is trying to get a message to you, check the aquarium. ■

CHAPTER TWENTY-EIGHT

Zoë wanted to ignore her injuries and just tackle the bitch. But sadly, she didn't have the magical movie power to ignore her aching broken arm or the sharp stabs of pain in her chest where her cracked ribs protested when she panted.

Still, she ran as fast as her battered body would allow her. Lucy's eyes were still closed as she concentrated on making the towering monster above them. As much as Zoë hated to go for the girl-fight stereotype, as she neared Lucy she reached out with her good arm and grabbed a handful of Lucy's sleek hair.

The zoëtist's eyes flew open and the pounding steps that followed Zoë faltered. Lucy's head snapped back and she fell backward as Zoë yanked again. Lucy splayed her arms to avoid being dragged, and Zoë continued to pull.

"Call them off!" Zoë shouted. "Or else your own creation is going to stomp you into the ground."

"Get off me, you slut," Lucy hissed, trying to pry Zoë's fingers from her hair.

"Make me. When that thing comes to step on us, I'm sure I'll let you go."

The plane golem had faltered briefly as Lucy lost concentration, but soon regained its footing. It stomped its slow way toward them while above them all the golem of the city howled again as it continued to form. Zoë could see frightened faces at the windows of the plane, and she realized she had no idea of how to deal with them.

No no no no no no—She gritted her teeth and tried to ignore the chanting in her head.

Then Zoë saw a slight movement in the cockpit of the plane. The blood splattered across the windshield changed as a hand passed over it, and the golem stopped in its tracks. Whatever magic was holding the plane balanced on baggage carts left it, and the legs buckled, the carts no longer able to support the tons of weight of the plane. Lucy let out a strangled cry as Zoë let her go and they ran away from the falling plane.

It hit the ground with a massive crash, and Zoë couldn't spare a moment to see if the people inside were all right. Lucy had made it free of the plane as well, and stood, murderous eyes on Zoë. She was so focused, in fact, that she didn't see Granny Good Mae coming. The old woman kicked the zoëtist in the face, launching her backward.

"Good. Backup," Zoë said, and ran to the plane's emergency doors.

Phil sped toward Lucy, who was being pummeled by Granny Good Mae.

The doors at either end of the plane opened and frightened people tumbled out, shaken and weeping. Some—the idiots—carried their luggage; others just jumped.

Arthur and Zoë managed to get under the doors and attempt to catch some of the people as they jumped out, but realized they were likely doing more harm than good—especially to their own injuries—so they stepped aside and just tried to help pick up people who had fallen.

Finally the yellow slide was lowered by two ashen-faced attendants, and the first person down was—

"Benjamin?" Zoë said in shock. The little man was covered in blood, but it didn't look as if much of it were his own.

Still, he looked exhausted. "Only she would make a golem with only *mem* and *tav*." They looked at him blankly. "Death. It means death. Usually 'death' makes a golem deactivate. But she's on another level. They were on the inside of the windshield in blood. Someone had to get in there to change it." He raised his bloody hand and smiled weakly.

"How the hell did you get up there?" Arthur asked, trying to support the zoëtist as he sagged.

"I made a flying golem," Benjamin said, mumbling into Arthur's shoulder like a drunken buddy. "Never done that before. It took a lot out of me."

"I didn't even know that was possible," Arthur said.

"Where's the bitch?" Benjamin said. "Didja get her?"

Arthur winced as the city above them shrieked again, sounding like amplified sirens, and took a step forward that took it half the width of the park. "Doesn't sound like it."

If Zoë had been hoping that Benjamin could give them some insight into how to stop a golem made from a city, she was disappointed as the man slumped against Arthur, utterly spent.

Granny Good Mae screeched so loudly that the strain on her vocal cords was obvious. "Emergency exit, emergency exit."

Zoë heard the words repeated in her head, but was confused, as the flight attendants had already exited the plane. The people from the plane walked into the park, supporting one another, and once they saw the other golem—Public Works was going to have a hell of a time doing damage control on this—the only people left were Arthur, the unconscious Benjamin, Zoë, and Morgen. Gwen had to be nearby, as sparrows flew in a flock above them, highlighted by the December moon.

Granny Good Mae sat on Lucy's chest, but instead of attack-

318

ing her, she chanted, "Emergency exit. Emergency exit!" until Phil dragged her off.

"Everyone got off the plane, more or less OK, Mae," Morgen said behind her. "Don't worry about them. We have bigger problems."

The ground shook as the city golem took another step, crushing trees beneath its massive weight. Sirens shrieked in the city as emergency crews approached. A helicopter buzzed overhead.

Zoë shook her head. She could hear it more clearly now. "No. She is talking to the golem. It's looking for a way out."

"Out?"

"Lucy didn't do a very good job. The city's pissed at being forced into a body like that. It's in agony." The golem shrieked again and turned, every step tearing great holes in the ground.

"Oh, that's all we need. A crazy golem the zoëtist can't control," Arthur said.

"Well, kill the zoëtist and it should stop the golem," Morgen said.

Arthur nodded. "That's what a vampire and apparently a martial arts master are trying to do. And failing."

Lucy had conjured another tree golem to protect her, and it knocked Granny Good Mae and Phil away as they tried to lunge toward her. Lucy looked bad, blood streaming down her face and one eye swollen shut.

"How come Chet hasn't taken a shot?" Zoë asked, spying their friend aiming at Lucy from behind the tail of the plane.

"He's got a bump on the head, it's dark, and there are three humanoids there. What if he misses?" said Arthur.

"No, two," Zoë said. Granny Good Mae had left the fight to Phil and was running behind the plane.

Zoë followed and found her sitting on the ground, rocking and babbling. She put her hand on the woman's head, and Granny Good Mae stilled.

"Granny, what's going on? Are you talking to the city?"

"You are too. She told me."

Zoë bit her lip. "Tell me about this."

"Whispers. They have always been whispers. Go here. Do this. At night it told me stories of the people here. Coterie. The animals. The rats." She smiled. "There have been many stories about the rats."

"Really," Zoë said, her voice faint.

"It sang to me, sometimes," Granny Good Mae's voice was far away. "Quiet lullabies that sounded like the wind sliding over water. Sometimes I could hear what the city had to say. Sometimes I could only guess. The whispers were always so quiet."

Her gaze hardened as she looked at the golem, the bastardization of her beloved city. "But not now. Now she's awake, confused and frightened. She's shoved into a small body, an uncomfortable body. And there was the woman, the tiny woman who told her what to do."

Zoë knew what Granny Good Mae was going to say next, knew it as the words appeared in her mind. "And she doesn't like that.

"You know. You know. She said you would know. She said you were like me. Just. Like. Me." The sixtysomething homeless assassin looked at Zoë eagerly, and the moment was quite surreal, having something so strange and personal in common with this woman.

"But I don't hear her like you do. I don't even know—"

"You will. She likes you."

"But I've never had an experience like this. Why didn't I hear Raleigh? I lived there all my life."

Granny Good Mae shrugged. "It probably didn't like you."

They turned to watch the city golem slowly trudge away from them, heard the sharp cracks as some idiot tried to shoot at a monster made of concrete and steel, and Zoë wondered how the hell they could stop it.

Stop Lucy. It all went back to that.

The zoëtist was weakening. Her defensive golem was falling apart. Phil was attacking the tree and split the willowy trunk in two, leaving it floundering in the grass. He darted in and was able to grab Lucy's shoulders and take her down. In an instant he was seated on Lucy's waist and over her neck. Zoë turned away: her boss seemed animalistic as he fed on Lucy. Just as when he had fed from Godfrey, he seemed like a dog over a food bowl, gorging and growling and daring anyone else to steal from him.

"It's best if you don't watch," Morgen said, appearing at her side.

"It's over now, right?" Zoë asked. "The big thing should just fall apart."

"I would think so," Arthur said.

The howling in Zoë's head didn't stop.

No no no no no no no exit exit exit—

The golem still trudged away from them, reaching the street and stomping on cars. As the messy, slurping sounds behind Zoë ceased, the golem did not fall apart as the plane golem had. In contrast, it seemed to gain strength and speed, heading toward Manhattan.

"Phil?" Zoë's voice sounded shrill to her own ears. "Is she dead yet?"

Her boss appeared at her side. Blood dripped from his chin and his eyes glowed a faint red. She swallowed her revulsion and her desire to take a step back from him.

He wiped his chin with the heel of his hand and licked the stray blood casually. "She's gone."

"You didn't turn her or anything, did you?"

"Yes, because that's what we need—a megalomaniacal zoëtist

vampire. There's a reason they're human—undead don't have the life force to control golems. And demons just don't bother to learn the arts."

"Then why is her golem wandering away? Do you think it wants to see a show?" Zoë pointed to the departing spirit of the city wrapped in cars, buses, construction materials, and a small library.

"I don't know. We need to get Benjamin on it. Where is he?"

"I think he and Arthur were taking care of the airplane passengers. Who have all run away in terror, by the way." Zoë winced as a large crash resonated from the direction of the golem. "We can't let it get away."

"Get Gwen to follow it. I will ask Benjamin about it." He ran off toward the airplane.

"Gwen? Where the hell has she been, anyway?" Zoë called after him.

"Watching Granny Good Mae," Morgen said, pointing at the sparrows, which had taken over a small cherry tree, making it look fully leafed out in December.

Zoë shivered involuntarily. Gwen appeared beside her, looking, like Phil, full of power and life. "Phil wants you to track the golem. The zoëtist is dead but we don't know why it's still going."

The death goddess nodded once. "I haven't fed this well in years. It's my pleasure."

Zoë shuddered again, trying to get used to looking at the world from a nonhuman perspective. Of course the potential for deaths went up with a huge golem wandering around the city. This was a smorgasbord for her. She took to the skies, transforming into a sparrow and disappearing into her flock, circling once and then heading into the city after the golem.

Zoë and Morgen went to find Arthur and Ben. Granny Good

Mae sat against the plane, holding her head in her hands. She crooned softly to herself.

Ben was supported by Chet, and seemed drunk. "Leave me alone. I got the plane down safely. I'm a hero." His eyelids drooped.

Phil slapped him. He jerked awake. "Listen to me, little man. The golem is still alive even though the zoëtist is dead. How is this happening?"

He staggered away from Chet and put his hands on his knees, catching his breath. "That golem. She put the spirit of the city inside it. I've heard of attempts to do that, but not sure if it ever worked."

"I'm not sure it worked now," Phil said. "The city is destroying itself."

"Emergency exit!" Granny Good Mae keened.

"It worked," Zoë said.

Phil looked sharply at her. "What did she say?"

Arthur waved his hand dismissively. "She's been babbling about emergency exits since the plane came down."

"You idiot," Ben said, blinking. "She's speakin' for th' city at this point. Wants a way out. S-scared."

"Out? Where would it go?"

"It wants free of its body, I expect," Chet said.

"Can you free it?" Phil asked Benjamin.

He shook his head. "I can't raise a golem the size of a cat at this moment." He held his hand flat above the ground and some dirt and grass swirled weakly in a tiny tornado, and then died back down.

"Wait a moment," Phil said. "I felt something. Do that again."

Benjamin took a step back. "Did you feed off of Lucy?"

"Yes."

Benjamin glanced at each of them and then looked at the ground. "I shouldn't say. It's forbidden."

Phil slapped him again. "Whatever you're protecting can't be as important as saving the city. We're about to lose everything here. Everything. The balance between humans and coterie, the very spirit of the city. I don't know what happens to a city if its spirit dies, but I don't want to find out."

"If an undead feeds on a zoëtist, he will get her life force—and powers—for a limited amount of time. So I can't raise anything to help stop that golem." He swallowed. "But you can."

Phil kept his vampiric composure, but Zoë was sure his red eyes widened slightly.

"So we have a strong zoëtist on our side again," Zoë said. "What do we do?"

All of them but Phil, who was focusing on his hands, turned to Granny Good Mae, who was still muttering to herself.

"Emergency exit, keep your head between your knees, and in the case of a water landing, kiss your ass good-bye," she said, her eyes glassy.

Arthur laughed dryly. "Of course. Like all coterie, it's wanting to go somewhere safe. Somewhere underground. Somewhere it won't hurt itself. It needs to be herded, though. It's too crazy."

Morgen grinned. "Smart city. It wants the water."

Zoë frowned. "That would be the Reservoir?"

"But it's walking into the city, parallel to the Reservoir. We have to make it turn ninety degrees," Chet said. "If it steps on MoMA, we're in a heap of shit. You do not want to wake up what's sleeping in there."

Zoë shook her head. This was insane. And what she was about to suggest was even more so. She looked at Arthur. "Does Public Works have power over the subways? I mean, if I told you to get everyone off the subways, can you do it?"

He scratched his shoulder near his wound and then winced.

"In theory, yeah. Although they're kind of dealing with more zombie problems right now. Why?"

She ignored him. "And you really think you have Lucy's power? All of it?" she asked Phil.

He nodded. "I have something, that's for sure. It's nearly intoxicating."

"Down, tiger," she said. She got on her knees with difficulty and touched Granny Good Mae on the shoulder.

"Mae," she said. "Are you ready to put her to bed?"

The woman nodded. "Prepare for a water landing."

"We're going to try. Will you come with us to help the city have its water landing? It might be scary."

Mae's eyes focused, and for a moment she was Zoë's stern teacher again. "I was a CIA agent for twelve years. I've assassinated coterie and humans. You can't scare me, girl. What do we need to do?"

Zoë looked at Arthur. "Get Fanny on the phone. Tell her we need a train evacuated. Preferably a long one, and preferably close by."

She put her hand on Phil and drew him away from the crowd. "Now let's talk about this new power you have."

Arthur shut the phone slowly. "They're still fighting. But Fanny was able to clear a train."

They all stood at the Central Park North Station at 110th Street and looked at Phil. The vampire held his hands out in front of him, palms down.

"So the magic protects the actual construct. That's how a couple of trucks can support a plane. Right?" Phil asked, staring at his hands.

Benjamin scowled, but there wasn't a lot of energy in his annoyance. "We don't call it magic. That's blasphemous. It's a mystical power from Adonai that we channel. But yeah, the rest is right."

Zoë grimaced. "Yeah. Now is when we want to pick nits. Just do it, Phil. I think she's coming closer."

They had cut down some side streets to get to the subway stop, having had to dodge some coterie already taking advantage of the chaos to come out in the open. Luckily, some street gangs had also taken the opportunity of the blackout to loot, and the two groups clashed violently, allowing Zoë and her friends to sneak by undetected.

The golem had staggered along Fifth Avenue, damaging buildings and stomping on cars as it did. The police had their hands full and were mainly doing their best just to keep frightened citizens away from the golem's path.

The vampire stared at the street, under which lay an empty subway train, according to Public Works. Zoë felt a little guilty at ejecting the confused and terrified people into a dark subway station and then onto a street with a rampaging golem, but no one else had come up with anything, not even the newly empowered vampire.

As Phil concentrated, Zoë took Granny Good Mae by the elbow and led her gently to his side. "Tell him how the city is doing as he works. But—" She bit her lip. "Don't tell him how you know. He's not aware you—we—can talk to the city."

"I love the library. All the books," Granny Good Mae said.

Zoë nodded slowly. "Right. You talk to Phil, and I'll just hope we can figure out what you're talking about."

"Stand back," Phil said, his face contorted in concentration. His eyes glowed redder and his fangs grew, turning him into a monstrous caricature of himself. Zoë backed up and ran into

Arthur, who grunted in pain as her head made contact with his wounded shoulder.

"Sorry," she mumbled. He put his hand on her shoulder to steady her and didn't remove it.

A rumbling came from underneath them, and Phil pointed to a spot in the road. "There."

The subway train burst forth from the street, spraying chunks of asphalt everywhere. Zoë ducked and Chet swore.

"I told you to stand back," Phil said, sighing.

The train lay on 110th Street, not moving at all. Phil frowned.

"It's all I can do. The power is there, but—"

"But you have no skill!" Benjamin said. "Did you think it was just child's play, just get some power and go?"

"It's all we had. I didn't hear you offering any ideas!" Zoë told Benjamin, who had the grace to look ashamed.

"Lost, so lost," Granny Good Mae said sadly. "Lost and lonely."

Lonely . . .

"Right. Encourage it toward the water, Mae. Tell it to turn around," Zoë said. Something caught the corner of her eye, in the shadows of the moon, and she glanced past Granny Good Mae. She swore.

Six vampires exited the deli behind them, followed by two demons and what looked like a fire sprite. They watched Phil with interest, and eyed the humans with leering grins.

Zoë looked up at Arthur. "I am guessing these guys aren't the kind who are interested in a balance between coterie and humans."

"Only in a balanced meal," Arthur said. He moved his hand from her shoulder and pulled his bag open. He pressed a short sword into her hand.

"Chet?" she asked.

"It's too dark. I can't shoot."

"Then take a sword."

Armed or unarmed, as they preferred, they surrounded Phil and Granny Good Mae, one who concentrated on getting the golem under control, the other who babbled incoherently.

"How many do we have?" Zoë asked.

"Ten, as far as I can tell," Arthur said. "One fire sprite. Seven vampires. Three demons."

"That's eleven, dumbass," Chet said.

"How about 'more than us,' then?" Arthur snapped.

Zoë tried to remember what Granny Good Mae had told her about fighting more than one opponent. How if she couldn't run away, her size was a benefit to her as long as she remained quick. Too bad her legs felt as if they were filled with wet sand.

She saw a fire hydrant in front of a store and wondered how she could open it.

The vampires attacked at once, seven of them against Arthur, Chet, Zoë, Morgen, and a nervous Benjamin. Gwen's sparrows perched in a tree, watching. Two vampires, a male and a female, went for Zoë; she ducked the male and clumsily sliced up with her blade, cutting a wide gash in his chest. The wounded vampire shrieked, and Zoë turned quickly, cutting across the female's arm. She was hoping to neatly sever her arm, but vampires were tougher than zombies, and the blade caught on her bone.

"Damn," she muttered, and howled in pain as the first vamp she'd cut grabbed her around the middle, pressing her broken arm to her body and compressing her cracked ribs. She struggled to free the sword from the arm of the flailing vampire. She threw her head backward and knocked the male vampire in the nose with her head, and he dropped her. She allowed the female vampire to wrench the sword from her hand as both vampires surprisingly fled.

"Where are they going? I know I'm not that much of a badass," Zoë asked. The other coterie, save the fire demon, were fleeing as well. "We can't be that strong," she said, panting. She turned around and craned her head up to see Phil's golem train swaying above her like a snake about to strike.

Her breath caught in her throat. "Phil?" she said in a small voice.

"Concentrating," he said, his voice rough.

"Right, great, I get that. But can you tell me if you're controlling this train, or if I should run away like those vampires?"

Arthur caught her hand and pulled her from the shadow of the train, which was turning to meet the trudging city.

"It's on our side," he said, "but that doesn't mean it's safe. He doesn't have the finesse most zoëtists do."

"What do we do about that one?" Zoë pointed to the fire demon, which was standing next to a building and forcing it to catch fire. "Morgen?"

Morgen shook her head. "It would evaporate me. It's too strong."

Granny Good Mae began to cry, and they all turned toward her. The light grew brighter as they realized the demon was coming forward in a wave of fire.

"Shit!" yelled Zoë. "Move to the sidewalks!"

They scattered, pulling Phil and the weeping Granny Good Mae behind them. The fire splashed over the street and re-formed itself. It came at them again, a towering wave ten feet high, determined to crash over and burn them all.

"Morgen!" Zoë cried, and a wall of water sprang up in front of them, looking like a waterfall with its gravity reversed. A great hissing noise came up and the demon retreated, much smaller. The remaining water fell, soaking them.

Granny Good Mae wept louder. "I just want to sleep. I'm so tired."

It was the city speaking through Mae. Zoë could feel it. Zoë studied the woman, who slipped in and out of madness with no warning. She sighed, wincing at her battered body's protests. "I have one more idea. But it could be risky."

"Unlike your last safe idea that had us turning a vampire into a zoëtist?" Arthur said.

"Yeah. But it should take care of all our problems. If it works."

Arthur shrugged. "I'm out of ideas. What's your plan?"

Zoë felt surprisingly gratified to have him on her side. "Mae, you love the city, right?"

The old woman nodded. "I just want it to stop hurting."

Zoë smiled. "I think we can do that for you." The fire sprite had nearly re-formed closer to the burning storefront, casting dancing shadows on the buildings around them. "We need to move. Let's go."

"Where?" asked Phil.

Zoë pointed toward the golem.

"Oh. Of course."

"I wish I'd known that about the bitch zoëtist who wanted to trap my city. I didn't see her coming," Mae said as Zoë pulled her toward the golem.

"No one did, Mae, till it was too late," Zoë said.

The city was in pain. Both Zoë and Mae held their heads when it screamed, hearing it both internally and externally. When Zoë opened her mouth she didn't know if her own wishes or the city's would come out. But as she got closer, she thought she'd never seen anything so beautiful, so pure. Instead of the tall, mangled, thrashing golem she saw nothing but the library that made its torso, and the door opened invitingly. She slowed her running to a halt and marveled at its beauty.

It wanted a companion.

Unfortunately, it was at that moment that the fire sprite caught up with them and embraced Granny Good Mae.

The old woman was on fire, the sprite literally devouring her. She burned, her eyes closed, her face enraptured. Arthur ran to her, calling for Chet to help him. He knocked her down and tried to smother her, crying out as the fire sprite turned its focus to him.

"Morgen—" Zoë said, but the sprite hadn't rejoined them. She thought fast, and started rifling through the weapons in Arthur's dropped bag.

"She told me to always carry a wrench," she muttered. "I didn't think she'd be right." But apparently Arthur was prepared, and his wrench lay at the bottom of his bag.

She grabbed it and hefted it to a nearby fire hydrant. She wrestled it onto the valve; it slipped off, and she got it on once more. When she got a secure grasp, she pulled the wrench with her one good hand and met with resistance.

"This was not tightened with the intent to come off for a one-armed small woman," she groaned, straining again. "Ben! Help me!"

The zoëtist, who wasn't much bigger than she was, staggered over and put his hands by hers. Together they pulled, and the valve finally gave way and the water gushed out the side, not even threatening the burning sprite.

"Give me your coat," cried Zoë. Ben struggled out of it and handed it over. She held it in the icy flow and ran over to the burning group on the street. She smothered them with the wet overcoat, and the weakened sprite went out for good.

Now. Yes. Now.

In the excitement, the golem had reached them. It stood over them, the metal in the great body groaning.

The demon was gone, and Granny Good Mae stood, her face still in calm rapture. Her bulky clothing had protected most of her skin from the fire sprite, but her hands and face were burned, and most of her hair was gone. She didn't register any pain, she just looked at the golem as if she saw the face of a god.

The door to the library that made the torso of the golem opened then. Zoë, who stood, sopping wet and shivering, gasped. The golem bent down with a scream of metal on metal and extended a hand created from a city bus. When it reached Granny Good Mae, she stepped aboard with no hesitation.

The golem straightened, and it brought its hand to the steps in its chest. She stepped off lightly, waved down to them, and walked inside.

The door closed.

Complete. The word was confident and pleased, and Zoë felt an overwhelming sense of wholeness.

The golem turned unerringly and, with a sense of purpose, walked south, back into the park. It was heading to the Reservoir, Zoë was sure of it. They lost sight of it in the darkness, but still heard it stomping. They remained silent until they heard a mighty splash, and then nothing.

Arthur lay unmoving on the street, and Morgen was still missing. Adrenaline left Zoë, and she crumpled onto the wet, cold street, and closed her eyes.

Let someone save us *for once.*

The Shambling Guide to New York City

MANHATTAN:
Lodging

The human cities are most welcoming to human sized coterie, whether you're demon- or human-originated. It's harder to find lodging for visiting dragons and other leviathan-class coterie. In Manhattan, the place to stay is the Museum of Modern Art.

MoMA was chosen for a number of reasons, the least of which being that one of the three mothers of the museum, Mary Quinn Sullivan, was a dragon who commanded great respect among coterie and humans, and she wanted to have a space where relatives could visit.

In addition, one gallery can always be closed on a variety of pretexts, making it easy to hide visiting coterie. And of course, dragons commonly loving lavish and artistic things, MoMA is a favorite vacation stop.

The museum is open on Tuesdays to coterie. ■

CHAPTER TWENTY-NINE

A month later, after a couple days in the hospital and many late hours at Underground Publishing, Zoë sat at Bakery Under Starlight and flipped through an advance reader's copy of *The Shambling Guide to New York City*. Her still-healing arm was in a sling, but all her stitches had come out and her limp from the gouge in her hip was barely noticeable.

The book looked really good. It came in at 230 pages, full color, and her writers had done an amazingly fast job. The Web team of air sprites Zoë had finally hired was creating the supplemental material for the website, and she was finally earning her pay doing actual book editing.

The really amazing thing about the events of the previous weeks was that the citizens of New York City blamed it all on an earthquake.

It had made sense, of course. Many crevasses had split the streets and park, chaos had reigned. You could call it an earthquake if you tried. And humans tried very hard.

Zoë smiled when Arthur came in. He had spent his own time in the hospital dealing with his cuts and burns, and then taken time off to heal and "reconsider his view on life." They'd agreed to hold off seeing each other until the New Year, to distance themselves from the incidents in early December.

Arthur joined her, bringing her a coffee and a croissant, then went back for his own identical order. "I think the baker was flirting with me," he said as he sat down.

"Well, of course he was. He's an incubus," she said. She took a sip of her coffee before venturing, "Are you doing all right?"

Arthur shrugged. "Healing is going fine. Dealing with my position as an 'almost zombie' isn't going so smooth, but Benjamin let me put his cell on speed dial, and he's helping me cope."

Zoë nodded. "Did you tell Fanny yet?"

He looked out the window. "No. As long as it's under control, she doesn't need to know."

She blinked. "She should probably know, Arthur."

He was silent for a moment, and then shrugged. "Yeah. Probably."

To cover the awkward silence, Zoë poured too much cream into her coffee and swore as it slopped over the edge. Arthur handed her a napkin.

"You know," she said, "I'm still baffled that the humans just explain away a walking library."

Arthur took a sip of his black coffee. "They can't comprehend the existence of coterie," he said.

"Do you ever wonder if there will be a great coming out?"

Arthur frowned. "We're terrified of that occurrence every day. The violence on both sides will be monumental."

Zoë considered this in silence, then shook her head, still holding on to the night in December. "I can't believe no one got any good pictures."

He shrugged. "There was a total blackout. Any pictures are very Bigfoot-like. You can't make out any details."

They sipped their coffee in companionable silence. Arthur's hair hadn't grown back since being burned, but Zoë preferred him bald. The shiny burn scars were still there, and likely would be forever, but he had his life.

"Any word from the water sprite?" he asked carefully.

Zoë shook her head. "But I'll tell you the weird thing. Guess who took a sabbatical to hunt for her?"

"I can't even guess."

"John. The incubus. I think he's trying to prove something. Who knows? Phil thinks she's…you know. Gone. But John doesn't."

"Huh."

"Do you think she's dead?" Zoë asked, nearly afraid of the answer.

"Sprites are elemental. They're very hard to kill, but you can hurt them badly by, well, removing their elements, like evaporating much of her body. I think she'll be back. Someday."

"Thanks," Zoë said, sipping her coffee. "I think the city's been calmer lately. I think the fact that the city is as at home as it can be, with Granny Good Mae, also helps people forget."

"You're connected to the city, right? What happened there?"

Zoë tried to make sense of the sensations she had gotten in the past weeks. "The city was fine connected to Mae when it was where it was supposed to be. Wherever that was, if it was a place. But when it was given a corporeal body, it went a little mad. Mae had to go sane to complement it, I guess. She and the city, together, gave it peace."

"Why the Reservoir?"

Zoë shrugged. "It was the only place that was big enough to hold the city. It couldn't have gone anywhere else safely, since it was trapped in the body. Where are you going to hide a golem that big?"

"So Mae is alive?"

"Definitely," she said. "She's happy now, and more lucid than ever. You'll have to take my word on that, though. I don't think she's coming out, and I'm not sure she's human anymore. I think she's part of the city."

They sat in silence for some time, neither talking about what was on their minds. Arthur cleared his throat.

"Now that your book is done, we could use you at Public Works, you know. Fanny asked me to ask you again. We have never had a citytalker on staff. I don't even think most people know what one is."

She frowned. "I don't feel like one. I don't have half the connection that Mae did. I have small blasts of knowledge. Danger nearby. How the city is doing, how Mae is doing. We don't have conversations. Besides, I like my job."

"Does Phil know your connection to Mae? Or the city?"

"Not too much, no. I don't want him to know everything about me. But I still enjoy working with the coterie. My life hasn't been this interesting in, well, ever."

"Public Works isn't uninteresting. You could do some good work."

She blushed slightly. "Isn't it dangerous to work with someone you're dating?"

"Well," Arthur said, smiling. "I've not asked you out yet."

"I know," Zoë said. "I'm asking you out. I got tired of waiting."

He took her good hand. "When I thought you were dead in the tunnels, it hurt worse than I ever expected it to. I didn't want to lose you."

"You didn't. I'm right here."

"What about that guy John who's obviously so interested in you that he's playing the gallant hero? Why would you agree to go out with plain old me?"

She squeezed his hand. "The last two men I was with were an idiot playboy and an incubus. Both of them such bad news that I can't even begin to explain. You're the first pure thing to happen to me in a while."

"Pure. I kind of like that."

She grinned. "You should. Now, will you go on a date with someone you know works for the other side?"

He answered by kissing her, and it was not as illicit as with Godfrey or as lust-fueled as with John, and had a soft insistence all its own. She could get to like this. Especially once they were both fully healed.

"You make life interesting, Zoë," he said, and kissed her one last time, lightly.

"We'll have to go on our date soon. I'll be traveling for work shortly," she said.

"Another book?"

She nodded. "I'm taking five writers with me and researching the new book. *The Shambling Guide to New Orleans.*"

"N'awlins," Arthur repeated. "That's like a coterie capital. It's thick with them."

Zoë sipped her coffee. "Uh-huh. I'm also looking for more citytalkers. I leave in a week."

Arthur checked his watch. "I think that leaves us six evenings to make life more interesting."

She grinned. "Sounds lovely. And you can always visit me down South. I hear Phil got me a penthouse suite."

The Shambling Guide to New York City

INTRO:
Welcome to New York, NY!

Before you do anything, even check in with your hotel, your first matter of visitation is to check in with your local coterie leader. If you planned ahead (using this fantastic book to guide you) then you should already be set, with your registration done ahead of time. As of this printing, the Coterie Council doesn't have a website yet, but it's working on that. For now, you can get all updated information on whom you should contact at their Fangbook page.

After you've registered, the city is yours! ▪

ACKNOWLEDGMENTS

The idea for a shambling guide was birthed in 2005 when David Wendt organized role-playing game writers to donate stories, art, and game components for *Beyond the Storm: Shadows of the Big Easy*, a book to support the Red Cross after Hurricane Katrina. Artist Angi Shearstone and I contributed art and a story called "The Shambling Guide to New Orleans." From there, my head wouldn't shut up with wondering what other shambling guides were out there.

Monster advice came from Richard E. Dansky. Medical advice came from Dr. John Cmar. Thanks to early readers Tom Rockwell and Jason Adams.

I want to thank the fine folks at Orbit, especially my editor Devi Pillai, who believed in the book and helped shape it into something better than I could have made alone. I can't forget DongWon Song, who initially brought the book to Devi's attention. Agents Nicole Tourtelotte and Heather Schroder provided constant support to this scattered author. I also want to thank my friends and mentors James Patrick Kelly and David Anthony Durham for everything from specific writing suggestions to fretful-author soothing.

It would be tragic if I did not take a moment to thank one of the biggest author influences of my life, the late Douglas Adams. I never got a chance to meet him, but his work still astonishes me to this day. I think of him whenever I stand and doubt.

Back in 2008, I read a portion of an early draft of this book to a tiny, packed room at Balticon. In the past four years, some of those who attended that reading have asked me repeatedly when they would be able to read the whole thing.

The answer: Now.

July 2012

extras

orbit

meet the author

JR Blackwell

MUR LAFFERTY is a writer, podcast producer, gamer, geek, and martial artist. Her books include *Playing For Keeps, Nanovor: Hacked!, Marco and the Red Granny*, and The Afterlife Series. Her podcasts are many. Currently she's the editor of *Escape Pod* magazine, the host of *I Should Be Writing*, and the host of the *Angry Robot Books* podcast.

interview

When did you first start writing?

I think I was around twelve, after reading Fred Saberhagen's Swords series and getting my first itch for fanfic. Then I began an epic story about all my best friends, featuring different-colored unicorns. This book is, thankfully, lost to the ages.

Who are your biggest writing influences?

As a child, I was most influenced by Anne McCaffrey and Robin McKinley. As an adult, it's been Douglas Adams, Neil Gaiman, and Connie Willis.

Where did the idea for The Shambling Guide to New York City come from?

I used to write for role-playing games, and in 2005 (post–Hurricane Katrina), I got together with some friends to do a print-on-demand RPG book about New Orleans to benefit the Red Cross. New Orleans has such a history with myth and magic, I had the idea to see the city from a zombie tour guide's POV, so I wrote a short story called "The Shambling Guide to New Orleans." After I wrote that short piece for the book, I began thinking of other cities that would have an underground monster population that might be in need of guidebooks.

extras

What was your inspiration for Zoë? Why publishing?

Embarrassingly enough, only after I finished the book did I realize how much Douglas Adams influenced my writing. One of my favorite parts of *The Hitchhiker's Guide to the Galaxy* is the actual travel book within the book. As for Zoë, she is a woman who thinks she can handle things bigger than herself; she has a reckless streak that I've always wanted to have.

How much of you is in your characters?

I think there's a little bit of me in all of them, else I wouldn't be able to write them. My protagonists are often braver than I am, though.

Why New York City?

I am from a small town, and currently live in Durham, North Carolina. While we have the cities of Raleigh and Durham, they suffer from sprawl, and so they never feel like proper cities to me. Cars are ubiquitous instead of subways and buses. And forget walking anywhere. Cities that pack their residents in create their own mythology with the layers from the ultra-rich penthouses to the squalor in the abandoned tunnels. I've always loved visiting cities, even though the small-town girl inside me fears getting hopelessly lost!

How much research did you have to do for this novel?

I did a lot of reading on different monster mythologies, especially those tied to different locations. For the city, I drew on media about New York, maps, and my experiences visiting the city. A lot of reading and a lot of Internet research.

extras

Worldbuilding is key in **The Shambling Guide to New York City,** *not only for the plot, but also for the travel guide excerpts. What was it like creating a whole new world within one we so closely relate to?*

It was the best part of the book! I love looking at something from a different point of view, how a graveyard can be terrifying, sad, romantic, or home, depending on who you are and what your experiences have been. It was a fun experiment to think about where a zombie would feel safe sleeping, or what kind of restaurant would best feed fairies.

Which coterie is your favorite and why?

One of the challenges in writing about existing mythology is trying to put your own spin on it. It's hard to say. I loved writing the zombies, tweaking their mythology to include celebrity worship, and the gay incubus who feeds on the love humans have for his food instead of sex.

But honestly my favorite was creating the human coterie members, the zoëtists, those who give life. I realized there was a parallel between the mystic Jewish story of the golem and the raising of zombies, and decided they were different schools of the same magic. And playing with the different kinds of golems the zoëtists could raise, that was awesome.

What is next for Zoë and the employees of Underground Publishing?

In the next book, I'm returning to give New Orleans the full treatment beyond what I wrote in 2005. Boston had a lot of problems with its urban project the Big Dig, and I'm pretty sure there was a big coterie issue with the delay. I also want to explore how the coterie influenced organized crime in Chicago. Internationally, I'd love to explore the history of London, and the strife between the relatively new coterie versus the native aboriginal coterie in Australia. I'd love to take this series around the world, if I can.

I think there's still a lot I can do in New York, revealing more behind the rats' and pigeons' influence on the city, as well as the fallout if a copy of *The Shambling Guide* falls into the hands of a human.

introducing

If you enjoyed
THE SHAMBLING GUIDE
TO NEW YORK CITY,
look out for

JILL KISMET:
THE COMPLETE SERIES

by Lilith Saintcrow

Every city has a hunter—someone brave enough, tough enough, and fearless enough to take on the nightside. Santa Luz is lucky. It's got Jill Kismet. With a hellbreed mark on her wrist and a lot of silverjacket ammo, she's fully trained and ready to take on the world.

1

Every city has a pulse. It's just a matter of knowing where to rest your finger to find it, throbbing away as the sun bleeds out of the sky and night rises to cloak every sin.

I crouched on the edge of a rooftop, the counterweight of my heavy leather coat hanging behind me. Settled into absolute stillness, waiting. The baking wind off the cooling desert mouthed the edges of my body. The scar on my right wrist was hot and hard under a wide hinged copper bracelet molded to my skin.

The copper was corroding, blooming green and wearing thin.

I was going to have to find a different way to cover the scar up soon. Trouble is, I suck at making jewelry, and Galina was out of blessed copper cuffs until her next shipment from Nepal.

Below me the alley wandered, thick and rank. Here at the edge of the barrio there were plenty of hiding places for the dark things that crawl once dusk falls. The Weres don't patrol out this far, having plenty to keep them occupied inside their own crazy-quilt of streets and alleys around the Plaza Centro and its spreading tenements. Here on the fringes, between a new hunter's territory and the streets the Weres kept from boiling over, a few hellbreed thought they could break the rules.

Not in my town, buckos. If you think Kismet's a pushover because she's only been on her own for six months, you've got another think coming.

My right leg cramped, a sudden vicious swipe of pain. I ignored it. My electrolyte balance was all messed up from going for three days without rest, from one deadly night-battle to the next with the fun of exorcisms in between. I wondered if Mikhail had ever felt this exhaustion, this ache so deep even bones felt tired.

It hurt to think of Mikhail. My hand tightened on the bullwhip's handle, leather creaking under my fingers. The scar tingled again, a knot of corruption on the inside of my wrist.

Easy, milaya. *No use in making noise, eh? It is soft and quiet that catches mouse.* As if he was right next to me, barely mouthing the words, his gray eyes glittering winter-sharp under a shock of white hair. Hunters don't live to get too old, but Mikhail Ilych Tolstoi had been an exception in so many ways. I could almost see his ghost crouching silent next to me, peering at the alley over the bridge of his patrician nose.

Of course he wasn't there. He'd been cremated, just like he wanted. I'd held the torch myself, and the Weres had let me touch it to the wood before singing their own fire into being. A warrior's spirit rose in smoke, and wherever my teacher was, it wasn't here.

Which I found more comforting than you'd think, since if he'd come back I'd have to kill him. Just part of the job.

My fingers eased. I waited.

The smell of hellbreed and the brackish contamination of an *arkeus* lay over this alley. Some nasty things had been sidling out of this section of the city lately, nasty enough to give even a Hell-tainted hunter a run for her money. We have firepower and sorcery, we who police the nightside, but Traders and hellbreed are spooky-quick and capable of taking a hell of a lot of damage.

Get it? A Hell of a lot of damage? Arf arf.

Not to mention the scurf with their contagion, the adepts of the Middle Way with their goddamn Chaos, and the Sorrows worshipping the Elder Gods.

The thought of the Sorrows made rage rise under my breastbone, fresh and wine-dark. I inhaled smoothly, dispelling it. Clear, calm, and cold was the way to go about this.

Movement below. Quick and scuttling, like a rat skittering from one pile of garbage to the next. I didn't move, I didn't blink, I barely even *breathed*.

The *arkeus* took shape, rising like a fume from dry-scorched pavement, trash riffling as the wind of its coalescing touched ragged edges and putrid rotting things. Tall, hooded, translucent where moonlight struck it and smoky-solid elsewhere, one of Hell's roaming corruptors stretched its long clawed arms and slid fully into the world. It drew in a deep satisfied sigh, and I heard something else.

Footsteps.

Someone was coming to keep an appointment.

Isn't that a coincidence. So am I.

My heartbeat didn't quicken; it stayed soft, even, as almost-nonexistent as my breathing. It had taken me a long time to get my pulse mostly under control.

The next few moments were critical. You can't jump too soon on something like this. *Arkeus* aren't your garden-variety hell-breed. You have to wait until they solidify enough to talk to their victims—otherwise you'll be fighting empty air with sorcery, and that's no fun—and you have to know what a Trader is bargaining for before you go barging in to distribute justice or whup-ass. Usually both, liberally.

The carved chunk of ruby on its silver chain warmed, my tiger's-eye rosary warming too, the blessing on both items reacting with contamination rising from the *arkeus* and its lair.

A man edged down the alley, clutching something to his chest. The *arkeus* made a thin greedy sound, and my smart left eye—the blue one, the one that can look *below* the surface of the world—saw a sudden tensing of the strings of contamination following it. It was a hunched, thin figure that would have been taller than me except for the hump on its back; its spectral robes brushing dirt and refuse, taking strength from filth.

Bingo. The *arkeus* was now solid enough to hit.

The man halted. I couldn't see much beyond the fact that he was obviously human, his aura slightly tainted from his traffic with an escaped denizen of Hell.

It was official. The man was a Trader, bargaining with Hell. Whatever he was bargaining *for,* it wasn't going to do him any good.

Not with me around.

The *arkeus* spoke. *"You have brought it?"* A lipless cold voice, eager and thin, like a dying cricket. A razorblade pressed against the wrist, a thin line of red on pale skin, the frozen-blue face of a suicide.

I moved. Boots soundless against the parapet, the carved chunk of ruby resting against the hollow of my throat, even my coat silent. The silver charms braided into my long dark hair didn't tinkle. The first thing a hunter's apprentice learns is to move quietly, to draw silence in tight like a cloak.

That is, if the apprentice wants to survive.

"I b-brought it." The man's speech was the slow slur of a dreamer who senses a cold-current nightmare. He was in deep, having already given the *arkeus* a foothold by making some agreement or another with it. "You'd better not—"

"Peace." The *arkeus*'s hiss froze me in place for a moment as the hump on its back twitched. *"You will have your desire, never fear. Give it to me."*

The man's arms relaxed, and a small sound lifted from the bundle he carried. My heart slammed into overtime against my ribs.

Every human being knows the sound of a baby's cry.

Bile filled my throat. My boots ground against the edge of the parapet as I launched out into space, the *arkeus* flinching and hissing as my aura suddenly flamed, tearing through the ether like a star. The silver in my hair shot sparks, and the ruby at my throat turned hot. The scar on my right wrist turned to lava, burrowing in toward the bone, my whip uncoiled and struck forward, its metal flechettes snapping at the speed of sound, cracking as I pulled on etheric force to add a psychic strike to the physical.

My boots hit slick refuse-grimed concrete and I pitched forward, the whip striking again across the *arkeus*'s face. The hell-thing howled, and my other hand was full of the Glock, the sharp stink of cordite blooming as silver-coated bullets chewed through the thing's physical shell. Hollowpoints do a lot of damage once a hellbreed's initial shell is breached.

It's a pity 'breed heal so quickly.

We don't know why silver works—something to do with the Moon, and how she controls the tides of sorcery and water. No hunter cares, either. It's enough that it levels the playing field a little.

The *arkeus* moved, scuttling to the side as the man screamed, a high whitenoise-burst of fear. The whip coiled, my hip moving first as usual—the hip leads with whip-work as well as stave fighting. My whip-work had suffered until Mikhail made me take bellydancing classes.

Don't think, Jill. Move. I flung out my arm, etheric force spilling through my fingers, and the whip slashed again, each flechette tearing through already-lacerated flesh. It howled again, and the copper bracelet broke, tinkled sweetly on the concrete as I pivoted, firing down into the hell-thing's face. It twitched, and I heard my own voice chanting in gutter Latin, a version of Saint Anthony's prayer Mikhail had made me learn.

Protect me from the hordes of Hell, O Lord, for I am pure of heart and trust Your mercy—and the bullets don't hurt, either.

The *arkeus* screamed, writhing, and cold air hit the scar. I was too drenched with adrenaline to feel the usual curl of fire low in my belly, but the sudden sensitivity of my skin and hearing slammed into me. I dropped the whip and fired again with the gun in my left, then fell to my knees, driving down with psychic and physical force.

My fist met the hell-thing's lean malformed face, which exploded. It shredded, runnels of foulness bursting through its skin, and the sudden cloying reek would have torn my dinner loose from my stomach moorings if I'd eaten anything.

Christ, I wish it didn't stink so bad. But stink means dead, and if this thing's dead it's one less fucking problem for me to deal with.

No time. I gained my feet, shaking my right fist. Gobbets of preternatural flesh whipped loose, splatting dully against the brick walls. I uncoiled, leaping for the front of the alley.

The Trader was only human, and he hadn't made his big deal yet. He was tainted by the *arkeus's* will, but he wasn't given superstrength or near-invulnerability yet.

The only enhanced human being left in the alley was me. Thank God.

I dug my fingers into his shoulder and set my feet, yanking him back. The baby howled, emptying its tiny lungs, and I caught it on its way down, my arm tightening maybe a little too much to yank it against my chest. I tried to avoid smacking it with a knife-hilt.

I backhanded the man with my hellbreed-strong right fist. *Goddamn it. What am I going to do now?*

The baby was too small, wrapped in a bulky blue blanket that smelled of cigarette smoke and grease. I held it awkwardly in one arm while I contemplated the sobbing heap of sorry manflesh crumpled against a pile of garbage.

I've cuffed plenty of Traders one-handed, but never while holding a squirming, bellowing bundle of little human that smelled not-too-fresh. Still, it was a cleaner reek than the *arkeus's* rot. I tested the cuffs, yanked the man over, and checked his eyes. Yep. The flat shine of the dust glittered in his irises. He was a thin, dark-haired man with the ghost of childhood acne still hanging on his cheeks, saliva glittering wetly on his chin.

I found his ID in his wallet, awkwardly holding the tiny yelling thing in the crook of my arm. *Jesus. Mikhail never trained me for this.* "Andy Hughes. You are *under arrest.* You have the right to be exorcised. Anything you say will, of course, be ignored, since you've forfeited your rights to a trial of your peers by trafficking with Hell." I took a deep breath. "And you should thank your lucky stars I'm not in a mood to kill anyone else tonight. Who does the baby belong to?"

He was still gibbering with fear, and the baby howled. I could get nothing coherent out of either of them.

Then, to complete the deal, the pager went off against my hip, vibrating silently in its padded pocket.

Great.